BLOOD OF VANRIS

THE WARDEN'S SON
BOOK TWO

NIKKI McCORMACK

ISBN: 979-8-9903922-0-5
First Edition 2024

Published by
Elysium Books
Bellevue, WA

Copyright © 2024 Nikki McCormack

Written by Nikki McCormack (https://nikkimccormack.com/)
Cover Design by Robert Crescenzio (https://robertcrescenzio.artstation.com/)
Map Design by Melissa Nash
Typesetting and Design by Brian C. Short
Editing by Alexander Lockwood

To my wonderous cat-god, Neko, and to all the companion critters everywhere. May you be loved deeply in life and remembered long after you are gone.

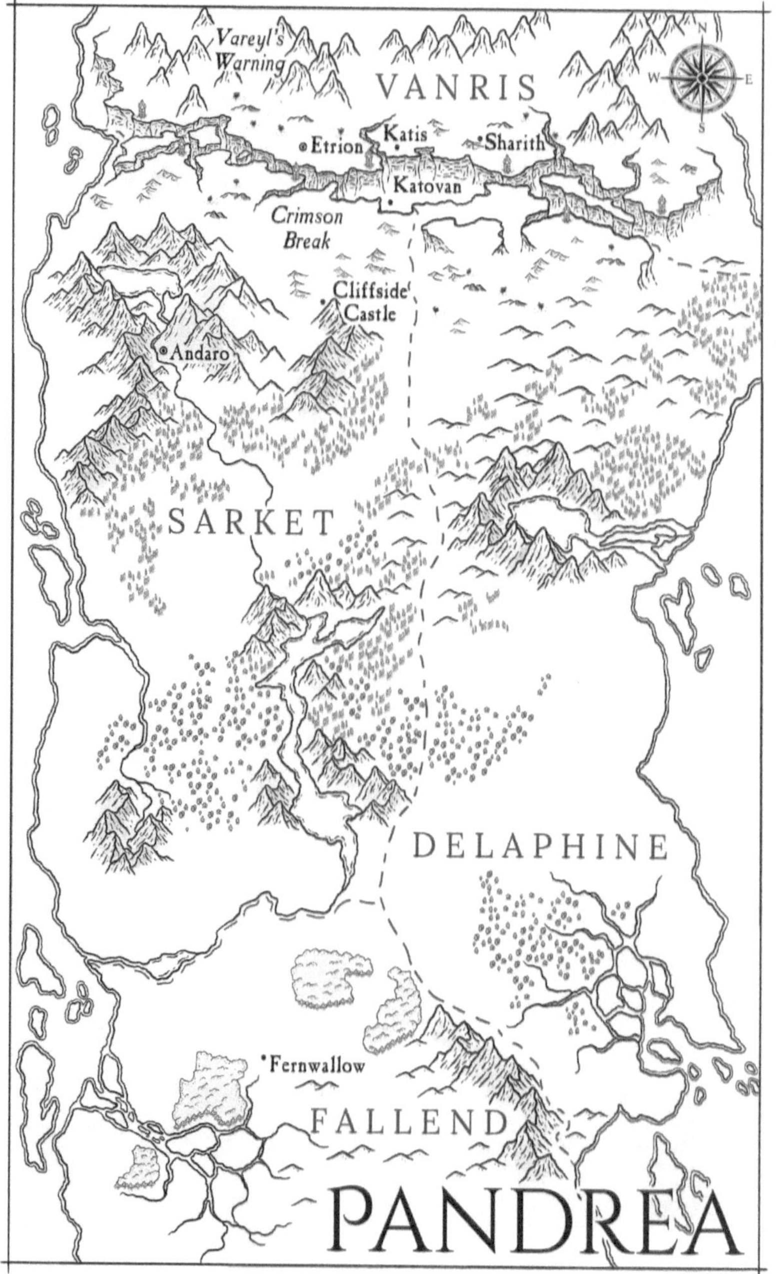

Vareyl's Warning
VANRIS
Etrion
Katis
Sharith
Katovan
Crimson Break
Cliffside Castle
Andaro
SARKET
DELAPHINE
Fernwallow
FALLEND
PANDREA
N
W
E
S

Muscle rippled beneath the kanodrak's silver-gray scaled hide, her long claws digging into the stone under her feet like it was clay. Her milky white eyes watched Kasiel while he watched her in turn, his gaze drifting to the elongated canine teeth that dipped below her lower jaw. She was a massive beast, larger than the average horse. Kasiel, by comparison, was rather unimpressive standing before her, his mind reaching out to hers in search of some connection. In fact, he couldn't remember when he had last felt as insignificant as he did now, facing that magnificent predator. Perhaps at that moment when he was almost five years old and Edmund, the man who would raise him as a son, had him pinned in the mud so they could cut the tops of his ears off.

A sweat broke out across Kasiel's forehead as he tried to stop the surge of dark hatred that thought brought up, but he wasn't fast enough. The kanodrak growled and rejected his presence, seeking welcome into her mind, with enough force that he staggered back a step. She lashed out with one paw, sweeping his legs out from under him. Kasiel hit the ground, curling around the flare of pain in his still-healing chest. The stitches were long gone, but the area over his heart where Edmund's dagger cut him remained sensitive.

The somewhat feline beast lowered her armored head, the tips of those extended front fangs almost brushing Kasiel's face. Her milky white eyes stared at the side of his face as she sniffed at him. Then she snorted, depositing a spray of mucus on his cheek, and loped away.

Kasiel stayed on the ground, waiting for the searing pain in his chest to pass. Once he managed to catch his breath, he wiped his cheek off with one sleeve and sat up. Adnar stood watching him from outside the bars that walled the front of the canyon off from the habitat where the kanodraks resided. He tossed his head, throwing his long blond hair back from his face, the corners of his mouth curling down.

Kasiel heaved a sigh and climbed to his feet. "That didn't go so well."

"Did she have her claws retracted when she struck you?" Adnar asked.

"Obviously. I still have all my parts." Kasiel struggled to keep the bitterness from his tone. Judging from the way Adnar's eyes narrowed, he failed.

"Then it could have gone much worse." Adnar unlocked the gate and held it open for him. "You need to focus."

"Maybe it's not me. Maybe she's the problem," Kasiel snapped.

Adnar's fist tightened on the bars. He slammed the gate behind Kasiel with a solid clang and slapped the lock into place. "Do you want to know how I know you're wrong?"

Kasiel drew a breath, trying to leash the quick temper that nagged him at every turn lately. "How?"

"Because a kanodrak is never wrong." Adnar doublechecked the lock, then faced him. "If you are still having this much pain, perhaps you should not be working with the kanodraks yet."

A white light of frustration burst behind Kasiel's eyes. "I'm fine. It's healing more every day. I can do this."

Adnar stalked up to him, glowering down at him with his head cocked to one side in a distinctly animalistic way. The ahndhomen wasn't that much taller than Kasiel, but his superior bulk and the intimidating way he moved, like a predator prepared to strike, made him seem bigger.

"You're right, Ahninveth Hahren. It isn't your injury that's the problem. It's your head. You need to be one hundred percent focused on this, and you're not even close."

Hatred for his Vanrian name piled on top of his frustration. "I don't care! I have to learn this!"

Adnar didn't react at all to his outburst, and Kasiel suddenly felt like an idiot. He reached out to the next canyon over with his mind and found Sylaryth, his tethdrak, basking in the last of the late afternoon sunshine. The large reptile responded instantly, welcoming his presence with a glimmer of excitement. Kasiel slipped into his head and looked out through his eyes, seeing several more of the beasts lounging in the sun nearby. He soaked in the tethdrak's contentment for a second before drawing back to himself.

"Apologies, Ahndhomen. It's not the kanodrak," he admitted. "I almost died in Katovan because I couldn't balance my awareness between myself and Sylaryth. Worse, Syl nearly abandoned the others when I got taken. They might have all died if I hadn't managed to turn him back. I need to get better at controlling my ability, so something like that doesn't happen again."

The aggression in Adnar's stance faded, and he gave a slow nod. "This is something you will struggle with as a Feral. Only through practice can you perfect being in their head and yours at the same time. Particularly in your case. The ability to see through their eyes, while it does give you some advantages, also puts you at greater risk. It is one thing to split your attention between more than one mind. Another entirely to try seeing through their eyes and your own at the same time. Balancing that will be difficult. I encourage you to be always reaching out to different beasts. Not just the ones you work with here, but any creature. Wild dogs, birds, rodents – practice finding them and linking with them. Look at the world through their eyes. Make it second nature."

Kasiel peered out into the habitat. The kanodrak was drinking from a stream that flowed along the floor of the canyon. As if aware of his scrutiny, she lifted her head and looked back at him. Her heavy tail swished once, and she flexed her long claws into the ground, then she trotted off deeper into the canyon.

"How do *you* do it, sir?" he asked, turning his attention back to Adnar.

Adnar's face could have been chiseled from stone for all the emotion it showed. "I cannot see through their eyes." He strode toward one of several doors embedded in the canyon wall. "We will work with the tethdraks tomorrow, Ahninveth."

Kasiel stared after him, at a loss for words.

His commanding officer, a powerful Feral and the only one in Etrion who could control the kanodraks, couldn't see through the eyes of his beasts. Adnar told him the gift was rare when Kasiel first mentioned seeing through Sylaryth's eyes, but Adnar was an ahndhomen. A mind-crafter of the highest rank under the dhomvalen himself, who answered only to the ruler of Vanris. It never occurred to Kasiel that he might be able to do something Adnar could not.

Kasiel walked along the tunnel that took him between the two canyons, rubbing at the long scar across the left side of his ribs. It hurt to rub it, but the scar tissue would limit his mobility if he didn't loosen it up. Edmund had intended the injury to be fatal. It would have been so if Sylaryth and Jethan hadn't burst through the door at that moment. Their timely arrival had saved his life.

In the other canyon, Kasiel took the key and let himself in to the tethdrak habitat. Sylaryth came bounding up before he had finished closing the gate. Nearly full-grown now, the tethdrak's back reached up to about mid-ribcage on Kasiel. The dusty tan and reddish scaling over his body had lightened as he matured, the mask pattern that ran around his eyes and up to his horns turned a pale rust color now. His massive claws dug runnels in the hard ground when he skidded to a halt, stopping a few inches shy of slamming into Kasiel, who made no effort to get out of the way. He trusted Sylaryth.

The powerful beast angled his nose toward the ground, his backswept horns pointing to the sky. Kasiel placed his palm against the heavy armor plating on the tethdrak's forehead and Sylaryth pressed into it with a surprising gentleness. A series of contented, deep clicks emerged from somewhere in his throat and a vibration moved through the closed frill around his neck. In response to his mental touch, Kasiel received a flood of affection from the beast and a weary smile curved his lips.

Overhead, the sky was picking up a hint of orange with the approach of sunset. He sent a quick thought to Sylaryth, showing him where he wanted to go. They turned together toward a large, flat formation of red rock that rose about ten feet above the canyon floor not far from the entrance. The tethdrak bolted ahead, lunging up the sloped backside of the formation to stand at the top. He flared the frill around his neck and called out with a high-pitched shriek, declaring the spot theirs. Then he leapt off the other side and came bounding back to Kasiel, dancing from one foot to the other with his impatience.

Kasiel chuckled and broke into an easy jog, trying not to jar his sore spots too much as he indulged the tethdrak. They climbed up together this time and Kasiel sat at the edge, secure on the gritty sandstone as he dangled his legs off the side. Sylaryth lay down beside him, resting his uncomfortably heavy, angular head across Kasiel's thighs. It was a discomfort he was content to endure for the bond they shared.

A few minutes had passed when Sylaryth's head jerked up again, and he turned to look back the way they had come. Kasiel slipped in behind his eyes, watching in the intense array of colors the tethdrak could see as Kenna and Jethan paused outside the gate, talking for a moment. Then Kenna let Jethan in and locked it behind him. Splitting his vision, Kasiel tried to watch his tehnaak, his spirit sibling, approaching through Sylaryth's eyes while also tracking the slowly changing sunset through his own. The effect was nauseating.

"Kenna promised you wouldn't let the tethdraks eat me," Jethan said, joining them on top of the rock.

Sylaryth returned his head to Kasiel's lap as Jethan sat on the other side. Orange light was spreading across the sky, a hint of pink bathing the clouds at their edges. The horizon itself shone a bright, searing yellow that was hard to look at. Layers of soil that formed the towering canyon walls began glowing a bloody gold.

"We'll see how it goes. Is she joining us?"

Jethan reacted with a look of mock offense. "We'll see how it goes?"

Kasiel fought a smile, though the twitch at the corner of his mouth gave him away. Jethan bumped his shoulder, earning a half-hearted growl from Sylaryth for the disturbance.

"She's not. I asked her to do a quick favor for me. How did training go with the kanodrak?"

Irritation flared in Kasiel and Sylaryth tensed in

response. Aware of how sensitive the tethdrak was to his moods, he tried to force it down. "Not great. Adnar wants me to go back to working with the tethdraks tomorrow. He says I'm not focused enough."

Jethan picked up a pebble and tossed it off the side of the formation. He gazed out, the brilliant sunset reflecting in his eyes as its colors gradually climbed the glowing walls. "He's right, Kas. I've noticed it too. You haven't been yourself since Katovan. Whatever's bothering you, you know you can talk to me about it, right?"

The irritation flared again, and Sylaryth lifted his head, claws digging into the rock. "I don't want..." he started raising his voice, then stopped himself. This was Jethan. No one deserved his temper less than his tehnaak did. "I'm sorry." Sylaryth's feet relaxed, his claws leaving behind gouges in the stone. "I'm just... I haven't been sleeping much."

Jethan was quiet until the tethdrak settled his head on Kasiel's thighs again. Then he asked, "Is it because of what happened with Edmund?"

Kasiel clenched his teeth and nodded. "Sometimes. I have nightmares where I stab him again like I did in that room. Only in my dreams, he grabs my hand that's holding the dagger in his chest and won't let go. He starts crying, telling me how he wishes things could have been different. I can't pull away, even though I know I'll bleed to death from the wounds he inflicted if I don't do something. Then I see bottles of my blood sitting on the table, fifteen or twenty of them, and I realize I'm already dead, I just haven't fallen over yet because he's holding onto me. The foolish thing is, even after that, I still feel guilty for stabbing him."

When Jethan opened his mouth to speak, Kasiel held up a finger to stop him. He slipped back behind the tethdrak's eyes to watch the sunset in that more brilliant array of colors, letting it distract him as he continued.

"That's not all. There are also the nightmares with Danica. We're back in the building where I met with her that night in Katovan. She's crying and screaming at me for killing her father. Her face is mangled. Torn open by the claws of a tethdrak." He set a hand on Sylaryth's shoulder. "My tethdrak. There's blood dripping from her jaw. I can see her teeth and tongue moving through the jagged rips in the side of her face, but she refuses to let me help her because I killed her father."

Jethan let out a low whistle. "By the Break, Kas, it's no wonder you can't sleep or focus."

Kasiel swallowed against the tightening in his throat. The searing light had climbed almost to the top of the canyon walls now, casting a red glow into the spreading darkness below. "I killed them, Jeth. I killed the man who raised me and the father of my childhood friend."

A sharp edge entered Jethan's tone when he spoke. "Technically, Syl killed Garrick, and you know why. Because they were killing you. They deserved it."

"Danica didn't deserve to lose her father. Her mother died of a sickness that ran through the village when she was seven. She didn't have anyone else."

"That may be true, but you didn't deserve to be kidnapped and have your ears cut as a child, either. They lied to you your whole life and used you for experiments. I know Edmund was the only father you knew growing up, but you've got to let him go. You have a tehsheyn now. A chosen family that won't use you or lie to you."

Kasiel glanced at his tehnaak, fighting the wave of nausea that came with trying to hold on to his split vision. "I know you're right, but I had never killed anyone with my own hands. Starting with the man who raised me..." He retreated fully behind his own eyes to stare down at his palms.

Jethan shifted closer and put an arm around his shoulders. "Hang in there. The power of those memories will fade in time. Until they do, you've got me, and you've got that big bastard." He gestured to Sylaryth with his free hand and the tethdrak lifted his head to snort at him.

Kasiel chuckled softly, the brief humor not quite penetrating the melancholy that hung over him.

Sylaryth stood then, staring at them expectantly.

Jethan looked from the beast to Kasiel. "I take it you're ready to head in?"

Kasiel nodded. Sylaryth was so tuned to his desires and intent now that he sometimes reacted to them before Kasiel had a chance to. They stood, and he paused long enough to place a hand to the tethdrak's forehead briefly before heading out through the gate with his tehnaak.

"Have you come up with any theories about why Edmund wanted your blood bad enough to risk dying for it?" Jethan asked while he waited for Kasiel to lock the gate behind them.

"No comforting ones, but I don't suppose it matters now. Unless you think he could have survived." Kasiel's chest seized at the thought. That idea had also haunted his dreams and sabotaged his tenuous focus of late.

Jethan shrugged, his gaze moving up to where the last hints of sunset were turning a dark purple on the horizon. "It isn't impossible. It would depend on how deep the wound was and how fast help arrived, if it ever did."

"That's not the reassurance I was hoping for to help chase away my nightmares," Kasiel muttered dryly.

Jethan waved his comment away. "I've got a plan for that. Let's get some food and I'll tell you all about it."

"All right. I can't object to a decent meal."

They strolled to the palace in comfortable silence. A private smile curved Jethan's lips now and then when he peered out into the evening streets. Kasiel considered asking about it, but he didn't quite feel like chatting. Perhaps that was selfish. His tehnaak was clearly pleased about something. Maybe after he had eaten, he would find the energy to be more social.

When they arrived at Kasiel's private chambers in the palace, Jethan stopped outside the door. "I almost forgot. There's something I need to grab from my room. I'll be right back."

The mischief in his grin captured Kasiel's curiosity at last, but he trotted off down the hall too fast for questioning. Kasiel vowed to give it the attention it deserved when his tehnaak returned. He entered the large sitting room outside his bedroom where a covered platter already sat on the table. Whatever delectable dish waited hidden within smelled fantastic. He closed the door and took a step in that direction, halting mid-step when someone knocked. Puzzled, he turned and opened the door. A slow smile crept across his lips.

Nerith stood there, one side of her silvery hair pulled up in a braid that showed off a pointed ear with several decorative cuffs and earrings upon it. Her lavender eyes glinted with delight when she smiled up at him. Then she put her arms around his neck and kissed him as she advanced into the room, moving him back. He slid one arm around her waist, pushing the door shut behind her with the other, and kissed her in return, frustration and sorrow melting away as she opened her soft lips to him.

After a moment, he drew back and met those captivating eyes. He had yet to see anyone else in Etrion with eyes quite that color. "I thought you were working late with the healers again tonight."

She stepped back against the door, her arms sliding away until her hands rested on his shoulders. "Someone convinced me that a night off might be good for me, especially with the right company."

He chuckled, recalling the mischief in his tehnaak's

eyes and that pleased little smile. "Someone being Jeth."

She grinned.

"He's not coming back tonight, is he?"

Nerith shook her head, tapping him on the nose with one finger. "Nope. You're all mine tonight."

They migrated to the couch and ate together while Kasiel asked about her last several days of training as a healer. Soon, she would undergo testing to see if she was ready to advance to the status of full healer. It was easy enough, given her nervous excitement around the coming assessment, to keep her talking about that. It allowed him to avoid burdening her with his troubles. Twice she tried to redirect the conversation to him, but he found ways to flip it back quickly. He didn't want to dwell on the dark places his mind had been stuck in of late. Better by far to let her dominate his thoughts for a few hours.

When they finished eating, they lingered on the couch sipping mead for a while. Nerith traced the coppery-red symbol tattooed around the scar on his right cheek with one finger. She had a similar scar on her cheek now, given to her by a trio of men who didn't approve of Kasiel's presence in Vanris. Those three loitered in prison cells now, however, while she sat here with him, warm and safe.

Her head came to rest on his shoulder. She ran her finger along one side of the chain of symbols and runes tattooed around his neck, the final symbol hanging like a pendant on his breastbone. Letting his head fall back on the couch, he closed his eyes, getting lost in the feel of her touch on his skin. Her hand sank from there down to the scar across the left side of his chest, finding it through the fabric of his shirt.

"Want me to massage this scar?"

He cracked one eye open to look at her. "Not really."

Anytime she suspected he may have neglected to

work on the scar tissue enough, she would do so, and she was merciless. Still, even with the threat of that torture, he wished they had more time to spend together. The long hours she dedicated to working in the healer's building to prove herself to her instructors left little opportunity for them. It wouldn't be much longer, though. After she passed her tests, as he was confident she would, she would have more freedom.

Nerith breathed a laugh. "Oh, so fragile."

"I'll have you know I was raised to be quite fragile," he answered, lightly tickling her side with the hand wrapped around her waist.

She squirmed, grabbing his wrist, and kissed his shoulder. "Then the man who raised you failed miserably."

He opened his eyes, regarding her as a flame of uncertainty ignited in his chest, sparking out to his extremities. "Are you tired?"

"Mm-hmm."

"Want me to walk you home?" That wasn't at all what he would like to do with her, but they were both tired and distracted. She deserved his full attention if they took their relationship farther. Besides, he had never progressed beyond kissing with anyone. What if he did something wrong and made a fool of himself?

Nerith shook her head and stood, pulling on his hand to draw him up with her. Then she led him into the bedroom and sat him back on the bed as uncertainty and longing waged war in his body. Slowly, she lifted his shirt off, pausing a moment to admire him, something he suspected she wouldn't have enjoyed as much before all the combat training beat the spindly teenager out of him. She removed her shoes while he pulled off his boots, then went to his wardrobe and got out a pair of soft sleeping pants and one of his longer shirts. The former she tossed to him. The latter, she took into the bathing room. He obeyed her unspoken order and changed into the pants. She returned a few minutes later wearing his shirt in place of her clothes. It hung almost to her knees.

Kasiel watched her walk around the bed and climb under the covers, hoping the hunger she sparked in him didn't show through too much. His apprehension lost power before his desire to touch her in so many ways, but her drowsy smile said tonight was not that night. He could be content just having her close to him. Taking a deep breath to calm his heart and the fire burning at his core, he slipped into the bed next to her. Nerith moved over against his side and rested her head on his chest. Kasiel wrapped his arm around her and placed a kiss on her forehead. Then he settled back and closed his eyes, waiting for his racing pulse to slow so he could sleep.

asiel woke to Nerith frantically pulling her apprentice healer's robe over her head. He rolled up on his elbow to watch her, catching the briefest glimpse of tattoos at the lower edges of her shoulder blades before his gaze moved down the curve of her waist, past her hips, and along her slender legs below the hem of the descending garment. Sudden arousal caught him by surprise. He shifted the covers, hoping she wouldn't notice.

She turned around to reach for one shoe and spotted him watching, her cheeks darkening to a rosy pink. "Oh."

"Don't worry, I didn't see..."

Her eyes narrowed, daring him to lie.

"Everything," he finished lamely.

"Shame on you," she scolded, the glimmer in her eyes erasing any conviction in her words as she walked to him and leaned down, touching her lips to his in a soft kiss.

He slid his arms around her, drawing her into a deeper kiss. Her mouth opened to him, her tongue brushing his. He pulled her over him and onto the bed, doing his best to ignore the sharp stab of pain in his ribs. He was accumulating quite the collection of scars on that side between the one Edmund gave him and the one the men who had attacked Nerith left him with. For the moment, with her in his arms, he had the fortitude to push that discomfort aside.

When he finally drew back, admiring the way her silver hair stood out against the black and purple of the coverlet, she grinned up at him.

"You're a wicked man, Kasiel Cavenos."

He adored the way she used his preferred name, and, somewhat unexpectedly, he didn't mind the way it sounded combined with his real father's surname. What he liked best, however, was having someone refer to him as a man and not a lad or a boy. Particularly when she was that someone.

"You bring out the worst in me," he teased, punctuating the comment with a light kiss.

"Oh?" Her brows lifted. "We should definitely explore that more thoroughly." She gave him a brief kiss this time before pushing him back. "But not right now."

Kasiel relented, sliding out of bed, and giving her a hand up. She straightened her clothes, then smiled up at him with an affection he found unfathomable.

"When do I see you again?" he asked.

"After my assessments. Give me a couple of days. I need to keep my mind on my studies, and being around you does exactly the opposite."

"Good luck then." He leaned in to steal one more kiss. "I know you'll be a full healer next time I see you, which I hope will be soon."

"I hope so too." Before stepping away, she poked his scar, eliciting a wince and a sharp intake of breath from him. "Rub this, or I will."

He smirked at her as she hurried toward the sitting room. "So cruel."

"You have no idea."

She vanished through the doorway. A few longing-filled heartbeats later, he heard the main door open and close. A glance out the window at the brightening light of a new day reminded him he had his own classes he was in danger of being late to. He cleaned up at the basin in the bathing room and threw on some clothes, then rushed out to his first lesson of the day at the mind-crafter academy.

Most days, Jethan met him on his way out of the palace if he hadn't spent the night on Kasiel's couch. Today, he didn't show, but that happened occasionally. Sometimes his tehnaak had other duties to attend to or merely needed a break from schooling. Jethan had taken these classes before they brought Kasiel back to Vanris. He only accompanied Kasiel as often as he did because their success was now inexorably intertwined.

Classes in the Vanrian language, history, and culture sped by, while some other subjects dragged on. He took advantage of slow moments and breaks to do what Adnar had suggested and reach out to birds, rodents, and other creatures inside the city, surprised by how many there were once he started seeking them out. With that to distract him, the day raced by. It was soon time for his afternoon combat lessons. For about another week, he would continue dedicating that time to strengthening the muscles affected by his injuries. The deep cut to his arm and the one across his ribs were both significant enough to require targeted rehabilitation. It wouldn't be long before things were back to normal though, and these sessions would once again be spent collecting bruises from Jethan and the other soldier he sparred with.

Jethan remained absent during combat training as well. Given that they weren't doing actual lessons, his absence didn't influence the outcome any, but it was unusual to make it this far along in the day without a word from his tehnaak. It made him a little uneasy, though Jethan could only get into a limited amount of trouble within the city walls.

When the session ended, Kasiel reached out with his ability, connecting with an enthusiastic Sylaryth in the canyon as he made his way in that direction. Adnar greeted him at the bottom of the lift, his tethdrak sitting beside him. Sylaryth waited next to the gate, prancing from one foot to the other like a massive reptilian dog as he watched Kasiel approach.

Kasiel grinned. "You're ridiculous, Syl, you know that?"

He put his hand through the bars, letting the tethdrak press his head into his palm. Then he turned and offered Adnar a slight bow.

"Ahndhomen."

"Ahninveth Hahren," Adnar strode up to him, his tethdrak staying close by his side. "I thought we would test out your grouping skills some more today. Step inside the enclosure. We'll see how many tethdraks you can gather while riding along behind Sylaryth's eyes."

He tossed the key to the gate to Kasiel, who caught it and unlocked the entrance. Sylaryth bounded backwards, making room for him to push in the gate. Kasiel touched on the tethdrak's mind, encouraging him to one side to make room for Adnar and his companion. The beast obliged instantly.

The four of them strode out past the rock platform where he and Jethan had sat watching the sunset and out to a large flat area before the stream. Without waiting for direction, Kasiel sent Sylaryth loping off into the canyon, easing in behind the tethdrak's eyes to see the landscape rushing by in vibrant color.

"Ahndhomen," he said, watching and feeling out for more tethdraks as he spoke, "I've been wanting to ask you something. Do you know why my father retroactively approved our effort to save the healers in Katovan?"

"Focus," the other Feral answered firmly.

"I am." Kasiel drew on three tethdraks, casting

his mental net wider as he watched them join up with Sylaryth.

"Do you think I have some special insight into the dhomvalen's decisions?"

Kasiel drew in two more, followed by another five, bringing the group to eleven with Sylaryth. Not enough yet. "If not you, then who could I ask?"

"Khevarin Seylin."

The answer threw him off for an instant, but he steadied quickly, managing to hold the tethdraks he had and draw in four more while the growing collection sprinted through the canyon. "I can't just go ask the khevarin about my father. She's the ruler of Vanris."

"Why not? Her nephew is your tehnaak. That makes her family."

The thought of Khevarin Seylin being family was a jarring one, but Kasiel's focus continued to hold strong. "Who's his tehnaak?" Two more.

"Your father's tehnaak died three years ago."

The comment brought Jethan to mind. Losing his tehnaak would be crushing, as it had been for Tath when she lost hers on their mission to bring him home from the south. How did one cope with a loss that devastating? Arhk's wife, his son, and his tehnaak had all been taken from him. No wonder he was such a calloch.

"How did they die?"

"*He* died in battle. It shouldn't come as much of a surprise to learn that mind-crafters are the most sought-after targets on a battlefield. It's why we try to make sure they don't stand out from regular troops. Although some, like your father, are far too infamous amongst Alliance forces to bother hiding at this point."

Kasiel tried to imagine Arhk blending in. Could his ego even handle being part of the crowd? "How do you hide a Feral surrounded by beasts?" Six more tethdraks.

Adnar's answering chuckle was devoid of humor.

"Why do you think we have so few Ferals? You have an advantage, however. Your ability to see through their eyes will allow you to operate at a greater distance from your tethdraks. Now bring them in."

Was that supposed to be comforting? Kasiel started drawing them back, pulling in another loner as the group circled around. "Is there anyone else I could ask?"

"Your father. Now focus."

"I am." Irritated, he reached out to Adnar's tethdrak, bumping the ahndhomen from the beast's head and taking control.

An animalistic growl came from Adnar. "That was amusing the one time you did it by accident."

The ahndhomen aggressively kicked Kasiel back out of the tethdrak's head. He reeled for a moment, nearly losing control of the group he was bringing in, but, with Sylaryth's unwavering reinforcement, recovered fast enough to keep any of them from slipping away. He dropped back behind his own eyes. The ground rumbled as twenty-four tethdraks came charging up the canyon, leaping the stream and slowing to a stop in the open area before them. Twenty-four massive, reptilian beasts with scales in varying shades of red and brown, each one capable of inflicting catastrophic damage on the human body. Something he had learned first-hand with Sylaryth in Katovan.

Kasiel grinned, scanning the tethdraks where they stood, breathing hard and waiting for his guidance.

Adnar considered him. "Well done, Cavenos, but don't get arrogant."

"Impressive, Ahninveth Hahren."

His father's voice behind him sent Kasiel into a spin. He flailed, grasping for the confidence and balance that skittered away from him, all too aware of the dangers of losing control of his subjects. With effort, he recaptured his focus, but not before three tethdraks slipped free of his influence. A soft sigh of relief escaped him when none of them moved, and he cast a discreet look of gratitude toward Adnar for his assistance as he turned to face his father. Sylaryth trotted up beside him, instinctively offering the support of his presence.

Kasiel inclined his head. "Thank you, Dhomvalen."

Arhk's gaze moved over the collection of tethdraks before coming to rest on Adnar. The sides of his long, white-blond hair were braided and pulled back from refined features that could have been carved from marble for all the emotion they revealed. "I need to speak with you, Ahndhomen Adnar."

"Of course, Dhomvalen." Adnar faced Kasiel. "Ahninveth Hahren, send the tethdraks back out into the canyon. If you can keep this level of focus over the next few sessions, we'll try the kanodrak again."

"Thank you, Ahndhomen." Kasiel reached out with his ability, reclaiming control of the tethdraks Adnar had snatched up when he lost his focus. He glanced up at the platform above that overlooked the canyon as the two men started turning away. Jethan often watched him working with the tethdraks from there or from outside the gate, but not today.

Arhk paused, his unreadable gaze returning to Kasiel. "If you are looking for your tehnaak, Ahninveth, I understand he will be spending a few nights in the deeps."

Kasiel's gut twisted. The deeps? What had Jethan done to get thrown into isolation?

He inclined his head to his father again. "Thank you, Dhomvalen."

The two turned away, continuing toward the gate. They began speaking in lower voices, so Kasiel couldn't quite make out the words. It occurred to him that, if he could see through the tethdraks' eyes, there was no logical reason he couldn't use their other senses too. He dropped into Sylaryth's mind, but instead of looking out of the beast's eyes this time, he focused on the surrounding sounds. Bird calls. The breathing of the other tethdraks. Voices.

"Do you think he can do it?" Arhk's voice sounded different through the tethdrak's ears, but the words were almost as clear as if Kasiel were walking beside him.

"Ride a kanodrak?" Adnar asked. He didn't wait for Arhk to answer. "I'm certain of it."

"Why so confident?"

"That tethdrak of his would lie down and die for him, and not because he compelled it to. He has a natural affinity with the creatures he works with. The kanodrak is already responding to that."

If Arhk said anything in response, Kasiel didn't hear it. He withdrew abruptly, glancing at the massive beast standing next to him. Was that true? Would Sylaryth be willing to die for him? That was a heavy burden to carry on his shoulders. It touched on that part of him that wanted to make sure no one ever died for him again. The healer Ahrin, Tath's tehnaak, gave his life bringing Kasiel to Vanris. That was already one death too many.

He turned to face the pack of tethdraks. For practice, he moved them back out into the canyon one at a time, encouraging them to return to a location they preferred. It was better that way when it worked because it meant that rival males were less apt to end up in each other's space, and females didn't get directed into the wrong male's territory. Most, aside from a few alpha males and females, were willing to cooperate with him. The resistant ones needed more complicated mental nudges and emotions to get them going. It required patience, but it was better than forcing them. The population here was beginning to accept his presence among them without him always having to resort to the Feral mind-crafter ability that let him control their minds. He wanted to encourage that.

When he finished, he left the enclosure, taking Sylaryth with him, and went to investigate what had become of Jethan. Before heading to the lower palace levels, he swung by the kitchens, collecting a flask that he filled with mead and a small pouch in which he packed a modest selection of cheese, fruit, and bread. He tucked the items under his jacket. If they offered any food in the solitary cells, it was unlikely to be especially edible.

Unfortunately, he had intimate knowledge of how to get to the deeps. He had spent part of a night there as punishment for cheating on his Feral mind-crafter testing only a week after arriving in Etrion. It was less intimidating descending into those dismal stone halls where the prison cells were with Sylaryth by his side, though it still gave him a chill. It was in the deeps, tormented by waking nightmares inflicted on him by his father, that he remembered Edmund looking on in approval the night they cut off the pointed tops of his ears. This place was a den of unpleasant memories.

When he reached the junction before the hallway full of cells leading to the isolation tower, a guard stopped him, eyeing Sylaryth uneasily.

"Can I be of assistance, Lord Hahren?"

It surprised him at first that the woman knew who he was, but with only three Ferals in the city, perhaps it wasn't that shocking. He obviously wasn't Adnar or Kenna, so that quickly narrowed down the options.

"I hope so," he answered, doing his best to convey the confidence of his position. "Lord Jethan Markanis is in the deeps. Before he got thrown in there, he was helping me collect some information for my father. I need to speak with him a moment."

Her lips pressed into a fine line, and her brows pinched together. "Visitors are expressly forbidden in the deeps."

"It *is* for the dhomvalen." He urged Sylaryth a small step closer to her. Hopefully, word of this attempted manipulation wouldn't find its way back to his father.

Her attention shifted to the tethdrak. Kasiel placed his hand, the one with the khevarin's mark of recognition tattooed on it, on Sylaryth's head, reminding her of what he was. Who he was. Those things had never mattered before, but now... they must be worth something.

"All right. I can give you five minutes, but he doesn't leave the cell. You can talk to him in there. I'll open a window to let in some light." She turned and marched swiftly down the hall toward the tower.

Kasiel followed, remembering the only other time he had been there. A lot had changed since that night. He could say without hesitation that he preferred being a visitor coming down here by choice rather than as a forced guest.

They went through a heavy steel door at the end of the hall into the large circular tower beyond. The top of the tower opened to the sky, letting in the fading light of late afternoon. A stone walkway circling the perimeter enclosed a patch of grass and flowers that gave the space a bewilderingly welcoming impression. In the center stood a statue of a Vanrian soldier, her head bowed so her forehead almost touched the haft of the spear she held. Her sorrowful countenance and the solid steel doors set at even intervals around the outer edge sucked all the warmth from the space.

The guard escorted him to the third cell. She flipped a lever alongside the door. "That will open the window in the back to provide you with some light." She unlocked it and rested her hand on the handle, giving him a stern look. "You have five minutes."

Kasiel nodded his understanding and gestured to Sylaryth to wait. The tethdrak settled in the grass and watched him enter the dimly lit cell.

Even with the narrow window in the back wall open to let in light, it was dark in the cramped, rectangular space. Jethan sat on the floor to one side, squinting against the newly introduced daylight. He looked diminished sitting there alone in that tall, black stone cell. His eyes widened when he saw Kasiel walk in, and he scampered to his feet.

"Kas?"

Kasiel flinched as the door clanged shut behind him, absently rubbing at the knuckles of one hand. At least no one would be able to overhear them now. These cells were soundproof. He had learned that firsthand.

"Jeth, what did you do?"

Jethan's lips twisted into something between a guilty smile and a grimace. He scuffed a shoe across the floor. "After I left you last night, I went to the Twisted Vine. Where else was I going to go, right? Anyway, Leysa was there."

"Nerith's tehnaak?"

Jethan nodded. "She had nothing else to do. I had nothing else to do. We had a few drinks. I invited her back to my rooms in the palace for something better to eat. A few more drinks later, I might have boasted that I could get us a special vintage out of the palace reserve. It seemed like a bit of innocent fun at the time, so we snuck down there."

"You're the khevarin's nephew. Aren't you allowed in the reserves?"

He averted his gaze, rubbing at the back of his neck. "Not after a minor incident a couple of years ago involving several bottles set aside for an important political dinner. My aunt holds a grudge."

Kasiel shook his head. "Go on."

"Well, they've only ever had one guard in the reserve when I've been down there before. We spotted the guard and snuck past when he wasn't looking. When we got back to the reserve section, I thought we were home free. I walked around the corner straight into another guard." He slapped his hands together for emphasis. "Literally."

"That doesn't seem like a deeps-worthy offence."

Jethan gave him that wincing, guilty smile again. "Oh, it's not. But then I used my Charmer ability on the guard to convince him I had come there alone while Leysa snuck out. As soon as she was clear, I started working to convince him it was also fine for me to be down there, and it would have worked if the other guard hadn't walked in. He twisted my arms behind my back and marched me to my ahndhomen. Never gave me a chance to engage him."

Kasiel glanced through the tiny window at the fading light. Even with it open, it would be almost black in the cell soon.

Using your mindcraft against one of your own people was a severe infraction. It had to be, or no one in Vanris would trust the mind-crafters any more than the people in the southern kingdoms did. Still, he couldn't help thinking of the night his father lost control and unleashed his Frightener ability on him. The ability of a Frightener as powerful as the dhomvalen could cause worsening aftereffects that would have driven him to his death if Evoker Setera hadn't expunged the memory from his mind. His father would never suffer punishment for that incident. Being one of the most feared and respected people in Vanris came with its privileges.

"I can't pretend you didn't bring this on yourself, tehnaak, but I do owe you one for last night." He took out the hidden food and flask and handed them over.

Jethan's eyes sparked with a hint of his usual mischievous humor. "I've taught you well." He slipped the items into a corner near the door, where the guard would be unlikely to notice them when she let Kasiel out. "Did Nerith stay?"

"Not that it's any of your business, but yes. We didn't do what your smile suggests we did, however."

Jethan chuckled and gave a little shrug. "There's always next time. Any nightmares?"

Kasiel hesitated a moment before slowly shaking his head. "No. Not a one."

The door opened, letting in a flood of light. "Time's up, Ahninveth Hahren."

Kasiel gave Jethan a brief hug. "Thank you, tehnaak."

Jethan returned the embrace, then pushed him away. "Get out of here. Don't get into any trouble."

"It seems far less likely with you in here." Kasiel winked at him before he stepped through the door. It shut firmly behind him, cutting off Jethan's undoubtedly pithy response.

For a time, Kasiel considered heading over to the Twisted Vine. Some of the rest of the unit might be there. Avris and Merrin sometimes visited the tavern outside their usual nights, and Darro and Kince dropped in whenever they got the notion, which seemed to be often. The other three – Tath, Wedro, and Chander – typically showed up only on the last evening of the work week, on the same nights he and Jethan did. The odds of running into at least one of the other pairings were decent. And yet... He had never gone there on his own before. The mere notion made him want to sneak back to the familiar comfort of the tethdrak habitat or his rooms.

The unit was Kasiel's chosen family now – his tehsheyn – bonded by the harrowing several-hundred-mile journey they embarked upon to bring him from Fernwallow to Vanris. And yet, he hadn't really spent any time with them without Jethan there. Jethan had been the leader on that mission, the rope that tied them all together until they started connecting on their own. In too many ways, Kasiel was still figuring out how to belong here, and Jethan was his foundation.

After mulling it over along his way out of the prison level, he decided he would spend the evening in. He took Sylaryth back to the canyon, lingering there with him for a time on one of the sun-warmed rocks while several more of the beasts joined them at a distance. Sylaryth's enthusiastic welcome didn't surprise him anymore, but receiving any positive reaction from the others without having to encourage it with a mental touch still came as something of a shock.

If only the populace of Etrion was as willing to give him a chance. Plenty of people continued to distrust him because he had been raised in the southern kingdoms. At least as many resented that the khevarin had provided him with quarters in the palace near his father's and allowed him to learn their ways. They were less open about it since he and his companions helped capture the trio who had attacked Nerith, but that didn't mean they weren't still out there waiting for an opportunity.

The way his thoughts were trending made the idea of walking to the palace alone a lot less attractive, but hunger had begun nagging at him. He had options, though, thanks to Jethan. His illicit trips to visit the juvenile tethdraks before his assessment testing that first week taught him an alternate route through a long tunnel up into the enclosed gardens off the west side of the palace. Tonight, he took that passage, avoiding the open streets that might make a tempting target of him on his own. His combat skills had improved drastically, but this was a military city. Most of the residents here had trained to fight their entire lives. His mere months of practice weren't going to hold up against that.

Once in the palace, he used less-frequented corridors to return to his rooms, trying to avoid anyone who might want anything at all from him. Despite that, he barely sat down to the tray of food waiting for him before someone tapped on his door. The previous night with Nerith danced to the forefront of his mind, and he smiled. Had she decided to visit again, after all?

He took a bite of succulent, if lukewarm, roast as he stood, following it with a swallow of water. Whoever waited outside knocked again.

He hurried to open the door. The woman standing there had long reddish-blond hair woven into a single braid that draped over her left shoulder. Her eyes were such a bright green it was hard to notice anything else about her, though the general impression was unremarkable aside from those striking eyes. The sword that rested on her hip sat there with an ease that suggested she was an active-duty soldier. But then, most people in Etrion were, regardless of how they looked otherwise.

"Ahninveth Hahren," she said, a soft breath of relief accompanying his name. "I hoped I had the right room."

"Sorry. Do I know you?"

She smiled, her green eyes drawing him in. "No. Not yet. But you've seen me in the tavern with Avris and Merrin before."

No. He would have remembered her eyes, at the very least. He started shaking his head when a vague memory plucked at his thoughts like a musician picking at the strings of a lute. Maybe he had seen her. Yes. Of course he had. She was friends with a few of his companions. Part of the extended group.

"Yes. I guess I have noticed you around."

"Treya." She offered her hand.

He glanced down as he took it, a moment of doubt creeping back in. Had he really seen her before?

She retracted her hand after a brief shake. Then she brought her thumb up and brushed it under his lip. A light, intimate touch. He jerked back in surprise, looking up to meet those impossible eyes again.

"Sorry. You had a little something there. I apologize if that was too forward of me. I'm kind of hopeless when it comes to personal boundaries." Her full lips parted in a nervous smile that sparkled into her eyes.

Kasiel found a smile curving his lips in response.

Perhaps he didn't know her, but she seemed like someone he might want to know. "It's fine. Can I do something for you?"

"Oh. Not for me. Darro asked me to come and get you. He had something he wanted to talk to you about. He said I should escort you back to his place so you wouldn't have to walk the streets alone. You will come, won't you?"

Kasiel couldn't bring himself to look away from her. "Darro?" He struggled for a moment. Again, something struck him as off about the situation, but he couldn't get his head around what it might be. "Why did he send you?"

"You know Darro." Her soft laugh chased away that lurking unease. "He's not one to go out of his way if he can get someone else to do the work for him. I have something to take care of, but if you meet me out in front of the garden entrance in a few minutes, we can walk together. It'll be nice."

Kasiel nodded. As pleasant as the evening was, it would be nice. "All right. I'll meet you there."

A delighted smile split her lips before she darted off. Kasiel grabbed his jacket and snagged one more quick bite of his dinner, then he struck out for the garden entrance. By the time he got there, however, doubt dragged at his footsteps. Why had he come? He shouldn't be wandering the city with a stranger, and this woman was a stranger. Just as he turned to head back inside, she came jogging up.

"Wait. Where're you going?"

Kasiel faced her, prepared to apologize for wasting her time and excuse himself. He met those bright green eyes, determined not to let her friendly smile sway him.

Her lower lip pushed out in a playful pout. "I thought we were going for a little moonlit walk together. To Darro's place." She gave a light laugh as she gestured for him to accompany her, the soothing sound chasing away his absurd paranoia.

"Well, I..." Whatever he had planned to say melted away on his tongue, fading from his thoughts. "Yes. Let's go."

They wandered out into the night together, Treya leading him on a meandering journey through the city streets. She chatted about combat training for a time, walking backwards in front of him for a few strides now and then to meet his eyes while she talked. He found the behavior charming in an eccentric way, appreciating the opportunity to gaze into those stunning eyes.

She was strolling alongside him when he began looking around and realized he no longer recognized the narrow, empty streets they were traveling down. Were they even going in the right direction? When had they left the areas he knew?

"What's your favorite drink at the Twisted Vine?" She stepped around in front of him, walking backwards again. "Mine's... Well, I have a little flask of it here." A conspiratorial smile tugged up the corners of her mouth when she stopped, forcing him to do the same, and pulled a flask out of a pouch on her belt. "Try some."

"Should we—"

She held the flask to his lips, those emerald eyes shining at him over it. "Everyone is always so obsessed with Vanrian Black Mead, but this is better. You'll love it."

He probably would. Kasiel accepted the flask and tipped it back, taking a long swallow. It had the burn of strong alcohol, with a slightly sweet aftertaste that reminded him of something he couldn't quite place through his muddled thoughts. "You're right, it is good."

He handed it back to her, and she sealed the flask, tucking it into her pouch.

"Aren't you going to have any?"

Treya stepped closer to him, brushing her thumb across his lips to wipe away a few lingering remnants of the drink on them. His pulse quickened. He stared into her eyes as she shook her head.

"No. I want it to last." A hint of satisfaction curled her lips now. "We should get to Darro's, don't you think?"

Kasiel nodded.

She turned and began walking, stealing away the comfort of her gaze. Warmth from the alcohol spread through him, unexpectedly potent for such a modest amount. He followed her, finding it increasingly difficult to keep track of her movements. His vision blurred, his legs growing unsteady. They had barely gone another two blocks before he stumbled and fell into the side of a building, bracing himself against it. He tried to shake away the thickening fog that filled his head, but the effort only made him dizzy.

Treya came back to him, something distinctly predatory in her smile now. A chill swept through him. He hadn't ever seen her before tonight. He was suddenly certain of that. Not with Avris or Merrin. Not with anyone he knew.

"You're a... Charmer." His words came out slurred.

She patted his cheek with one hand. "Yes, darling." Her gaze flickered to something behind him, her expression turning cold. "He's all yours."

Kasiel tried to turn to see who she was talking to, but his legs gave out, and he fell into a bottomless darkness.

•

The sound of voices slowly penetrated that darkness. His head was pounding. His hands and feet were bound.

Whatever he was lying on was cold and hard, the grit of packed dirt and sand rough against his cheek. A light breeze told him he was outside, somewhere away from the cobbled city streets he had blacked out in.

Fighting panic, he kept his eyes closed and his breathing steady, listening to the voices. Horses were approaching. At least three, moving at a canter from the cadence of their hoofbeats, the creak of wagon wheels accompanying them. Odd how he could feel every strike of a steel-shod hoof vibrating up through the hard ground beneath him. The sensation helped him focus past his rising dread.

"Took them long enough. The bastard's going to wake up soon."

A male voice, speaking in Vanrian. One he didn't recognize. This was bad.

You're not helpless, he reminded himself, reaching out with his mind. Blindly searching was far more difficult than being able to look around for a target or at least knowing a direction, but his captors clearly weren't eager for him to wake up. That meant things were probably going to get worse for him the instant they realized he already had. If he could convince them he was still out, he could buy himself time.

There. A sandhawk. He slipped behind the raptor's eyes. It sat perched on top of a rock, busily tearing strips of flesh from a dead snake. It took little encouragement to drive it up into the sky. The arid landscape and sections of scorched ground were enough to tell him they were in the Crimson Break – the wide swath of devastated land between Vanris and the Pandrean Alliance kingdoms to the south.

Sweeping the bird around, he spotted the group he was with. Two Vanrian men waited on foot, their horses ground tied a few feet away from where Kasiel lay in the dirt. Treya, the Charmer, wasn't with them. The approaching riders were southern. Three men with four horses. The fourth animal was a stockier beast, drawing a wagon with an empty cage affixed on it, partially covered in canvas. The newcomers slowed to a stop about ten feet back. Their movement stirred a cloud of dust that the breeze sent over him and his captors.

"Callochs," one of the Vanrians muttered under his breath.

Kasiel watched with the bird's eyes, hearing saddles creaking and feet hitting the dirt through his own ears as two of the new arrivals dismounted. The separation of senses was at once both disconcerting and fascinating. But he didn't have time right now to become caught up in that experience. Investing himself deeper in his connection to the raptor made it easier to let his physical body appear unconscious. He turned the bird, looking for anything he could use. The horses were an option, but he might not be able to create enough chaos with just them to keep these men off him. Sending it further out, he continued his search.

"You brought what we asked for?" one southerner said in Pandrean Common.

After so many months in Vanris, Kasiel noticed the southern accent a lot more than he had before. He could hear the two men walking closer now, their feet grinding grit into the hard ground.

"Just like you asked," one of the Vanrians answered, also switching to Pandrean Common.

Someone flicked Kasiel's hair out of his face, the unexpected sensation almost making him break his ruse. There was a moment of silence, then they pushed his hair back further, exposing one cut ear to the cool morning air. He heard whoever it was make a hasty retreat.

"Havaad's mercy! You brought us that Break-blasted Feral. The Warden's son."

The raptor flew over a deep spot in a nearby canyon,

and Kasiel noticed something moving in the shade. He swept the sandhawk around and dipped lower.

"Yes," one of the Vanrians answered. "He doesn't belong in Vanris."

"Then kill him. Don't bring him to us."

"You wanted a mind-crafter," the Vanrian returned, a smug edge to his tone. He almost sounded like he was enjoying himself.

"We specifically asked for a mind-crafter we could control long enough to get them to the stronghold. One of your Charmers or something else easy to manage. How are we supposed to keep him from calling in beasts to help him while we're traveling?" The southerner was shouting now, his ire suggesting that he felt the Vanrians had betrayed whatever arrangement they had made between them.

In the shadows of an overhang, Kasiel found what he needed. Five large wildcats rested outside their den. Their dark tawny coats blended with the dusty terrain, making them easy to miss when they weren't moving. They had undoubtedly done their hunting at dawn. Dragging them out now might anger them, but he kind of wanted them to be a little angry. Splitting his awareness between them, he eased into their minds, using only as much force as he had to. He didn't have time for a great deal of finesse.

"Don't let him wake up then," one of the Vanrians was saying, a lilt of amusement in his voice that was unlikely to make the southerner happy.

"We keep him knocked out the entire way and he won't survive the journey. And we won't get there alive if his fucking father comes after him."

"You wanted a mind-crafter. We brought you one."

"This isn't what we asked for, and you know it," the southern man shouted. "You're trying to unload your problem on us. Kill him if you want to. We're not paying you until we get what we asked for." Kasiel could hear the man walking back to his companions now, muttering under his breath, "Drag us all the fucking way out here for this bullshit."

The cats were on the move now. Unwelcome humans had invaded their territory, and Kasiel was happy to guide the beasts to them. He flew the sandhawk ahead, sweeping down to check on his situation. The two southerners who had dismounted were returning to their horses. The Vanrians watched them for a moment, then one raised his hand and called after them.

"Fine. This little calloch's tehnaak is a Charmer. We can bring him to you in two days, but our price goes up fifty percent."

One southerner stopped and faced them. "Only things I got out of that were Charmer and two days. Sure, we'll take a Charmer, but the payment stays the same."

Rage flashed through Kasiel like wildfire. They weren't getting their hands on Jethan. Not ever.

The Vanrian who had done most of the talking shook his head. "No. We both know there are people in the Alliance who will pay for dead mind-crafters. You can still make a tidy sum off this one's corpse. You want another one, you're paying more."

Sudden pain flared through Kasiel. Pain that wasn't his. He pulled out of the raptor's mind. His eyes snapped open, and he spotted the third southerner still sitting on his horse, lowering a crossbow.

The man's gaze shifted to Kasiel, and their eyes met. "Shit, he's—"

Kasiel jumped into the horse's mind, sending the animal into a wild panic. It reared and twisted sideways with enough force that the man lost his seat. He hit the ground with a pained grunt. The others were turning to Kasiel now, so he frenzied the rest of their mounts. It was easier than usual, given that the cats had emerged from the sunken area and were sprinting toward them now. One of the southern horses reared and struck out with its front hooves at the man standing next to it, catching him in the face with the loud crack of breaking bone. The man collapsed instantly.

The horse hitched to the wagon also reared and kicked out. One leg became caught in the rigging, and it fell, busting the wagon shafts with its thrashing. Freed of its burden, the animal lunged back to its feet and bolted, lines from the harness flying out behind it. Kasiel lost his tenuous control over one cat as it gave chase.

One of the Vanrians swung a kick at Kasiel's head. He brought his arms up fast enough to take the blow to the backs of his forearms. It still hurt, but at least it wasn't incapacitating. One failed attack was apparently all the man was willing to risk. He was Vanrian. He knew enough to recognize that, even if he killed Kasiel now, the cats were likely tuned to their targets. Giving up the effort, he bolted after his companion, almost certainly his tehnaak, who was about to their horses. Just before the man reached the animals, Kasiel sent them running.

Two of the cats sprinted past him. One took down the first Vanrian soldier from behind. The other soldier turned to fight, but he wasn't fast enough to draw his blade before the cat slammed into him. He screamed as claws and teeth ripped into his flesh. The last two cats raced the opposite direction, attacking the two remaining southerners who were trying to get clear of their panicked mounts. When the cats charged in, the horses bolted.

In a moment of forethought, Kasiel reached out and drew one of the Vanrian animals back around. If he managed not to die here, wherever here was, he was going to need a ride home.

The last human scream cut off abruptly. The snarling of the cats carried on in a less frenzied manner now. Kasiel laid in the dirt and took a deep breath, a dizzying sense of relief flooding through him. He wasn't out of danger yet, though. With a careful mental nudge, he sent all but one cat over to where the beast he had lost control of was feasting on the wagon horse. Guilt twisted in his chest for the poor animal, but its death would give the other horses time to escape and keep the wildcats off the mount he had retained for himself.

The one remaining cat he compelled to drag the closest of the two dead Vanrian soldiers to him. The cat snarled at him when he reached out to the body, but he redirected it, sending it to join the others. Then he took the soldier's dagger and wedged the hilt between his bound feet, using the blade to cut through the bonds holding his hands. With that done, he made quick work of cutting his feet free.

Keeping a respectful distance between himself and the cats, he checked the three southerners, looking for anything that might tell him more about what their purpose was in trying to purchase a living mind-crafter. The most he found was compelling evidence, based on their mismatched leather and chain armor and lack of declarative insignia or colors, that they were mercenaries. Anyone could have hired them. He uncovered a hefty sack of Vanrian coin tucked in a back corner of the wagon. Probably payment for the mind-crafter. Taking that, he carried it over to the waiting horse.

The poor animal was trembling, the whites of its eyes showing as it stared at the deadly cats. It couldn't overpower his mental grip to flee, but the desire to do so was apparent in the way it alternately stomped its feet and leaned forward, as if trying to pull a heavy wagon. Kasiel sent soothing into the horse, calming it while he added the sack of coins to its saddlebags. Then he reached out with his mind again.

He immediately found what he was looking for. The raptor had gone down in a patch of dry grass a few yards away. The crossbow bolt had skimmed its side and damaged one wing. He pulled the shirt off one of the Vanrian soldiers, trying not to think about the fact that he had killed the man. Filling the bird's mind with a sense of safety, protection, and help, he carefully wrapped the sandhawk in the shirt. Cradling the living bundle in one arm, he climbed up on the horse. Then he turned the animal north and kicked it up to a canter, leaving the cats to their feast.

This section of the Crimson Break was unfamiliar to Kasiel. That wasn't especially surprising, given how little time he had spent outside Etrion since his arrival in Vanris. The terrain here varied dramatically, with an abundance of slot canyons and raised rock formations. It wasn't more than a few hours before he came around the side of a plateau and spotted a Vanrian watchtower ahead. About the same time, he caught sight of a group of riders coming in his direction, sending up a cloud of dust in their wake. They appeared to be following something large that was also charging toward him.

He reached out, relief easing the tension from his shoulders and back when he met up with Sylaryth's enthusiastic welcome. He hugged the sandhawk against him and urged his mount faster, pushing a sense of calm down over the horse to keep it from spooking when they met up with the tethdrak.

When they were a few yards apart, Kasiel eased his mount to a controlled canter. Sylaryth bounded past him and came around on the other side. The tethdrak's excited leaping was enough to startle the horse even through his soothing. Breathing a shaky laugh, he tightened his grip on the reins and sent a flood of affection and calm to Sylaryth, managing to tone the large beast's exuberance down a little.

They slowed to a stop as they met up with the approaching riders. Kastus was in the lead, with Wedro, Chander, Avris, Merrin, and Tath following along. It surprised him to see so many of his companions there.

Avris shook her head at Kasiel as they drew together. "We came here to save you, right? You're supposed to be in distress."

If only she knew how much distress he was in beneath the surface. Keeping that hidden, Kasiel shrugged. "You took too long." He glanced down at Sylaryth. "How did you manage to bring him?"

"Adnar's here," Chander said. "He stayed back at the tower so we wouldn't be putting another Feral at risk coming out here. Even he apparently didn't have to do much to manage Syl. Your tethdrak knew something was wrong before anyone else did. He started searching for you the minute Adnar pulled him out of the enclosure."

Wedro rode up next to Kasiel. He glanced down at the raptor in his arms, his brows pinching together. "What happened? You disappeared and Syl was frantic when Adnar checked on the tethdraks first thing this morning. Now here you are in the Break with blood spattered across your shirt and..." He grabbed Kasiel's arm, provoking a defensive shriek from the sandhawk, and held it up to take a better look at the irritated rubs on his wrist. "And it looks to me like someone had you tied up."

Kasiel glanced down at his shirt. He hadn't noticed the now-dry spray of red across the front of it. The image of a desert cat tearing open the chest of one of the Vanrians flashed behind his eyes and his stomach turned. "The blood's not mine." A tremor moved through him. He was back among people who not only didn't want him dead, but who cared enough to come searching, regardless of what danger might be waiting for them. His eyes started to sting. He adjusted his hold on the raptor to give himself an excuse to keep his gaze down. "I'll explain everything when we meet up with Adnar."

Tath circled around and came up alongside him, using her horse to edge Wedro out of the way rather than attempting to move Sylaryth. She put a hand on his arm. A gesture of comfort. "We should get moving then."

He met her eyes and nodded, grateful for the compassion in her gentle gaze. The rest of the group circled around him, and they struck out for the watchtower at a canter.

Kastus led for a while, then he fell back alongside Tath as they neared the enormous black structure. "How did you get past the watchtower without being seen?"

How had they gotten him past the tower? "I don't know. I wasn't conscious at the time."

Tath's lips pressed together in a hard line, her hands tightening on her reins.

Kastus looked up at the structure, his eyes narrowing. "Perhaps that's a question for the tower guards, then."

"You think someone here might have been involved?" Kasiel asked.

Kastus gave a curt nod. "Involved, or at least bribed to look the other way."

The tower loomed over them now. The first time Kasiel had seen one of the Vanrian watchtowers, he was still learning who and what he was. He had known nothing of the language and next to nothing of the culture here. The awesome black stone structure had been the embodiment of his fears. Overwhelming. Insurmountable.

This time, he took comfort from the imposing strength it represented. Maybe some people didn't want him in Vanris, but those who did mattered more. They were the ones who made this place his home.

One of those people emerged from the tower as they rode up. Adnar's long strides consumed the ground between them, his tethdrak close beside him. Man and beast both moved like predators on the hunt.

Kasiel was sure he saw a flicker of relief in the ahndhomen's expression before he turned to Kastus. "You found him fast."

"We didn't exactly find him. He was already heading this way when we met up with him."

Adnar looked at Kasiel. His keen gaze moved from the blood on his shirt to the hawk in his arms, then to Sylaryth, who hovered as protectively close as he could with the horse in the mix. "Rough night, Ahninveth Hahren?"

For some reason, the question amplified his urge to break down and cry. The result of hunger, pain, and the ultimate release of fear now that he was among allies. He wouldn't let himself break down, though. This experience wasn't over. Not yet. He needed to hold himself together, at least until it was. "You could say that, sir."

"Let's go inside. I need you to tell me exactly what happened." He approached Kasiel and held his hands up, his gaze resting on the bundle in Kasiel's arms.

Kasiel passed the sandhawk gently down to him, keeping a steady flow of calm and safety feeding into the injured raptor. Then he swung off. He stood next to his mount and peered over the saddle at the city of Etrion rising like a black storm on the horizon. Jethan was there. Nerith too. His home.

"Ahndhomen Adnar," he began. Something in his voice stopped Avris and Tath as they started to dismount. They settled back into their saddles, and affection surged in him in response to their perceptiveness. He faced Adnar, who stood watching him, waiting for him to continue. "If you could check the hawk and make sure it's stable enough, I would prefer to proceed to the city. I can tell you everything along the way."

Adnar held his gaze for a long moment. Then he offered the bird back to Kasiel, letting him hold the creature while he opened the bundle. He looked at the light graze that had sheered away some feathers and drawn a thin line of blood on the raptor's side. After a few seconds, he gently pulled out the wing, inspecting where the bolt had damaged a few feathers, grounding the bird. When he finished his examination, he let go of the wing so the sandhawk could fold it in and wrapped the shirt back over.

"With a little help, it should recover. In the interim, it will need someone to hunt for it. By the time it can fly again, it is possible that you will have earned yourself a remarkable set of eyes, Ahninveth."

"Thank you." Kasiel adjusted his hold on the bundle and swung into the saddle again.

Kastus dismounted. "Take your horse, Adnar. I'm going to stay here. I suspect someone in the tower may have been involved. If so, they might panic now that they know Hahren's back. It's the perfect time to ask a few questions."

Kasiel winced inwardly at the use of his Vanrian name. At least he was becoming better at not visibly reacting to it.

Adnar took the reins. "I can send a full rotation of guards out if you want to bring this bunch back to the city for additional questioning. Do you need help?"

Kastus glanced over their group. "If you can leave me Merrin and Avris, I'll bring them back to the city with the tower guards once the rotation arrives."

The two women dismounted when Adnar nodded. The Feral ahndhomen swung up into the saddle. "We will see you then."

Avris tapped Kasiel's leg as she led her mount past

him. "I expect to be regaled with the full story at the tavern later."

"You can count on it." It surprised him that he could manage a wink and a grin for her, given that his insides felt like quivering mush.

They rode out then, leaving the three behind. Sylaryth stayed close on one side and Adnar moved up next to him on the other, his tethdrak creating a compelling barrier on his far side. They kept to a slower pace while Kasiel recounted everything he could recall from the moment the Charmer showed up at his door to when he met Kastus and the rest riding through the Break.

When he finished, Adnar looked ready to rip someone's throat out with his own teeth. Next to him, his tethdrak was emitting angry clicks and occasional growls that were riling up Sylaryth. Kasiel sent calm and affection to his companion, doing his best to keep the two tethdraks from feeding each other's aggression.

Adnar drew a deep breath and his tethdrak immediately settled. "You did well, Ahninveth. You kept your head about you and used your ability as skillfully as any Feral with years of experience and training would have."

"I should have known better than to trust Treya to begin with." Kasiel tightened his grip on the reins, the leather straps pressing uncomfortably into his palm.

"You didn't have to trust her. She is a Charmer. You should know from seeing Jethan work that all she had to do was get you to look her in the eyes a few times."

Sylaryth growled next to him, reacting to Kasiel's rising anger. "I'm starting to understand why the southern kingdoms hate mind-crafters so much."

Adnar gave him a hard look. "That's a dangerous sentiment to speak aloud, Ahninveth. I do not want to hear those words cross your lips ever again. Understood?"

Kasiel swallowed, pushing down his anger. "Yes, sir."

They kicked the horses up to a canter from there, riding in silence the rest of the way to the city. Before they entered, Adnar handed Kasiel his cloak and had him pull the hood forward to hide his face. Once they were inside, the Feral ahndhomen charged Tath with finding Kenna and sending her to the palace entrance to meet him. He then turned to Wedro and Chander.

"Do you two know how to get to the private quarters within the palace by way of the inner wall passages?"

Wedro nodded, an uncommon intensity in his glacial-blue eyes.

"Good. I expect you to get Ahninveth Hahren to his rooms without him being seen by anyone." He considered the sandhawk a moment, then looked up into the hood at Kasiel. "Keep yourself hidden in my cloak. We don't know yet who else could be involved in this. I will take the raptor and Sylaryth with me. If I'm seen crossing the city with your tethdrak, that will encourage the assumption that we didn't find you."

"Yes, sir." Kasiel reluctantly allowed Adnar to assume control of both beasts and handed over the hawk.

The Feral ahndhomen signaled a pair of guards standing alongside the large double doors on their right. They opened to an enclosed passage that followed along the inside of the wall. It was designed to allow riders to move unhindered and unobserved around to the palace in situations where discretion was required. The guards let Kasiel, Wedro, and Chander enter. Adnar trotted off into the city with the two tethdraks, the sandhawk bundled in his arms. The doors closed behind them, dropping them into the limited light of torches placed at intervals along the length of the concealed way.

They held to a controlled canter while riding single file through the passage with Wedro in the lead and Chander bringing up the rear. The two took their task seriously, which made the weight of the circumstances that much greater, given that both tended to lean into humor even when it was inappropriate.

The long, monotonous route extended ahead and behind, always the same, making it seem as if they were making no progress for a time. Then an entrance to the palace was before them and they left their horses with a guard who asked them no questions. The halls they followed inside the palace were stark and unfamiliar at first, until they climbed a narrow stairwell and slipped through a hidden door, emerging in the private quarters. As soon as they stepped into his rooms, he took a deep breath and pulled off Adnar's cloak. A mild disappointment crept through him at finding no food waiting. It wasn't a surprise under the circumstances, but he mourned the lukewarm roast he only got two bites of the night before, given that he hadn't eaten since.

His stomach growled and he grimaced. "Sorry."

Wedro glanced over at him. "Shit. You probably haven't eaten for a while. I can go try to find something."

Kasiel shook his head. "I think we should stay here until we hear from Adnar. I'm going to get washed up."

"All right. We'll hold the couch down." True to his words, Chander plopped onto the couch and put his feet up on the elegant table.

Kasiel wandered through his bedroom into the bathing room. He took his time cleaning up and getting dressed in clothes without bloodstains on them. When he came back out, Wedro and Chander were playing a round of dice at the table. He joined in, pretending, for the moment, that nothing out of the ordinary was going on.

A knock on the door interrupted their third game. Before anyone could answer it, Adnar entered with Jethan on his heels. Kasiel stood. His tehnaak met his eyes and darted around Adnar, engulfing him in a fierce embrace.

"You Break-blasted calloch! I told you not to go getting into trouble without me."

"I got out of it without you too," Kasiel teased, though he returned the hug with equal intensity, closing his eyes for a second to bask in the comforting strength of the bond that linked them.

"Lord Markanis." Adnar cleared his throat. "I got you out of the deeps for a reason."

Jethan stepped back, a somewhat self-conscious grin turning his lips. "Yes, thanks for that, at least."

Kasiel answered his tehnaak with a chastising look before facing Adnar. "What about the sandhawk and Syl?"

"Sylaryth is in the hall." Adnar gave him a mental nudge, offering control of his tethdrak back to him. "Kenna took the raptor to get a better look at the damage and get it some food."

Lucky bird.

Kasiel reclaimed Sylaryth from Adnar, receiving that welcome wave of uplifting enthusiasm from the tethdrak. Excited clicking from the hall brought a faint smile to his lips.

"Jethan, do you know a Charmer by the name of Treya?" Adnar asked, moving them on to the matter at hand.

Jethan shook his head. "Doesn't sound familiar."

"She had red-blond hair," Kasiel said, her features etched in his mind in vivid detail. "Very pale skin and a narrow face. Her hair was done in a single braid that she kept pulling forward over one shoulder. She was about my height, and she had some of the brightest green eyes I've ever seen. Like gemstones."

Jethan had started nodding while he was speaking. The moment Kasiel mentioned her eyes, he snapped out a finger. "Ilsa. That's definitely Ilsa."

"You are certain?" Adnar's tone was deadly serious.

"Yes." For an instant, Jethan's expression was as

sober as the ahndhomen's. Then his brows pinched, and he exhaled dramatically. "I don't have to go back to the deeps now, do I?"

Adnar scowled at him. "I'll think about it. Ahninveth Kasiel, come with me. The rest of you need to stay here until we return. I don't want anyone outside the palace finding out about this until we've at least got Charmer Ilsa in custody."

Kasiel grabbed Adnar's cloak and threw it over his shoulders, pulling up the hood as they left the room. With Sylaryth at his side, someone might guess it was him, but since Adnar was also a Feral and would have been seen outside the palace with the tethdrak, it was still worth being discreet.

They strode along several halls and down a few floors to a sparsely furnished, stone-floored chamber. A scarred wooden table stood in the center of the room. Only one chair sat near the table, though two more waited, pushed up against the black stone wall on the far side next to another door. The flickering light in the room came from simple, dark metal sconces along the walls.

Setera, the Evoker who questioned Kasiel after his arrival in Vanris and who had removed his memories of Arhk unleashing his Frightener ability on him, entered through the door opposite the one Kasiel and Adnar came through. Arhk strode in behind her wearing his customary long black jacket with its dark metal accents. It was unfair how that single article of clothing significantly amplified the man's already intimidating presence. Kasiel's courage wanted to shrivel up and crawl away, but he wasn't going to let it. He was hungry, tired, and shaken. Not the best state to deal with his father in, but he had saved his own life several hours ago. He deserved some credit for that.

Setera inclined her head to each of them.

Kasiel removed Adnar's cloak, handling it back to

him, and returned the gesture. Technically, he and Setera had the same title now, though she had considerable seniority as a fourth-level ahninveth. He couldn't help wondering if she found his abrupt advancement offensive. If so, she wouldn't be the only one.

The dhomen of the city guard walked in through the back door then. He had one side of his head shaved with some of the symbols of his ke'hanoath, his identity, tattooed along that part of his head. Two dark metal cuffs wrapped the upper edge of his pointed ear on that side. His long, dusty blond hair hung down over his ear on the other side.

Arhk nodded to Adnar, though his gaze settled upon Kasiel first, lingering there for a few seconds even after he began speaking. "Ahndhomen Adnar, do we know who the Charmer was?"

"Her name is Ilsa, Dhomvalen," Adnar answered.

Arhk looked back at the guardsman. "Dhomen Branith."

Branith bowed. "Consider it done, Dhomvalen." The man strode across the room and out the front door.

When he was gone, Arhk's gaze came back to Adnar. "Yesterday, we got word that an Evoker went missing from the military camp near Katis. Given these events, I want that disappearance to be investigated more thoroughly. If someone on the Alliance side is making use of traitors within our ranks, we need to weed them out. I want more Evokers brought down from the north immediately. See to it."

"Dhomvalen." Adnar offered a partial bow and turned, leaving the room with his tethdrak.

Kasiel barely stopped himself from calling after the other Feral. He didn't want to be left here alone with his father and Setera, especially not as rattled as he was. Sylaryth shifted closer, bumping into him. Kasiel placed a hand on the tethdrak's shoulder, grateful for his strength and devotion.

When the door shut behind Adnar, Setera and Arhk both looked at Kasiel. Arhk gestured to the chair at the table. "Ahninveth, if you would sit and share with us the relevant events leading up to this moment."

"Adnar already told you everything, didn't he?" Kasiel held his position, refusing to even look at the indicated chair.

Setera nodded. "He did, but we need—"

Kasiel cut her off. "To make sure I'm not lying."

"A formality," Setera said, her icy blue eyes at least warmer than his father's. "It will also give me an opportunity to see some of what you remember and possibly catch details you may not recognize as important."

Kasiel heaved a sigh and settled into the seat. Sylaryth sat next to him, staring intently at the Evoker.

Setera gave the tethdrak a wary look as she collected a second chair and sat across from him.

He narrowed his eyes a fraction. "No stealing." Sylaryth growled softly to emphasize his words.

Setera pressed her lips together in a tight line, glancing briefly up at Arhk. The dhomvalen remained silent, though his surface thoughts may have offered her some response. After a second, she said, "I promise. You keep all your memories this time."

Kasiel told them everything as precisely as he could recall. Setera took notes while he spoke, sometimes nodding to herself. A few times, she prompted him for more information about details he mentioned in passing. The color of the clothes the two Vanrians were wearing. The equipment on the southern horses. Arhk leaned against the wall and watched in silence.

Going through it all again left Kasiel drained. He wanted to eat and sleep, but he got the disappointing impression they weren't close to finishing with him yet.

Arhk placed a hand on the back of Setera's chair and

leaned over her shoulder. She pointed several things in her notes out to him, letting whatever she had written do the talking for her. Whether they intended to share these thoughts with Kasiel, they didn't get the opportunity before someone knocked on the door. Arhk glanced at Kasiel and gestured behind him. Hoping he understood, Kasiel got up and moved to stand at the back of the room with Sylaryth.

"Enter," Arhk called, his voice somehow soft and commanding at the same time.

The door opened and Treya – Ilsa – entered the room. Her eyes widened the moment her gaze fell upon Kasiel. She backpedaled into the guard following her, obviously not expecting what waited for her in that small space. Arhk gave a nod, and the guard grabbed her arms, pulling them back behind her while a second guard stepped in and clapped manacles around her wrists.

Ilsa struggled, trying to twist free of the two guards. "Let me go! I did nothing wrong."

Arhk took a step closer to her, sweeping one hand toward the waiting chair. "Then sit and prove your innocence."

Pressure filled the room, and the lights seemed to dim. Ilsa flinched away from him. She stopped fighting and stared at the table as one guard moved the chair back from it and the other shoved her into it. The two guards separated then, one going to stand beside each of the entrances to the room.

"You know who I am?" The dangerous edge to Arhk's soft voice made Kasiel almost feel sorry for the Charmer. Almost.

"Yes, Dhomvalen."

"And you know Ahninveth Hahren, don't you?" he asked, gesturing to Kasiel.

Ilsa said nothing. She stared at the table as if the key to her salvation lay in the lines of that fine woodgrain.

"Your eyes admitted your guilt when you walked into the room. There's little point in trying to deny it, especially with Evoker Ahninveth Setera in attendance."

Ilsa started looking up, and Sylaryth growled. She froze.

Arhk glanced over at Kasiel and his tethdrak, the barest trace of a smile curving his lips. "As the tethdrak so elegantly implied, if you attempt to use your ability on anyone in this room, I will sentence you to death immediately. Understood?"

"Yes, sir." A tremble entered her voice now.

"Good. Who hired you to go after Ahninveth Hahren?"

"No one, Dhomvalen. They didn't ask for him specifically. They just asked me to help them get a mind-crafter."

"Who are *they*?"

A tear slid down her cheek, and Kasiel realized the pressure had never left the room. The light still appeared muted. What was his father doing to her? The Frightener ability hadn't struck him as a subtle one, but maybe it could be. Having been on the receiving end of it before, the implications were unsettling.

"I don't know. A couple of Vanrian soldiers approached me. They didn't give me details, just asked me to use my ability to help them capture a mind-crafter to deliver to interested parties outside the city. They told me that if I did so, they would give me a cut of their earnings and make sure I wasn't one of those taken." Her hands were trembling now too.

"What did these *interested parties* want a mind-crafter for?"

"I don't know." More tears were streaming down her cheeks now as she cringed away from him, pressing as far back in the chair as she could with her hands still bound behind her.

Arhk glanced at Setera, who nodded. The muscles in his jaw jumped. A tiny glimpse of frustration. He faced Ilsa. "And you chose my son because?"

I get to be your son now, do I?

Kasiel hastily suppressed the flood of cynicism, realizing Sylaryth might react to it if he wasn't careful.

"I chose him because he doesn't belong here. Even

you don't think he belongs here." She spat the last words at him. A flash of defiance that vanished instantly as the pressure in the room increased and the light dimmed more. She cringed back into the chair again with a whimper.

Kasiel caught himself as he was about to nod in agreement. She had a point.

For a moment, silence prevailed, then Arhk took another step closer to her. "What makes you think that?"

An aggressive sniffle did little to slow the snot now creeping toward her upper lip as she continued to tremble in the chair. She started looking up at Arhk, then caught herself and kept her gaze lowered. "It's obvious. He's your son, but there was nothing when he returned. No celebration. Not even an announcement. You're never seen together. Not even by the palace staff. You brought him here and tucked him away in the palace like some embarrassment."

The truth in her words was a blade in Kasiel's chest. He placed a hand on Sylaryth's shoulder, searching for comfort even the tethdrak couldn't provide. When Arhk looked over at him, he kept his head high, refusing to hide the tears that stung his eyes or the anger that tightened his jaw.

Arhk strode to the chair and placed a hand on the back of it, leaning over Ilsa. From the side, Kasiel could see blackness creeping across the whites of his eyes. She squeezed her eyes shut, whimpering.

"The fact that I have wronged my son doesn't give you or anyone else permission to do the same." Arhk stepped away from her, turning to look at Setera now, though his words, when he spoke, were for the guards. "Take her to the deeps. No food, water, or light. We'll question her again in the morning. Bring her tehnaak in next."

"No!" Ilsa screamed as the guards came in from

both sides of the room and hauled her to her feet. "She doesn't know anything!"

Arhk regarded her dispassionately. "We shall see."

"Leave her out of this, you calloch!" She fought the guards, still shouting protests as they dragged her out.

When they were gone, the pressure disappeared, and the light seemed to brighten. Even knowing that Arhk's ability only changed his perception of reality, not reality itself, the return to apparent normalcy still made it easier to breathe again.

"Did you get anything useful?" Arhk asked Setera.

She shook her head, folding her arms as she leaned back in the chair. "She doesn't seem to know much more than she said. I did get the images of the two soldiers she mentioned, but they are the same as the men in the images I got from Ahninveth Hahren of the two he dispatched out in the Break. If there are others involved, it is likely that she does not know who they are."

"We will see what she remembers after twelve hours of waking nightmares."

A shudder swept through Kasiel. He didn't envy her the night she was going to have. He took a few steps toward the table, Sylaryth staying protectively close to him. "What will happen to her after she's questioned tomorrow?"

Arhk faced him, his eyes now their normal color, a gray-green several shades lighter than Kasiel's. "Her ke'hanoath will be removed and she will be put to death as a traitor."

"Removed?"

"Cut away."

Kasiel recalled seeing some tattoos of her ke'hanoath peeking out around the collar of her shirt. He cringed inwardly, struggling not to envision the removal process. "You can't just kill her."

A hint of pressure moved through the room as Arhk's

expression hardened. "She was willing to use her ability to get you killed. There are few crimes more severe than using your ability against one of your own people with the intent to bring them harm. And selling a mind-crafter to the enemy is treason, without question. Do you believe she would have hesitated a moment if they had asked her to help them take Jethan?"

A hint of the anger he had experienced when the Vanrian soldiers offered Jethan to the mercenaries flared up again. He would kill them himself before he let that happen.

Arhk nodded as if he had gotten a satisfactory answer and turned back to Setera. "Did you get any indication of what the Alliance is trying to achieve by taking these mind-crafters alive?"

Setera glanced at her notes and shook her head. "No. I don't think she knows. At this point, we don't know for certain that Alliance forces are behind this."

Kasiel's stomach did a flip. He remembered Edmund risking death in Katovan to obtain some of his blood. Back when they saved Kasiel from the mercenaries outside Fernwallow, Jethan had guessed that the professor put Vanrian runes and symbols on Kasiel's armor and weapons to try awakening his ability. Whatever Edmund was hoping to discover back then, he appeared to believe the awakening of Kasiel's ability might help him find it.

"It's their blood."

Setera and Arhk looked at him, two sets of pale eyes demanding answers.

Kasiel drew a breath and made himself continue. "I don't think Edmund ever found what he was looking for in my blood when I was growing up because my ability hadn't awakened. When he took my blood at Katovan, that was no longer true. Whatever he was looking for, I think maybe he found it, and he's trying to get more."

"I thought you killed him."

That deadly calm in Arhk's voice set off alarms in Kasiel's head, but he didn't think he was necessarily the one in danger. At least he hoped he wasn't. "I'm not so sure now. Jeth and I were talking about it the other day. If someone got to him fast enough, he might have survived his injuries."

Arhk's eyes darkened along with the room. Learning that the man who had killed his wife and stolen his son might still be alive apparently didn't sit well with him. Kasiel almost wished he hadn't said anything, but keeping this to himself wouldn't help the situation.

"Dhomvalen, this could be very useful information."

Setera's gentle voice broke through to Arhk and he drew a deep breath, reining in his ability. "Yes, it could. You are free to go for now, Ahninveth Hahren. We may need to call on you again as we investigate this. Try not to get abducted in the interim."

The hint of dry humor in Arhk's words caught Kasiel off guard, but it gave him the courage to press for something else. "Can I ask one thing first?"

"What is it?"

"Why did you authorize our mission to save the healers in Katovan?"

Arhk's gaze flickered to Setera.

The Evoker stood abruptly, collecting her things. "I'll gather the officers and the khevarin and meet you in the council room," she said, excusing herself. She nodded to Kasiel on her way out through the door at the back.

Arhk picked up the chair Ilsa had been sitting in and tucked it in against the table. It was probably the most mundane thing Kasiel had ever seen him do. It made him markedly more human in that moment. Approachable.

He met Kasiel's eyes. "When we found out you might be alive, we had to make a choice whether to attempt a dangerous rescue mission or merely hire an assassin to eliminate the risk you posed. There were many convincing arguments to support the latter. Rescue would require putting some of our people at risk. We also had concerns that you would be unable to successfully integrate into our culture and that your spirit bond with Jethan would never recover from so many years apart." He paused, giving Kasiel too much time to consider that they had seriously weighed the option of having him killed.

"Our culture," Arhk continued, "was founded on the idea that our strength comes not from our technology or mind-crafters, but from our community, families, and friendships. That is why the practice of spirit siblings is such an integral part of who we are. You and Jethan have proven the power of those bonds. On top of that, the connection developing between you and the members of the unit that brought you back here represents everything we value at the core of our society. Your mother, Ellaris," he said her name with an aching reverence that resonated in Kasiel, "always believed that those values would be what eventually ended this war. The way you and your companions pulled together in Katovan and put yourselves at risk to protect those you care for was reckless."

He turned toward the table, placing his hands on the back of the chair. Kasiel held his breath, afraid the smallest distraction might disrupt the candid moment.

"However, you brought honor to your mother's memory through your selfless devotion to your companions. I was not willing to see any of you punished for that." Arhk stared at the empty spot where Setera had been sitting. He took a deep breath and let go of the chair back, glancing in Kasiel's direction. "Go. I imagine you could use some food and rest."

Kasiel lowered his gaze, uneasy at seeing vulnerability

in the one person he thought had none. Hating his father was easier than hoping for a relationship that might never be possible. This moment dangled that hope in front of him, and he couldn't bring himself to reach for it.

"Yes... Dhomvalen."

He strode to the door he had entered through, taking some comfort from Sylaryth's shoulder brushing against his hand.

"You handled things remarkably well today," Arhk said.

Kasiel paused with his hand on the door handle. He could turn around. He could try to build something from this.

"Thank you, Dhomvalen." *Father.*

He opened the door and walked out. Every step of the way back to his quarters, Kasiel considered turning around. Eventually, though, he had to acknowledge the reality that his father would have left the room anyhow, rendering the impulse pointless. He needed to return Sylaryth to the tethdrak enclosure, but going there alone would be a poor choice under the circumstances. If the others were still in his chambers, he could ask one of them to accompany him.

When he turned down the hall his rooms were in, Ahndhomen Adnar stepped away from the wall, cutting him off. "I'll take Sylaryth back to the habitat. You shouldn't be out alone by yourself yet, especially not at night."

A little of the tension in Kasiel's shoulders released. "Thank you, sir."

He didn't need to pass control to Adnar. He hadn't been actively influencing the tethdrak. Sylaryth's devotion to him meant that he responded to Kasiel's desires and needs without the necessity for prompting much of the time. A light connection was enough to ensure that he could intervene and take charge of the tethdrak if required. Before the beast left with Adnar, Kasiel held up his palm and Sylaryth pressed his head into it. A slight approving smile curved the ahndhomen's lips before he turned and led the tethdrak away. Kasiel watched them for a few seconds, feeling that ache of separation, then he continued to his rooms.

The quantity of laughter he heard coming from within surprised him. He opened the door to find their full unit inside. The group consisting of Jethan, Wedro, and Chander when he left had since grown to include Tath, Avris and Merrin, and Darro and Kince as well.

Kince, sitting in one of several unfamiliar chairs that they must have confiscated from another room, lifted his mug. "If it isn't the vanquisher of foul villains!"

Kasiel found himself the unexpected recipient of a hearty cheer from around the room as they all raised their mugs to him. Jethan hurried forward to present him with his own mug, its contents easily identified by the familiar scent as Vanrian Black Mead. The more important aroma came from a fresh platter of food resting on the table next to another similar tray that they had picked nearly clean in his absence.

He couldn't stop a smile as he shook his head at them. "Why do I get the feeling you didn't exactly keep quiet about my presence?"

"Your lack of faith wounds me," Jethan said, gesturing to an empty chair next to the table. "When I ordered this meal, I told the kitchen we were in your rooms hoping for your return and could use something to eat while we wiled away the hours worrying."

"You're the worst," Kasiel said, sinking gratefully into the chair.

"Also, kind of the best, right?" Jethan dropped into another chair next to him.

"Maybe." He began piling food on a plate, casting

a quick glance up at Merrin. "What happened at the watchtower?"

Merrin was leaning against one corner of the fireplace in a pose similar to Darro's where he stood on the other side. She looked at Avris, making it clear she was going to leave the talking to her tehnaak.

Avris washed a bite of roasted beet down with a swig of mead before answering. "Kastus used his Enkindler ability to make the tower guards feel confident and at ease before he questioned them. He got one of them to admit to seeing the riders with you pass by just before dawn. None of the other guards knew anything about it, so he arrested that one. We brought all of them in with us when the rotation arrived so they can undergo additional questioning with Setera there, but we know at least one deliberately allowed the soldiers to pass through with you."

"Calloch," Darro growled from his spot by the fire.

Kasiel turned his attention to the food. The others continued chatting while he did so, offering him a chance to focus on that need as he considered the information they had so far. Knowing Kastus had found a complicit party in the watchtower brought no comfort. How many more people might be involved? How many were willing to risk having their ke'hanoaths cut away and being put to death to give these mercenaries what they wanted? Ilsa had done it to protect herself from the same fate and had chosen him because, like a fair number of others, she didn't believe he belonged here. But what motivated the other two? Their comments to the mercenaries showed they were happy to get rid of him, but they hadn't asked Ilsa for him specifically. Was it just the coin, or was there something else?

His appetite faded, though he forced himself to eat more, recognizing that he would regret not doing so later. He set the plate, still partly full, on the table and rubbed at his jaw to ease the tightness of stress that had settled there. Most of his muscles ached. He wasn't sure how they had transported him from the city out into the Break, but his body suggested they hadn't been especially considerate about it.

Jethan leaned close, his hand coming to rest on Kasiel's shoulder. "You want us to go?"

"No." He sat up straighter. "I'm glad you're all here."

"Hear that," Wedro said, "he does like us."

Kasiel tossed a wedge of evalis fruit at Wedro that the other man deftly caught. "Maybe not all of you," he teased.

"We do need to talk about this, though," Darro said, his somber tone alone bringing the mood down. "They tried to get rid of you, Kas, and they made it clear that, among the mind-crafters in Etrion, you and Jethan are at the greatest risk. They may have failed this time, but others in the city might look at this as an opportunity."

Kasiel leaned back in the chair and glanced around at them. He didn't want to worry them more, but this problem might be bigger than they realized.

"What is it?" Jethan asked, tuned to his change in mood.

"A mind-crafter recently went missing over near Katis," Kasiel explained. "They think it could be related to this."

"Shit," Darro hissed under his breath.

A knock came at the door then, and Kasiel reflexively got up to answer it. "There's more," he added, holding up a hand to indicate that he would continue once he discovered who was outside. Remembering what happened the previous night caused a twist of apprehension, but he had his friends here now. No one would dare try anything.

He pulled the door open and Nerith stood there

beaming, her bright smile giving him a burst of renewed energy. She took a step toward him before noticing the gathering in the room.

Her smile faltered, and she shifted her foot back. "I'm sorry. Is this a bad time?"

His companions moved in near perfect unison, as if they shared a single mind.

"Nope," Kince said. "We were all just leaving."

Kasiel stepped back into the room, bringing Nerith along with a touch on her arm. He glanced around at them. "You don't have to go."

"It's time," Kince said, patting him on the shoulder as he headed out the door.

Darro gave Kasiel a nod on his way out. "We'll pick this up again tomorrow, danro."

Chander grabbed a few pieces of cheese off the platter on his way past and strode out with Wedro.

Tath stopped and put her arms around Kasiel, pulling him into a brief hug. "Stay safe, country boy."

Merrin and Avris followed Tath out. On her way past, Avris gave him a side hug and a peck on the cheek.

Jethan also hugged him, whispering in his ear. "If Nerith leaves, I can come back. Don't let anyone else in here."

Kasiel caught his arm as he continued out. "You be careful too, tehnaak. I'm not the only one in danger here."

Jethan nodded. "Promise." He glanced at Nerith and winked. "Have a good night, you two," he said before leaving.

When the door closed, Kasiel slid the bolt into place.

"What's going on, Kas?"

"It's nothing. How did—"

She pushed him back with a hand against his chest, her eyes narrowing. "Don't lie to me, Kasiel Cavenos."

He stared down at her, her lavender eyes alight with

anger, and couldn't help smiling. "Do you have any idea how beautiful you are when you're mad?"

Her jaw tightened.

"All right. Come on." He led her to the couch, sat her down beside him, and proceeded to tell her everything that had happened. When he finished, she sat staring at him in silence, unshed tears shining in her eyes. One slipped free, and he wiped it away gently. "I'm fine," he murmured. "The burning question is, did you pass your assessment?"

She nodded.

It was easy to find a genuine smile for her. "So, you're a full healer now. That's wonderful!"

She brushed away another tear and a coy grin crept across her lips that made his pulse race. "Yes. I'm fully qualified to care for all of you now."

Taking his hands, she stood and led him into the bedroom. There, she sat him down on the bed and pulled his shirt off as she had done before, then she kissed him. Kasiel welcomed her kiss, reaching for her, but she caught his wrists and pushed his arms back to his sides. Pulse racing, he watched her untie the belt of her dress and drop it. His core turned molten as she slowly lifted the garment over her head, exposing all the soft curves of her ivory skin that he yearned to touch.

When he started bringing a hand up, she stopped him with a shake of her head. Then she tugged off his boots and undid his trousers, helping him out of them. His entire body vibrated with longing. She slid back onto the bed, taking one of his hands and drawing him with her, her intense gaze holding him captive.

He moved over her and a surge of panic froze him there. What if he did something wrong? What if he hurt her?

"Nerith, I've never—"

She stopped him with a finger to his lips. "Neither

have I." She met his eyes, holding him captive. "I'm here because I want this, Kas. I want this with you."

"I don't want to hurt you."

Her soft smile melted him. "You won't. Not if you do it from a place of caring."

He held her gaze for a long moment, then he gave a small nod, his red hair falling forward to create a curtain that shaded their faces from the flickering light of the wall sconce. "I can do that," he whispered.

Their lips met, and she slid her hands up his arms and down along his back, setting his blood on fire.

Kasiel rolled onto his side. Nerith slept peacefully next to him, her back to him. The sheets had slipped down, revealing the silver-blue symbols of her ke'hanoath tattooed along her shoulder blades like a pair of wings. He shifted closer, gliding one hand over the curve of her waist to her belly. The side of her mouth curled slightly up.

Bringing his lips close to her ear, he whispered, "Good morning."

Nerith rolled onto her back to smile drowsily up at him. She lifted one hand, sliding it into his hair. "Good morning, handsome."

Her fingertips brushed the scarred edge of one cut ear, and he reflexively flinched back.

She jerked her hand away, brows pinching together.

"Sorry, I just..." He averted his gaze, frustration threatening to destroy what had the makings of a perfect morning.

"You don't have to explain." She lifted herself up enough to place a soft kiss on his lips.

With that simple act, she set off that fire that she was so skilled at igniting within him. Ears forgotten, he deepened the kiss, pulling her against him. It was a heady sensation, knowing she found him attractive and realizing he could be considered worthy by such an engaging and wonderful woman.

A knock on the door broke the moment.

Nerith giggled, touching a finger to his lips as he drew back. "That would be breakfast."

Kasiel recalled bolting the door after Jethan left. Sighing, he kissed the finger against his lips, then threw off the sheets. Rolling out of bed, he grabbed the long black dressing robe he had learned to leave draped upon the chair there and strode out through the sitting room to open the door for the palace attendant.

The man standing outside with a tray in hand ducked his head in a slight bow. "Good morning, Lord Hahren. I apologize if I woke you."

Kasiel waved it off. "No need to apologize. I'm the one who bolted the door."

He picked up one of the platters still on the table from last night, providing a space for the man to set down the fresh one. Feeling somewhat guilty for the mess they had left, he helped the attendant gather the remains of their meal onto a single tray. By the time they finished, they had the two old platters neatly stacked, making it possible for the attendant to remove them in one trip.

Nerith stepped into the doorway from the bedroom, wearing another of Kasiel's dressing robes. The hem dragged the floor. She had taken a moment to brush out her silvery hair, letting it drape over her shoulders, the points of her ears peeking out through it.

The attendant's eyes widened the slightest bit, and he ducked his head, perhaps attempting to hide the astute smirk that briefly curved his lips. "Nerith. I hope the morning finds you well."

Her gaze lingered on Kasiel when she spoke, a hint of flush in her cheeks. "Quite well, thank you."

The attendant glanced around the room. "Do you need me to return these chairs to... wherever they belong, my lord?"

"I'll figure it out later," Kasiel said. Where had they snatched those extra chairs from? He might have to ask the others when he next saw them. It was a free day. At least some of them were bound to show up at the Twisted Vine.

The attendant nodded. "Have a lovely morning," he said, hastening from the room.

Kasiel shut the door behind him and gestured to the table. "I made you breakfast."

Nerith laughed. "Did you now? You're remarkably quick." She walked to her satchel and pulled out a small stoneglass flask.

"What's that?" Kasiel asked, his gaze riveting upon her lips as she uncorked it and brought it to them.

"A little precaution. It prevents conception." She moved the flask away from her mouth, her lips quirking up on one side in a faint smirk. "That is, unless you were hoping for children now?"

"I..." He swallowed.

Nerith laughed and took a sip from the flask.

"How do you have that on you?" he asked, feeling far out of his depth.

"In a city full of soldiers, it's easy to come by. They don't allow children in the military towns and strongly discourage them anywhere this close to the Break. Policies partly inspired by what happened to you as a child."

He shook his head, trying to pull his thoughts back from the scattered state of momentary panic. "No, I mean..."

"Do I carry this around with me all the time?" She arched a delicate brow at him. "No. Did you think I was joking when I said I wanted this with you? Women can't often afford the luxury of spontaneity."

His cheeks grew warm. "I suppose that makes sense. If there's anything I really don't get, it's why—"

"I'd choose you?" Her expression darkened, and she

shoved the flask back into her satchel. "Because your southern upbringing and cut ears somehow make you unworthy?"

She was annoyingly perceptive. Kasiel turned his attention to moving the cover off the platter. She strode over and placed a hand on his arm. He relented to her gentle pull, reluctantly facing her.

"You are so much more than you think you are, Kas. Besides, no one gets to tell me who I can love. And that includes you."

He looked into her lavender eyes and couldn't hold in a smile. She was so beautiful when that fierce side came out. As unstoppable and exquisite as the sunrise. He slid one hand along her jaw and into her hair.

Nerith met his gaze, drawing away a fraction. "What?"

"Remember when I told you that you're a lot stronger than you think you are?"

"Oh, hush." She took his hand and kissed his palm, then went to sit by the table.

Another knock sounded just as Kasiel started to sit next to her. He straightened and went to answer it. Jethan stood outside the door, his grin making it obvious he suspected Nerith was still there.

"I won't keep you. I just wanted to see if we could arrange to meet up when you're through here."

"Come in, Lord Markanis," Nerith called.

Kasiel stepped back from the door, extending one arm with a flourish to direct Jethan through. Looking like a thief who had been caught stealing, the other youth ventured warily inside.

"Nerith, I like the new outfit." Jethan winked at her.

She narrowed her eyes at him and gestured to a seat across the table from her with the apple slice she was holding. Kasiel kicked the door shut and wandered over to join them, sitting next to Nerith on the couch. She was watching Jethan like a hawk might watch a mouse. It was almost fun seeing his tehnaak shift uncomfortably before that shrewd gaze.

"I'm glad you're here, Jethan," Nerith said. "I've been wanting to talk to you about trying to get Leysa thrown into the deeps the other night."

Jethan dropped the piece of cheese he had taken back on the platter and held his hands up in a gesture of surrender. "Hold on. I had no intention of getting her in trouble. We both had a little too much to drink, and I just wanted to—"

Nerith arched a brow at him. "Show off? Lure her into your bed with your rebellious charm?"

He winced. "Maybe use a word other than charm. Besides, it's not like that. I'm not that kind of guy."

"Oh? Are you not?"

Jethan turned his pleading gaze to Kasiel. "Help me out here."

Kasiel enjoyed seeing his tehnaak squirm enough that he felt a little guilty about it. That didn't mean he was going to let him off easily, though. "It's true. He's not that way. I mean, he does break the rules, and he has been known to use his ability when he shouldn't. Now that I think about it, if I were in your shoes, I probably wouldn't want my tehnaak spending time with him, either."

Jethan's eyes widened. "What? Whoa! That is not the kind of help I was hoping for."

Kasiel offered him a fond smile then. "But, knowing him like I do, there's no one I would trust more with my life."

Jethan picked up the cheese and sank back into his seat, shaking his head at Kasiel. "Love you too, you calloch."

"You two are disgusting," Nerith said, taking a few

pieces of the evalis fruit and handing one to Kasiel.

An hour later, Nerith retreated to the bathing room to clean up and dress. When she was ready for her day, Kasiel walked her to the door.

She stopped in the doorway and turned, stepping closer as she slid her arms over his shoulders. "Any chance I can see you later?"

"Not that I'm listening," Jethan called, "but we'll be meeting up with the others at the Twisted Vine this evening if you want to join us."

Nerith met Kasiel's eyes, and they both laughed. Then she leaned in to kiss him, her lips soft and warm with a hint of sweetness from the fruit. Kasiel slid his hands around her waist, pulling her closer, and deepened the kiss, somewhat surprised that he could still be so hungry for more of her. She opened her mouth to him, coming up on the balls of her feet, her body pressing flush against his. His pulse quickened, certain other parts of him rising to the occasion, eager for a repeat of last night. For a few seconds, he forgot they weren't alone, until a low whistle from inside the room jarred him back to reality.

Nerith drew away, laughing softly as she delicately wiped her lips, her cheeks flushed as brightly as he suspected his own were. "You really are the worst," she murmured, moving closer again, so her breath warmed his lips when she spoke.

"Are you sure it's me?" he countered, keeping his voice low enough that Jethan wouldn't hear this time.

"Not entirely." She gave him another quick kiss. "I'll see you later."

With that, she bounded off down the hallway, turning back halfway to the crossing hall to blow him a kiss. He watched her until she rounded the corner, then retreated into the room.

"That definitely topped the kiss in Katovan," Jethan

remarked, slathering a piece of bread with jam.

Kasiel rolled his eyes at his tehnaak, trying to hide how much the comment pleased him.

A short while later, they wandered down to the canyon together. Kenna didn't waste a second before reprimanding Jethan for the infraction that earned him time in the deeps. Within minutes, the two became engrossed in a philosophical debate about using one's ability in more harmless ways on your fellow citizens. Kenna was adamantly opposed, something Kasiel found a little surprising given how often her tehnaak did it. Jethan, attempting to defend his behavior, tried to convince her it wasn't always a bad thing. With his recent experience in having the Charmer ability used against him by Ilsa and his early encounter with his father's Frightener ability, Kasiel found it hard to agree with his tehnaak. Rather than take Kenna's side, he left them at the juvenile enclosure and excused himself, saying he wanted to practice with his Feral ability since they were down here.

Instead of going around to enter the tethdrak habitat, he wandered through the tunnel to the kanodrak habitat in the next canyon. Adnar had entrusted him with a key to the tethdrak gates. The Feral ahndhomen didn't feel he was ready yet for that level of responsibility when it came to the kanodraks. An assessment Kasiel couldn't disagree with.

When he emerged from the tunnel, he was surprised to see the female kanodrak he had been attempting to connect with lounging near the front of the habitat, watching him as he came through the door. She didn't get up, but she tracked him with her milky white eyes as he went to the bars that sectioned off the front area from the rest of the canyon. When he stopped at the barrier, she looked away, seeming to lose interest.

Kasiel reached out with his ability, cautiously seeking

admission into the mind of the massive predator. He tried passing along trust, confidence, and respect. The kanodrak got abruptly to her feet and came toward him. Her strides were lazy, her huge paws spreading as they pressed against the ground, the tips of lethal claws visible even when retracted.

As the beast prowled closer, one ear turned to him while the other swiveled in different directions, always attentive to the world around her. Muscles rippled under her thick silver-gray hide. When she was less than a foot from the bars, she growled. It wasn't the usual growl of threat, though. More of a slow rumble rising from deep in her chest.

Kasiel resisted the urge to step back. Instead, he put one hand between the bars, holding it out with his palm facing her. The kanodrak stopped a few inches away and sniffed at the offered hand. Kasiel looked into her strange eyes, giving only respect now as he continued his delicate effort to gain entrance to her mind. She lowered her head, still keeping it a few inches back from his hand. He didn't move. She brought one paw forward, her weight shifting onto it, the natural armor that covered her face coming up against his palm. Kasiel's breath caught in his throat.

The kanodrak withdrew her paw and turned away, loping out into the habitat. Kasiel watched her depart, muscles rippling with each step. He left his hand hanging in the air for a moment where she had touched it. Then he drew it and his ability back.

"You do like to push your luck, Cavenos."

He startled, turning to see Adnar emerge from the hidden alcove in the front wall. The ahndhomen was grinning.

"I came down to visit the sandhawk. I just thought I'd see if anyone was over here." He had planned to check on the hawk. That part wasn't a lie, but he had come to this side hoping to see the kanodrak, and he suspected Adnar knew as much. He wasn't sure why he was trying to hide it, other than perhaps a desire to preserve the intimacy of that moment of contact.

Adnar chose not to call him out on it. Instead, he joined Kasiel at the bars to watch the kanodrak, who had found a spot to stretch in the sun a little further out. "I'm just glad she didn't decide you were offering her something to eat."

Kasiel looked at his hand. He would have missed it terribly. "You and me both. How did you get the kanodraks to let you in?"

Adnar met his eyes. "I'm not going to tell you that, because I think you can do it better on your own. Continue to do this your way, and you will get more than just her permission. You will earn her trust and her devotion. The connection you have with Sylaryth and some of the other tethdraks now is far stronger than what many Ferals ever achieve. You are patient with them. You give them your respect and listen to what their minds tell you better than anyone I've ever seen, me included. Keep doing this your way, and you will be to Ferals what your father is to Frighteners."

A calloch?

He kept that sentiment to himself. After casting one last long look at the kanodrak, he turned to Adnar. "Where is the sandhawk?"

Adnar gestured toward the tunnel leading back to the tethdrak canyon. "It's in one of the rooms where we care for injured tethdraks. The first door on your right after you exit the other end of the tunnel. Not the nicest creature, but Kenna tended its injuries, and we gave it some meat from the supply we keep for socializing juvenile tethdraks. I expect you to visit it and feed it at least twice a day. Get into its head. Encourage it to bond with you. Having such a companion with your sight ability could prove invaluable."

In battle.

Adnar didn't say that part, but Kasiel knew that was what he meant. "I will. Thank you, sir."

"We will try working with the kanodraks a few days this coming week. I suspect she's almost ready to let you in."

Kasiel glanced back out at the awesome creature. She might be about ready to let him into her mind, but was he prepared to be let in? After seeing the damage a tethdrak could do in combat, the idea of taking a kanodrak into battle was several times more intimidating. To be in charge of her outside the controlled environment of the canyon. To ride upon her back like he would a horse. The prospect was at least as terrifying as it was exciting.

He inclined his head to Adnar, then headed out through the tunnel.

The sandhawk was in a tall cage at the back of one of several rooms carved into the cliff wall. A collection of wood, rocks, and soil had been added to the enclosure to provide the bird a few comforts from its usual habitat. When he came in, the raptor hopped up on a raised branch and spread its wings, exposing a gap in the feathers on the injured side.

Kasiel eased into its mind, offering a sense of soothing and safety. A few chunks of raw meat waited on the counter with a set of heavy leather gloves lying next to them. Kasiel pulled the gloves on and picked up the meat. So equipped, he entered the enclosure. The sandhawk moved sideways up the branch, inching closer. Kasiel held one gloved hand up to his feet, and the bird stepped onto it, accepting the first morsel of meat with enthusiasm.

The door opened, and the raptor spread its wings again, nearly smacking Kasiel in the face. It shrieked at

Jethan and Kenna as they walked in.

Kenna sneered at it. "Break-blasted bird."

Kasiel ran a gentle finger over the raptor's head, smoothing down his ruffled feathers. "That's not a nice thing to say, is it?" he cooed at it.

Kenna stuck her tongue out at him. "Little monster tried to bite me no less than twelve times last night. Adnar ordered me not to get in its head. He wants it connecting to you and you only."

Invaluable.

Kasiel pushed down the dread that accompanied that thought and fed the raptor the rest of the meat before returning it to the branch.

"Adnar has a few of our scouts keeping an eye out for recently deceased sandhawks so we can try imping the damaged feathers," Kenna said.

"Try what?" For a second, Kasiel worried it might be a stupid question, something he should know, but Jethan's blank look reassured him.

"It's a method for repairing their flight feathers. I'm sure Adnar will be thrilled to walk you through it if they find any."

Kasiel sensed an edge of bitterness in her last words. Was that jealousy?

"Have you seen Syl yet?" Jethan asked, dragging him away from Kenna's flat regard. "He's out there lying by the gate, looking like his world is coming to an end. Where did you wander off to?"

Kasiel stepped out of the enclosure and put the gloves back on the table, cleaning his hands in the basin there. "I wandered over to the kanodrak side. Spoke to Adnar." Worked toward becoming even more of a military asset, he added in his head, forcing a smile. "Why don't we take Syl for a walk around town? Maybe we can find a traitor for him to eat."

"Sounds like a brilliant plan." Jethan turned to

Kenna. "Are you coming along?"

She shook her head. "I'll catch up with you at the tavern. Save a bit of traitor for Raxxa. My cliff cat," she added in response to Kasiel's questioning look. "Maybe I'll bring him, and we can see how he and Syl get along."

Jethan glanced from Kasiel to Kenna and shook his head. "Sure. Let's take two terrifying predators to the tavern. You Ferals are all a little insane. Not sure how I ended up with two of you in my life."

"Just lucky." Kenna threw an arm around his shoulders and steered him out of the room.

CHAPTER SEVEN

When Kasiel and Jethan entered the Twisted Vine with Sylaryth as evening drew near, they found it bustling with activity. Avris and Merrin, Kince and Darro, and Tath had claimed the usual table in the back. Darro and Tath sat together, lost in a conversation of their own. Kasiel had suspected that something was building between them, and their body language now – the way they leaned into each other, how their eyes locked, their smiles – all supported that.

The tavern staff had moved the tables near the end Kasiel sat on farther away to accommodate Sylaryth. The tethdrak might be an inspirational symbol of good fortune, but few people were comfortable sitting that close to the deadly beast. Wedro and Chander strolled in behind them, gathering with the rest of the unit around a tray laden with mugs of Vanrian Black Mead.

Kince lifted a cup as they settled into their seats. "Welcome. We thought we might start with a few drinks here. After that, Darro suggested that we should..." He trailed off, glancing at his tehnaak, who appeared entirely unaware that anyone other than Tath was there. Kince smirked. "Well, assuming these two don't disappear into a dark room somewhere, he suggested that we—"

He winced when Darro kicked him under the table

without breaking his engagement with Tath. Laughter burst out through the group and Tath tried to fight a grin, her cheeks turning as red as her hair.

A hand came to rest on Kasiel's shoulder. "You have room for a few more?" Nerith asked.

Jethan moved aside, bumping Avris and Merrin down to make space for Nerith and Leysa between them. The two women stepped over the bench, Nerith sliding her hand along Kasiel's arm and into his hand as she sat next to him. He twined his fingers through hers, even that modest contact stoking a desire to be alone with her.

Kince leaned down to rub his leg where Darro had kicked it. "Welcome, ladies. Come to share a few rounds with us before we head back to Kasiel's room to discuss recent *events?*"

The emphasis he put on the last words made it apparent what events those were. They had to assume Kasiel and Jethan, and possibly other mind-crafters, were at risk until the guards and Evokers managed to dig up any remaining threats within the city. If the incident at the military camp near Katis proved to be connected to what happened to Kasiel, every mind-crafter in the vicinity of the Break could be in danger. All that aside, whether or not the southern mercenaries wanted a Feral, Kasiel appeared to still have a solid target on him that increased Jethan's risk because of their bond.

Nerith met Kince's eyes, her expression hardening. "I'd like to join you for that discussion, if that's all right." She squeezed Kasiel's hand under the table.

Kince nodded. "The more people keeping an eye out, the less likely we are to lose someone."

"We won't be losing this someone." She leaned in to give Kasiel a kiss on the cheek.

"Aren't you two sickeningly cute?" Avris fake-gagged at them.

"Don't be a calloch," Kince said, though the roll of his eyes undermined his half-hearted effort to come to their defense.

Give her a kiss. A wet, sexy one. The kind you need a nap after.

The voice in Kasiel's head made his cheeks grow warm. Alongside him, Sylaryth stood, turning to face the rest of the room behind them. When a group moved out of the center, Kasiel spotted Kenna near the bar with her cliff cat beside her. The beast was a little more than waist high at the shoulder, with a deep blue-gray coat. Slate blue stripes extended the length of its spine along either side of a ridge of longer, spiked fur. Its bright sapphire eyes glinted like stars in the flickering light from sconces and candles in the room. A puff of hair the same slate blue as its stripes tipped its long tail. Other patrons were trying to stay clear of that swishing appendage.

If Kenna was there, that meant her tehnaak, Therin, was also somewhere in the building, which explained the voice in his head. Kenna shifted back from the bar, and he spotted Therin behind her, covering his mouth and laughing. Kenna glanced from Therin to Kasiel, then punched her tehnaak in the arm before striding over. Kasiel spun fully around on the bench, putting a hand on Sylaryth's shoulder to keep him calm.

When Kenna and her beast companion got close, Sylaryth tensed. The cliff cat stopped and leaned forward, sniffing the air in front of the tethdrak. Sylaryth lowered his head, nearly touching the cat's nose with his own. His tongue darted out, smelling this new creature. The cat growled in response, and swiped out with one paw, smacking Sylaryth across the side of the face.

Kenna's eyes popped wide. "Raxxa!"

Kasiel tensed, ready to stop Sylaryth if he attempted to retaliate. The massive tethdrak bounced on his front feet, to the right, then back to the left, sending people closest to them scattering with startled cries. Then he splayed his front legs out wide, sinking his head down level with the cat's.

Kenna looked at Kasiel, a mystified smile tugging at her lips. "Is he... trying to play?"

The surge of excited energy from the tethdrak confirmed her suspicion. Kasiel laughed and nodded. "It appears so. I don't think he took Raxxa's message the way it was intended."

Raxxa snarled and pressed closer to Kenna's side. Kenna stifled a giggle. "Maybe we'll go sit on the other end for a bit and let them get used to each other from afar."

"Is Therin joining us?" Wedro asked. "I need to get a count for the next order."

Kenna glanced over at her tehnaak. She lifted a hand to point at their table. Therin made no visible response, but Kenna smiled and gave him a thumbs-up. Speakers did specialize in communicating from a distance. It was odd to consider that the man could speak into anyone's head, but was it really any stranger than controlling the mind of a beast with your own?

"He's not going to keep dropping inappropriate comments in my head, is he?" Kasiel asked in a low voice, hoping Nerith wouldn't hear.

Kenna's grin picked up that edge of predatory threat. "Not unless he wants to be cat food." With that, she wandered down to sit at the other end of the table.

Sylaryth watched them leave, emitting a few low, sorrowful clicks.

Kasiel placed a hand on the tethdrak's head. "I think you were a little much for Raxxa, my friend." He turned around on the bench again and urged the beast to relax beside him.

Nerith leaned close, her breath warming the hair over his ear. "What inappropriate comments were they?"

Kasiel grinned, wishing he had the nerve to kiss her the way Therin had suggested. This wasn't the proper place for it though. "I'll show you tonight."

About an hour later, their group, twelve in all, with Nerith, Leysa, and Kenna joining them, got up to leave the tavern, the two beast companions clearing a quick path to the door for them. Sylaryth watched Raxxa hopefully as they strolled through the nighttime streets toward the palace. The cliff cat pointedly ignored the tethdrak, his long tail twitching irritably every time Sylaryth let out a few invitational clicks.

About halfway there, near the entrance to the canyon habitat, the group stopped. Darro wandered over to Kasiel, gesturing for Kenna to join them. "I assume Jethan will accompany you to the tethdrak habitat to drop off Syl. Kenna, we can send someone else with you." His brows pinched. "Why didn't Therin come?"

Her tight-lipped expression suggested irritation with her tehnaak. Whether over his illicit use of his ability or something else remained unclear. "He was a little muddled. Had too much to drink, I suspect. Some girl he was flirting with offered to see him home."

Alarms sounded off in Kasiel's head before she finished speaking. The southern mercenaries wanted a mind-crafter they could control. Like a Speaker, perhaps? Next to him, Sylaryth tensed, a low growl rising in his throat. "Did he know her?"

Kenna looked from the tethdrak to Kasiel, a hint of unease creeping into her regard that brought Raxxa's hackles up. "He met her tonight. Why?"

Jethan met Kasiel's eyes. "You don't think—"

"I do."

"Shit." Jethan turned to Kenna. "Can that cat track Therin?"

Kenna narrowed her eyes at him as Raxxa hissed. "That cat's name is Raxxa, and yes, he can, but why would he need to?"

"Back to the tavern," Darro ordered. "We can explain along the way."

Kasiel caught Nerith's arm. "Why don't you and Leysa go on to the palace?" His gaze moved to Wedro and Chander. "You two go with them. A group this big retracing our steps will draw too much attention anyhow."

"No." Nerith gave a firm shake of her head. "I can help. What if you need a healer?"

"I'll be there." Tath met Kasiel's eyes over Nerith's shoulder. "I've got plenty of field experience."

Nerith scowled up at him. "Fine. I'll go, but we're talking about this later."

"Thank you." He ducked down to plant a quick kiss on her lips before she could pull away. Then he waved the rest to follow, leaving Nerith and the other three behind.

"How would they have gotten me out of the city?" Kasiel asked anyone who might answer as they hurried back toward the tavern.

Darro glanced toward the main entrance to Etrion. "The front gate has too many guards. They can't have paid them all off."

"But there are the two smaller exits on either side of the city," Merrin offered. "They're secure enough that there's usually only one guard. Two if there's active fighting in the nearby sections of the Break."

Kasiel nodded thoughtfully. Next to him, Jethan was bringing Kenna up to speed.

If they had bought off a guard on one of the side gates, they could have slipped out of Etrion without raising alarms. That would suggest at least one or two more traitors among the city guards. If the woman who offered to take Therin home turned out to be involved, she undoubtedly had help waiting for when she lured him away from the crowds. That meant another two or three additional traitors within the city for this effort alone.

Of course, it was also possible they would track Therin down and interrupt a perfectly ordinary tryst. That would be embarrassing, but far better than ignoring it if it the woman turned out to be something other than what she seemed.

As they approached the tavern, Kenna sped up and Raxxa loped ahead, startling a few people standing outside as he began sniffing around the area. Kasiel held Sylaryth back, waiting until Raxxa bolted off toward the western side of the city. He let the tethdrak follow, slipping in behind the beast's eyes while attempting to maintain enough awareness of his own body to keep pace with his companions as they hurried after the two creatures. Jethan, cognizant of the problem, took hold of Kasiel's wrist to guide him.

Sylaryth had excellent night vision, his view of the streets brighter and richer than what Kasiel could see through his own eyes. He watched Raxxa pause and dart briefly down a dark alley before continuing west again. They were traveling away from Therin's house. It was still possible that the woman lived somewhere on this edge of town, but a comment from Merrin confirmed they were on a direct track for the west gate now.

Kasiel distanced himself from the tethdrak enough to focus on moving up beside Kince.

"Want me to see if there are any guards in the area?" Kince asked, picking up on his intent before he could put voice to the request.

Kasiel gave him an appreciative nod. "If you could."

Kince broke off from the group, disappearing down a side street.

The black stone wall loomed over them when Kasiel motioned his companions to halt in an unlit, narrow alley a block away from it.

"Pull Raxxa back," he whispered to Kenna.

When she did so, he encouraged Sylaryth to continue, creeping slowly forward in the dark now. He didn't have to go much farther before he heard people talking through the tethdrak's ears.

"This better go smoother than the last one," a man's voice was saying.

Sylaryth crept up alongside a building, hanging back in the shadows. Ahead, near a large door in the wall that stood slightly ajar, was a group of three men and a woman Kasiel thought he might have seen in the tavern earlier. Two of the men were wearing guard uniforms, one of whom was helping the third support a barely conscious Therin between them.

"What do you care?" the woman asked. "You're getting paid in advance."

The man who had spoken first, one of the gate guards, gave her a nasty sneer. "I care because things don't go well for us when these bastards come back. Ilsa's been sentenced to death along with a couple of watchtower guards."

The woman shrugged. "No great loss. Ilsa was a mind-crafter too."

"She was a friend," the guard snapped.

Sylaryth looked to his left suddenly, the unexpected motion making Kasiel briefly dizzy. Off in that direction, less than a block away, someone was creeping through the darkness, watching the figures by the wall. The individual leaned into a patch of moonlight and Kasiel recognized him. Tarik, an inveth in the city guard who had helped them with Nerith's assailants.

Kasiel urged Sylaryth to step out in the light of a street torch before shifting back into the shadows. As he had hoped, the movement caught Tarik's attention, his eyes widening when he saw the tethdrak. After a moment, he gave a sharp nod and held a hand up, palm out, gesturing for them to hold back. Then he hunkered down next to the building, listening. Through Sylaryth's eyes, Kasiel spotted another guard lurking in the darkness beyond Tarik.

They waited.

"You can't just pick and choose which mind-crafters you're all right with," the woman at the gate snapped.

"I can do whatever the fuck I want," the guard countered.

Kasiel started to wonder if they would need to do anything at all. The two sounded ready to take each other out.

"Maybe you could want to open the fucking door and let them through. This bastard isn't weightless," the guard helping hold up Therin snapped.

"Right." The first guard turned toward the door.

Tarik gestured for Sylaryth to move around the left flank as he and the guard with him started advancing on the right. Kasiel gave Kenna the same signal and urged Sylaryth forward as directed. Raxxa came loping silently up alongside the tethdrak. With Kenna and Kasiel guiding them, the two ignored each other.

The beasts broke into a sprint around the side of a building and charged the group. Kasiel lost track of Raxxa as Sylaryth rushed in, sweeping out with his claws to rip through the ankle of one of the men holding Therin. Not missing a stride, the tethdrak lunged into the woman, taking her to the ground. Kasiel barely stopped him before his jaws could snap shut on her face, but his claws dug deep into her shoulders, pinning her beneath him. Kasiel and Kenna sprinted out behind their beasts. Without the advantage of being able to see through Raxxa's eyes, Kenna had less fine control of the cliff cat. Raxxa had already torn out the throat of the gate guard who had been holding Therin.

The other guard attempted to dash back through

the door in the wall, but a crossbow bolt fired by Tarik sank into his thigh, hobbling him before he could make his escape. Tath came running out and crouched down to attend to the torn open ankle of Sylaryth's first victim, who lay in the dirt wailing and holding his leg. Kasiel reached the tethdrak and urged him off the woman. The damage to her shoulders left her writhing on the ground, in too much pain to get up. Kenna and Darro moved Therin away from the others and sat him against a building. He was minimally responsive but appeared unharmed aside from the effects of whatever they had drugged him with.

As Tarik's companion grabbed the wounded guard, Tarik stood regarding Kasiel as he might a promising new recruit. Kince jogged around a building then, bringing three more guards with him.

Tarik took charge of the new arrivals, freeing Kasiel from his intense gaze for a moment. "You two check outside the gate for any accomplices." He pointed to the third as the first two jumped to follow his orders. "You, shackle those three then help the healer stabilize their injures. We'll need to send for a wagon to move the body." With the other guards engaged in their assigned tasks, he strode over to Kasiel, his gaze lingering on Sylaryth. "He's grown a lot since the last time I helped you take down criminals in the city. You've got a knack for this. It's a shame you're a Feral, I'd enlist you in the city guard in a heartbeat."

It was uncanny how easily the man appeared to tune out the moans and wails of the injured. Attempting to act less bothered by it than he was, Kasiel asked, "Were you already following them?"

"We've been staking out all the city exits since you were taken. Dhomvalen Arhk wanted to verify if this was an attack on you specifically, or if we really have traitors in our midst trying to sell our mind-crafters to the south. I guess we have our answer." He gestured toward Therin with a jerk of his head. "That one's a mind-crafter, I presume."

Kasiel nodded. "He's a Speaker. When they tried to sell me, the southern mercenaries expressed an interest in mind-crafters they could more easily control."

"Speakers and Enkindlers, maybe some Charmers and Evokers too." Tarik's gaze wandered over the scene. "Since it's going to come up when I report this, how did your group end up trailing them?"

Kasiel barely held back a groan. The last thing he wanted was to have to go before the khevarin and his father for something like this again. "Therin is Kenna's tehnaak." He gestured to her. "We weren't sure he'd been taken, but we had a bad feeling about it when she said he was acting odd, and an unfamiliar woman offered to walk him home."

"Good instincts you lot have. Since I can't recruit you, maybe I could lure some of your companions into the guard."

"You could try," Kasiel said, though he doubted it. With the exception of Tath, his companions were all over helping Kenna with Therin now. They left the traitors to the guards and to Tath, who would always be a healer first. They were a unit. Assisting the guards was merely a side effect of their desire to protect the people they cared about, not the goal. "What happens now?"

"We'll drag them in and let Ahninveth Setera and the dhomvalen question them. I suspect Khevarin Seylin will put the city on full lockdown after this."

That didn't sound great, though it made sense. "Have they learned any more about the missing Evoker from the base?"

Tarik took a few steps back away from the others, gesturing Kasiel to follow him. When they had put enough distance between them and everyone else, he leaned closer to Kasiel and lowered his voice. "It was a similar situation. They've arrested a few soldiers involved, but the Evoker is still missing. We also received reports of a few mind-crafters missing from other bases and from one town east of here."

Kasiel swallowed, a chill sweeping through him, raising the hair on his arms and the back of his neck. "This is a widespread issue, then?"

"It's looking that way. I should get back on the job here. Take your companions and go get some rest. I should be able to keep the palace off your back for tonight, but don't be surprised if you get summoned in tomorrow morning."

Kasiel inclined his head to the guard inveth. "Thank you."

After they got Therin safely home, Kasiel took control of Raxxa so Kenna could stay with her tehnaak and returned the cat and Sylaryth to their enclosures. The others came with him, not leaving his and Jethan's company until they were securely back in the palace.

When they reached the private quarters, Jethan turned off toward his rooms.

Kasiel stopped. "No company for dinner tonight?"

Jethan held his hands up and backed away, a smirk quirking up the corners of his mouth. "I saw the look in Nerith's eyes. I guarantee she's waiting in your room with a collection of thoughts she'd like to share with you."

His chest tightened, a ripple of anxiety crawling up his spine. "I don't understand why she got so angry. I just didn't want her getting hurt."

Jethan laughed and shook his head. "You know she's combat trained, right?"

"She is?" He met Jethan's eyes, a sinking sensation in his gut.

"Our healers go out in the field with us. They're all

combat trained."

Kasiel hung his head, rubbing at the bridge of his nose. "I'm an idiot."

Sympathy softened his tehnaak's answering chuckle. "You're not. You're still learning our ways. But I'm afraid angry girlfriend falls outside my purview."

Kasiel glanced down the hall toward his rooms. He wasn't sure angry girlfriend fell within his purview either. "I thought spirit siblings were supposed to support each other."

Jethan took a few steps closer to him. "Tell her you're sorry. Listen to her. Follow your instincts. You've won over deadly predators. I'm sure you can handle Nerith."

He hoped his tehnaak was right. "I guess I'll never know until I try."

"Exactly." Jethan backed away, grinning. "Good luck. I'll come pick up the pieces in the morning." With that, he chuckled and strode off toward his own rooms.

Kasiel trudged to his door and eased it open. As Jethan predicted, Nerith was waiting for him. She stood by the fire, the flames reflecting ominously in her lavender eyes as he crept in.

"Is Therin all right?"

He appreciated that her first thought was for the well-being of the mind-crafter, even if the sharp edge in her tone carried a warning for him. Peeling off his jacket, he discarded it on the back of a chair on his way over to the fire.

"We caught up with them before they could get him out of the city. Some guards were staking the area out. They took charge from there. Therin's home now. Kenna's watching over him while he recovers from the drug they used on him. I'll probably be called in with the others about it tomorrow, but Inveth Tarik said he would try to buy us the night to rest."

"I'm glad Therin's safe." The way she clipped her

words was enough to tell him his heroics weren't getting him off the hook.

"Nerith, I'm sorry. I just didn't want you in danger."

She closed the remaining distance between them with a few abrupt strides and poked him firmly in the chest with one finger. "And you think I want you in danger? We live in Etrion. A Feral and a healer in Vanris's army. We're going to be put in danger. The best thing we can do is learn to look out for each other when the opportunity allows it. Why don't you trust me?"

"It's not about trust—"

"Isn't it?" Her eyes flashed, a hint of moisture rising in them. She put her back to him.

Trust your instincts, Jethan had said. Kasiel stepped forward, sliding his hands around her waist. She stiffened and moved to push him away, but he leaned in, brushing his lips against her neck in a gentle kiss. She drew in a sharp breath of surprise and ceased trying to pull free of him.

Encouraged, he trailed more kisses up her neck, then he let his lips lightly brush her ear as he whispered, "Show me what I can do to make it up to you."

She turned in his arms to face him, meeting his eyes. "Trust me."

He leaned down to her, stopping just shy of her lips. "I do."

Nerith responded with a deep, demanding kiss. Her hands pulled up the sides of his shirt and slid under it, warm and soft against his bare skin. Not breaking their kiss, Kasiel moved them toward the bedroom.

The expected summons didn't come until later the next morning, after Kasiel and Nerith were up and dressed. Their breakfast was nearly gone. Having gotten distracted by interests other than food during the night, they had woken up ravenous. Kasiel swallowed his last bite of bread and stole a kiss from Nerith before going to answer the knock on the door.

The waiting attendant offered him a partial bow. "Lord Hahren, your presence is required."

"Of course." He glanced at Nerith. "Will you be around later?"

When she opened her mouth to answer, the attendant cleared his throat with intent. "Healer Nerith is also required."

"She wasn't there," Kasiel objected.

"Those are my orders, my lord."

Arguing with the attendant would serve no purpose, so Kasiel held a hand out to Nerith. "Care to join me?"

She breathed a laugh and walked over, accepting the offered hand and twining her fingers through his.

They followed the attendant to a room that had become increasingly familiar to Kasiel. It was a large circular chamber with a curved dais reaching out from the back wall, on top of which sat a similarly curved table. To his surprise, none of the others involved in the evening's events were there when they arrived. Khevarin Seylin and his father, Dhomvalen Arhk, were on the dais in front of the table. Arhk waited off to one side, his expression as unreadable as always, while the khevarin stood near the center of the table, tapping her long silver fingernails on its polished surface. The leader of the city guard, Dhomen Branith, sat behind the table on the end closest to the door with Evoker Setera a few seats down. At the opposite end, Ahndhomen Adnar sat with his tethdrak lying next to him.

Kasiel and Nerith knelt before the dais, their hands no longer linked and an appropriate distance between them. The khevarin regarded them in silence for a few seconds. The pale blue stone in the woven silver and dark metal tiara she wore perfectly matched her eyes. A few similarly colored gemstones were worked into her white-blond hair and added as ornaments to her long silver dress.

"Healer Nerith, please step to the side." The khevarin gestured to one end of the dais with a slender hand, fingers elongated by her tapered nails.

"Majesty." Nerith inclined her head and rose, going to stand in the indicated spot, her hands folded politely before her.

"Ahninveth Hahren, we have already spoken with most of the others involved in preventing the abduction of one of our mind-crafters last night. An event that has, unfortunately, required us to lock down the city and order a curfew." She strolled to the edge of the dais, gazing down on him. He resisted the urge to look up at her, having not yet received permission to rise. "By all accounts, you were instrumental in stopping these traitors and protecting one of our own."

The khevarin's ensuing silence suggested that she wanted a response. "I wasn't willing to see someone else taken the way I was, Majesty."

"You survived the experience."

He almost looked up at her then but caught himself. What did his surviving have to do with this? Was she fishing for a particular reaction or admission from him? "Not everyone has the resources at their disposal that I do," he answered cautiously.

"Because you are a Feral?"

A low grunt came from Adnar that he had no idea how to translate. His gaze moved up for a second, and he noticed a slight widening of Setera's eyes where she sat staring at the back of the khevarin's head, as though something caught her by surprise.

He lowered his gaze. "Yes, Majesty."

"This is not the first time you have put yourself at risk to protect our people. Your efforts on their behalf have not gone unnoticed. We leave it to Ahndhomen Adnar to determine an appropriate form of recognition. Know that you have our considerable gratitude... yet again." She gestured with her hand for him to rise, her silver nails and several rings flashing in the light. "You may be called upon as we continue our investigation of these events, but for now, you may go enjoy your free day, Ahninveth Hahren."

"Thank you, Majesty." He stood and turned away, his gaze locking with Nerith's for an instant.

She took a step forward, as if intending to join him when he headed for the door.

"Healer Nerith."

The khevarin's voice stopped Nerith in her tracks. She turned back toward the dais. Kasiel slowed his strides, curiosity stalling him.

"Majesty?"

The tremor in Nerith's voice drew his full attention. He glanced over at her, puzzled by the hint of dread in her eyes and the wringing of her hands. She gave a small shake of her head, as if asking the khevarin not to say or do something.

"Given how Ahninveth Hahren and his companions continue to be frequent targets of malicious parties in Etrion, we require that you cease spending time in his company. You are a full healer now and not a resource we care to risk unnecessarily." Kasiel glanced up at the khevarin, an argument rising in his throat, but she had not finished speaking. "We also feel that he has proven himself to be a loyal citizen. More so, it would seem, than some who grew up within these walls. As such, there is no longer a need for you to carry on reporting his activities to us."

Her words struck Kasiel like a punch to the gut. He looked at Nerith. She was staring at him with wide eyes, her brows pinched together, lips parted as if she might speak. Where only a few seconds ago, he would have delighted in hearing anything she had to say, now he wanted nothing more than to be anywhere she wasn't.

Adnar's tethdrak stood, growling.

Kasiel tore his gaze away, pressure building around him as he strode swiftly from the chamber, yanking the door shut behind him. He made it all the way to the hall his rooms were in before Nerith came racing after him.

"Kas! Stop!"

He increased his pace.

She sprinted forward and grabbed his arm. "Kas!"

He turned on her, yanking his arm away. "All this time, you've been spying on me for the khevarin. What was that horse shit you were feeding me last night about trust?"

The door to Kasiel's room opened. Jethan stepped into the doorway and stopped there. Nerith glanced at Jethan, wringing her hands again. Then she turned to Kasiel and moved closer to him.

He stepped back.

Moisture rose in her eyes. Her hands were shaking.

"Yes, Khevarin Seylin did ask me to spy on you. The first time I came here, it was on her orders, and I was furious. I could think of nothing worse than being forced to play friends with someone I didn't give a whit about. But when I met you, I instantly liked you. I started feeling like this could be the best job I'd ever been given." She lowered her gaze, staring down at his feet.

"Then I was attacked because of my association with you." One hand came up, her fingers absently touching the scar on her cheek. The one that matched his. "The khevarin called it off. She didn't want to risk a future healer. But I couldn't stay away. After Katovan, I decided to ignore her order and keep seeing you. When she found out, she said that, if I insisted on putting myself at risk, I could at least be useful and resume reporting to her." She looked up at him, pleading in her eyes. "What was I supposed to do? She's the khevarin."

He met her gaze, Edmund's face looming his mind. "You could have been honest with me."

"It's not like it matters, Kas. There was never anything to report. It's obvious you have no loyalty to the south. Even she believes that now."

He turned away, fighting the urge to yell at her. How could she not see the problem? "It matters because I can't trust you now. I spent my entire childhood being lied to by the man who raised me. I thought I left that behind in Fernwallow."

He stormed toward his room. Jethan moved into the hall, clearing his path.

Threatening tears gave a raw edge to Nerith's voice when she called after him. "Please, Kas. I love you."

He stopped at the doorway, unable to look at his tehnaak, and turned slightly in her direction, though not quite far enough to see her. He couldn't bear to look at her, either. "Right, Edmund said that too."

A hollow ache spread through his chest. He hurried

into the room and slammed the door shut behind him, stopping just inside. He couldn't focus on his surroundings. All he could see was her face when the khevarin exposed her for the liar that she was. Exactly like Edmund. His body shook with rage, and he clung to that roiling emotion, letting it form a shield to protect him from the pain lurking beneath.

"Kas!" She was right outside the door now, where he had left his tehnaak. "Please, Jethan, let me in. I need to talk to him. I need to make him understand."

"I don't think that's a good idea." Jethan's tone was cold and unyielding. Angry. "You should go."

"Not like this." Her voice broke with a sob.

"Go."

Kasiel could hear her crying now, but the sounds grew distant, along with her hasty footsteps as she departed. He continued to his bedroom and slammed that door. The outer door opened and closed. Jethan didn't knock or try to follow him into the bedroom.

Kasiel threw himself back on the bed and stared up at the ceiling. Reaching across the palace and into the canyon with his ability, he sought out Sylaryth. The tethdrak welcomed him in with his joyful enthusiasm. Slipping behind the beast's eyes, he felt a flicker of hope as Sylaryth turned toward the entrance to the enclosure, waiting to see if he had also come to visit in the flesh.

Kasiel was distantly aware of tears streaming into his hair. "Carry me, my friend," he whispered, encouraging the tethdrak to run.

Sylaryth did so, sprinting exuberantly along the floor of the canyon in the dazzling midmorning sunshine. Kasiel let go of himself and sank fully into the beast, watching the canyon walls rush by, listening to the chatter of other creatures, feeling the cool autumn breeze brush across his scales.

•

After riding through the habitat with Sylaryth for a time, Kasiel drifted off. When he woke, he wandered out into the sitting room to find Jethan dozing on the couch, a book laying open on his chest. His tehnaak had bolted the door, undoubtedly, to keep Nerith from coming in if she returned. Kasiel leaned over the back of the couch and nudged him awake with a hand on his shoulder. Jethan was on his feet in an instant. He came around the couch and pulled Kasiel into a firm hug.

"I'm so sorry, tehnaak," he murmured.

Kasiel let himself sink into that embrace. The hollow ache in his chest settled, not growing anymore, but not shrinking either. Jethan was the one person he absolutely believed would never betray him. He hadn't realized how rare a gift that was.

"Thanks for staying," he muttered, extracting himself from the hug.

"I'm here for you, Kas. No matter what comes of this, you're the one whose well-being I'm most concerned with." He tilted his head, regarding Kasiel with a sympathetic smile. "With that in mind, what do you need of me? Should I stay? Go? Drag you out into the canyon, or maybe the tavern?"

Kasiel managed a half-hearted chuckle. "Might be a little early for the tavern yet. I am supposed to be taking care of the sandhawk though. The last thing I need right now is Adnar upset with me."

Jethan nodded. "Let's go then. A little fresh air would do us both good, and we can check in on Kenna if she's down there. Find out how Therin's doing."

Jethan threw an arm around Kasiel's shoulders and steered him to the door. Before exiting the room, he peeked out into the hall to make sure it was clear. Then he led the way from the palace, taking the back route through the garden and down the long tunnel that came out near the juvenile tethdrak enclosure.

They found Kenna at the other end throwing chunks of meat to the young tethdraks currently in the fenced off area. The new group was only about a month old. Small, clumsy, and covered in sharp points. Even as awkwardly cute as the reptiles were at that age, Kasiel found little pleasure in watching them. If anything, the way they wrestled and tumbled over one another with carefree abandon somehow heightened his sorrow.

Despite the heartbreak consuming him, he noticed the deep circles under Kenna's eyes and the sloppy braids in her dark-blond hair. Combined with her sluggish movements, it all suggested a rough, sleepless night, so he dredged up the best smile he could for her, fake though it might be.

"How's Therin?" Jethan asked.

She leaned against the bars as if standing required too much effort. "A little shaken." She grimaced. "A lot shaken, honestly. He asked me to thank you if I saw you today, so thank you, from him and me."

"You're family," Kasiel said. "That makes him family too."

Jethan gave him an appreciative smile. With Kasiel missing for twelve years of their youth, Jethan was raised and educated alongside Kenna and her tehnaak. For him, the two really were part of his family. That made them a part of Kasiel's now too. That was how spirit sibling bonds were meant to work. It was one of his favorite aspects of Vanrian culture. They went out of their way to try to ensure that no one went through life without someone to support them.

"Thanks, Kas."

Kenna's weary smile warmed something in him, if only a little. As with the playing tethdraks, it also made the sorrow that much more intense.

Down here, at least, it was easy to find a reason to excuse himself. "I'm going to check on the sandhawk before I bring Sylaryth out."

"Want company?" The fact that Jethan asked rather than simply joining him told him his tehnaak had already tuned in to his desire to be alone.

Kasiel shook his head. "Stay and chat. I won't be long."

He made his way around to the front of the main tethdrak enclosure, keeping to the back of the observation area. If Sylaryth spotted him too soon, he would only become distraught when he didn't come to visit right away.

Why couldn't Nerith have told him the truth? Maybe not at first, when they barely knew each other, but once things started growing serious, at least. The question was a blade spinning in his chest, bringing fresh pain with every pointless revolution and a sinking sensation that left him feeling dejected and broken.

It wasn't even the spying on him that bothered him the most. It was keeping the truth of it from him. Edmund had kept his entire past from him. Constructing a house of lies around him, of which letting Kasiel believe the professor had found him abandoned was the worst. Edmund had orchestrated his abduction, the killing of his mother, and the cutting of his ears. That was the pinnacle of his lies and secrets. It was miraculous that he kept track of it all well enough to keep the story going over the course of twelve years. Every moment of Kasiel's childhood Edmund had woven together using a combination of deception, careful misdirection, and precisely cultivated ignorance.

The urge to scream surged up in him, but before he could relent, another mind reached out to his. A gentle, inquisitive contact that carried with it an overall impression that was curiously maternal. It retreated as abruptly as it had come. Captivated, Kasiel followed his sense of that presence, heading past the room where they were keeping the sandhawk and down the tunnel to the next canyon. He wandered out into the observation area of the kanodrak habitat and up to the barrier.

None of the massive beasts were out where he could see them. He took hold of the bars and pressed his forehead against them, closing his eyes. Reaching out with his ability, he connected with Sylaryth and shared the tethdrak's vision briefly. The beast was drinking from the stream that meandered through the habitat, his head lifting the instant Kasiel slipped into his mind. He left the tethdrak and touched on the sandhawk, getting a brief glimpse of the inside of the room the raptor was in and a flash of impatience from the bird.

As he pulled back to himself, he collided with that maternal presence again. Hot air blew into his face. He jerked away, his eyes snapping open, and looked up into the milky white eyes of the female kanodrak, his heart racing. She leaned in, pressing her head against the two bars he had been holding. Kasiel moved forward, placing his forehead between the same two bars until it touched the natural armor that protected hers. He closed his eyes, afraid that even so much as breathing might break the moment. The unexpected warmth of her mental presence moved in, folding around him like wings, comforting and gentle.

Tears slipped down his cheeks. He reached through the bars with one hand, resting his palm against her neck, awed by the iron hard bands of muscle beneath her thick, scaled skin. A rumble rose in her chest. He opened his eyes as she raised one massive paw and touched the pads against his forearm, her deadly claws curling around it without harming him. Closing his eyes again, he yielded to the pain of what had happened between him and Nerith. The loss. More tears trickled silently down his cheeks, the hollow in his chest splitting wide like a chasm, threatening to drive him to his knees.

Those careful mental wings folded in tighter, drawing his ability to her, bringing him into her mind. Comfort. Protection. Safety.

Kasiel gasped. She was projecting emotions and sentiments to him the way he did with other beasts. He got no sense of structured language, at least not the way he understood it, but this creature possessed an intelligence not that different from his own.

He passed back a wave of gratitude.

They stood that way for a time, her paw a heavy yet comforting weight against his arm. After a time, her claws retracted, and she removed her paw. The mental embrace released him slowly as she backed away from the bars. Kasiel opened his eyes, letting his hand sink to his side. The kanodrak shifted her weight enough to peer past him for a moment. Then that white-eyed gaze returned to him, and she inclined her head before wandering out into the enclosure.

Kasiel stood watching her. He didn't have to turn to figure out what had drawn her attention behind him. They only allowed a few people to come down here. "You didn't tell me how intelligent they are."

"I thought it better for you to find that out on your own," Adnar said, a low reverence in his voice. "But in all my years working with kanodraks, I have never seen something like that."

"She's remarkable," Kasiel said, speaking primarily to confirm what he had discovered for himself.

Adnar moved up beside him. "She may not be the only one."

Kasiel didn't respond to that. He didn't think he was remarkable, at least not in most respects. What he did feel was greatly honored that she had granted him that moment.

"I was going to suggest doing some less challenging

activities in the coming week," Adnar said, "but I see I was wrong in assuming you might not yet be ready to work with the kanodraks again."

Kasiel glanced at him. The Feral ahndhomen was still watching the retreating kanodrak, reverence shining in his blue eyes. "Why wouldn't I be ready, sir?"

Adnar drew in a deep breath and let it slowly out, his jaw tightening for a moment. "What Khevarin Seylin did this morning—"

"I know why the khevarin did what she did." She had manipulated him. Nerith wouldn't follow orders to stay away from him, so the khevarin exposed her duplicity, using his predictable anger to solve the problem for her. Kasiel swallowed hard, trying to keep the resentment from his voice when he continued. "I reacted exactly the way she wanted me to. But none of that matters down here." Anger pulled his shoulders tight, and the kanodrak stopped, turning back to stare hard at Adnar as if he might be responsible.

Adnar eyed the beast, his brow furrowing. "I'd argue that the kanodrak thought it mattered. Enough so to require her intervention."

Kasiel calmed himself, passing the sensation along to the female. After a few seconds, she resumed walking away. "She led me here. I wasn't even trying to connect to her."

"Then she had already accepted you. I suspect she just wanted to be certain you recognized it as her decision and not yours. Any idea what you'll call her?"

The first name that popped into his mind was his mother's. Ellaris. It didn't strike him as right somehow, though he imagined she must have been as fierce as a kanodrak to keep Arhk in line. "No. Not yet."

"It's a free day," Adnar said. "Visit the sandhawk, then take your tethdrak out and enjoy what's left of the afternoon. There will be time to consider such things."

"Yes, sir." It was a free day, and he had to find some way to navigate it without losing himself to the ache in his chest or the anger threatening to bury him. Now, he at least had the kanodrak's acceptance to help balance that.

After a little over a month of working with the kanodrak, Niskenya, Kasiel was growing more proficient at putting her saddle and harness on. At least when she wasn't in the mood to toy with him by lying down or wandering off in the middle of the process. The equipment was disturbingly simple, considering it was all he had to keep him from falling off the massive predator's back. The saddle and chest collar were light and form fitting, designed to offer stability to the rider while – and this was the priority – providing the least possible amount of discomfort for the kanodrak. Adnar explained from the start that, in this relationship, Niskenya's needs always came first.

A bridle was unnecessary. Direction came from the mind of the rider. Anyone who wasn't a Feral bonded to a kanodrak would never ride a kanodrak. Not that he had done so yet. He wasn't about to try mounting up without her express invitation. It was enough of a victory merely finding a name she was agreeable to.

Niskenya turned and nudged him on the shoulder with her head. He staggered back several steps, sending a gentle chiding to her in response to her amusement.

Moving up next to her again, he checked that the saddle girth wasn't too tight. "Take it easy on me, Niske. You know I'm tired."

Exhausted might have been a better choice of words.

A few days after the khevarin exposed Nerith's duplicity, she and Leysa were transferred to one of the military bases along the Break. The official statement was that Nerith needed to build up healing experience in the field, though Kasiel wondered at the exact timing. He tried to keep his mind off her. He tried not to worry about her. As angry as he was with her, he couldn't help wishing they had sent her someplace safer. Preferably a place that also wasn't Etrion.

During the last month, he'd had little time to dwell on what happened between them. Inveth Tarik somehow convinced the council to let Kasiel and "his unit" – a designation they had given his companions despite his objections to the implied leadership role – help patrol the streets after hours to enforce the new curfew and scout for more traitors. His ongoing practice with connecting to other creatures proved to be immensely useful on patrol, though he did find himself unintentionally spying on a few intimate moments. Trying to explain his sudden blushing to his companions inspired him to start listening before he looked through another creature's eyes.

They split into two groups, with Kince and Darro joining Kenna, Raxxa, and Therin for the first half of each night. Avris and Merrin took the second shift with Kasiel, Sylaryth, and Jethan. Tath did her part by working that earlier shift in the healer's building. Khevarin Seylin, not surprisingly, didn't want one of her healers wandering the nighttime streets with them. Apparently, acceptable risk levels were different for healers inside Etrion than for those stationed outside the city.

Clandestine lovers and rambunctious youths frequented the streets during that first shift. Most of the illegal activities they uncovered occurred between midnight and dawn, when Kasiel's team was out. Among those, only a few ended up being related to the yet unknown party's attempts to obtain mind-crafters. Setera, along with the other Evokers Adnar had summoned to the city, had also exposed a few traitors through their efforts.

The rest of the time, when he wasn't busy with regular classes, combat training, or trying to sneak in a nap, Adnar had him practicing with the tethdraks, Niskenya, or Kitrix, the sandhawk. Niskenya was typically less cooperative with Adnar watching, so Kasiel worked with her on his free days too in an effort to make more progress. Now she permitted him to initiate physical contact with her, even to the point of letting him put the riding gear on if her mood was right. One of her favorite activities was escorting him around the canyon while protecting him from the other kanodraks, as if he were a prized pet she enjoyed showing off. She allowed him into her mind only by invitation, and she had yet to let him see through her eyes, but they were developing a gradual rapport.

One of the scouts had found the feathers needed to repair Kitrix's wings using the imping process Kenna had mentioned, which Adnar required Kasiel to learn in case the raptor got injured again. After the procedure, Kitrix could soar through the sky once more. Adnar insisted he return the sandhawk to the enclosure when he wasn't training with him until their bond became secure enough to keep the bird coming back. For now, working with him mostly involved flying him out to become accustomed to seeing the world using his eyes and feeding him to help build that bond.

As for the tethdraks, Adnar had him practicing increasingly complex commands and formations with them, typically from afar while using Sylaryth as his eyes. The ahndhomen had started introducing distractions to some of their sessions, going so far as to pit Jethan against him in armed combat while he was controlling groups of tethdraks. Splitting his vision and attention still caused significant nausea, which also made it harder to maintain an awareness of multiple creatures and activities at once. With time, he hoped that would improve. Until then, he was collecting enough bruises that a rotten banana looked better.

"I'm beginning to suspect you'll never get up the nerve to ride her." Adnar's voice held an edge of taunting.

Niskenya growled at the ahndhomen.

"I agree," Kasiel murmured, earning another bright flash of amusement from the massive beast. "We'll get there when we're both ready," he added loudly enough for Adnar to hear. "Sir."

Niskenya took a step forward, bringing the stirrup up next to Kasiel, and turned to look at him through those milky white eyes. A rumble rose in her chest. Not a growl this time.

He put a hand out, resting it on her head. "You're sure?"

She gave a slow blink, her mental touch urging him toward her.

The idea of climbing up on her still landed with a lump of icy apprehension in his gut, though it was a smaller lump than it used to be. And yet, he could imagine very few things he would enjoy more in that moment than making Adnar eat his words.

Adnar had fallen silent and statue-still beyond the bars. Kasiel's nerves danced, or perhaps screamed was a better term for what they were doing. He had to bring his knee up almost to his chest to get his foot in the stirrup. Swallowing against the threat of panic, he took hold of the saddle.

No reins. No control. Not even mentally unless she chose to allow it. This was the ultimate show of trust.

He drew in a deep breath and swung up on the saddle,

settling into the security of a seat made specifically to fit him.

An instant of furious rage swept out from Niskenya, her fiercely independent nature compelling her to fight this indignity. To be free. For a few heartbeats, her muscles bunched under him. Her tail lashed, claws digging deep into the ground. She shuddered, at war with her baser instincts. Kasiel sent calm and affection to her. Trust. Respect.

The moment passed. Her muscles slowly relaxed. She lifted her head. Kasiel put a hand on her shoulder, twining the other one into the grip on the front of the saddle to be ready if she moved unexpectedly. It was a long way down.

She struck out then, turning toward the open canyon behind them. Everything about being on her was peculiar. Different from riding a horse. Not only in the basic mechanics of her gait. She moved like a predator. Something in the free and fluid motion of those powerful muscles radiated threat and brutal strength. It was a heady sensation to sit up on the back of such a beast.

A brief mental embrace wrapped around him. A warning. He settled deeper in the saddle and took hold of the grips with both hands. She broke over into a faster gait, pacing along. The vertical aspect of the motion increased, but her flexible joints absorbed most of the shock, her body sinking into it in a way that kept him from being jarred by the impact.

The walls of the canyon sped past. Niskenya took them around several rock formations, heading toward the stream that wound through the habitat. When she reached it, her muscles bunched, and he gripped with his legs, leaning low over her back as she leapt the water. The landing jarred him, but, once again, her awesome musculature absorbed the brunt of it. Now a long flat stretch lay before them.

Kasiel stayed low, braced and ready when she surged forward, breaking into a full gallop. The wind whipped around them, stealing his breath and bringing tears to his eyes. He hugged her sides with his legs, awestruck by her raw power. Her mental presence enveloped him, lifting his confidence the way an Enkindler might. He sat up straighter, letting go of the grips one at a time and holding on with only his legs and seat in the custom saddle. She fed him more encouragement until he drew a deep breath and spread out his arms, cutting through the wind as he flew upon her back. Niskenya rode with him on the wings of his exhilaration.

Adnar was standing at the front watching for them when they returned a short time later, moving along at a more casual pace now. Niskenya took them up to the bars, her attention turning to the tunnel coming from the tethdrak canyon as the door opened. Kenna, Jethan, and an unfamiliar female soldier in military uniform emerged. All three slowed when they saw Niskenya there with him on her back. Kenna and Jethan smiled, eyes shining with wonder.

Niskenya, not one to miss an opportunity, opened her mouth, letting out a loud roar. The three new arrivals jumped back a step. Even Adnar flinched in surprise.

Sharing Niskenya's amusement, Kasiel grinned and rested a hand on the thick, scaled hide over her shoulder, as reluctant to dismount now as he had been to get on in the first place. Still, the appearance of the other three here suggested that something important was up. They rarely allowed any non-Ferals in the kanodrak habitat unless it was for official business of a kind that couldn't wait.

He swung down and strode up beside Niskenya's head, placing a hand on her neck.

The soldier cast an uneasy look at the kanodrak as she straightened and took a step toward Adnar. "Ahndhomen

Adnar, the dhomvalen has requested that all Ferals report to the council chamber immediately." She glanced at Jethan, who had casually drifted closer to the bars, his eyes on Niskenya. "Tehnaak may also be present."

"Dhomen Nevias?" A note of inquiry lifted Adnar's voice as he spoke his tehnaak's name.

The soldier inclined her head. "Your tehnaak is already there, sir."

"We will be there momentarily." As the soldier bowed and took her leave, Adnar turned to Kenna. "My guess would be that this isn't good news. Do you want Therin there?"

Kenna's gaze encompassed Kasiel and Jethan. "He's training with a unit today. I'll be fine with these two."

Kasiel unfastened the chest collar and girth.

Jethan stopped a few inches from the bars, gawking at Niskenya. "So, this is your new girl, huh?"

Niskenya, still breathing hard from their run, huffed at him.

"Yes, I don't like his tone either." Kasiel patted her shoulder before pulling off the saddle.

The kanodrak nudged him in the arm with her head, then trotted off to find a place to relax in the sun. Kasiel stepped out and handed the saddle to Jethan. Caught off guard, his tehnaak took it, staring at it in puzzled surprise as Kasiel, chuckling to himself, turned to lock the gate using the key Adnar had recently entrusted him with.

"What am I supposed to do with this?" Jethan asked, holding up the saddle.

Adnar pointed to a door in the canyon wall. "Put it away."

Jethan shook his head at Kasiel and started for the indicated door. "When did I become your servant?"

Kasiel followed him, jogging ahead to open the storage room. "I don't know, but I could learn to like it."

"Hurry up, you two," Adnar called.

They hung the saddle on a wall rack, then joined Kenna and Adnar heading into the tunnel. Kasiel hesitated before going in. Glancing back at the massive kanodrak basking in the sun, he sent her a surge of gratitude. Her responding emotions made him feel like a kitten being affectionately groomed by its proud parent. For an instant, delight and amusement at the ridiculous yet somehow fitting notion bubbled up in his chest. Those positive feelings faded when he stepped into the tunnel. He jogged a few strides to catch up with the others, apprehension creeping in. What could the dhomvalen want that required all the city's Ferals?

In the next canyon, Adnar stopped them at the enclosure. He collected his tethdrak and waited for Kasiel to bring out Sylaryth. From there, they made a side trip to the cliff cat habitat to get Raxxa, reasoning that Kenna should have her companion since she would be the only one of them reporting to the palace without her tehnaak.

People in the streets stopped to watch them pass after that. With only three Ferals in the city, all of them traveling together with their beasts garnered plenty of attention. Once inside the palace, those they encountered turned down side halls or ducked into rooms to move out of the way of their group. Kasiel glanced behind him, noting the prints the beasts left in their wake. Little specs of dirt and debris from the outdoors. Who would have to clean that up?

The only other time Kasiel attended a council meeting, when they were planning the delegation they sent to negotiate in Katovan, it had occurred in a smaller room. This time, they entered a large oval chamber with an elegant oval table taking up the center under a similarly shaped stoneglass and crystal candelabra. Even knowing how little stoneglass weighed, Kasiel caught himself eyeing the extensive, ornamental piece nervously as he approached the table set beneath it.

The walls around the room were pale cream, continuing the uniformity of shape with oval paintings in gilded frames hung upon them at intervals. The elegance at first glance began to lose its appeal when he noticed that all the paintings depicted scenes of battle. A unit of tethdraks tearing through everything in their path. A Frightener riding into enemy forces as they trampled each other trying to flee the terror. A figure seated upon a kanodrak at the edge of a rise overlooking a battlefield. Scene after scene of war with mind-crafters featuring prominently.

The one exception hung at the back of the room. The painting, three times the size of the others, depicted a coastal setting with fishing boats unloading a bountiful catch. One of the fishermen was tossing a large fish to a tethdrak lounging on the dock. A young boy sat fishing off the end of that same dock. The people in this image were all smiling. Far in the background, a great mountain towered over it all. A scene from the Vanrian homeland before its volcanoes drove them to Pandrea and eventually to war.

Adnar's tehnaak, the formidable Dhomen Nevias, waited at the table among a gathering of other officers, very few of them mind-crafters. Arhk, wearing his long black jacket with its dark metal armor accents stood at the end of the table with the homeland landscape hanging behind him. He inclined his head to them as they entered, his expression more grim than usual.

Once they were all standing at the table, he spoke. "We have had twelve mind-crafters go missing in just the last month. Thanks to the efforts of the city guards, with help from Ahninveth Hahren's unit, none of these disappearances have occurred in Etrion." His gaze flickered to Kasiel, the barest hint of appreciation in it before he moved on.

"Now we have an additional problem. We received

word last night that Pandrean Alliance forces overtook the base near Katis early yesterday. According to reports from the few who escaped, the abilities of our mind-crafters, specifically a Frightener and two Dampeners stationed at the base, had no effect on those Alliance troops. This morning, we learned that an altercation south of here met with the same results. The Frightener in the group could not influence the Alliance's soldiers."

Kasiel's skin tightened with the chill that swept through him. Katis was where Nerith and Leysa were stationed.

"The surviving residents of Katis are on their way to Etrion now, fleeing ahead of the force that took the base. Another Alliance force has been spotted crossing the Break, on track to intercept them sometime tonight. Our people will not make it here unless we intervene. Given these reports and the brazenness displayed by going after our people this close to Etrion, we must assume that the Alliance forces have found a reliable method of blocking us out of their minds."

Kasiel looked at the men and women assembled around the table. They hung on Arhk's words, faces darkening with anger and perhaps a hint of fear. None of them attempted to speak. He held them in thrall, all waiting for his solution to this new and terrifying threat.

"We have always relied heavily on our mind-crafters, so the Alliance may not realize how plentiful and well-trained our basic soldiers are. Until we figure out what they are doing to block our mind-crafters and how to counter it, we are going to have to rely more heavily on those troops. We also have one group of mind-crafters who may still be effective against them." He looked at Adnar.

"The ones who don't work with human minds," Adnar stated.

Arhk nodded. "Our Ferals. We have already sent for additional reinforcements from up north. Specifically, basic troops and all the Ferals with their beasts that we can get. For now, it is up to those of us here to assist the people from Katis." As he spoke, his gaze drifted around the table, picking out each officer individually. "I want as many troops as I can get ready to march within the next three hours. I mean to have our force intercept the Alliance before they can cut off the people from Katis. You will have two Ferals to assist your troops, a few Enkindlers to boost morale, and as many Speakers as we have available here. There will be no Frighteners and no Dampeners, so plan your troops accordingly." His gaze settled on the last of the officers standing next to Adnar. "Go prepare your rosters. I must speak with my Ferals."

The other officers bowed and exited the room. All except Dhomen Nevias, given that one of the Ferals was her tehnaak. When the room had cleared, Arhk singled out Adnar again.

"Ahndhomen Adnar, can Ahninveth Hahren manage the kanodraks if you and Ahninveth Kenna go to fight?"

Kasiel set a hand on Sylaryth's shoulders, as much to keep the tethdrak calm as to stop himself from reacting to a burst of anger at his father's assumption that he couldn't handle battle. The truth was, he didn't even want to fight. This was a good thing. And yet, it still served as a reminder that he was lesser in his father's eyes.

Adnar cocked his head in that animalistic way of his and regarded Arhk. "Yes, Dhomvalen, I believe Ahninveth Hahren can handle the kanodraks. He won't need to, however, as I intend to send him out with Ahninveth Kenna this time."

Kenna sucked in a sharp breath of surprise next to Kasiel. On his other side, Sylaryth stood abruptly, reacting to the alarm that exploded in Kasiel's chest.

Arhk inclined his head slightly, a hint of challenge in his eyes. "And you think this is the right choice because..."

Adnar stood straighter, facing down Kasiel's father with unshakable confidence. "Because he has a more empathic connection with the tethdraks than any other Feral I've ever worked with, and his ability to see through their eyes will allow Dhomen Nevias to keep him back out of the fighting while he is commanding his beasts. I may have experience, Dhomvalen, but Ahninveth Hahren's unique talent alone is worth a great deal more than my experience."

Arhk looked at Kasiel, his pale eyes hiding any feelings he might have on the subject. After several seconds, he nodded. "Very well. Make certain he is ready."

The hour following the meeting they spent discussing the mission with Nevias, who would lead their company into battle, and Adnar, who would remain behind in a role Kasiel would have happily filled. After Nevias left to prepare her other troops, Adnar continued to drill Kasiel, Jethan, Kenna, and Therin – who they had summoned to join them – on their roles in the coming battle. Kenna would run her cliff cats and Kasiel would manage a unit of tethdraks. The Ferals and their beasts were to remain out of sight at the rear of the Vanrian force until they engaged the Pandrean Alliance company. Once the fighting began, Kenna was to bring her cats in on the eastern side and Kasiel would stay behind, attacking with his tethdraks from the west using Sylaryth as his eyes to direct them.

They assigned a group of guards to protect Kasiel to allow him to focus the majority of his attention on his tethdraks through Sylaryth. Jethan would also be there to support him. He and Kenna would maintain a passive connection with each other's companion animal, so they would know immediately if either of them got into trouble. If something happened to one of them, the other would take control of their beasts to ensure they didn't attack the wrong side in the frenzy of battle. They trained the beasts to recognize colors and patterns in the Vanrian uniforms, and soldiers also carried scent pouches when working with Feral units, but an abandoned beast could still become confused and strike out at the wrong person. A large part of a Feral's job in battle was keeping their beasts calm and focused as they moved them around on the battlefield.

Adnar had a meal delivered while they planned to make sure they ate before marching. Kasiel yearned for a little time to rest first, but he probably couldn't fall asleep under the circumstances anyhow. He had seen fighting in Katovan, but this would be his first genuine battlefield engagement, and he wasn't that excited about it. He hated that Sylaryth would be in the heart of the battle, but the strength of his connection to the tethdrak made him the obvious choice for Kasiel to use as his eyes.

It was still several hours ahead of nightfall when they struck out, heading southeast. The goal was to intercept the Alliance force after dark as they were coming out of the Break. The Ferals stuck to the back of the company as planned, where their beasts were less apt to be spotted before the battle engaged. Attacking at night would also help with that.

He and Jethan rode beside Kenna and Therin, the tethdraks and cliff cats spread out to either side. The four guards assigned to Kasiel followed immediately behind him. He always expected it might be comforting to have some of his friends with him as they rode toward battle, but now that it was happening, it was mostly just upsetting. Their presence meant they would be in danger. He spent much of the ride working through scenarios in his head to come up with ways to keep them safe. No matter what he did, Kenna and Therin would be out of his reach unless he disobeyed orders, which could put a lot more people at risk.

"Do you think Nerith made it out?" Kasiel asked as

dark crept across the landscape, a warning that battle wasn't far away. He wore a cloth over his mouth and nose to help with the dust churned up by the company. The poor horses and other creatures didn't have that benefit.

Jethan glanced at him, the dark fabric covering half his face making him look like a bandit. "If she did, she'd be with the group riding in from Katis. The only way we'll find out for sure is if we succeed in protecting them tonight."

"Right." He focused on Sylaryth for a few seconds. The tethdrak practically vibrated with the nervous energy around him. The other beasts were the same. That charge of anxious expectation would make controlling them more difficult. "Not that it matters."

Jethan snorted a laugh. "You're riding into your first proper battle and you're worrying about her. It must matter some."

Kasiel clenched his jaw and stared ahead.

Jethan's tone was gentle when he spoke again. "It's never wrong to remember what you're fighting for on the way into battle."

Kasiel looked at Jethan, considering everything his tehnaak had gone through to bring him to Vanris and help him find a home here. While his ideas didn't always work out for the best, his efforts all stemmed from an earnest desire to see Kasiel succeed. He smiled. "I know what I'm fighting for, tehnaak."

Jethan grinned. Before he could speak, a bolt of tension swept over the force, and Therin lifted a hand, slowing them to a smooth stop with the rest of the company. The Speaker's focus turned inward for a second, then he glanced around at them.

"The Alliance company is just ahead."

Silence hung over them for a moment, as if they were all waiting for the clap of thunder after a lightning strike. Then the front of their force surged forward, the next rank and the next following behind in a ripple of motion. The first battle cries and clangs of weapons striking weapons or armor rang out in the night. Therin's focus turned inward again, awaiting word from the Speaker with Dhomen Nevias. All too fast, Therin signaled their line to move. The battle had begun. Kasiel had missed his opportunity to throw up.

Kenna gathered her reins, glancing over at him. "You can do this, Kas."

Before he could collect his thoughts to respond, she was galloping toward the eastern side of the company, her cliff cats sprinting after her like a stream of silent death.

Kasiel yearned to charge in. Not because he believed he could do better in the middle of the chaos, but because it felt cowardly hanging back out of the fray. Still, their success depended, in some part, on him doing what his commanding officers ordered him to do.

A sudden surge of confidence boosted him, the Enkindler's influence at work. For once, he was happy to be manipulated. He had a role in this battle, one that could be pivotal to the outcome. It was time for him to prove he deserved that. He slipped behind Sylaryth's eyes and set the beast running, leading the unit of tethdraks along with him. They swept wide, their ground-consuming strides bringing them past the Vanrian company and around the western flank of the Alliance soldiers in seconds.

Kasiel sank fully into his unit of beasts, trusting the guards, and primarily Jethan, to watch over his physical self. The encounter in Katovan taught him how much damage a tethdrak could do in a matter of seconds. Even with that experience, it caught him unprepared when one beast rushed past Sylaryth and laid open a horse's belly with a swipe of its claws. A whirlwind of ferocity, his unit of tethdraks sent that flank of the Alliance company into chaos. The armored scales of his beasts deflected all but the most powerful or well-aimed attacks while they tore apart everything within range, using teeth and claws that could kill with a single savage strike.

He held Sylaryth behind the rest of the tethdraks. Partly to make it easier to keep watch over them and guide them in the correct direction, but also to protect his companion from harm as much as possible. Sylaryth had the same natural armor as the others, but the right hit could still inflict severe damage and Kasiel wasn't willing to lose him.

He heard screaming from the battlefield now. Not cries of rage or forced courage but screams of terror that came from being attacked by a creature as lethal and unstoppable as the beasts the Ferals brought. His gut twisted, so he sank even deeper into his connection with Sylaryth, relinquishing himself to that wild ferocity as he guided the tethdraks into the heart of the opposing force.

A deafening blast rang out nearby, and something slammed into Kasiel. Everything went dark.

•

Kasiel tasted blood and dust. He lay face down in the dirt. Darkness surrounded him. He could still hear the sounds of battle, but they were hollow and distant, as if he were deep inside a cave with the fight raging outside. Something extremely heavy had him pinned. He strained, digging his fingers into the hard dirt to pull free of whatever lay on top of him. His horse, perhaps, given the weight of it.

Much of his body hurt, but nothing stood out as particularly dire. As he dragged himself out, his eyes slowly adjusting to a dark night thick with smoke and dust, he touched his fingertips to a stinging spot on his head. They came away sticky with blood. He struggled to bring his hands and knees under him and sat back on his ankles. Then he turned and saw what had fallen on top of him. His chest seized.

Sylaryth lay there, a spear driven in deep behind one front leg and another piercing up into his side below his ribs. The tethdrak was straining to draw in shallow, rasping breaths. Kasiel crawled to him, leaning over him to see blood pooling next to the beast's mouth.

"No." His voice broke. "No. Syl. Please."

The tethdrak drew a wheezing breath, and Kasiel placed a hand on his shoulder. He wanted to make the spears go away but removing them would only cause him to bleed out faster. There was nothing he could do for him.

Or maybe he could do something.

He closed his eyes and wrapped love and comfort around his companion, trying to hold back the sorrow that threatened to rip him apart. Sylaryth answered with fear, fear and pain... and hope. The last because Kasiel was with him now.

Tears streamed down Kasiel's cheeks. He sank in the dirt next to the tethdrak, bringing his face to rest against Sylaryth's neck.

"Syl. I can't fix this."

The fear faded. Fierce, unconditional affection took its place, washing over Kasiel. A stubborn, uncompli-cated form of love. Then the tethdrak exhaled and his mind fell silent.

Kasiel screamed, a cry of anguish and rage lost amidst the sounds of fighting that were growing clearer as his hearing returned to normal.

"Kas!"

He lifted his head and glanced around, his vision

blurred by tears. Beasts appeared out of the smoke-filled night. Not just his tethdraks, but the cliff cats too. Kenna rode into sight, Therin not far behind her. She swung from her mount, her face twisting with sorrow when she looked down at Sylaryth.

"Oh, Kas. I'm so sorry." Moisture welled in her eyes as she knelt next to him. "Are you injured?" She brought a careful hand up toward the wound on his head as he sat back on his heels again.

He pulled away. Something else was wrong. An absence that Sylaryth's silence amplified. He peered around them, panic rising through the grief. "Where's Jethan?"

Alarm sparked in Kenna's eyes. She hurried to her feet, scanning the area. "I don't know. I felt your connection to Sylaryth break a short time ago, and I managed to take control of your tethdraks, except for Syl. He wouldn't let me in. But I was in the middle of the battle. I couldn't get over here right away. Where are your guards?"

Taking his hand from Sylaryth's still-warm neck was like tearing a chunk of flesh from his chest. It was hard to breathe, and not because of any physical injury. He peered around. Two of the four guards lay a few yards away, both dead. On the other side of Sylaryth, Kenna crouched next to two bodies, their gaping, ragged wounds obviously the tethdrak's doing.

"These aren't Alliance soldiers, Kas. These are mercenaries. It looks like Syl was protecting you from them." She glanced around, shaking her head briefly as if to clear it. "Can you take your tethdraks back? I can't manage them and the cliff cats in this chaos. They're too different."

He didn't want to. With Sylaryth gone, he wanted nothing to do with them, but he made himself do it for her sake. The instant he reconnected to them, he recognized that they had lost two other beasts in the fighting. When he had full control again, he set them searching, passing images of Jethan through to them. A little farther out, they found a third guard and another dead mercenary who appeared to have dragged himself away from where Sylaryth lay before bleeding to death from a thigh torn open to the bone.

"He's gone, Kas." Kenna stood staring forlornly into the smoky darkness. "They hit your group with a blackout bomb to stun you and create a smoke screen. Then they took Jeth and killed everyone except you because Sylaryth got here fast enough to protect you."

At the cost of his life.

Therin walked up behind Kenna and put a hand on her shoulder. "The fighting's not finished," he said, his tone gentle, but insistent.

"How did they know we'd be back here?" Kasiel glanced over at Sylaryth, lying so devastatingly still. "How did they know who to take?"

Kenna turned to him, rage kindling in her eyes. "There are *three* dead guards. Why would they take an ordinary guard?" Her tone said she wasn't asking for her benefit. She had already figured it out.

"One of my guards was a traitor." Fury burned through him. A cleansing fire of pure loathing. His gaze moved to Sylaryth again, the intense pain of that loss fueling the flames.

"Our company needs its Ferals," Therin said.

Kasiel dove in behind the eyes of one of the other tethdraks, vaguely aware of Kenna telling Therin to stay with him. He sent his beasts charging back into the heart of the battle, directing them straight down the center of the Vanrian company. They plowed through toward a group of Alliance soldiers who were holding out against the Vanrian force now that the beasts were off the battlefield. The tethdraks plunged in among them, driven to frenzy by his rage. They took down soldiers and horses indiscriminately, leaving a path of blood and carnage in their wake.

It was over before he had even begun burning through his anguish. The cliff cats arrived in time to pick off a few stragglers on the edges. Kasiel pulled the tethdraks back to his position. The world spun when he looked out of his own eyes again. Therin caught his arm, steadying him. Sylaryth still lay dead a few feet from where he stood and Jethan was still missing. This was a nightmare he would give anything to wake from.

Kenna and Dhomen Nevias rode up together a few minutes later, a large number of Vanrian soldiers following behind them.

Nevias looked down at him, a hint of sympathy in her solemn regard. "Some of the uninjured soldiers are going to help clean up here and transport our wounded back to the city. The rest are coming with me to ensure the other Alliance force doesn't overtake our people from Katis before they reach Etrion. I need my Ferals for this."

Kasiel looked down at his hands. They were shaking. Was that rage? Fear? Sorrow? "I have to find Jethan."

"Kenna told me what happened. I am sorry. I believed you would be safe back here." She paused, glancing at one of the dead guards, her hands tightening on her reins. "You don't know which way they went or how many there are, and I can't let one of our Ferals go off after one man when we have a whole town's worth of people to protect. I'm sorry, Ahninveth Hahren, but this must be handled the right way."

What am I fighting for now, Jeth?

The anger faded. Everything faded. Numbness set in as he finally nodded.

Nevias released a relieved sigh, as if she had expected him to refuse, and scanned over the troops behind her. "Someone bring Ahninveth Hahren a horse. We're moving out."

The night wore on endlessly. Their company intercepted the people fleeing from Katis and surrounded them in a defensive shield of Vanrian soldiers. Kasiel and Kenna rode at the back. Their beasts, sensitive to danger, fanned out to create a buffer between the townsfolk and any threats that might come up behind them.

Kasiel didn't look at the people they were protecting. He didn't search for Nerith among them or even care much if they were happy to see the Vanrian company. He wanted this to be over, though he wasn't sure what came next, or if it mattered. The connection he had to maintain with the tethdraks was a constant reminder of what he had lost. One he couldn't wait to rid himself of. He had stopped watching through their eyes. Being that intimately linked to any of them now only made him yearn for the bond he had shared with Sylaryth.

The first light of dawn was creeping over the horizon when they reached Etrion. The Pandrean Alliance force coming from the east hadn't caught up with them. It was possible they received word of the decisive battle the Vanrians had won in the night and chose to hold back and reassess. Regardless of the reason, the townsfolk from Katis became much more animated once they were within the long, dark shadow cast by those massive, black walls. Most of their company waited outside the gates until the people from Katis passed through.

Kasiel sat silently on his mount, watching the sun rise. He didn't want to enter the city, not without Jethan and Sylaryth.

Kenna rode up beside him. She took a cloth and a waterskin from one of her saddlebags. After dampening the cloth, she nudged her mount closer to his. When she reached toward his face with it, he shifted away.

"Kas, there's very little I can do for you at the moment, but I think Jethan would prefer that we try to help each other. Let me at least clean the blood off your face."

He heard the aching weight in her voice and met her eyes, unsurprised by the tears welling in them. She had lost Jethan too. He nodded and sat still while she wiped away the blood from the cut on his head. The cloth was stained red when she finished, and the company was now making their way through the gate. They waited until last with their beasts.

Kasiel gestured for Kenna to go in ahead of him. He lingered, staring off into that awful sunrise, until he heard Adnar calling to him.

"Ahninveth Hahren." The Feral ahndhomen strode out to him, reaching up to place a hand on his arm. Kasiel could see by the sympathy in his eyes that he already knew everything. That meant the other part of their company had made it back during the night with the wounded. He supposed that was good news. "I'll take the tethdraks. Your father would like to speak with you. Go up the inner wall passage. I've already approved your entry."

Kasiel nodded and relinquished control of the tethdraks to Adnar. With a squeeze of his legs, he urged his mount through the gate. He wanted to speak with his father too.

When Kasiel arrived at the palace entrance by way of the concealed side passage, an attendant was there waiting for him. The woman inclined her head and bade him follow her. She led him not to one of the council rooms as he had expected, but directly to Arhk's private chambers. That meant it would almost certainly be just the two of them. For once, a chance to confront his father alone was exactly the encounter Kasiel wanted.

Arhk's elegant sitting area was nearly twice the size of the spacious one in Kasiel's rooms. A long couch and four chairs sat around a polished dark wood table before the gaping maw of a black stone fireplace. His father, dressed down in simple black trousers and a silken ivory shirt, stood gazing out one of several large arched windows along the far wall when Kasiel entered. His hand rested absently on a long, polished wood box that lay on a table next to him.

He glanced over at Kasiel, his annoyingly perfect brows rising a fraction. "You have looked better."

Kasiel bit back a flurry of angry retorts and skipped directly to the reason he was here, which was not because his father had summoned him. "I'm going after Jethan."

Arhk nodded thoughtfully and strolled over to rest

his hands on the high back of one chair, his gaze picking Kasiel apart with more interest now. "I expected no less. Your unit is already gathering supplies for the mission."

"You can't stop..." He trailed off, hearing what his father said as opposed to what he had expected him to say. "What?"

"You cannot take your kanodrak or any of the tethdraks, but the sandhawk might prove useful. I have given my permission for you to borrow one or two of the hunting hounds out of the kennels if you want them for tracking. You are not supposed to leave the city with them, but, so long as you keep your intentions to yourself when you collect them, you should not have a problem."

Maybe he had hit his head harder than he realized. It sounded like Arhk was not only accepting his resolution to search for Jethan but helping him accomplish it. "The khevarin doesn't object to one of the city's three Ferals running off right now, possibly into Alliance territory?"

Arhk tapped a finger on the chair. "The Alliance was not expecting the resistance they met up with last night. We showed them that their new advantage is not as impactful as they believed it to be. They will pull back and reevaluate the situation before attacking again. That should buy us time for the Ferals and other troops from up north to reach Etrion." A faint smile curved Arhk's lips. "All that aside, I did not ask Khevarin Seylin for her permission to let you go after your tehnaak any more than you came here to ask for mine."

Tears stung Kasiel's eyes. He had come to Arhk ready for a fight. Anger and confrontation were what he needed to keep the anguish and hopelessness at bay. The one person in all of Etrion he thought he could count on to meet that need was his father. He had no idea how to deal with this.

Arhk wandered over to look out the window,

providing Kasiel a measure of privacy in which to gather his composure. "While I cannot pretend to understand the bond you had with your tethdrak, I do know what it is like to lose your tehnaak. I already knew the pain of losing you and your mother when mine died. Given the chance, I would have done anything to save him." He took a slow, even breath before speaking again, as if preparing himself for something. "I made the wrong choice all those years ago. I should have gone to search for you when you were taken, no matter the orders I was given. I have no desire to see you repeat my mistakes."

He turned to face Kasiel, setting aside the moment of candor. "Given that Healer Tath has not taken a new tehnaak, I have arranged for someone else to fill the empty space in your unit – your tehsheyn, as I believe you have started calling them. They are all aware of the need for discretion. You will depart after dark tonight. I warned the night guards on the eastern gate to expect you. They are aware that you are embarking on a clandestine mission on my orders. Until then, you should eat, rest, and have your injuries seen to." His gaze flickered up to the cut on Kasiel's head where blood still darkened his hair. "You will need your strength in the days ahead."

Kasiel drew in a shaking breath and exhaled slowly, doing his best to quiet the tempest of emotion that threatened to crush him. "I'm not sure what to say, Dhomvalen."

Arhk approached him, meeting his eyes. "Say you will not make me regret this. I expect you to return, with Jethan or without."

Kasiel fought the urge to take a step back from him. Even without his ability active or the benefit of his embellished attire, something about his father perpetually warned of danger. "What will happen here?"

Arhk returned to the window, picking up a letter

that sat on top of the box on the table. He skimmed it briefly before answering. "Here is not your concern right now. Go prepare for your departure."

"You won't regret this," Kasiel said, the conviction of his anger strengthening his words. "I will bring back Jethan, and I'm going to find out what they're doing with our mind-crafters while I'm at it."

Arhk gave a slight nod of approval, the barest hint of a smile curving his lips as if he had been waiting for that bold declaration. He waved toward the door dismissively with one hand and returned his attention to the letter he held.

A selection of food arrived minutes after Kasiel entered his rooms. Healer Iatan showed up at about the same time. He checked Kasiel over while he ate. The wound on his head turned out to be mostly superficial. Kasiel also had a plethora of substantial new bruises, undoubtedly a result of being thrown from his horse when the blackout bomb exploded, and a cut on the back of one hand he hadn't noticed. Fortunately, it wasn't on the side with khevarin's tattoo of recognition.

He stared at the tattoo as Iatan cleaned the cut on his other hand, chewing at a bite of grilled quail. What would happen when Khevarin Seylin discovered they were gone? Even with more Ferals coming, he couldn't imagine she was going to appreciate one disappearing this way. Would Arhk admit his part in their departure or deny his involvement?

"Not quite good as new," Iatan said, leaning back to look Kasiel over, "but I've seen you in far worse condition."

"You have." Kasiel wished he could find a smile for the healer. "Thank you, Iatan."

"Of course, Lord Hahren." He gathered his supplies and walked to the door. When he opened it, he stopped and glanced back over his shoulder. "You have company, my lord.”

Kasiel stood up from the couch. Avris entered as Iatan left. She bumped the door shut with her heel and crossed the room, pulling him into a firm embrace. He could almost hate her for it. The warmth and comfort of her arms around him gave the relentless heartache permission to rise above the anger that sustained him.

“Avris.” His voice sounded rough with the emotion he was trying to keep back. He pushed her away.

Undeterred, she moved into his space again, sliding a hand along his jaw. “We’ll find Jethan,” she said, effortlessly digging out his pain. “I just wish—”

He put a finger to her lips. It was hard enough to think about his tehnaak knowing there was a strong possibility he might not get him back. He couldn’t cope with the passing of Sylaryth, who would never be with him again, no matter what anyone did. The two losses together were too much.

“I can’t talk about—”

She didn’t let him finish the sentence. “Then don’t.” She took his hand and moved it away from her mouth, her pale green eyes searching his.

He wasn’t sure who leaned in first, but their lips met in a hard, demanding kiss. She opened her mouth, inviting him in. They pulled his shirt off together and discarded it on the floor, his hands roughly yanking at the fastenings on her shirt. She slid her palms down his bare chest, descending to the waist of his trousers.

This wasn’t how he felt about her, not to say that he didn’t find her attractive, but he was confident she didn’t see him as a romantic partner any more than he did her. Somehow, in that moment, none of that was relevant. Neither spoke as they hastily removed each other’s clothing. They sank onto the couch, joining with a desperate need that had nothing to do with love. As bruised and sore as his body was, the act of coupling hurt, but he welcomed the distraction of interwoven physical pain and pleasure, selfishly taking whatever she was willing to give him.

•

Kasiel woke in his bed sometime later with a vague recollection of moving to the bedroom after the frenzied encounter on the couch. The waking world was stark and gray. Jethan was somewhere in the hands of the enemy. When he closed his eyes to that anguish, smoke-filled darkness swept in around him, Sylaryth's body lying before him, pierced with the weapons of those same enemies. He pressed a fist to his forehead and squeezed his eyes shut tighter, jaw clenched against the overwhelming wave of grief.

The bed sank a little as someone sat on the edge next to him.

"We can do this, Kas." Avris placed a hand on his shoulder. "We got you back, didn't we?" Her hand moved away, then the backs of her fingers brushed across his cheek. "You don't have to deal with this alone."

He opened his eyes. She had gotten dressed. Her pale eyes gazed down at him with an affection that stirred unease in his gut. Did their frenzied coupling earlier mean more to her than he thought? In the moment, he had convinced himself they were using each other as a mutual distraction. Now he wasn't so sure. That uncertainty didn't make any of this easier.

"Avris—"

"Shh." She put a finger to his lips to silence him. Then she leaned down, replacing the finger with her lips in a soft, brief kiss that brought the sting of tears back to his eyes.

When she straightened and moved to stand, he caught her wrist in a gentle grip. "Where are the others?"

She arched a brow at him. "You mean, why did I come here alone? Kince and Darro pulled out their dice sets, and we all rolled to see who got to come check on you. I won," she added with a coy smile.

"At least it was who *got* to come and not who *had* to come." He released her wrist and sat up, resisting the brief, modest urge to keep the sheet pulled up. She had seen everything at this point.

"Are you kidding? We all wanted to come. We were worried about you, country boy. Besides, the others are at Kince and Darro's place packing supplies for our *mission*. Who wouldn't want to get out of that? But just so you know," she said, tracing a finger down one side of the chained tattoos of his ke'hanoath around his neck, "I didn't come over here expecting to have sex with you. That just kind of happened. But you certainly slept well after." She nodded toward the windows.

Kasiel followed her gaze. The light streaming in through the glass had the fading glow of evening. He had slept nearly the entire day. At least while asleep, he hadn't had to face... things.

She stood. "There's hot water in the tub and a platter of fresh food in the sitting room. I'm going to go collect a few supplies I need for our journey. Do you want to join us at Kince and Darro's when you're ready?"

He slid one leg out of the bed. He must have slept deeply if they filled the tub in the bathing room without waking him. "I'll meet you outside the eastern gate after dark."

Her eyes tightened, her casual posture going rigid. "I feel like we should all head out of the city together."

"I'll need to collect Kitrix and the hounds. It'll be easier if I meet you outside the gate."

She rested her fists on her hips, resistance rising in her eyes. "At least one of us should go with you."

He shook his head. "No. I'll be fine."

Her lips pressed into a tight line, and she made no move to leave.

Kasiel exhaled a heavy sigh and met her eyes. "I'll be there, promise. I just need some time alone."

She took his hand, rubbing her thumb gently across the back of it. "If you change your mind, we'll be in and out of Kince and Darro's until it's time to leave. We're here for you, Kas. Don't forget that."

He nodded. "If you could get a horse for me, that might make it easier."

"Consider it done." She leaned in, placing another light kiss on his lips, and gave his hand a squeeze before leaving him there.

Kasiel wandered into the bathing room and soaked his sore muscles in the hot, scented water. He tried not to think about anything except what he would need to take with him. Not Jethan, or Sylaryth, or whether what had happened with Avris would complicate his relationship with her and the others. Just the requirements of the coming journey. One he hoped would end quickly with his tehnaak back by his side.

He had little desire to work with the hounds. They weren't his creatures, but he didn't have permission to take any of his beasts other than Kitrix. Not that he had official permission for any of this. The hounds would be excellent trackers, and he had to believe he could learn to appreciate working with them if it helped him find Jethan.

He heard the main door open and close again a few moments later. Curious, he climbed out and dried off, throwing on a set of clothes designed to be worn under his leather armor. In the sitting room, he found the long box he had seen in his father's chambers lying on the couch with a letter on top of it. He picked up the letter and broke the official-looking purple wax seal displaying a curved sword wreathed in flame.

It read: *These were intended as gifts for a later occasion, but it appears that you may have greater need of them now. Dhomvalen Arhk Cavenos.*

Not a man to waste time on sentimental words.

Kasiel put the letter aside and pulled the top off the box. A set of black leather armor similar to his father's lay within, strategically reinforced with dark metal plates. Alongside the armor rested a curved, dark metal sword and a black leather sheath embossed with many of the same symbols that formed his ke'hanoath. Not that long ago, though it felt like years now, Edmund had gifted him a much more basic set of leather armor and weapons. They had taken those from him when he arrived in Etrion. Now his real father replaced those items with far superior equipment.

He brushed his fingers over the flawless chest piece of the armor, then reached for the blade, lifting it cautiously from the box. The dark metal sucked in the light, barely reflecting it. He wasn't an accomplished enough swordsman to do justice to such an exceptional piece. It was his now, though. Perhaps he would grow into it one day.

As he set it back down, he noticed another little box nestled in the bottom of the larger one. It had a second letter tucked through the strings that tied it shut. This one bore a different seal. A stylized kanodrak in silver wax. He broke that seal and opened the letter.

It read: *Ahninveth Hahren Cavenos, we wish to present you this gift of gratitude for protecting our people. You have more than proven to us that you are Vanrian in your blood and in your heart. These are merely an ornament through which you may, if you so choose, proclaim that truth when you face our foes. Your khevarin, Seylin Markanis.*

He opened the box. Resting on a bed of purple silk lay a set of dark metal ear cuffs that extended back into fierce looking decorative wings meant to sweep out behind each ear. A symbolic replacement for the missing ends of his ears.

He closed the box. How would the khevarin feel if she knew Arhk had given these to him now? Did this mean that his father intended to acknowledge his involvement in this clandestine mission?

Setting the little box on the table, he turned to packing the few items he would need for the journey. Once he had done that, he sat to eat, watching the light gradually disappear outside his windows. When it was nearly dark, he donned the new armor, noticing as he did that the wrists of the gauntlets were thicker than normal, the leather reinforced against a raptor's talons. He sheathed the sword at his waist and tucked the little box with the earpieces in his bag, though he doubted he would have any need of them.

With all of that done, he slipped out of his rooms, sticking to the smaller side hallways typically used by palace attendants. The few he passed along the way didn't question his attire or the bags he carried. They might mention it to someone else later, but he suspected they wouldn't go out of their way to do so now. He was the dhomvalen's son. Whatever he was up to, it really wasn't their business.

He cut across the enclosed garden alongside the palace and out to the tethdrak canyon through the tunnel there. When he entered the front section, he avoided looking into the enclosure itself, hurrying past to the room where they were keeping Kitrix. He connected to the sandhawk as he walked in and unlocked the cage. The raptor flew to his arm when he held it up and landed there. He immediately began preening his wings, as if confinement had sullied them.

Kasiel took him outside and sent him up, encouraging him to watch for prey while he waited. The raptor didn't have the best night vision, but it would keep him occupied, and he might get lucky enough to catch something. That done, he turned and cut through the tunnel to the kanodrak enclosure. He wasn't about to leave Etrion again without saying goodbye to Niskenya first. Who knew when, or if, he would make it back this time.

He peered into the viewing area at the front before exiting the tunnel, looking for any sign of Adnar. The Feral ahndhomen spent most of his waking hours in the canyons, but he did typically leave at night. Kasiel reached out to Niskenya while he waited a few minutes in the doorway. By the time he decided it was safe to head out, the female kanodrak was by the bars, pacing. She stopped when she saw him, watching his approach with her milky white eyes. She looked restless, and the touch of her mind when she welcomed him in confirmed that.

Kasiel entered the enclosure, and she stopped before him, lowering her head to let him rest a hand on the armored plating above her eyes.

"What's wrong?" he murmured. "You know I'm leaving, don't you?"

Niskenya pulled his awareness in, dragging him deeper into her mind. Caught off guard, Kasiel threw a hand against her shoulder for balance. Before he could react, he found himself looking out through her unusual eyes. Those milky white eyes could see better in the night than even the tethdraks. The colors were strange, though, all a little different from the colors as he saw them with his vision. How much of that was the dark, and how much was an actual variation in the way her eyes processed light?

Niskenya took several steps back from him, holding him captive behind her eyes in a way he hadn't known was even possible for a beast. She looked at him, standing there armed and wearing the darkly elegant armor his father had gifted him. His long red hair hung straight down about shoulder-length, parted more to one side, though he still made certain it covered both of his ears. There was a haunted look to the man they were staring at that left him feeling like he was observing a stranger.

Niskenya inclined her head, bringing his attention to the space between them. Her gaze moved along a faint thread of blue light stretching from his chest into hers. Kasiel watched disjointedly as he passed a hand through that thread of light. The bond connecting them was more than a mental or emotional construct. It had a physical aspect, too. Did Adnar know that?

She thrust him back behind his own eyes, making that thread no longer visible, and regarded him expectantly. He moved closer to her, running one hand along the thick scaled hide of her neck.

"You're right, my friend," he murmured. "I need you."

asiel rode along, watching ahead through Kitrix's eyes. Despite the raptor's unfortunately poor night vision, its excellent hearing and his foreknowledge of where his companions had exited the city helped him locate them quickly. They had stopped to wait for him on the far side of a natural rock arch. The sandhawk landed quietly on top of the arch and looked down on them. He could see Avris, Darro, Wedro, and Kince sitting near the base of the formation, a compact travel lantern on the ground dimly illuminating the space between them. The others he could hear moving around by the horses, though he couldn't see more than shadows of them through the bird's eyes.

"Someone should have stayed with him," Avris said before going back to biting the end off a fingernail.

"We're doing this to find Jethan," Darro said. "He'll be here."

"What if something happened?" Wedro asked, shifting his feet as he stared into the darkness. "What if someone caught him trying to leave the city?"

"What if you all sit down and shut up?" Kince snapped, as charismatic as always, his unease manifesting as anger.

Kasiel retreated from the bird's mind. He had no desire to eavesdrop on his friends. At this point, he just wanted to be with them. Without him having to ask, Niskenya moved into a casual lope, consuming the remaining distance with long, powerful strides. In minutes they slowed to a walk again, the arch a few yards away, dimly backlit by the lantern. He reached ahead, calming the horses to keep them from panicking when the kanodrak arrived.

Once they were close enough for the light to pick them out of the darkness, Darro spotted them first, hopping to his feet. The other three followed suit, the alarm in their eyes fading a little when they noticed Kasiel on the beast's back. Niskenya stopped and Kasiel swung off. He stepped up alongside her head, placing a hand on her neck.

"Nice armor. It's very flattering on you," Avris said, looking him over with unabashed appreciation.

Her compliment took him back to his room and their heated encounter. Had she mentioned that to anyone? He would proceed as if she hadn't. "Thanks. It was a parting gift from my father, I suppose."

Darro was staring at Niskenya. "And he let you take your kanodrak?"

Kasiel glanced at the massive creature next to him. He refused to indulge any sense of guilt. Niskenya wanted to be here. "Not exactly."

"Then how did you get her out of the city?"

Kince came up beside his tehnaak, offering Kasiel a conspiratorial wink. "There's a way out through the kanodrak enclosure. They keep a key out in the canyon near the gate. It's well hidden, but he is a Feral. I assume he would know about it."

Darro looked at Kince, brows pinching together. "And how do you know about it?"

Kince shrugged. "I've done a lot of work with the guards. It's their job to know every way in and out of this city."

"I actually didn't know about it," Kasiel said, taking comfort from the low rumble in Niskenya's chest. "Niske showed me."

"So, this was her idea?" Darro asked.

Kasiel nodded.

He smirked. "See what happens when you listen to the ladies?"

Avris punched Darro in the shoulder. "Don't be an ass."

"What about the hounds?" Kince asked.

"Niske can track for us." The kanodrak sent confidence and comfort to Kasiel as he spoke. He lifted his arm and Kitrix swept down to land on it. "And we have a scout."

"He gets all the best stuff," Wedro muttered, though his grin told Kasiel he was at least happy to have that stuff working for them.

"All right then." Darro turned back toward where the lantern was waiting. "If we're stealing a kanodrak, we probably shouldn't linger. The Dhomvalen provided us with maps of mercenary activities along the Break that Setera's interrogation team and our scouts have compiled. Come take a look, Ahninveth."

The rest of their unit approached from over by the horses. It was a punch to the gut when Nerith stepped into the light, dressed in armor like the others. The flames of anger ignited in him, burning away the chill of the night. Nerith lifted her head, her jaw set and defiance flashing in her eyes, daring him to object. But this was his mission. She was a Break-blasted fool if she thought he was going to trust her with the lives of his companions.

Just as he opened his mouth to say something, Kince hurried over, placing himself in Kasiel's line of sight with one hand lifted in a subtle gesture to stall him. He eyed Niskenya warily as he walked up close to

Kasiel, speaking low enough that the others wouldn't hear.

"Before you object, you should know that her tehnaak was killed in the fighting outside of Katis. Your father sent her to fill the opening left by Ahrin's death. This way, we can have two healers again without having to risk someone else losing their tehnaak in the arrangement."

Kasiel drew a deep breath. Another broken pairing. At least his tehnaak might still be alive, though it was hard to cling to the hope that they would find Jethan before that changed. And yet, no matter how much sympathy he had for what Nerith must be going through, he couldn't pretend to forget what she had done.

"I want people I can trust with me in this. Jeth's life could depend on it."

"And I agree with that." Kince's expression was uncommonly sympathetic for him, but his placating tone implied that he had made his decision and intended to stand by it. "Your father may be a serious ass, but he's not stupid. He's putting a lot on the line to give us this opportunity. He wouldn't have chosen her if he thought we couldn't rely on her. Besides, Tath says she's a talented healer, and we don't have the luxury now of finding someone to take her place. It's up to you. This is your mission, but I urge you to use your head for this one, Kas, not your heart."

It was his decision. A fact he didn't find all that reassuring. He outranked the rest of them, although Kince and Darro were inveths, so he only outranked them because he was a mind-crafter. An advantage he gained merely through having the right lineage. Every one of the others, even Nerith now, had more genuine experience than he did. Had Jethan felt this out of his depth when they put him in charge of this unit to retrieve Kasiel from Fernwallow?

Kince took a quick step back when Niskenya moved closer. The kanodrak nudged Kasiel's shoulder with her nose. Comfort and patience flowed through their link. He looked into one of her milky eyes. If she agreed with Kince, how could he argue? He still didn't have to like it, though.

"All right, Nerith stays. Let's look at these maps."

Niskenya lurked at the edge of the light as Kasiel and Kince joined the group. Nerith also stayed back beyond the lantern's reach on the opposite side from the kanodrak, watching silently as they unrolled two maps. One showed several locations in the Break where the traitors Setera and the other Evokers had questioned either had met with or were supposed to meet mercenaries to hand off captured mind-crafters. The second map marked places, most close to the Pandrean Alliance side of the Break, where Vanrian scouts had spotted southern mercenary groups or found evidence of their passing. They crouched around the maps, Merrin, Kince, and Darro falling into a debate over where they might be taking the mind-crafters based on the triangulation of those locations.

Merrin reached in to point something out, but Kince waved her hand away. "I got a chance to talk to Inveth Tarik earlier," he said. "From the information the city guards pulled together, they think an outside party is behind this. Someone not directly working for the Alliance who is hiring these mercenaries to collect mind-crafters. Whoever they are, they seem to be operating with the approval and occasional support of Alliance troops. Jethan's disappearance wasn't the first one to occur during a battle. The mercenaries move in after the fighting starts knowing many mind-crafters work from the edges of the battlefield. Given that our mystery party appears to function apart from the Alliance, we can't assume the mercenaries are taking their captives to an Alliance stronghold. Something that might ultimately work in our favor if we can track them."

Kasiel leaned in closer, pointing to a spot on the map. "This is where last night's battle took place." He moved his finger south and a fraction east. "And this seems about central to most of the sightings and rendezvous locations. We'll cut in toward the battlefield to see if Niske can pick up Jethan's scent there. If not, we'll head toward the southern border here."

Merrin crossed her arms and stepped back, giving him an assessing look. "That's what I tried to suggest a minute ago, if Kince could be bothered to listen."

Avris grinned at her. "That's my tehnaak, full of great ideas no one ever hears."

Kasiel gave Merrin a nod, acknowledging her attempted guidance. "I know. How do you think I picked the border location?"

Merrin straightened. "Thank you, Ahninveth."

He turned to Kince and Darro. "Any objections?"

Darro stood. "None. We just need to be wary of the Alliance watchtowers. There are some slot canyons near the southern edge of the Break that could help keep us out of sight. The area we're talking about crossing is one of the wider sections. We're unlikely to make it over the border before daybreak, especially since it will take time to try picking up the trail."

"We'll see what Niske can find at the battlefield and go from there." Kasiel glanced over his shoulder, spotting the kanodrak's shape in the darkness.

Kince folded the maps and got to his feet. "We brought you a horse, Ahninveth."

"None of you need to use my title. This isn't an official mission. Besides, we're still tehsheyn out here." He avoided looking at Nerith as he said it. They were *mostly* family. "As for the horse, I doubt Niske is going to want me on her back all the time. She'll need to hunt and be free to investigate leads, so we'll have need of it. Let's get moving."

Kasiel returned to Niskenya while the others retrieved their mounts. They couldn't afford to waste more time if they expected to have any hope of tracking Jethan before the trail went completely cold, assuming it wasn't already. He also didn't want to be anywhere near Etrion when Adnar discovered Niskenya's absence. The Feral ahndhomen and his father weren't going to care that she had insisted on coming.

Keeping the horses calm and Kitrix close overhead, Kasiel led the unit out into the desert. Darro offered to guide them, but it wasn't necessary. The churned ground from Kasiel's passage with the Vanrian company was difficult to see in the dark, but every minute of the ride to the battlefield with Jethan and Sylaryth at his side remained etched in his mind. The last time he had with them before everything fell apart. Less than a year with his tehnaak and Kasiel already couldn't imagine life without him. If anything, he needed him now more than ever.

Niskenya loped easily along, keeping a pace that the horses could sustain. They traveled in focused silence, moving steadily away from the city. Hours slipped past, every heartbeat hopefully bringing him a step closer to finding Jethan. He tried a few times to drop behind Niskenya's eyes to see better in the dark, but the kanodrak brushed him off like an annoying fly, easing her rejections with a touch of comfort or affection. That part of their connection was something he would have to leave at her discretion.

The stench of death greeted them before they reached the scene of the battle. Several tents were arranged upwind, and a bonfire burned out on the northern edge of the battlefield. Kasiel brought them in as close as he dared, then stopped the group and climbed off Niskenya.

He pulled a shirt that belonged to Jethan out of his pack for her to smell, passing images of his tehnaak through their connection.

"See what you can find," he murmured, "but stay out of sight."

Niskenya nudged his shoulder with her nose before trotting off into the darkness.

Darro rode up next to him, handing him the reins for the extra horse. He stared after the kanodrak. "I really hope she comes back. They'll put us to death very slowly if we lose her."

"She'll come back." Kasiel swung up in the saddle. He felt uncomfortably close to the ground on the horse's back after riding the kanodrak for a few hours.

He considered the others for a moment, briefly inclined to bring Tath with him, but she was a healer. Taking the khevarin's healers without her leave was a less dire infraction than sneaking off with a kanodrak, but still a significant offense. "Avris. Merrin. You two come with me. The rest of you see if you can find any sign of the mercenaries retreating from this side of the battlefield, heading south or southwest. Don't wander too far, though. I imagine there are predators nearby."

"None bigger than the one you brought." Kince waved him away. "We can handle it."

Trusting them to manage things, he urged his horse to a trot, heading toward the bonfire with Kitrix scouting overhead. The fire burned a little southeast of where he had controlled his tethdraks from during the battle. Odd how crisp his memory of the spot was despite how similar the desert landscape appeared here. Through the raptor's eyes, he saw a lone figure standing near the fire on the upwind side. More soldiers waited farther back, stationed at intervals facing away from the blaze to keep watch for danger.

The soldiers on the near side noticed them immediately

when they got close and ordered them to halt. The figure standing near the fire glanced in their direction, squinting into the darkness. Kasiel recognized her at once through the sandhawk. It was Dhomen Nevias, Adnar's tehnaak.

One soldier approached, drawing her sword while another leveled a crossbow at him. She looked him over in his Vanrian armor, her gaze lingering briefly on the dark red tattoo on his cheek that stood out against his pale skin even at night.

"Who are you, and what are you doing out here?"

"Stay with the horses," he said, passing Avris his reins. Turning to the soldier, he held his hands away from his weapons and took a few steps toward her. "Ahninveth Hahren Cavenos." He hated to give that first name, but only those close to him knew him as Kasiel.

The soldier lowered her sword and gestured for the man behind her to move his crossbow enough that it was no longer pointing directly at him. "Apologies, Ahninveth Hahren. We weren't expecting anyone else out here tonight."

"I need to speak with Dhomen Nevias."

"Of course." The soldier waited for him to reach her, then she turned and escorted him toward the figure by the fire.

Nevias noticed them coming when they were still a few yards away and strode over to intercept them. Her eyes narrowed suspiciously. She dismissed the soldier back to her post before addressing him.

"You shouldn't be out here, Ahninveth." She looked past him, peering toward where Avris and Merrin stood with their mounts.

He watched the searing flames licking around the bodies of humans and horses, spotting what might be the leg of a tethdrak sticking out near the edge, though it was becoming hard to tell for certain. The heat made it difficult to be even this close. How did Nevias stand it?

"You're burning the dead?"

"We took most of our dead back to the city. The horses and tethdraks are too heavy to move that far. We're also burning the Alliance dead. We won't leave them to rot this close to Etrion and we're not about to let the Alliance venture this close to collect them."

Kasiel nodded. He loathed the idea that Sylaryth might be in there sharing his pyre with Alliance soldiers enough that he wanted to scream at Nevias for the insult. But none of this was her fault, and making a scene would increase the chances of the dhomen trying to interfere with his current objective. He was taking an enormous risk in speaking with her at all.

Biting back the anger that coiled in his gut, he asked, "You collected *all* our dead?"

Her wary regard softened a fraction. "Lord Jethan was not among them."

"Thank you." He needed to be sure. There would be no point in searching for him if they had found his body.

"Does your ahndhomen know you're out here?"

He had the information he came for. The longer they spoke, the greater the chance of her prying too deeply. "I should go."

"You and your companions can stay here tonight. We've got room in the tents. You can ride back to the city with us in the morning." When he didn't respond, her gaze shifted to Merrin and Avris with the three horses. She took a step closer to him, one hand sinking toward her blade as if she meant to challenge him. "You don't intend to go back, do you?"

Kasiel said nothing, turning his side to her to signal his intention to leave.

"You can't go after him. You're a Feral. We need you here." When he still didn't respond, she peered out at his companions again, perhaps noting the packs on the horses this time. "I could have my soldiers drag you back to Etrion. But... it's not just the three of you, is it?"

"Thank you again, Dhomen Nevias." He moved to walk away.

"Wait. I collected something for you." She strode to a row of horse blankets laid out with various items piled on them and picked up a large gray claw. "I thought you might like to make something with it," she said, holding it out to him as she returned. "To remember Sylaryth by."

Kasiel took it from her and lowered his gaze, unprepared for the burst of sorrow. His hand tightened around the claw, the point digging into his palm. "I appreciate this," he said, his voice catching. "We need to get moving."

"I'll see you back in Etrion tomorrow, right?"

She had to know he was going to lie to her. He tucked the claw into his belt pouch and gave a curt nod. "Tomorrow."

He strode away into the welcoming embrace of darkness that would help him hide his pain. It didn't work as well as he hoped, given Merrin and Avris's sympathetic looks. Avris put an arm around his shoulders and gave him a brief side-hug before handing him the reins to his horse.

As he was swinging up, he received a sudden flood of accomplishment and enthusiasm from Niskenya. Kicking his mount up to a trot, he struck out in the direction of her presence.

"Come on. Niske's found something."

CHAPTER THIRTEEN

Kasiel stayed on the horse after they joined up with the others, allowing Niskenya the freedom to pursue the trail she had discovered. It started at Jethan's lucky dagger found lying in the dirt, which had obviously not lived up to its reputation. They followed the kanodrak west a short distance before cutting south, heading into a tall slot canyon. Kasiel breathed a little easier when they could no longer see the bonfire. He didn't want to give Nevias an opportunity to come to her senses and send someone after them.

He wasn't going back. Not without Jethan.

The canyon's winding passage was narrow, though still wide enough in most places for two horses to travel abreast, which allowed Darro to ride with Kasiel behind Niskenya much of the time. Kince and Darro were more familiar with this region than anyone else in the group, and since Kince typically deferred to Darro in matters of importance, the latter became Kasiel's advisor here.

Their purpose limited the speed at which they could travel. Niskenya paused any time they came upon a branch within the canyon or possible exit to ensure she was still following the correct path. The group they hunted had come through this way on horseback, but at greater speed, judging from the depth of the hoofprints and the spread between them. Trying to hurry away from the Vanrian force and get across the border to safety.

Kasiel kept Kitrix soaring up above the slot canyon, watching for any human activity in the area and keeping an eye out for the Alliance watchtowers in the distance. The raptor wasn't especially effective in the dark, but he was better than nothing.

The first hints of dawn were brightening the sky when the canyon came to its end, the trail continuing beyond the protection of its walls. Kasiel called Niskenya to him, coaxing her back with a sense of caution. He stopped the group and looked out through Kitrix's eyes to see what the rising sun would show them.

The first thing he noticed was the unwelcome presence of an Alliance watchtower almost directly south and a little east of them. The surrounding land was rocky and broken, riddled with other canyons like the one they were traveling through. Between the termination of the slot canyon and the border, the terrain smoothed out, the landscape gradually changing to a flat, dry expanse of exposed desert. Beyond the watchtower, it gave way to grasslands and sparse, dry forest. With the sun coming up, the tower guards would have no trouble spotting them if they tried to make a run for the border. The cloaks they carried, designed to blend with the colors of the desert, might help them do some cautious scouting alone or in pairs, but they wouldn't be enough to hide the group and their mounts in the daylight.

He set Kitrix loose, encouraging the sandhawk to hunt before the sun finished rising. The poor creature had earned a meal and rest. That done, he turned to his companions.

"If we leave the canyon now, we'll be an easy target for the guards at the nearest watchtower."

Tath, riding toward the rear, pointed behind them.

"We passed a branch in the canyon about fifteen yards back. There was a large open area on the eastern side, with plenty of room for all of us to dismount and rest."

Kasiel nodded. "Let's take a look."

They turned around, a few of them having to back their horses to get to a place wide enough to do so. The branch Tath had mentioned widened out into a larger space where the high red walls curved in closer together toward the top, promising areas of shade even when the sun reached its peak. With a brief exploration a little further down that way, Chander and Wedro found a shallow stream trickling along part of the canyon floor before it disappeared beneath the wall. If they were conservative about it, they could water themselves and the animals there over the course of the day.

After caring for their horses, most of the group settled in to catch up on sleep, since they couldn't move on until dark. Kasiel, Avris, and Merrin stayed up to keep first watch and partake of what food they had brought that didn't require cooking. Tath stretched out next to Darro to rest, their hands touching. Nerith lay down a few feet away from her, looking uncomfortable amongst them.

Niskenya approached Kasiel as he sat to eat, growling low in her throat. Hunger snapped across their link. He set his food aside and stood, placing a hand on her forehead. She was hungry, but smart enough to recognize that hunting here while it was light was out of the question. A kanodrak near the border would draw watchtower guards down on them in no time. It fell upon him to find another way to feed her. She was his responsibility.

He led her a short distance away from the others, passing patience back to her. Once he located a large enough flat spot, he sat cross-legged, encouraging her to rest next to him. With a little persuasion, she lay down, watching him intently. He closed his eyes and reached out with his Feral ability.

Footsteps and a low grumble from Niskenya pulled him instantly back. He opened his eyes to see Avris stopped mid-step a few feet from him, staring warily at the kanodrak.

She met his eyes. "Can we talk a minute?"

A touch of apprehension fired through his nerves. He pushed it back. No matter what she wanted to talk about, it had to wait. "After I feed Niske."

"How are you going to accomplish that?"

He closed his eyes again. "This is perfect habitat for desert wildcats. The watchtower won't notice anything unusual if I have them hunt something down for her."

"Hmm, that's actually a clever way to solve the problem." Her boots scraped over the rock as she came to sit next to him.

"Maybe you could try not to sound so surprised that I would come up with something clever," he said, reaching out with his mind again. He touched on Kitrix to see if the bird might help him find what he was looking for, but the raptor had made a kill, so he left him to eat it in peace.

Avris bumped his shoulder with hers. "Want me to feed you while you search?"

"No."

"Fine."

It took several minutes to find what he needed, during which he could hear Avris crunching on root vegetables beside him. It was the scent of the dried meat she pulled out next that made his mouth water. Then he touched upon a trio of desert wildcats already out hunting in the predawn light. He let himself sink fully into them, leaving his body and any sense of hunger behind.

About fifteen minutes later, he had one cat drag the carcass of a small deer to the edge of the canyon and drop it over. It landed with a meaty thwack, startling everyone in their party, judging from the gasps and a few alarmed cries. He sent the desert cat on its way and returned to his body, opening his eyes as Niskenya leapt to her feet and went to claim the prize. The others were all awake now, watching as she grabbed hold of it with a snarl and dragged it around the corner. They all looked at him then.

"By the Break, Kas," Wedro muttered, curling up again to go back to sleep.

Darro smirked at him and stretched out, giving Tath's arm a tug to pull her down with him. She tucked in a little closer this time, resting her head on his shoulder.

Nerith didn't lay down again with the others. She cast a sorrowful glance around at them and slid back against the sandstone wall, pulling her knees to her chest. Kitrix dove into the canyon, capturing her attention as he settled on a sharp rock near Kasiel. Her gaze drifted from the raptor to him, their eyes meeting for an instant before they both looked away.

"Eat something." Avris gestured to an array of food items she had laid out in front of him while he was traveling with the wildcats. Then she shifted a little closer to him, speaking in a low voice. "You should talk to her."

He focused on the food, picking up a strip of dried meat. "Not yet."

"Fine, but you should talk to someone. She's in a better position to understand what you're going through than most of us, except for Tath, obviously. Besides, if you don't put your differences with her aside for this, it's going to make it hard for some of the others to accept her as part of the group."

He looked at Avris, appreciating the way her pale green eyes picked up a glow in the gradually brightening morning light. "Hard for *some* of the others?"

"I'm no hypocrite. I understand that what she did

may have been the worst form of betrayal given your past, but we all mess up. Given all the things I've done that I regret, I'm not about to condemn her for being fallible."

A glimmer of insecurity crept in. "You don't regret—"

She laughed, pressing her shoulder to his. "Sleeping with you? No. I'd do that again in a heartbeat. For a novice, you're not so bad."

Warmth spread up his neck and into his cheeks.

She met his eyes and her expression turned more serious. Her gaze drifted to his lips for a moment, her body leaning a little closer. Then she abruptly shifted away, twisting a lock of her red hair around one finger. "You're no idiot, Kas. You know we need to be a unit to pull this off. You're part of our tehsheyn, but you arc also our leader right now. It's your job to bring us together. All of us." She reached up, brushing her thumb across his lips, her gaze lingering there again for a moment before she broke the contact and stood up. "Eat and get some rest. There are enough of us awake to keep watch."

She wandered over to where Merrin sat and gave her a hand up. Together, they walked to where Nerith huddled against the canyon wall. Kasiel couldn't hear what they were saying, but after a brief exchange, the two sat down with her.

He drew a deep breath and let it out slowly, wishing the tension and heavy sorrow would leave with it. It didn't.

I don't know if I'm cut out for this, Jeth, but I'll make it work. I have to.

He slid back and leaned against the canyon wall, yearning to talk to his tehnaak or reach out to Sylaryth and experience that always enthusiastic welcome. Digging into his belt pouch, he pulled out the claw Nevias had given him. He closed his eyes, clenching his hand around it until the point penetrated the skin of his palm. A different type of pain to focus on. One that ultimately hurt less than the gaping hollow in his chest.

When Niskenya came back and sprawled alongside Kasiel after finishing her meal, he could finally fall asleep. Darro woke him in the late afternoon to take a shift on watch. Nerith had stretched out to rest with Avris and Merrin. Now that she was sleeping, he dared to observe her for a moment, noticing the deep shadows and puffiness around her eyes. When Tath's tehnaak died, Jethan said they needed to keep an eye on her for a time, to make sure she survived the loss. Here, away from the city with his unit, Nerith had less support than Tath did back then. Avris was right. He had to show them that he considered her a member of their unit, no matter what personal conflict existed between them.

Nerith moved in her sleep and his attention caught upon how unfortunately well-defined the curve of her waist and hip were in the fitted leather armor she wore. Parts of her body he had gotten to experience intimately a few times. Was it wrong to notice such things now when they were both mourning? When they were no longer a couple?

"That's not what I meant by your turn to keep watch."

Darro's voice next to him made him jump. "I know." He dragged his gaze away from Nerith, glancing back to where Kitrix still dozed. Like the rest of them, the sandhawk had pulled a long night. He would let the raptor and Niskenya sleep for now.

"How are you holding up?"

The uncommon gentleness in Darro's voice left Kasiel wishing he could run away from them all. He didn't want their sympathy. It forced him to acknowledge the ones that were missing. "We're all worried about Jethan," Kasiel answered, emotion giving a rough edge to his voice.

"Not the way you are. It's different when it's your tehnaak. And I know you lost Sy—"

"Please don't."

Darro looked away, light brown hair falling forward to shadow his face. "Sorry. If you need anything, you know that any one of us would be happy to help." The seriousness gave way as a mischievous smile tugged at the corners of his mouth.

Kasiel took a step back, a vague horror rising in him. "Don't say it."

The smile grew. "Maybe not the way Avris did, but..."

Kasiel turned away, trying to hide the intense burn spreading up his neck and into his cheeks. "Does everyone know?"

Darro gave his shoulder a brief, almost painful squeeze. The man had a grip like a vice. "Don't panic. She didn't say anything, I made an educated guess based on how well I know her and a few recent observations." He chuckled. "Nothing to be ashamed of, Ahninveth. It's not like Tath and I are being discreet."

Darro's words did little to ease the embarrassment, but Kasiel forced himself to face him. "You two are in a relationship, though, aren't you?"

"And? Don't overthink it. If Avris chose to share herself with you, that's between you two. I wouldn't let it affect how we all work together. We're still tehsheyn, and right now one of our number needs rescuing."

Kasiel exhaled heavily. He had to focus on what mattered. Darro was right about that. "Thanks. I'm going to see if I can find a bird to take a look up top."

"I'll check over the horses. Make sure we're ready to go when dark falls."

Kasiel nodded absently as Darro walked away, part of his awareness already reaching out to locate a suitable scout. He quickly found a smaller bird hopping amongst the branches of a thorny shrub in another area of the canyon. For reasons he didn't understand, birds were especially easy to dominate, but incredibly resistant if he tried to persuade them into doing what he wanted. Given the danger of their current position, he opted for simply seizing control, though he attempted to be gentle about it.

Riding behind the eyes of the swift little bird, he flew up above the canyons into the blazing sun. The Alliance watchtower looked larger in full daylight, though still not as imposing as the Vanrian watchtowers across the Break. The architecture wasn't as severe, and these were built with a pale gray stone. Different from the towers on the Vanrian side that were designed with intimidation in mind and constructed of the black stone common to the region with an abundance of sharp angles evocative of bladed weapons.

He swept around, surveying the landscape for threats. A lone rider patrolling to the west of the watchtower off in the distance provided no immediate concern. He brought the bird in close to their current location and began a systematic search of the slot canyons, scanning for any dangers that might be hidden within those steep walls.

Speeding along with the little bird, he darted down the southernmost branch of the canyon they were in. Then he tracked back, passing through their location and down the eastern branch over the trickling stream. The erratic movements of the tiny flier made his head spin, but he forced himself to stick with it. They flitted around one bend, and another, and a third, dodging at the last instant to avoid slamming into a horse coming the opposite direction.

Kasiel sent the bird up and turned it, darting back in for a second look. Two horses ridden by Alliance soldiers were moving along the passage at a leisurely pace. The men were alert, constantly scanning their surroundings, yet unconcerned enough that their hands rested well away from their weapons, their reins hanging in relaxed grips. A routine patrol of the slot canyons that was heading toward the Vanrian group's current location.

Kasiel pulled back from the bird. He got up, sending a quick touch out to Kitrix and Niskenya to wake them while he strode to where Kince and Darro were chatting over the saddle on one horse.

"Company coming down the east passage." He strengthened his control of their horses when Niskenya loped over to join him. "Two mounted Alliance soldiers. They don't look like they expect trouble, so I'd guess it's a routine patrol."

Kince's jaw tightened, eyes narrowing as he cast a glance east. "We'll have to kill them. Even if we bolt, they're going to notice we've been here and call more troops in."

"Can you stop their horses?" Darro asked. "If the animals balk at coming down here, we might at least be able to get them on foot where they're more vulnerable."

"I can." Kasiel started reaching out again. "Kince, grab your crossbow and come with me. Darro, get someone to wake the others, then join us."

"I'll handle waking everyone and send Merrin to join you. She's our best fighter."

That was new information. Useful knowledge to have given the opportunities for conflict in the coming days. He gave a curt nod. "Do it."

They jogged off to take care of their assigned tasks. Kasiel eased into the minds of the soldiers' horses, wary of startling them too soon, and strode toward the eastern branch of the canyon. He encouraged Niskenya to remain behind. The kanodrak answered with irritation, but, to his relief, she stopped following him.

Kince jogged up beside him a few seconds later, loading his crossbow. The weapon took Kasiel back to the day Ahrin died. He had told Jethan that day that he didn't want anyone to die for him ever again, and yet Sylaryth had done exactly that. He set his jaw and pushed the memories away.

"Keep me on course," he said in a low voice as he slipped in behind the eyes and ears of one of the Alliance horses. "Around the next bend there's a wide spot where we can tuck in to wait for them."

Trying to look out through the eyes of a creature and his own at the same time was still difficult. Doing it while moving added an extra element of challenge. He felt Kince's hand on his elbow, prepared to guide as needed. Another set of footsteps came up on his other side as Merrin joined them.

He compelled the two horses to stop and refuse to move forward when their riders urged them on. Guilt twisted in his chest as the soldiers tried to force them, driving their heels into the animals' sides and slapping them with the ends of the reins to push them onward. Still, he maintained control, making the animals resist while he listened and watched through one.

"Worthless cowards." The soldier in the front swung off his mount. "Probably one of those wretched desert cats up ahead."

The second soldier dismounted, patting his horse's shoulder. "You might not be so eager to confront them if you were on their menu."

"I'm not a coward." He glared at his horse before facing his companion and drawing an axe from a loop on his belt. "Let's take care of it. We can chase the bastards out of the way and get on with this. I hate patrolling these Havaad-cursed canyons."

They dropped their reins, ground tying the horses, and continued forward on foot with weapons out now.

Kasiel retreated into himself as his trio moved to a wide spot in the passage. They pressed against the red sandstone wall near the end where the soldiers would come through. Kince pointed to his crossbow, then to the corner they had just come around. Kasiel nodded and watched him jog back there, disappearing behind the bend.

They waited, breathing softly, listening to the crunch of gritty sand and rock shifting under the soldiers' feet as they approached. Kasiel's pulse quickened. They were standing here preparing to kill these men. He put his hand on the hilt of his sword, flashing back to that morning in Fernwallow before the mercenaries arrived. His biggest concern had been whether or not Danica wanted to kiss him again. A time when he never would have dreamed of killing someone. How dramatically his life had changed since then.

His fingers curled around the sword grip.

The blade of the first man's axe came into view. Merrin held a hand out flat by her waist, a signal to wait. The man paused mid-step, and Kasiel's heart stopped with him.

His grip tightened on the ax, and he shifted his weight back. "Something doesn't feel right."

"Picking up the nervousness from the horses?" the man behind him teased.

Merrin leapt in fast enough that Kasiel could barely follow the movement, yet somehow, the man with the axe twisted and blocked her strike. The reaction also moved him out of the path of the bolt Kince fired at the same time. A grunt behind the first soldier told Kasiel the projectile had at least found another target. The second man lunged into view, Kince's bolt embedded in the metal pauldron over his left arm. He raised his sword to swing at Merrin from the side while the first soldier had her attention.

Kasiel drew his sword and rushed in, forcing the man in back to redirect his weapon to block his attack. As their blades collided, the man's foot came up and struck Kasiel hard in the stomach, sending him sprawling. The soldier wasted no time bringing his sword down in an arc intended to finish the job.

Everything happened in a matter of seconds. Merrin dodged a swing of the axe and spun, thrusting her sword into the second man's side through a join in his armor as he was bringing his weapon down at Kasiel. She ripped the blade free and twisted back in time to catch the first man's axe with the edge of her blade mere inches from her head.

The second soldier dropped his weapon and sank to one knee next to Kasiel, both hands now trying to stop the blood gushing from his side. The man with the axe let loose a furious cry, driving Merrin back against the wall of the canyon with sheer brute strength. She slammed into it hard. Attempting to take advantage of her momentary stun, he raised the axe and brought it down again. Merrin still blocked him. They locked in a battle of power and will with her sword crossed in front of her to hold back the blade of his axe.

Kasiel scrambled to his feet and swung. His dark metal blade cut through the man's arm at the elbow effortlessly, like a knife slicing warm butter. The abrupt loss of pressure on the lower part of the haft sent the axe flipping forward and the edge of the blade nicked Merrin's cheek, drawing a line of red down it. The soldier stumbled back, looking on in horror as his forearm fell to the ground, the axe still gripped in that hand.

A crossbow bolt appeared in his throat. He stared at Kasiel, blood blossoming brightly on his lips, then he staggered a few steps and toppled. Merrin, a trickle of red streaming from the cut on her cheek, spat at the dead man. In one smooth motion, she turned and drew her blade across the neck of the other man, who was still frantically trying to halt the blood pouring from his side. He made a wet choking noise before he slumped to the ground.

Kasiel's stomach did a flip. He swallowed and focused on Merrin. "Are you all right?"

"Yes," she growled, breathing hard.

"Nice sword." Kince strode up, admiring the bloodied, dark metal blade hanging in Kasiel's hand. "Was that a gift from the dhomvalen too?"

It was entirely indecent that he could be so calm. Kasiel drew a long, shaky breath before meeting his eyes. "Yes."

Merrin wiped her blade on the closest man's surcoat. "We should probably get their horses. If the animals wander out of the canyon without riders, it's going to draw attention."

Kasiel reached out to the two animals, focusing on bringing them in to avoid giving too much thought to what he was doing when he wiped his own blade clean on the dead man's garment. Kince and Merrin tensed, raising their weapons when the two horses came trotting up behind them.

"Handy trick," Kince said, lowering the crossbow again. "Also, a little unnerving."

Merrin wiped her cheek, scowling at the smear of blood on her glove. Her eyes narrowed at Kasiel. "I didn't have a single scar from enemy combat before this. Not one. If you had given me another second, I'd have solved him."

"Sorry." Kasiel sheathed his sword, stepping away

from the bodies. "From my vantage, you know, sitting on my ass in the dirt, it seemed like you might need help."

Merrin's dark look vanished, and she laughed. "It's fine. I was teasing you. You handled yourself well. Technically, since you caused this injury, the enemy is still standing at zero."

Kince gave him a good-natured grin before glancing up at the sky. "There's still a couple of hours until dark. We should probably find another place for the unit to hole up until then. We can leave their horses at our current spot. What do you want to do with these two? It's pretty obvious what killed them." He kicked the leg of the closest man.

"I'll bring the wildcats in once we're out of here. If we're lucky, it'll be hard to tell what killed them by the time they find the bodies." Bodies. Not people. He couldn't think of them as people.

Kince practically beamed at him. "Good idea, Cavenos. We'll make a soldier out of you yet."

Perfect. He forced a smile.

Merrin sheathed her sword and placed a hand on his shoulder, turning him away from the dead men. "Let's get back before the others worry."

With Merrin's guidance to keep him on track, Kasiel put his ability to work bringing the two horses along. He split off another portion of his awareness to reach out in search of the wildcats he had used to hunt for Niskenya. They deserved an easy meal after he made them give up the last one. He just needed to not think too hard about what they would be eating.

*

Night could hardly come fast enough. Every minute they had to wait, Jethan was out there, possibly suffering, certainly getting farther away. As the shadows of dusk stretched across the landscape, Kasiel, watching through the eyes of a wild dog, spotted three soldiers riding toward the canyons from the tower. Their speed suggested a sense of urgency. If they were looking for the two dead men, they had substantial territory to cover. They undoubtedly had a few routine patrol routes. What mattered now was how far into that route the two men had been when they encountered Kasiel's unit. If these soldiers followed the same route, they at least wouldn't begin their search near where Kasiel and his companions were.

He considered checking in with the wildcats to see if they had done sufficient damage to the two corpses to mask the actual cause of death, but he couldn't bring himself to look. Just the thought of what he might find peering through their eyes was enough to turn him off wanting to eat for the evening.

While waiting for full dark, he sat away from the others and closed his eyes, bouncing restlessly between the minds of various desert creatures. It was a pointless exercise. He was looking for something he wouldn't find. A particular exuberant welcome that he would never experience again.

Niskenya curled around him, her head coming to rest on her forelegs on one side of him while her hind legs and tail stretched on the other. Her presence wasn't only comforting, it kept his companions from approaching. Sensing his desire to be alone, she growled softly at anyone who dared to wander too close. For now, they heeded her warnings.

Eventually, he settled behind Kitrix's eyes, watching his unit as the last traces of daylight faded from the sky. Avris and Merrin continued making an effort to involve Nerith in their conversations and activities. The others paid little attention to her. Most notably Tath, who needed to work closely with her as a fellow healer and someone who also had no tehnaak among them. He needed to figure out how to change that, but how could he when he didn't want to interact with her himself? Arhk had been there when the khevarin exposed Nerith's deception. He had to have known sending her was a poor choice. So why had he done it?

Kasiel noticed Wedro heading his way and opened his eyes. It was finally time to move on. He stood and grabbed hold of the saddle, slipping his foot into the stirrup, and swinging up as Niskenya surged to her feet. As he settled on her back, he sent Kitrix up to check where the three riders from the tower were in their search.

Wedro stopped several feet away, his gaze drifting to the long upper canines that curved down well below the kanodrak's lower jaw. "We're ready to move if you are."

Already soaring with Kitrix, Kasiel held up a hand for him to wait a moment. The raptor spotted the soldiers in a section of passage that would lead them to the aftermath of the fight. They had another five minutes at most before the trio got to that location. Chasing off the wildcats and investigating the scene should hold them up for a time. Long enough, he hoped, for his unit to cross the last stretch of the Break and make a run across the open field beyond. They could angle toward where the sparse forest almost reached the border, but that would require passing closer to the watchtower than he dared. The shortest distance to the border would leave them out in the open longer once they crossed, but keep them farther from the tower, making it more difficult for the guards to spot them in the dark.

In the end, it depended on where their search took them. If Jethan's trail veered west from there, they would be out in open plains for a while where it would be harder to hide. If it continued south or turned east, the dry desert forest that stretched out toward the back of the watchtower would provide an opportunity for cover once they put enough distance between themselves and the tower itself.

He looked down at the lanky red-head and nodded. "Let's go."

Wedro jogged to where the others had gathered near the horses. "Kas says it's time to go. Mount up."

Sensitive to Kasiel's wants, Niskenya followed Wedro, stopping back far enough to keep from making the mounts or their riders too uncomfortable. Had they caught on yet to how little control he had over the massive predator? For now, he saw no value in bringing it up. They had enough to worry about.

"There are soldiers in the canyons," Kasiel announced. Everyone tensed, a few reaching for weapons. Perhaps he should have framed the information differently. "They're not a threat right now. They're about to find their missing comrades. We should be able to slip out through the southern passage before they're done driving off the wildcats."

Merrin swung up in her saddle. "If the cats did their job, we should have nothing to worry about."

"That's what I'm hoping, but we still don't want to waste time getting out of here. Niske has the best night vision. She can avoid hazards. Follow directly in her path and I'll keep the horses calm. I want everyone riding in pairs with our healers toward the center of the line." Not Tath and Nerith. Our healers. It was a legitimate way to refer to them, but he had done it specifically because he wanted to avoid saying her name. It was going to be much harder to integrate her into the group if he couldn't move past his own hangups.

"We'll be right behind you, Ahninveth." Darro inclined his head. "Kince and I will take the rear."

Kasiel gave them a few minutes to mount and line up, then he encouraged Niskenya to head out. Since she alone could follow the scent of their target, she would determine their direction, assuming doing so didn't put them in immediate danger. He refocused part of his attention on the horses and another portion on Kitrix, who sat perched on a scraggly shrub near where the Alliance soldiers were. The raptor was his early warning on the off chance their misdirection failed.

They made their way along the slot canyon back to the branch that cut south. Niskenya tracked directly to where Jethan and the mercenaries had exited the canyon and took a few tense minutes finding the scent before breaking into an easy lope heading south. She moved with her head low, making the perch on her back feel less stable, but with the saddle customized precisely to her form and his seat, he only had to stay properly centered to maintain his balance.

After a few minutes spent adjusting to her movement, Kasiel let himself sink deeper into Kitrix, listening to the Alliance soldiers through him. The raptor's perch was around the corner from where the dead men were, close enough to hear the three tower guards without having to view the carnage the cats left behind.

"Havaad-cursed beasts," one soldier growled.

"Where's his arm?" someone else asked.

"How should I know? Maybe they took it back to the den for their cubs to chew on."

He missed the other guard's response because the third man was coming in from the opposite direction, leading the two dead men's horses. He didn't notice Kitrix off to one side in the darkness.

"Found their horses," he called as he rounded the corner. "I also found a bunch of hoofprints in the crossing canyon. More of those idiot mercenaries may have passed through without checking in at the tower again."

"We should start shooting the bastards when we see them," one of the first two snapped. "If they can't act like allies, we should stop treating them like they are."

"They're working for that professor," the man with the horses countered. "As long as his research is helping the Alliance, I say let them go."

Something dark coiled in Kasiel's gut. He didn't want "that professor" to be Edmund, but the dread spreading through him said it was. Next time he saw the man, he would kill him properly.

"Sure, but why doesn't he want to use Alliance troops if he's so keen to help us? What's he hiding?"

What was he hiding?

Kasiel pulled back from Kitrix, encouraging the bird to join them. The soldiers didn't appear to suspect anything yet. Inspecting the bodies in the dark would make it that much harder to identify a cause of death other than the apparent wildcat attack. If they believed the tracks were mercenaries passing through, all the better. With him leading the way on Niskenya, the horses behind them would trample her unusually large paw prints leaving the canyon and continue to encourage that assumption.

They kept a fast pace, crossing the border marked by the watchtowers without incident. Trusting Niskenya to follow Jethan's trail, Kasiel bounced his awareness to different creatures throughout the area – an owl, wild dogs, long-legged sandhoppers – watching for other tower guards in the dark.

Everyone stayed precisely in their formation behind him, riding silent and alert. Kince had Kasiel's horse on a lead trailing him. The path angled east after they crossed the border, trending through the brown grasslands to the dry forests beyond. Niskenya increased the pace, silencing his concerns about her ability to track at that speed with confidence and a gentle sense of reprimand she sent along their bond.

By the time predawn light crept across the sky, trees

as brown as the grass in the fields they had galloped through surrounded them, offering the limited protection of the sparse, dry forest. Exhaustion, hunger, and thirst nagged Kasiel, coming from his link to the horses he still maintained control over. It seemed safe to assume that the same issues plagued their riders. When he pulled more of his awareness into his body, he found that it also suffered from the lack of food, water, and rest.

How far behind the mercenaries and Jethan were they? How unrelentingly did he dare push himself and his unit? From an emotional standpoint, he didn't want to stop until he had his tehnaak back, but they would be in no shape to deal with danger if he drove them too hard.

He raised his left arm, bringing Kitrix in to land on it as Niskenya slowed and turned. The raptor lit upon the gauntlet and settled instantly, too weary to bother with posturing or preening. The others reined their mounts in. He could sense that familiarity was reducing the fear the horses had of Niskenya. If she continued to regard them as part of his unit and not meal options, the animals would eventually reach a point where he didn't have to force them to be calm around her.

"It seems as if we could all could use a break."

"Yes, please," Chander said, his words accompanied by tired nods from the dust-covered group.

"Let's..." Kasiel trailed off, his awareness dragged away from him by the kanodrak. For a second, the crisp smell of fresh water, something his less keen human senses hadn't registered yet, joined the scents of dirt and dry grass. Then the kanodrak dumped him back into himself. Shaking his head to alleviate the dizziness caused by the abrupt transitions, he patted her neck with his free hand. "Thank you." If only he could convince her to stop being so aggressive about it.

His companions were watching him with wary curiosity.

Tath leaned forward to scratch her horse's neck. "You know, Kas, the way you just disappear from yourself periodically is disconcerting. I've seen Kenna do it, but not quite like that."

"You think it's disconcerting for you?" he responded absently. "Niske smells water nearby. Let's go a little farther and see if there's a place to set up a camp near it."

Not waiting for a response from the others or his prompting, Niskenya struck out again, following her nose. The ground was rocky here, making it more precarious for the horses. The kanodrak barely noticed. They wove amidst straight, narrow evergreens with rough gray-brown bark. Brown grasses and shrubs picked up hints of green as they approached an opening where a shallow river raced through the forest.

Niskenya continued past the shoreline, immersing her tired paws in the water before she ducked her head down to drink. Kasiel hopped off, landing in the water next to her. He crouched there and splashed the refreshing liquid into his face, rinsing away the dust of the desert. Then he cupped his hands and brought some up to drink. While the others followed suit, taking the opportunity to quench the thirst of themselves and their horses, Kas removed Niskenya's saddle and carried it up to the tree line.

"We can set up camp in the trees here," Darro said, leading his horse over. He had dunked his head, and his light brown hair was soaked, the water leaving trails through the accumulation of dust as it dripped down his leather armor.

They all wore the same armor reinforced with strategically placed steel plates in a style similar to Kasiel's, though his was black and used the stronger dark metal that made his sword so deadly. He didn't like that he had better equipment when most of them had been at this far longer, but being the dhomvalen's son had its benefits. This was his opportunity to earn what he already had, which struck him as a backwards way of going about it, but he would do his best to prove himself worthy. For Jethan's sake, more than his own.

Kasiel wasn't ready to pause their search, but he needed to rest too, assuming he could sleep under the circumstances. "I'm going to have Niske show me where they crossed with Jethan, see if there's any sign of them stopping to camp."

A strained smile touched Darro's lips for an instant. "All right, but take someone with you."

Avris walked over and handed her reins to Darro. "I'll go. Come on, country boy. Let's see what we can find."

Kasiel turned his back on Darro's suggestive smirk and strode toward where Niskenya stood watching them, her paws still submerged in the river. Avris fell silently into step beside him. He didn't have to say anything to the kanodrak. As soon as they were close, she started downstream along the riverbank, maintaining a slow pace that they could keep up with on foot.

Avris gestured to Niskenya with her chin. "Just how smart is she?"

He watched the apex predator moving a few strides ahead of them, lean muscle rippling under her silver-gray hide. "As best I can tell, at least as smart as any of us."

"That's intimidating."

"You could say that. It's a little disconcerting feeling like the dumb one in the relationship."

Avris chuckled. "Well, if you didn't want that, you probably should have bonded with a male."

For a split second, a smile pulled at his lips. Then Sylaryth, the male beast he had bonded with, came to mind and the expression faltered. Niskenya turned her head to look at Avris and growled.

"It's all right, Niske. It's not Avris's fault."

The kanodrak faced forward again, a hint of lingering tension shortening her strides.

"Protective of you, isn't she?" Avris reached out and gave his hand a gentle squeeze. "Though I suppose I can't blame her." She was silent for a few seconds, then she looked over at him. "So, are you going to do something about Nerith?"

Niskenya saved him from answering when she turned and crossed the river in two powerful bounds. Kasiel forged out after her. The water was shallow and not too fast, but the rocks were slick under his boots. He slowed his advance, picking his footing with care.

"Watch your step. It's slippery."

"I can handle myself," Avris said behind him. "It's your stubborn ass I can't handle."

Kasiel ignored the comment, appreciating the coolness of the water flowing around the feet and ankles of his boots. The leather was treated to protect it from moisture, though he imagined submerging it wasn't something he should make a habit of.

Niskenya continued to the top of the sloped bank on that side and a few yards in before she stopped. Climbing up after her, he found her standing next to the remains of a campfire. He strode over to place a hand on her neck.

"Jethan was here?" he asked, glancing at Avris, who halted a little farther back from the kanodrak.

Niskenya nosed his shoulder, sending certainty across to him. She followed it up after a few seconds with an insistent jab of hunger.

"Well done. Go hunt, but be careful."

She nosed him again before loping off into the trees, leaving him alone with Avris.

"This is where they camped?"

"Yes."

Aside from the cold campfire, the ground was churned up in places where people and horses had left their marks. The mercenaries hadn't tried to hide the remains of their fire or spread the manure piles where they tied their mounts. That suggested thoughts of hostile pursuit were far from their minds now that they were in Alliance territory. An encouraging observation as it meant they might not be traveling at any great speed, either.

Kasiel wandered to where the hoofprints left the camp and stared off into the woods. How far and fast would he have to ride to catch them? How was Jethan? Were they feeding him? Had they hurt him?

A shudder moved through him, remembering how the mercenaries in Fallend had treated him. If this group had harmed his tehnaak, he would show them no mercy.

CHAPTER FIFTEEN

Avris came to stand beside Kasiel, her gaze following the tracks into the trees. She leaned her head against his shoulder. "You think he's all right?" she asked, echoing his fears, worry adding weight to her tone.

"I have to believe he is." He turned to face her, intentionally moving his shoulder away. "I thought you were the one always reassuring me."

She retreated a step, glancing toward the camp. "Sorry. I let myself get comfortable around you. Now my insecurities are showing."

He slid a finger gently under her chin, drawing her gaze back to him. "It's all right. In a way, I feel less alone knowing others are as worried as I am. I know how much you all care for him and how far you're willing to go to rescue him, and that helps me believe it's possible."

"Thank you." She leaned in and placed a light kiss on his lips. "I know you won't give up on him, Kas. You don't believe you're strong, but that doesn't matter, because I know you are. I've seen it in you for a while. Jethan's lucky to have you."

He wanted to kiss her in return, to steal the comfort that contact could offer, but she moved away, heading down the slope toward the river before he could give in to that urge.

She glanced back, beckoning for him to follow. "Come on. Everyone needs rest and food. That means you too. The better you take care of yourself, the more useful you'll be to Jethan when we find him."

After a few seconds spent staring at the trail that led to his tehnaak, he turned to join her. She was wading out into the water, the sun making her rich red hair glow like fire. Then her feet slipped out from under her. She landed with a loud splash and furious string of curses, a few of which he hadn't heard yet. Kasiel rushed to her, scrambling down the slope and into the water to help.

He grabbed her hand and elbow, lifting her to her feet. "Are you hurt?"

"I'm definitely cleaner than I was a minute ago." She flipped over her other hand. Bright blood welled from a cut on her palm. "Figures. Merrin gets a minor scratch fighting two watchtower guards and I slice myself open falling on my ass."

"I told you—"

Threat gleamed in her eyes when she looked up at him. "If you value your life, you'll stop there."

He grinned. "It's slippery."

Avris shoved him and he threw one leg back, barely avoiding falling in the river himself. "Nice try."

"Calloch," she grumbled, though a faint smile tugged at her lips.

He placed a hand on her elbow and guided her toward the far shore. When they made it back, the others had a rough camp set up. A modest fire crackled in a low spot in the trees. They didn't need it for heat, but to take advantage of an opportunity to cook a more filling meal.

Avris's palm still bled.

Kasiel took her wrist, bringing her hand up to inspect the cut. "A healer should tend that."

"It's not that deep."

"It could still infect." He gave her a stern look, and she shrugged, sighing when he didn't release her.

He stopped them at the edge of the camp, catching sight of Tath near the horses. Movement beside the fire drew his attention to Nerith, and he clenched his teeth. He could feel Avris watching him, waiting for him to make what she clearly believed was the right choice.

He met her eyes. When she arched her brow, he exhaled heavily and called out, "Nerith."

Nerith's gaze jumped to him, a hint of surprise in her eyes. A few of the others paused what they were doing, watching with unabashed curiosity as she stood and walked to them. She noticed Avris's hand before he could say anything and took her wrist from him, leaning in to inspect the wound.

"So, you do remember my name," Nerith said, not looking up from her task.

His chest tightened, frustration spinning his thoughts into chaos. "Is now the time for this?"

"Well, you aren't hiding behind your beasts for once."

Avris chuckled. "She's got you there."

He gave Avris a sharp glower to let her know she wasn't being helpful.

She just smiled.

Kasiel drew in a deep breath and let it out. He looked at Nerith, who was explicitly avoiding looking at him. "When you're done with this, we can talk," he said, his voice low enough that only the two women would hear.

Nerith answered with a curt nod.

He left them and went to find a seat with the others, settling against a tree to partake of the hearty stew they had cobbled together. The food landed heavy and satisfying in his stomach. When he finished, he rested his head back, trying not to let the stillness of the moment drive him mad.

Kitrix swept in, alighting on a nearby branch. Kasiel reached out to the raptor with his ability, receiving a powerful sense of weariness that muted the bird's underlying hunger. He wasn't a nocturnal beast, and the long hours of flying in the night had thrown off his feeding and sleep schedule. If he was going to make it through this, he would need assistance.

Kasiel reached out around them, easily finding a selection of mice, rabbits, and squirrels within the immediate area. Struggling not to think too deeply about what he was doing, he urged a squirrel up onto a log at the edge of the camp under where the raptor was resting. The typically wary rodent barely resisted, wandering obligingly out into the open. Kasiel mentally nudged Kitrix, bringing the sandhawk's attention to the waiting meal.

"How cute."

At Tath's words, Kasiel looked at the small critter he had summoned. It was cute, sitting there on the log with a puffy tail curled up behind it, its little black nose twitching. Panic rushed through him. He tried to drive it away before it met a dismal end, but it was too late. Kitrix dove and snatched it up, taking it back into the branches. For a few seconds filled with desperate squeaking, no one spoke. Finally, the squirrel fell silent.

"Kasiel." Tath waited until he was looking at her. "Did you just lure that creature to its death?"

"Do you really want me to answer that?"

She stared at him.

"Kitrix was too tired to hunt."

"We can't let our scout starve," Chander said, coming to his defense. "He's a necessary part of the unit."

She shook her head at Kasiel. "I can't argue with that. But maybe not next to the campfire where we're eating next time."

"Point taken." Kasiel gave Chander a look of gratitude

before leaning back to close his eyes for a minute.

It was about five hours later when Nerith nudged him awake. "Come on. Last watch is up. You're patrolling with me."

Technically, he didn't have to move a muscle to cover more ground than the entire group of them could at once. The abundant wildlife in these woods was ideal for that. He almost said as much, but she was aware of that, and he knew that keeping watch wasn't the reason she selected him to join her.

"We should get moving." He got up and glanced around, spotting Niskenya stretched in a patch of sunshine. Five hours was too long to have slept with Jethan still out there. "Why didn't someone wake me sooner?"

"Because you needed sleep. We should be able to make better time once we've all gotten some rest." She swept one arm out to include everyone at the camp, pointedly pausing at their horses.

He forced his frustration down and walked with her away from the others, casting out a wide net with his ability to check for danger as he did so.

"I'm sorry... about Leysa." He tried not to feel the words as he said them, given how close he danced to the edge of the same loss. His voice still cracked with emotion.

She gave a fierce shake of her head. "Don't, Kas. I can't talk about what I've lost. Not yet."

He mentally kicked himself. How many times had he said something like that to the others when they tried to comfort him? He should have known better.

They strode along a little further in silence. He watched the ground, noticing the occasional black beetle or trail of ants amidst the needles fallen from surrounding trees. His hand moved to the pouch that held Sylaryth's claw.

"Neither can I." He looked over at her, finding it

unexpectedly easy to recall how happy he had been with her before.

She glanced at him, the warmth of understanding in her soft lavender eyes. Then she averted her gaze. "Are you and Avris a couple now?"

He almost missed a step. Had Avris said something to that effect? They weren't a couple, were they? "I don't believe so," he answered cautiously.

"She says you're not."

"Then why are you asking me?" He bumped up against a strange presence at the edge of his ability and let his focus turn toward that, avoiding giving too much attention to the uncomfortable turn their conversation had taken.

"I'm not sure I believe her." Nerith scuffed her foot through the dirt, bringing up a cloud of dust even this close to the river. "There's an intimacy between the two of you that wasn't there before."

He didn't know how to respond to that, so he opted for silence. The distant presence he had found felt dark and unclean. Threatening. The way approaching lightning felt when the forest around Fernwallow was dry from too little rain, raising the fire risk.

"What happened between us—"

"Doesn't matter here," he interrupted, his unease with that distant presence making him terser than he meant to be. He softened his tone. "We have one purpose. Jethan is all that matters right now."

A hint of sorrow tugged down the corners of her lips. She lowered her gaze. "I agree."

That was what he wanted to hear, wasn't it? Then why did he find her agreement so disappointing? For that matter, why did she?

He pushed harder at the distant presence, turning his attention to figuring out what it was. Abruptly, he broke through into a tempest of anguish and mindless rage, realizing as he did that the sense of distance had been entirely a mental illusion. Now that he shattered that false separation, the source of the corrupted darkness wasn't far away at all, somewhere in the trees to their right. It announced its presence with a low growl.

Kasiel placed a hand on Nerith's arm as they turned toward the sound.

A hulking, emaciated bear lumbered out of the trees less than ten feet away. Drool hung from its jaws and a swollen gash split open its snout, continuing up onto its forehead. The wound oozed blood and puss. It growled again, and he drew Nerith back a step with him.

"You can control it, right?" Her voice shook.

He attempted to do so, but the fevered haze of pain, infection, and some other illness lurking beneath the rest made its mind slippery, like trying to hold on to a wriggling, wet fish with his bare hands. The beast sensed his effort to find a way in, and it didn't appear to appreciate it. Rising on its hind legs, it let out a ragged roar. When it dropped back to the ground, it charged.

"I can't." Kasiel grabbed Nerith's hand, pulling her with him as he turned to flee. "Run!"

He sprinted in a direction that would take them near camp. He didn't want to lead the beast straight into the others, but passing close enough that someone might come to their aid struck him as a sound tactic. The ground was uneven and rocky, making for poor footing, at least for them. The bear had no trouble gaining on them, even sickly as it was.

He angled them toward the more open area along the riverbank. The bear roared again, a terrifying sound he nonetheless appreciated since it would alert the others. When they were near the water, the beast's huffing loud enough behind them that he expected to feel the heat of its breath on his back, he pushed Nerith to the side and spun, drawing his sword. The bear didn't react as expected. Instead of facing the obvious threat, it veered toward Nerith.

For a split second, his vision changed, the colors altering, and he was looking at their backs through Niskenya's eyes. He barreled into Nerith, taking her to the ground with him. The kanodrak leapt over them, massive claws ripping open the bear's hide as she latched onto it and pulled it down with her momentum. The instant it hit the riverbank, she broke free and bounded to her feet, lunging for his neck to finish the job.

Kasiel slammed into the kanodrak with the full force of his ability, sending her reeling back with a powerful surge of warning. Danger. He didn't know what other underlying sickness the animal had, but he wouldn't risk exposing her to it. Niskenya snarled at him, her rage, heightened by adrenaline, pounding across their bond.

Climbing to his feet, he took a step toward her. The bear lay between them, its ribs showing through the long tears Niskenya's claws made in its side. It was still trying to get up. Kasiel, daring to take his eyes from the enraged kanodrak, drove his blade into the beast's neck.

The others came sprinting toward them, most with weapons ready. They stopped when Niskenya snarled her fury at them. Kasiel pulled free his sword, letting the bear bleed out faster.

"Niske," he called, nudging her mind gently this time. When she turned her anger on him again, he pointed to the dying creature at his feet. "Smell it. It's sick."

Gradually, her snarl disappeared, and she lowered her muzzle, sniffing at the bear. After several seconds, she came around the dead beast and inclined her head to him, sending gratitude and affection now. He drew a shaky breath and leaned into her, pressing his forehead to the natural armor over her brow.

"We're all right," he murmured. "I just wanted to protect you."

Feeling her calm, he turned his attention to the rest of the group. Darro was sheathing his sword and walking toward Nerith, who still sat on the ground, staring at the bear, and brushing her trembling hands together to clean the dirt from them. Kasiel hurried across the short distance between them to reach her first and offered a hand to her. Darro stopped and retreated a step, inclining his head to Kasiel.

The deference in Darro's gesture made him uncomfortable, but this was his chance to lead by example with Nerith. "Are you hurt?"

She looked at his hand, then up at him, and shook her head. For a second, he thought she might refuse his help. She brushed a lock of hair from her face. He was the only one at the proper angle to see the tear she also wiped away. Taking a deep breath, she reached up and accepted his hand, letting him pull her to her feet. He met her eyes, searching them to see if she really was all right. She gave an almost imperceptible nod before releasing his hand and moving a few inches away.

"You're a Feral. What happened?" Kince asked, nudging the bear with his boot. "Wow, this thing stinks."

It did stink, like urine, feces, and rot. Aside from the raging infection in the wound on its face, filth matted its fur, as if it had stopped tending to itself.

"It was sick. I couldn't get into its head." Kasiel glanced around at them. "Since we're all awake, shall we get back on the trail?"

Darro nodded. "Let's get away from that."

As everyone left to gather their supplies and mounts, Kasiel called Tath over. She joined him, wrinkling her nose at the bear.

"I need you to help Nerith out. She's a talented healer, but she doesn't have a lot of experience, and she's going through a significant loss right now, one that you can unfortunately understand." He saw resistance building in her eyes and moved to head it off. "She's not supposed to replace Ahrin any more than you're supposed to replace Leysa, but I need you both for this. Jethan needs you. Help her. Let her help you. Please."

"And what she did to you? That's forgiven?"

No. It wasn't. He wanted it to be, but every time he thought about it, Edmund came to mind. She had betrayed his trust in a manner that reminded him far too much of what Edmund had done.

"All that matters right now is that we get Jeth back. What happened between me and Nerith can be addressed when we're home safe again."

A weight lifted from his chest when she nodded.

"I'll try, Kas."

"Thank you."

●

It was barely past noon when they left the river. Niskenya picked up the trail with ease, keeping them moving at a swift pace. They could see from the tracks they followed that the mercenaries weren't in a rush now. They spent long periods at a walk with comparably brief stretches of trotting. Wherever they were going with Jethan, they didn't seem to be on a tight enough schedule to want to push themselves and their mounts in the rough terrain. Nor did they appear at all concerned about pursuit now that they were securely behind Alliance lines, something that worked in the Vanrian unit's favor.

The day grew hot, but the rugged forest provided a modicum of shade. Not knowing how soon they would find water again, Kasiel's group tried to maintain a balance between not pushing the horses too hard and still progressing fast enough to gain ground on their quarry. A rocky creek gave them a place for a break in the evening where they could eat and water the animals before they pressed on again.

Niskenya was as restless as Kasiel, perhaps because he was. They kept going, riding into the night until the rough terrain made it too risky for the horses to continue safely in the dark. When they stopped to rest, Kasiel didn't dismount right away. He stayed on Niskenya's back, staring out at the black forest in the direction Jethan was likely to be.

After a short time, Wedro came to get him. "Hey, Ahninveth, you going to join your subordinates?"

Kasiel managed a slight smirk at the jesting in his tone.

Niskenya shifted her feet.

He glanced down at Wedro. "We're going to do a quick scouting run around here close. It shouldn't take long."

Wedro nodded. "Be careful. We don't know what's out here or how close we are to catching up with those mercenaries."

Close. Very close.

Kasiel placed a hand on Niskenya's shoulder. "I won't be alone."

He touched on Kitrix's presence as Wedro returned to the group. The raptor had caught his own meal this time and was resting now. Kasiel directed him to stay behind. His poor night vision would make him nearly useless in the inky darkness. With a thought, he encouraged Niskenya to take him wherever she wanted to go.

The kanodrak moved south at a lope. After less than ten minutes, she dropped to a slow, prowling stride, weaving through the trees like a shadow of death despite her great size. Eventually, she stopped, and Kasiel hopped off, continuing cautiously along behind her. The dark forest was full of small creatures, most of which scurried away to hide from the awesome predator. An owl hooted overhead, and the occasional bat flitted past, backlit by dim moonlight.

Niskenya sent him a warning before she darted off to one side, disappearing into the deeper shadows among the trees. He ducked down alongside some large rocks, searching for danger. A few seconds later, the sound of a twig snapping drew his gaze to a man wandering through the forest. The figure peered around as if keeping watch, though both hands were busy picking apart a chunk of bread, giving the impression that he didn't expect any trouble.

He stopped close enough to where Kasiel crouched that he could see the man's pointed ears poking out through his long blond hair. He was Vanrian, and familiar. The missing fourth guard who had been assigned to Kasiel the night of the battle.

Traitor.

Kasiel swallowed back bile as his hand sank to his sword, rage rising red around the edges of his vision. Before he could act, a huge form stepped out of the shadows behind the man. Niskenya's jaws snapped shut on his head, crushing his skull. The bread fell to the ground, rolling to a stop inches from Kasiel's hiding spot. The kanodrak dragged the body away, vanishing into the trees.

It couldn't have happened to anyone more deserving, but that didn't keep Kasiel from wishing he could forget the sound of bones cracking between those mighty jaws. Swallowing against a wave of nausea now, he crept forward, sneaking in the direction the traitor had come from. A few yards further along, he spotted a campfire, burned down mostly to coals now.

Three figures lay stretched out asleep near the fire. A fourth bedroll was empty. Sitting against a tree a little way from the fire, his hands bound behind him and tied to the trunk, was Jethan. He was also dozing, his head drooping to one side in a manner that would leave him with a nasty kink in his neck in the morning.

elief and joy surged through Kasiel, making him almost giddy. He continued to creep forward, nearly falling on his face when Niskenya dragged him briefly behind her eyes to show him she was in the trees nearby, also watching the sleeping figures. He dropped back into himself and sent her patience. Once Jethan was free, they would deal with the mercenaries. He wanted to take at least one of them alive.

When he reached Jethan, he placed a hand over his mouth to keep him from making noise. Jethan's eyes snapped open, one of them bruised and swollen partially shut as if he'd taken a punch. For a second, he looked panicked, then he focused on Kasiel, the good eye going wide with surprise.

Kasiel took his hand away to reveal a delighted smile that rivaled his own.

"Kas," Jethan whispered, "what are you doing here?"

"Saving you. I thought that would be obvious."

Jethan glanced uneasily around them. "That turncoat guard is keeping watch somewhere."

Kas shook his head, examining Jethan's tightly bound hands. "Niske took care of him."

"Kas."

Jethan's abrupt change in tone captured his attention. Kasiel met his tehnaak's eyes. "What?"

"They did not let you take a kanodrak across the border for this." It wasn't a question.

"No, but she wanted to come. She's been tracking you for us."

"Us?"

"The unit's back together." He grinned, finding it much easier to do now that Jethan was there.

"Couldn't you have just used Syl to track me?"

The grin shattered.

"They killed him." Kasiel's voice caught, pain raking through his chest.

Jethan's brows pinched together. "Kas... I'm sorry." Anger tightened his voice then. "I saw that guard – one of our own blasted guards – throw a blackout bomb at us and run. I woke up later in a slot canyon in the break. The mercenaries taunted me with how three of them had stayed back to kill you and the other guards. When those three never showed up at their rendezvous, they didn't seem so pleased anymore. I dared to hope that meant you survived. I couldn't bear to believe anything else."

"I wouldn't be here if not for Syl. He lost his life protecting me and giving me the chance to come after you." Kasiel glanced at the sleeping figures, watching for a few seconds to make sure they weren't stirring while he blinked away threatening tears.

"Don't worry. They drink too much and sleep like the dead. Bastards." Despite his words, Jethan kept his voice to a whisper. "Kas, you do realize the kanodrak is on all our heraldry, right? They're the most revered creatures in Vanris. To ride one is an incredible honor. To steal one... That's a death sentence. The least they're going to do is demote you."

Kasiel shrugged it off. "At least I'll have earned that." He pulled his dagger and reached to cut the rope from the tree to give them some slack to work with.

"Wait."

He drew the dagger back. "What?"

"If we could find out where they're taking our mind-crafters, maybe we could help our country and turn this into something worthwhile."

Kasiel nodded, impatient now to get his tehnaak away from here. "I told the dhomvalen I would find out what they were doing with our mind-crafters, but we can worry about that later. First, I'm cutting you free. Then we take one of these bastards hostage and see what we can learn."

"No."

Kasiel stared at him in the dark, his dagger poised to cut the rope, the presence of the men sleeping nearby plucking at his nerves. "No?"

"What if we can't get the information out of them?"

"You can use your ability?"

Jethan gave him a dour look. "I'm not gagged. If my ability worked on them, I wouldn't still be here. It's like they're immune. I can't get in their heads."

The statement sent a chill through Kasiel, but he pushed it down, hiding his dread behind a show of humor. "I'm surprised they didn't leave you gagged anyway, just to shut you up."

Jethan gave him a mock glower. "You're lucky I'm still tied."

"You shouldn't be." He reached for the rope again and Jethan shifted his hands away.

"What if you leave me with them?"

Kasiel stared at him, finding it hard to believe what he was hearing. "No. We'll figure out another way."

Jethan watched Kasiel for a few seconds, both freezing still as statues when one mercenary shifted in his sleep. Once the man settled and was breathing evenly again, he said, "Hear me out, Kas. They're apparently supposed to deliver mind-crafters in good condition, so they're feeding me and not treating me that badly. You can continue tracking us while they take me to wherever we're going. Then we'll know where our mind-crafters are."

Kasiel sat back on his heels. "We might also find out how they're shielding themselves from your ability." This professor was behind all of it, of that he was certain. "But what if it's a place we can't get you out of once you're there? What then?"

"I get the impression we're close to their destination. A day away. Maybe two. At least leave me with them until we know where that is. Then you can rush in and free me before they complete their delivery."

He settled the hand with the dagger in his lap, not willing to sheath it yet. "I have Kitrix. I can use him to keep watch and check in with you."

Jethan nodded. "This could work, Kas."

Niskenya was growing restless again. He could feel her rising urge to attack the sleeping men. The fact that he shared that desire made it harder to hold her in check.

"What about the guard? I can't have Niske un-kill him."

"Take his bedroll and his horse. The bay mare on the far end. I won't even need my ability to convince them he deserted. They aren't that fond of him. Mostly because he's Vanrian, but they also have a strange intolerance for him because he betrayed his own people, ironic as that is."

Kasiel nodded thoughtfully, watching the sleeping mercenaries. He didn't move.

"Kas, you need to go now if we're going to pull this off."

He met Jethan's eyes. "I'm not sure I can leave you here. I didn't know if I was going to get you back at all."

A hint of fear finally broke through in Jethan's eyes. "I don't really want you to, to be honest, but I believe we can pull this off. I wouldn't suggest it if I didn't think so. Imagine going back with this knowledge. Or, better yet, with our missing mind-crafters. That'd be one powerful argument against them executing you for stealing a kanodrak."

Kasiel gave him a wry smile. He always intended to find the other mind-crafters, but he hadn't planned to worry about that until after Jethan was safe. "I don't know if risking you is worth even that, but we'll try it. I'll use Kitrix to keep a close eye on you. The minute I think you're in too much danger, I'm getting you out, whether or not we have our answers."

"I'm counting on it."

Fighting the intense desire to cut the rope anyway, Kasiel sheathed the dagger. He crept to the campfire and held his breath as he picked up the empty sleeping roll. One of the men stirred, and he froze. He could feel Niskenya's muscles move when she shifted in the shadows as if they shared the same flesh. It was an odd sensation. The man settled again, and Kasiel snuck away from the fire. When he had the guard's horse, he looked back at Jethan. His tehnaak.

How could he leave him here?

Jethan gave him a nod, his jaw set with determination.

Gritting his teeth, Kasiel led the horse into the trees, calling on Niskenya to help him find a safe path in the darkness. Now, to explain this to the others.

·

Kince stood up from his seat near the subdued campfire. "You can't be serious."

Kasiel stayed standing back from the fire, a hand still on Niskenya's neck for the comfort and confidence her presence offered. "It was Jethan's idea."

"That doesn't make it a good one," Kince snapped.

Avris poked at the fire with a stick. "It's not that bad either."

Kince gave her a sour glare.

"It's not," Nerith offered, stepping up to Avris's defense. She looked at Kasiel. "Kas would never have left his tehnaak with them if there weren't some considerable advantages to be gained by doing so."

The comment made his gut twist. If anything went wrong... "I almost didn't regardless, but I think we have an opportunity to do something worthwhile here, and not just because I absconded with a kanodrak. This could be important to Vanris. We're in a position to do good here."

Darro chuckled dryly. "About Niske. None of us tried to talk you out of taking her or turn you in, so we're not exactly innocent." He looked at Kince, holding his tehnaak's gaze until the other threw up his hands and sat down. Then he glanced around at the rest of them. "Whatever is going on with these mercenaries taking our mind-crafters, it's connected to the Alliance's sudden resistance to mind-crafter abilities. They've figured something out."

"Exactly," Kasiel said, finding the courage to move away from Niskenya in Darro's support. "If we could figure out what they're doing, we could help Vanris fight this and maybe rescue some of our mind-crafters in the process. We could save lives."

"Our own included," Chander muttered.

"I'll keep track of Jethan with Kitrix. The minute we know where they're headed, or if it looks like anything is going wrong, we take him back. It's not as if we'll have any trouble overwhelming three mercenaries."

"Especially with our stolen kanodrak," Chander muttered.

Wedro kicked his tehnaak's foot. "This is serious, calloch," he snapped, trying not to grin, and failing.

Tath rolled her eyes at them and slid her hand into Darro's. "I can't believe I'm saying this, but I think it's worth a shot. This is the greatest threat Vanris has faced since the fighting started. Our unit is in a better position right now than anyone else to get to the bottom of it."

Darro beamed at her, twining his fingers through hers. "I can't help wondering if the dhomvalen hoped this would happen when he sent us out here."

Kasiel recalled the nod of approval his father had given when he said he was going to find out what they were doing with the mind-crafters. "I suspect he at least considered it."

"Do you think he expected you to take the kano-drak?" A hint of hopefulness lifted Chander's voice.

Kasiel glanced back at Niskenya. She sent a flash of hunger to him before turning to lope off into the trees. At least that meant she probably hadn't eaten the Vanrian guard. He faced the others again. "No. I'm pretty sure that will have come as a surprise."

"We keep tracking the mercenaries, then." Darro gestured to an empty spot on one of several logs they had pulled up near the fire. "Settle in and eat something. Sounds like we're not heading home for a few more days."

The instant it was light enough the next morning, Kasiel sent Kitrix to watch over Jethan. He encouraged the raptor to keep out of sight as much as possible, but that wasn't particularly difficult. The mercenaries weren't checking the sky for danger, which meant the bird mostly had to stay up above, landing high in the nearby trees any time they stopped.

Based on Kasiel's eavesdropping through Kitrix, the three men were not only willing to believe that the Vanrian guard deserted, they assumed as much before even bothering to confront Jethan about it. They celebrated the fact that they could speak more openly without the man there. Jethan apparently didn't qualify as a threat in their eyes. They mentioned "the professor" numerous times throughout the day. First speculating around why he was offering sanctuary to Vanrian traitors and later attempting to terrorize Jethan with speculation of terrible experiments he might be performing on the mind-crafters they were bringing him. Kasiel tried to imagine this professor was someone other than Edmund, but the man who raised him and this professor had become the same person in his head.

As evening drew near, the group settled in for the night. The Vanrian unit set up camp about a mile to the north of them, ready to move if the need arose. Kasiel lingered with Kitrix, listening in on the mercenaries' campfire conversation. He had barely been present with his unit during the day, keeping his awareness with Kitrix while Niskenya carried him along, the kanodrak holding a steady distance between them and their quarry. When the mercenaries finally stretched out to sleep, Kasiel lured a rodent to feed Kitrix, then retreated into his physical self.

He was sitting on the ground with Niskenya wrapped partially around him. Most of the Vanrian party was asleep, except Merrin and Avris, who stood watch, and Nerith, who got up to bring food over the moment he returned to himself. The weary kanodrak didn't move when Nerith crouched next to him to give him the bowl.

"Is everything all right with Jethan?" she asked, her gaze drifting to Niskenya's head.

"All right enough, considering he's still in enemy hands." He took a bite of the stew they had constructed. After swallowing, he forced out an awkward, "Thank you."

"Actually, it's me who needs to thank you." She met

his eyes. "That bear would have killed me."

"That was Niske. If not for her, I'm sure it would have killed us both."

She offered a nod to the kanodrak. "Then, thank you, Niske."

Niskenya lifted her head, a low rumble in her chest.

Nerith reached a hand toward the kanodrak, then pulled it back and looked at him. "May I?"

Kasiel shrugged, focusing on his meal. "It's not up to me. She makes her own decisions."

She moved her hand out again, stopping a few inches from the kanodrak. Niskenya brought her face forward into Nerith's palm and Nerith gasped, her fingers sliding out over the solid bone plating that protected the kanodrak's head.

"Such a remarkable creature," she breathed. "Leysa will be... would have been so jealous." She swallowed, tears rising in her eyes.

The intense desire to pull her into his arms and hold her caught Kasiel unprepared. He perfectly recalled the wing shape of her ke'hanoath tattooed on the soft skin of her back, the light that sparked in her eyes when she teased him, and the comfort of her body pressed against his when they embraced.

He set down the bowl and stood, stalking out into the darkness. Breathing the cooler night air helped clear his head, though not as much as he would have liked. It wasn't even the physical closeness that he missed most about being with Nerith. That was just the least painful part to remember. He missed her boldness and the way she laughed. He missed a million little behaviors and quirks. But how much of it had been authentic? How many of those memories he cherished were merely her attempts to fulfill the khevarin's orders?

Footsteps alerted him to Avris's approach a few minutes later. "You're needed," she whispered, stopping next to him.

"What do you mean?"

She took his hand and led him out past the other side of the camp. Nerith sat against a tree alone in the dark, her arms wrapped tightly around her legs, shoulders shaking with quiet sobs.

"It's not my place," he whispered.

"Then whose is it?" Avris hissed back at him.

He had no answer for that, so he made his way out to Nerith and sat down beside her.

She didn't look at him. "I miss Leysa so much." Her voice cracked and more sobs shook her.

Kasiel slipped an arm around her shoulders and pulled her close. "I know," he murmured.

•

The mercenaries were up and off with the first light of dawn, so the Vanrians were too. When Kasiel slipped into Kitrix's mind, he got an increased sense of agitation from him, the raptor responding to a heightened mood and energy coming from the group with Jethan. About four hours into the day, the three men began boasting of their plans to spend the evening drinking at the professor's table and one broke out in a bawdy tavern song. That meant they were near their destination. Kasiel sent Kitrix up and ahead. A little over a mile past their location, he spotted a division in the trees that might be a river or road. On closer inspection, it proved to be the latter. To one side of where Kitrix crossed it, the road trended west and gradually south. It curved to the northeast, going the other way.

Venturing a guess, he sent the raptor west toward where the landscape appeared to dip gradually down alongside some rocky crags sticking up out of the trees. Keeping near the treetops, he followed the road across a bridge and to the crags where it started to descend, curving along the side of a cliff. As Kitrix soared above the roadway, a modest castle came into view, tucked up against the cliff overlooking a large plunge pool and the continuation of the river below. A waterfall cascaded over the cliff near the front entrance, the water rushing under a drawbridge covered in enough dust and gravel that he suspected it didn't get taken up often. Another branch of the falls disappeared beneath the castle farther in. Guards stood atop the walls, a few of them wearing Alliance colors, though most lacked any distinctive affiliation in their attire. Two of them appeared Vanrian, although he didn't venture close enough to be certain.

Kasiel made Kitrix circle overhead a second time, noting a large stack of wooden crates in one corner of a nicely maintained courtyard. Two gardeners tended to a collection of decorative trees and shrubs that benefited from mist off the nearby waterfalls floating in over the wall on a light breeze.

This was where the mercenaries were heading. That meant it was time to take Jethan back from them, preferably before they reached the road. He turned Kitrix around, flying swiftly toward where he had last seen them.

He was about to return to himself when stark terror flashed across the link, sending him reeling. Something slammed into his back – Kitrix's back – the ends of long wings flapping forward on either side of him as talons dug deep in his flesh. The raptor thrashed to break free. A blinding flash of agony cut through the back of his neck, making Kasiel double over in his saddle. Kitrix's presence fell silent.

Niskenya halted beneath him, snarling in response to his distress, her claws sinking into the dirt.

"Kas!" Darro was the first to reach him, his horse balking at getting too close to the upset kanodrak.

Kasiel gripped the saddle with one hand, his vision blurring. He brought the other hand up, expecting to find blood on the back of his neck. The physical pain hadn't been this intense when Sylaryth died, but then, he hadn't been conscious when the tethdrak sustained those injuries. His fingers came away dry. The memory of the agony lingered. He clenched his teeth against it, struggling to gather his wits about him so he could respond to his companions.

"Kas?" It was Avris this time, coming up on his other side. "What happened?"

He met her eyes. "Something killed Kitrix. A larger raptor, I think."

"Shit," Darro muttered behind him.

"I'm sorry, Kas," Avris said softly.

He ignored her. He couldn't afford to mourn the loss right now. "I think I found where they're going. More importantly, there's a road not far ahead. We need to take Jethan back before they reach it."

Kince came up beside Darro. "Let's go then. Just keep in mind, Niske can cover this terrain a lot faster than our horses can. Don't get too far ahead or you could end up in trouble."

Niskenya could probably also take down all three mercenaries by herself, but he refrained from pointing that out. This wasn't the time to provoke an argument. He simply nodded and gripped the saddle, encouraging the kanodrak to move. As they broke into a lope, he reached ahead, seeking any flying creature that might serve his purpose. It didn't take long. The forest teemed with wildlife here.

He seized control of a tiny songbird and went in search of the mercenary group. They had increased their pace sometime after he took Kitrix away from them. Panic burned through him when he realized they were almost to the road already.

Kasiel leaned low over Niskenya's neck, urging her faster. The unit would have to catch up. Even with the kanodrak's ability to navigate the rough terrain at speed, the mercenaries were going to reach the road before he could intercept them. Taking them on in the open was an option, albeit one with greater risk. At least he could try to stop them from getting within sight of the castle.

Through the bird's eyes, he watched the mercenaries. They were about to emerge onto the road when they slowed, and the lead rider put his hands up in the air. Ahead of them, a group of Alliance soldiers escorting an armored wagon along the roadway had rolled to a stop. Two of the mounted soldiers and a third sitting in a seat at the top of the wagon had crossbows trained on the approaching mercenaries.

"Halt and state your business," a soldier in the front demanded.

Kasiel brought the songbird up and around, taking a better look at the heavy wagon and its guards. Four horses pulled the fully enclosed conveyance. It appeared built for cargo rather than passengers, though he couldn't guess what, if anything, was in it. Ten mounted Alliance soldiers rode along with the wagon, and two more armed with crossbows sat on seats in the front and back. The driver was also in uniform and wore a sword at his hip.

The mercenary leader raised his hands higher and urged his mount a few steps forward with a nudge of his heels. "Just a few hired swords delivering a present to the professor." He pointed to Jethan without lowering his hands. "Happy to ride along with you, if you don't mind."

No!

Kasiel cursed under his breath, urging Niskenya down to a walk. The kanodrak was an impressive beast, but even she couldn't take on those numbers.

The soldier sneered at Jethan, though his regard for the mercenaries wasn't much more respectful. "Follow along if it pleases you. Just stay out of our way."

The Alliance soldiers lowered their bows and continued, the ease with which the horses moved the wagon telling Kasiel that it was empty or carrying something exceptionally light. The three mercenaries with Jethan fell in behind the group. Kasiel landed the songbird on Jethan's leg, tapping his arm once with its sharp beak. Jethan gave a subtle nod, the faint sheen of sweat on his brow exposing his fear.

Reluctantly, Kasiel set the bird off again and retreated into himself. He turned Niskenya to rejoin the rest of his unit. They needed to come up with a new plan of action fast. He wasn't leaving here without his tehnaak, but he wouldn't blame any of the others if they reconsidered, given this new development. He and Jethan had taken a gamble and lost, significantly complicating the rescue mission. If he hadn't wasted those crucial minutes flying Kitrix ahead, he might have the raptor and Jethan with him now.

When he reached his companions, they were farther back than he expected and minus one horse. Kince's mount had caught its leg in a hole hidden by a loose rock and gone down. Kince had fresh bruises and an abundance of curses to share but came out of the incident otherwise unharmed. The less fortunate horse had broken its leg. They killed the animal to end its suffering and moved Kince to Kasiel's mount.

After Kasiel shared his unfortunate news about Jethan, they turned and fell in together, heading back toward the road at a more subdued pace.

"What now?" Merrin spat the question, manifesting the frustration and anger that simmered in all of them.

Kasiel stopped them inside the tree line, staring at the now empty road. "First, we find out why the Alliance company is here," he answered, already darting along behind the eyes of another songbird.

"Does that even matter?" Wedro growled.

Darro stopped alongside Kasiel. "Shut up and give him a minute."

"Let's not start snapping at each other," Tath said. "We're all on edge, but we can't do this if we don't work together."

Kasiel gave an absent nod in the direction of her voice. "Thank you, Tath."

He brought the bird into the castle courtyard, landing on a tree near where the wagon had come to a stop. Two of the Alliance soldiers were lifting a chest out of the back.

The lead soldier gestured to the stack of wooden crates in the corner. "Start loading these up. I want to be out of here first thing in the morning. They need these elixirs on the front lines if they're going to keep those Vanrian mind-fuckers scrambling." He glanced up and smirked at one of the Vanrian guards on the wall before leading the two carrying the chest inside.

Kasiel was distantly aware of Niskenya growling in response to his own immediate loathing for the man.

The three mercenaries followed the Alliance group through the front doors, shoving Jethan ahead of them. Several castle guards started moving the wooden crates into the wagon, the care with which they handled them suggesting fragile cargo.

Kasiel dropped back to himself and looked around at his companions. "I've got an idea."

Kince arched a brow at him. "Is it a good one?"

"Probably not."

Kasiel watched through the eyes of another inconspicuous little bird as the wagon left the courtyard the next morning. It moved slower now, laden with the weight of its fragile cargo. He kept the bird close, flitting from tree to tree along the side of the road, staying far enough away to avoid drawing attention. He had made the mistake of losing sight of Jethan the previous day when he scouted ahead with Kitrix. An error that cost him the raptor and an opportunity to rescue his tehnaak. One he might never forgive himself for if he couldn't find a way to make it right. This time, he would track every step the horses took as they pulled the wagon closer to the ambush.

Wedro and Chander had selected a location about three miles up from the castle, where the road was carved through a rocky rise in the landscape. The trees provided them cover. Higher ground gave them an advantage. A place where they could get a good angle not only on the riders, but on the crossbowmen in the seats on either end of the armored wagon.

Kasiel split his awareness as they drew closer, sending patience to Niskenya where she waited poised to flank the wagon, and to two bears positioned around a bend in the road to intercept any Alliance soldiers who attempted to escape. He had a raptor waiting in the trees as well. A large enough bird that it could have been responsible for Kitrix's death, though he tried not to let that possibility influence his connection to it. The rest of their unit hid in the trees on either side of the road, ready to move at his signal. The horses they left tied to a line deeper in the forest where the passing soldiers wouldn't see or hear them.

The sound of hooves grinding along on the gritty roadway and the creaking of the wagon wheels reached them first. Kasiel kept his position, setting the songbird free once he could see the Alliance group approaching through the eyes of the raptor. Niskenya's rising anticipation was as effective as any Enkindler's ability for boosting his confidence. The kanodrak was ready to fight.

He waited.

The lead soldiers passed under his position. He could smell their horses and the dust they churned up from the roadway. The front of the wagon moved past beneath him. He drew in a breath and let it slowly out. The second the archer on the rear seat was below him, he sent the raptor in, diving in the face of the driver, its razor talons digging at his eyes. That was the signal.

The driver screamed, dropping the reins to try fending off the airborne assault. Both the wagon's crossbowmen turned toward the sound, and bolts shot from the trees, sinking through the open faces of their helmets. As the soldiers grabbed for their weapons, Kasiel seized control of their mounts, provoking the animals into a frenzied fight against their riders.

His companions swarmed into the chaos, Merrin and Darro leaping in first on either side of the roadway to pull two riders off their uncontrollable horses. The rest were right on their heels, except for Nerith and Tath, both armed with crossbows, so they could stay out of the melee in their primary roles as healers. Niskenya charged in from behind, nearly decapitating one soldier with the swipe of a massive paw. In seconds, they had switched the odds, cutting thirteen Alliance soldiers down to seven.

Kasiel also stayed out of the physical altercation. His task now was to move horses away from the fighting to keep the animals from harming any of his companions once their riders were thrown, pulled off, or jumped clear on their own. The raptor had effectively blinded the driver, leaving the wagon horses with no guidance other than Kasiel's encouragement to wait out the battle. Next, he sent the bird into the face of another soldier who appeared to be gaining the advantage with Chander, distracting the man enough for Chander to strike a killing blow.

A man toward the front jumped off his uncontrollable horse and ran. Kasiel moved the bears in to intercept him, dropping behind their eyes long enough to confirm the kill. When he pulled back to himself, the fighting was all but finished. Niskenya stood over a pile of three bodies, blood on her teeth and claws. Only one Alliance soldier remained standing, a man whose horse had thrown him off into the side of the wagon. His sword arm hung useless, bent in an unnatural place. He was retreating from Kince, who had someone else's blood spattered on his face. Kasiel glanced away when Darro stepped up behind the soldier. It didn't help. He could still hear the wet choking after Darro dragged his blade across the man's throat.

Swallowing against the sick feeling in his stomach, he brought the riding horses together alongside the wagon and skidded down the slope onto the road. Nerith and Tath came with him, calling for a tally of injuries.

Kasiel scanned around the wagon. One of them had finished off the driver. The man lay in the roadway, his eyes bloody, gaping wounds in his face. "Someone who's not injured, move the wagon into the trees. Let's take these horses and tie them out near ours. We don't want them wandering to the castle."

Merrin jogged over and climbed onto the wagon seat. Wedro, Avris, and Kince began gathering the waiting horses. Kasiel strode to where Tath was putting pressure on a cut above Darro's eyebrow. Nerith turned her attention to a wound on Chander's arm.

"How are we for injuries?"

Darro nodded to him. "Surprisingly good. A few superficial injuries. A few fresh scars on our armor. Nothing serious. I think your beasts did most of the hard work." He gestured to Niskenya with a point of his chin.

"If you move your head again, I'm cutting it off," Tath snapped.

Darro smirked at her. "Yes, dear."

"I should just let you bleed," she grumbled under her breath.

Kasiel glanced at Nerith. "How's your patient?"

"Not too bad. I think we can get away with a snug bandage for the moment."

Niskenya prowled up next to him, and he absently placed a hand on her shoulder. "All right. Let's get off the road then."

Merrin already had the wagon in the trees, maneuvering it through an area they had plotted out earlier. Because of the rough terrain, they wouldn't be able to get it as far in as he wanted, but there wasn't much they could do about that. When everyone else was off the road, he took one last look around at the bodies, trying not to consider the lives and families these soldiers may have had, then followed his unit.

Several minutes later, they completed their various tasks and met up by the wagon. Kasiel broke open a crate and pulled out one of the flasks packed in straw within. He removed the cork, sniffing at the reddish liquid inside. It smelled sharp, almost acidic, with a faint hint of metal underneath. When he held it out to Niskenya, the underlying scent took on the distinctive stench of blood through her superior senses. Vanrian blood, no doubt. He sealed it again and picked up two more flasks before facing his companions.

"Darro, how do you feel about taking on the role of ranking officer for this next part?"

Tath took Darro's hand, pulling him protectively close.

The corners of Darro's mouth curved up a little, as if her reaction pleased or amused him. "I'm fine with it, though you don't exactly look like my subordinate at the moment."

Kasiel glanced down at his exquisitely crafted black leather and dark metal armor. "Excellent point." He peered around at the others. "Wedro, we're about the same size. Can I borrow your gear?"

Wedro immediately began working at the buckle on one bracer. "If you die, I'm keeping yours."

Avris punched him in the arm. "Not funny."

Kasiel considered the contents of the wagon. If this was how Alliance soldiers were resisting their mindcraft, these elixirs were far more dangerous than the south's alchemical bombs. "We'll take a few flasks with us to prove we have them."

Kince stepped forward, his eyes narrowing. "If you get my tehnaak killed—"

"He won't," Darro interrupted. He met Kasiel's gaze, the wound above his eyebrow fresh and angry, but no longer bleeding. "Let's get this over with."

They returned to where their horses waited. While Darro selected two mounts and packed the flasks of elixir, Kasiel stripped off his armor and sword. Nerith accompanied Wedro when he brought his gear over. He set it in a pile and put a hand on Kasiel's arm, leaning close.

"I'm hoping I don't actually get to keep your armor and sword, my friend," he said in a low voice before leaving them.

Nerith said nothing. She simply picked up the first piece of Wedro's armor and helped him buckle it on. When they finished, he turned to face her. She met his eyes, still silent.

"Why are you here, Nerith?"

"Because your father sent me." She reached up as if intending to brush back the lock of hair that had fallen in his face, then stopped short, returning her hand to her side. "I told him you wouldn't want me here, but he insisted I was the best available fit."

"You were wrong."

Her eyes picked up a hopeful gleam. "I was?"

Kasiel nodded. "I'm glad you're here."

Nerith barely let him get the words out. She popped up on the balls of her feet and kissed him. When she moved away, Kasiel caught her in his arms, pulling her close and kissing her back as if he might never get another chance. How he had missed the way she felt in his embrace. She slid her fingers into his hair, letting her body soften against his. Her lips were supple, warm, and welcoming. He tasted salt on them and drew back. Bringing his hand up, he cupped her cheek and brushed away a tear with his thumb.

"Don't do that. I'll be all right."

"You better be." Her lavender eyes flashed with defiance, as if her fierce will alone could protect him.

That fiery spirit was probably his favorite thing about her.

"Ten out of ten on the kiss," Darro said, sauntering by with two horses in tow. "We should get moving, though."

"Calloch," Nerith muttered. She gave Kasiel a last warm, fleeting brush of her lips against his before extracting herself from his embrace.

He didn't want to leave her, but until Jethan was back, he had one overriding purpose. Turning away, he strode over to Niskenya, passing patience and calm into her. She brought her head close to his face, and he leaned in, closing his eyes as he touched his forehead to the armor plating.

"Wait for me, Niske," he murmured. "Protect them until I come back."

She answered with a rumble in her chest and a wave of affection.

He drew a breath, searching for courage. Finding it in the kanodrak's steady, milky-eyed gaze, he steeled himself and went to swing up on the horse alongside Darro. He glanced around at the others. "If one of us hasn't returned in an hour, destroy the contents of the wagon and get out of here."

Resistance sparked in the many eyes looking back at him. No amount of arguing was going to change that. He had to hope they would do the smart thing if this went badly, but he couldn't force them to.

He breathed a wry laugh. "At least destroy the contents of the wagon. We don't want that ending up in Alliance hands."

"Yes, Ahninveth," Wedro said, a smirk quirking up one side of his mouth.

Avris regarded Kasiel and Darro, her fists resting on her hips. "Just don't be late for supper, all right, kids."

"Never," Darro answered.

They left the group, heading out to the roadway. Kasiel called in the two bears and the raptor to linger beyond the tree line for additional help if they needed it. It wasn't as if they were trying to be discreet, and if the professor was who he believed he was, hiding his ability was pointless. But Merrin had pointed out that the soldiers and mercenaries might not be aware of what he was capable of, a fact that could give them an advantage if things did go awry. They trotted down the road, riding in uneasy silence until they were almost to the drawbridge. Two guards on top of the wall aimed their bows at them. Another stepped out of the shadows of the entryway and shouted for them to halt.

Kasiel slowed his mount, letting Darro pull a few strides ahead of him before they stopped to encourage the idea that the other man was the ranking officer. The bears he brought up alongside their position, still hidden in the trees. The raptor circled once, sweeping down to land on a nearby branch at his direction.

Darro pulled one flask from the satchel he carried and held it up. The noise of the waterfalls forced him to raise his voice to almost a shout. "We've got something of yours. We were hoping the professor would be amenable to discussing an exchange of property."

The gate guard took a few steps toward them, casting wary glances at the surrounding forest, correctly suspecting that there might be more of them out there somewhere. He narrowed his eyes, peering at the flask, then let fly a few curses.

"Wait right there." He looked up at the guards on top of the wall as he turned. "Shoot them if they come any closer," he called, before jogging back into the courtyard.

Kasiel kept his breathing steady, reaching out with his mind to touch on creatures throughout the area. Specifically, he sought those residing within the keep. Rodents sneaking along less used corridors and nesting in the backs of deep cabinets. He jumped from one to another, slipping into a world of muted colors as seen through their eyes, searching for the mind-crafters he knew must be in there.

"Any luck?" Darro asked under his breath.

"No." Kasiel jumped to yet another rat, gazing out

its eyes from behind the bars of a cell. He made it look around, taking it from the crumbs it had been feasting on. Upon turning, he saw a Vanrian woman sitting on a cot at the back of the cell, leaning against the wall, her eyes closed, a tight bandage wrapping one forearm. "Yes!"

Before he could investigate further, Professor Edmund Danovan strolled out under the arch of the courtyard entrance. Kasiel's gut went sour. If there was anyone he wanted to see less than the professor, he couldn't think who it might be. Then again, the effectiveness of his plan had hinged somewhat on Edmund being behind this, so being right wasn't unfavorable, just unsettling.

Edmund had his dark hair cut short and neatly combed. He wore a heavy, deep blue tunic with gold brocade down the front and along the hem. A black cloak with similar gold accents hung in folds over the tunic, a large, jeweled broach clasping it at his right shoulder. An ensemble more luxurious than anything Kasiel had ever seen him in.

Edmund's gaze skipped past Darro, focusing on Kasiel. "Kasiel, how nice to see that we both survived our unfortunate injuries from Katovan."

Kasiel clenched his teeth, trying not to let the man's taunt get under his skin.

"Professor Edmund Danovan." Darro inclined his head, though his tone conveyed less respect than the gesture implied. "We happened upon a little shipment of yours we thought you might like returned."

Edmund's false smile tightened. "And what is it you hope to gain by offering me this merchandise you've stolen?"

"Oh, I think you know." Darro's answering smile picked up a predatory edge. "You have several things you've stolen from us. We'd like to discuss an exchange."

Anger lit Edmund's eyes. Stepping closer to his guard,

he engaged in a hushed conversation with the man for a few minutes, during which Kasiel turned his attention back to the rat. He sent it out through the bars, peeking into different cells as he sprinted past, and quickly found more Vanrians. Sitting on their cots. Pacing. Exercising. Sleeping.

Jethan!

He spotted him toward the end of the run, lying back on his cot. Like the first prisoner, a heavy bandage wrapped his forearm from the elbow halfway down to his wrist. He looked paler than normal, other than the bruise over his eye. Kasiel hurried past the cell, searching now for the exits.

"I am willing to discuss an exchange of goods," Edmund said, "but I will negotiate with Kasiel and only Kasiel. Perhaps we could conduct our conversation over a decanter of wine in a more civilized setting." Edmund gestured behind him at the castle.

"No. We settle this out here. With all of us."

Darro's curt response drew Kasiel fully back from the rat. He urged his horse up alongside the other man's and leaned in, keeping his voice low. "Yes."

Darro met his eyes. "No. I'm not letting you go in there, especially not alone."

"Yes, you are. I've found Jethan and the others. I need to work out where in the castle they are. Negotiating with Edmund will give me the time I need to do that."

"And if this is a trap?"

Kasiel glanced at his former father figure. Edmund looked eager now. Hopeful. "It almost certainly is, but whatever he's after, he still wants those elixirs. The Alliance paid him for them. They won't be pleased about paying for goods and not receiving them. Besides, even if he takes me prisoner, I can use the rats in the castle to help me break out. Niske will let you know if I get into trouble."

"What if he just wants to kill you?"

"He doesn't. I remember how he looked at me when he wanted me dead. This is different. He wants something else now. Besides, killing me won't get him his elixirs back." Kasiel's nerves were dancing like he had lightning under his skin. If he was wrong, he might never have the chance to regret it.

His horse pranced in response to his heightened anxiety despite the calm he had forced on it to deal with the nearby bears. He held a hand out to Darro.

Audibly grinding his teeth, the other Vanrian tucked the elixir he was holding in the satchel with the rest and passed it to him.

"Return to the unit. I'll keep the bears close by until you're clear of here. Give me another hour from now before you destroy the elixirs. If it gets to that point..." He was going to tell him to lead the group back to Vanris, but he could see the argument rising in Darro's eyes already, so he let it go. "Just don't do anything too reckless."

"Be careful, danro, and we won't have to."

Kasiel nodded, saying nothing. If his voice shook with the fear he felt, he would have a harder time convincing Darro to leave. He urged his mount forward. When Darro didn't follow, Edmund signaled the archers on the wall to lower their bows. Kasiel kept his gaze ahead. He didn't need to look back. Shifting behind the eyes of one bear, he watched himself arrive at the entrance to the courtyard.

Edmund offered a slight nod as Kasiel dismounted. "Osric can take your horse." He turned toward the castle and gestured to a burly man dressed in common attire. "Osric, give the animal some food and water, but keep it ready for our guest to depart."

The man nodded, and Kasiel handed over the reins

with a confidence that didn't extend beyond the surface. Back on the road, he saw Darro turn and trot away, his lips pulled into a grimace as he went. Kasiel kept the bears moving parallel to him, alert for anyone trying to follow.

Being close to Edmund put Kasiel's hackles up. He yearned to pull the dagger he wore and drag that sharp blade across the man's throat. That wasn't like him. He rarely wanted to draw blood, but Edmund had earned a special place in his hate.

A guard jogged ahead and opened the castle door. Edmund led them inside an entry hall floored in swirling white and pale gray marble. The same stone formed a curved staircase leading up from one side of the hall. A massive decorative candelabra hung overhead from the ornate, arched ceiling.

"This is quite the change from Fernwallow. Was this what you were working toward all along?"

Ignoring the question, Edmund stopped inside the door and gestured to a polished side table. "If you would be so kind as to leave your weapons here. A precaution."

Two more guards joined them.

Kasiel answered with a derisive smirk. "Do you really think I can take out an entire castle by myself?"

Edmund glanced down at his dagger. "No, but I am concerned that you might try to finish what you started in Katovan. I'm not wearing armor under my clothes this time."

Armor. That explained why he'd had such a difficult time trying to drive in the blade, and why Edmund survived the injury.

"I think you're remembering that wrong," Kasiel said, infusing his tone with false affection. "I'd never hurt you. You know I loved you like a father." The words were meant to mock similar sentiments Edmund had expressed at their encounter in the woods after Kasiel fled Fernwallow, but the broken truth in them cut back at him.

Edmund's eyes tightened, but he didn't move.

With the odds currently stacked against him, Kasiel removed his sword belt.

Edmund continued toward the rear of the entry. "Kasiel..." He stopped and turned. "Or is it Hahren now? That was the name they used in Katovan, wasn't it?"

For the first time, Kasiel considered choosing his Vanrian name, but no one was going to take his identity from him. Especially not Edmund. "Kasiel is fine."

Edmund nodded, a pleased smirk curving his lips. He resumed his walk toward the rear of the hall. "Thirteen alliance soldiers were guarding that wagon. There must be a fair number of you here to have defeated them."

A not very subtle dig for information. "Maybe our soldiers are simply that much better than theirs. I don't see how our numbers are relevant to current negotiations."

"Hmm." A guard opened a door in the back wall for them, leading into a darker hallway traveling perpendicular to the entry. Edmund stopped again as they passed through the doorway, turning to look at him. "I'm not so fond of this foolishness." He gestured to Kasiel's cheek and the portion of the chain tattoo that showed at his collar.

"My ke'hanoath? I don't recall asking for your opinion."

Edmund drew in a breath, his eyes narrowing. "You seem to have grown a spine since your time in Fernwallow."

"No thanks to you." Hatred spread bitterly across his tongue. Perhaps it was good that he had dropped his weapons at the entrance. Edmund might be dead now otherwise, and so, in all likelihood, might he, given the accompaniment of guards.

Edmund turned to the right and resumed walking. "Danica's here," he said, and Kasiel somehow managed not to stumble at that gut punch of information. "I took her in after her father's untimely demise. Perhaps you'll get to see her before you go." He stopped in front of a door and held a hand out to Kasiel. "I'd like to start some tests on those elixirs you brought. Make sure they haven't been tampered with. You understand."

Kasiel gave him the satchel.

"Give me just a moment to get these going, then we'll find a more comfortable place to conduct our business." He disappeared through the door, one guard going with him.

Once that door shut, the remaining two guards retreated down the hall a short distance and stopped there, watching him. The lightning beneath his skin crackled, thunder pounding a warning in his head.

Edmund wouldn't try something yet, would he? Not when he had no idea how many Vanrians he was dealing with or where they had hidden his goods.

Kasiel reached for the door Edmund had disappeared through. A sudden blast sent him slamming against the opposite wall. Smoke billowed around him, filling his lungs. He coughed, staggered a step, and fell into blackness.

CHAPTER EIGHTEEN

The pounding in Kasiel's head could have put a drum circle to shame, but it was the sharp, stabbing pain in his arm that dragged him awake. His stomach churned as he eased upright, unsurprised to find himself locked in a prison cell. Someone had removed the upper pieces of his borrowed armor and rolled up one sleeve. A bandage wrapped around his arm at the elbow, hiding the source of that nagging pain. Anger scalded its way through him, making his upset head spin, which consequently worsened the churning in his stomach.

The cell across from him was empty. A young woman stood in front of it, staring at him with wide eyes. When he looked at her, she scurried out through a metal door at the end of the hall.

A few minutes later, Edmund entered the hallway. "There you are, lad. I was starting to wonder if you would ever wake up."

"Don't call me that," he snapped, wincing at the flare of pain in his head.

"Did you know that something in a mind-crafter's blood changes when their ability awakens?" Edmund's tone was conversational, as if they were having a chat over tea. "I wish I had known that before we put so much effort into kidnapping you and raising you in Fernwallow. Though I did ultimately learn it from you. The blood

I took in Katovan was different from the samples I'd taken over the years before your awakening. Fascinating how the very thing that gives you your abilities is the key to protecting our soldiers from them. I'd like to try dissecting some bodies of pre- and post-awakening mind-crafters to see what other changes might occur, but I can't really afford to spare any of you for that right now. Maybe once the war is over."

"This is why you killed my mother and took me from my home? So you could find a way to fight mind-crafters and sell it to the Alliance?"

Edmund nodded, looking immensely pleased with himself. "The only child of a mind-crafter like your father was practically guaranteed to have a powerful ability. The problem was that we simply couldn't figure out how to awaken it. It has worked out in the end, however, and proven quite lucrative."

Kasiel glanced at his arm. The scar from where Edmund cut it open to collect his blood in Katovan extended out below the bandage. "So, you hire mercenaries to bring mind-crafters here. Then you extract their blood to create an elixir that makes Alliance troops resistant to our abilities?"

"Yes. It only works for a limited amount of time, however, so I must keep my resources alive and healthy. It's like farming cattle. I milk them for their blood, then let them recover until I can do it again."

Hatred boiled up in him so potent it made his head spin. "We're not cattle, you calloch!"

Edmund's eyes sparkled with malicious delight. "Oh, but you are to me, lad, and I'm going to need more of you to keep up with demand."

Kasiel glared at him. He would escape here, and the professor would regret every choice he had ever made. Not taking his eyes off the hated man in front of him, he tried reaching out to rodents in the castle. Any creature he might use to bring him the keys or something else to break him free of this cell.

Silence met him. He couldn't sense any animals at all. Not inside the castle or beyond its walls. Not even Niskenya. His blood turned to ice. His breath caught in his throat.

Edmund smiled. "And there it is, the panicked look that tells me my experiment worked."

"What experiment?" Kasiel had to choke the question out past the constriction in his throat.

"The greatest remaining threat to Alliance troops is Ferals like you, Kas. My last problem to solve. I added an experimental mixture to some blackout bombs that I was hoping would deaden the Feral ability, but I had no one to test it on. My mercenaries are too scared to try transporting a Feral. But you delivered yourself to my door. I no longer need to fear your father, thanks to my ingenuity, so now we can take our time and wait to see how long it lasts." His self-satisfied smile was a dagger in Kasiel's chest. "It should work against other mind-crafters as well. I'm eager to see how effective it is in combat."

"You'll never get your elixirs back if you don't let me go." Kasiel fought the panic that urged him to plead for his freedom. He needed to be patient. This would wear off, and he didn't have to tell Edmund when it did. He forced slow and steady breaths, trying to calm the racing of his heart, but it refused to be soothed.

"I don't know about that, but I do know it's not your concern anymore," Edmund said, much too confident for Kasiel's liking. "You may notice that I took a little of your blood after your exposure to my modified blackout bomb. I need to know if exposure to the substance in it alters its effectiveness for my elixirs. If so, I'm afraid you may be of little use to me once this experiment is over. You will cooperate while I figure these things out, won't you?"

"What do you think?" He growled the question, his lip lifting in a hint of a snarl.

The door Edmund had come in through opened and a mercenary entered. Edmund hurried over to intercept him at the entrance. They spoke in hushed voices. A dark rage twisted Edmund's features. He made a sharp gesture as he said one last thing, then he returned to Kasiel's cell, glaring in at him, his upper lip twitching.

"Your companions destroyed my elixirs. How wise was it, do you think, to get rid of the only thing they had worth bargaining for?"

Kasiel grinned. If they had destroyed the elixirs, maybe they also had the sense to flee this place.

"Don't make the mistake of looking at this as a victory, lad." Without breaking eye contact, Edmund made a beckoning gesture toward the mercenary.

The man opened the door and two more men forced Chander into the room, holding his arms twisted behind his back. Kasiel lunged to the bars, gripping the cold metal.

Chander's eyes widened.

"No!" Kasiel choked on the word, panic closing off his ability to breathe.

"Kas! The oth—"

Before Chander could finish speaking, one mercenary drew a blade across his neck. Blood spilled bright red from the wound, spurting out to spray the gray stone wall. Chander's mouth moved, more blood streaming over his lips as he struggled to say something. Then his legs gave out, the light fading from his eyes as he sagged between the two men.

Kasiel gripped the bars, pressing his head to the cold metal. He clenched his teeth and closed his eyes, unable to fight the tears spilling forth. More than ever before, he yearned for Niskenya's comforting presence, but this time, he couldn't have it. Edmund had taken her from him too.

"That is payment for the elixirs and to ensure your future cooperation. Should you wish to watch more of your companions die, you have merely to remain defiant."

Kasiel clenched the bars, despair creating a heavy pressure in his chest. He had failed. He had failed completely. Arrogance and naivety led him to assume his ability could save him. Without it, he had nothing.

"I'll do anything you want. Just let the others go." He opened his eyes, staring at the floor. Blood streamed along a groove between the stones, creeping into the edge of his field of vision.

"Their fate will be entirely up to you, Kasiel." Edmund followed the mercenaries out as they dragged Chander's body from the room.

Kasiel turned, putting his back to the bars, and slid slowly down them until he sat on the hard, cold stone floor. He pulled his knees into his chest. Sylaryth had given his life protecting him, and for what? So he could condemn his family to death. So he could sentence Jethan to a fate that was arguably worse than dying. He should have recognized that they were too inexperienced to pull this off and rescued his tehnaak when he had the chance. Even with the threat of whatever punishment awaited him back in Vanris for taking Niskenya.

But the kanodrak wasn't why he went along with Jethan's idea. He had always wanted to find the mind-crafters and discover how the Alliance was blocking their abilities. For the sake of the lives they could save, and because it was his blood that enabled Edmund's research. What a fool he had been to think their small unit could do this alone? To believe that he could help them pull it off simply because he was a Feral?

Now Edmund knew how to combat the Ferals too.

Not only had he failed, but he had actually succeeded in making the situation worse for Vanris.

He let his head fall back against the bars hard enough to increase the pounding in his skull. Tears crept down his cheeks. He could hear the waterfalls outside. They were close to this part of the castle. Aside from that noise, it was silent. No other prisoners occupied this short corridor of cells. Edmund was keeping the rest of the mind-crafters and Kasiel's companions elsewhere in the structure. He was alone. Alone and blind to the world without his Feral ability.

A door opened, though not the one Edmund had come through. This sounded like it was somewhere to the left of his cell. He stayed where he was, staring at the stark stone wall at the rear of the cell. It was better than seeing Chander's blood drying on the floor and wall behind him.

"Why did you have your beast kill my father?"

Danica.

He lifted his head from the bars but didn't turn. "Sylaryth killed your father to protect me. Probably his first mistake." He brushed the tears from his face.

"Why would my father try to hurt you, Kas?" Her voice trembled.

"For Edmund. For this." He gestured vaguely toward the main door.

"Please look at me."

Drawing a deep breath, he turned enough to grab a bar and used it to pull himself to his feet. Then he faced her. She wore her long black hair woven into its myriad little braids hanging loose around her warm, dark face. The shadows of sleeplessness created bruising under her bloodshot brown eyes. She had on a simple tan dress with ivory and amber details worked along the bodice and hem of the skirt. Outside their encounter in Katovan and a few festivals in Fernwallow, he had never seen her willingly don a dress. She hated them.

"I'm sorry about your father. I believe he was a good man. Edmund just led him down a corrupted path." Kasiel wasn't sure that was true. He had a feeling Garrick was involved in Edmund's plan from its conception. That wasn't what Danica wanted to hear, though. What harm could there be in indulging her now?

She nodded, brusquely brushing away a tear that slipped free. Her eyes moved over him. Scrutinizing. Wary. "All those tattoos. Mindcrafting. You really are one of them now, aren't you?"

He sighed, too heartsick to keep the niceties going for her sake. "Don't you get it, Dani? When we danced around the harvest bonfires as kids or chased dragonflies in the marshes, I was one of them. When we helped Edmund hunt for medicinal plants in the woods, I was one of them. That day after sword practice, when you kissed me, I was one of them. I have *always* been one of them. Edmund killed my mother and took me from them when I was a child."

"Why would he do that?"

He gave her a hard stare.

She lowered her gaze. "For this."

"Yes."

She murmured something too quietly for him to make it out.

"What?"

"I said Edmund doesn't have the others. The one..." She glanced toward the blood on the floor and hastily away, swallowing hard. "The one they killed was the only one they caught."

Kasiel's knees gave out. He sank to the floor, gripping the bars, fresh tears running hot down his cheeks. Edmund had lied. Of course he had. That was his way. Relief flooded through him, followed by an immediate crushing guilt. The others were alive and still free, but

Chander was dead. Like Tath and Nerith, Wedro was now part of a broken whole that could never be mended.

Danica came to the bars and sank down on her knees in front of him. "You always had kindness in you, Kas. That's one of many reasons I liked you so much."

Her hand wrapped over his on the cold metal. It was softer than he remembered. The callouses from working in the forge with Garrick were fading. Her fingernails, though she had always kept them trimmed, were chewed down to raw nubs. When had she started biting her nails?

He met her eyes. Maybe he could still recover from this disaster. "The mind-crafters, do you know where he's keeping them?"

She nodded. "Edmund turned most of this floor into prison cells. He doesn't have much time for me, and his mercenaries ignore me, so I help the servants. They started letting me bring food down to the prisoners. I'm not supposed to talk to them, but I do."

"You use his elixir?"

"Everyone who goes around the prisoners does. He has a stronger version of it he makes for our use. One that lasts longer. He says it's more profitable to give the Alliance the weaker version."

"Keep them coming back for more." His stomach turned as he said it. Greed. This was all for greed. He sank down to sit by the bars.

"Mm-hmm." Danica sat alongside him on the outside. Her lips pressed into an irritated line as she adjusted her skirt. "I saw them bring in your friend." That caught his attention. "I remembered him from that night in Katovan, so I asked him about my father's death. Edmund said you attacked them unprovoked, setting your beast on them. I couldn't believe you would do that. Jethan told me a much different story. It rang truer than what Edmund told me, no matter how much I didn't want to believe my father was part of such things." Her gaze moved to the white scar that extended out below the bandage on his arm. "The evidence supports his story too."

"Is Jethan all right?"

"As all right as any of them. No matter who they fight for, no one deserves to be harvested like an animal." She let out a brief, humorless laugh. "I guess I can see why I wasn't supposed to be talking to them."

He slipped his hand through the bars and placed it on her arm. "Help me, Dani."

She pulled her arm away and stood, moving back from the cell. Kasiel followed her up.

"Please."

She looked away, toward whatever door she had come in through, wringing her hands. That confidence he always admired her for had fractured over the last several months. "I can't. I'm Edmund's ward. I have nowhere else to go."

"He's going to kill me or keep me in a cell to harvest my blood like the others. Don't let that be my end."

A few tears fell from her tired eyes. She brushed them roughly away and bolted from the corridor, vanishing through the door he couldn't see. He leaned his head on the bars and tried again to reach out with his ability. Silence and emptiness met him. The metallic scent of Chander's blood crept up from the floor. Defeated, he trudged back to the cot and lay down, staring at the ceiling. All he could do now was wait for his ability to return.

He had hoped to see Danica again, since she said she was helping deliver food to the prisoners, but it was a guard who brought him his evening meal. That didn't come as much of a surprise. He had a feeling Edmund wouldn't want her talking to him. The guard asked him if his ability had come back, ignoring him once he confirmed that it hadn't. His appetite was absent, but he forced himself to eat. He needed sustenance if he was going to have the strength to do anything when he recovered his mindcrafting.

And if it didn't return? If Edmund's additive to the blackout bomb had permanently broken his ability?

Kasiel shuddered. For a time, he lay on the cot, eyelids drooping with fatigue as he watched a rat that had come in to clean up the crumbs of his meal. A creature whose head he should have been able to reach inside of with ease. Still, when he tried, he felt no different than he had before his awakening. No matter how hard he focused, nothing happened.

The lock on the main door clicked, and Kasiel sat up, waiting to see who would enter. Danica slipped in, glancing nervously over her shoulder as she did so. Her secretive manner sent a burst of energy through him, snapping him wide awake. She left the door standing slightly ajar and made her way to the front of his cell, stepping around the still-drying pool of blood on the floor. In one hand, she held a ring of keys. She grabbed the bars with the other.

"The door next to your cell leads to a garden balcony looking out at a level of the falls. You can hop over the railing into a natural pool there and go under the castle to fall into the plunge pool below. It's a long drop, but I've done it a few times. It's safe enough." She glanced at the main entrance again, listening for a second before continuing. "Edmund's in his laboratory. Most nights he's there until at least midnight. That should give you a few hours to meet up with your companions and get away from here before he knows you're gone."

Kasiel wrapped his hand over hers, stepping closer. "I can't leave here without Jethan."

A scowl tugged at her lips. "No. Promise me. If I let you out, you will leave here. More people will get killed if you try to rescue the others." Her gaze darted back toward the door again, her hand tightening on the bars under his.

He didn't want to be like Edmund, and yet, how could he do anything but lie to her? It was his freedom she held in her hands. His chance to right his egregious wrongs. "Dani."

"Promise me."

He curled his fingers, sliding them under her hand and pulling it away from the bar. She resisted for a moment, then let him take it, staring down at their hands as he moved his so that their palms joined, twining his fingers through hers. Her lips parted as she looked into his eyes again. Already, he was lying to her, and he hadn't said a word.

"I promise."

He could see her pulse racing in her neck. She cast another glance at the door. Her fingers tightened on his hand for a second before she pulled away. He watched in tense silence as she slid the key into the cell lock. Uncertainty charged the air between them.

Her gaze sank to the key. "Never come back here, Kas," she whispered.

"Never," he repeated, reinforcing his lie.

When she turned the key, the door disengaged, opening a fraction. Danica yanked the key out and bolted through the main door, shutting and locking it behind her. Kasiel pushed the cell door open and hurried around to the door she had told him about. Beyond it, he found a quiet garden balcony. A collection of potted plants added color to the space around the cushioned bench that stared out over a swirling pool at the cascading waterfall.

Leaning out over the balustrade, he spotted a place past the far edge of the pool where the corner of the castle didn't quite meet up with the cliff. He might be able to climb out and sneak through that gap, though he would need to be wary of archers on the walls.

He glanced over his shoulder at another door that led back into the structure. Somewhere beyond that door, Jethan and the other mind-crafters were imprisoned. Gritting his teeth in frustration, he jumped the balustrade into the pool. Any plans he had to swim to the outer edge vanished as a swift current dragged him under the overhanging balcony and into darkness beneath the castle. He inhaled water, struggling to orient himself as to which way was up. He still hadn't figured it out when the violent flow spit him over the next drop.

For a few heartbeats, he was in free fall. He got his body straightened in time to plunge feet first into the pool below. Upon surfacing, he coughed up water, and sucked in a breath of precious air. He paused there, treading water while he tried to orient himself. A glance up at the castle on the cliff above helped him do so, and he swam to shore. When he climbed out of the pool, the bandage on his arm had soaked through, the wound bleeding again. He pulled it off and threw it aside. Clamping a hand over the cut, he struck out in the direction that would take him to his companions. He could only hope they hadn't left the area.

CHAPTER NINETEEN

Fatigue dragged at Kasiel, but months of consistent physical training had its benefits. He broke into a jog, heading up the hillside as fast as he could without entirely exhausting himself. The gradual ascent took him out around the cliffs. Staying deeper in the trees gave him more cover from the castle guards. It also added time to his journey that he resented every minute of. When he reached the level of the road, he followed it from a distance, keeping to the shelter of the woods. Despite his attempts to stay hidden, he didn't make it far.

"Nice try, Vanrian mongrel," a voice growled from the trees ahead of him.

His heart stuttered, a metallic taste spreading across his tongue as two mercenaries stepped out of their hiding places, both holding crossbows aimed at his chest.

"Looks like you went for a swim. Lucky for us, we spotted you climbing out of the water from up on the wall and came down to escort you back to the castle." A wicked grin curved the second man's lips.

Despair, held at bay by the faint hope his escape earned him, swept in with crushing force. He raised his hands. The wound on his arm had stopped bleeding, not that it mattered much. If his blood proved useful, Edmund would open it up again.

One mercenary set down his crossbow and came

forward, unhooking shackles from his belt. A rustle in the trees drew the man's attention, and he hesitated, turning an instant before Niskenya surged from the darkness. Her powerful claws laid open his chest, cutting easily through the leather and chainmail armor.

The other mercenary aimed his crossbow at her. Kasiel charged, slamming into the man and wrenching the weapon from his hands as they both hit the ground. Niskenya lunged in, her jaws closing on his throat and crushing the lower half of his face, spattering Kasiel with his blood.

Kasiel rolled to his hands and knees and threw up. Hot breath warmed the back of his neck as he spit and wiped his mouth. He shifted out from under the kanodrak's head and climbed to his feet, staring at the awesome predator. When he tried his ability, there was still nothing, and yet...

"How did you know to find me here?"

Niskenya growled and butted her head into his chest hard enough to knock him on his ass. He sat there for a second, looking up at her, remembering the link between them she had shown him. Was that still active, even with his ability muted?

He rubbed the tender spot on his chest where she had struck him. "I definitely deserved that." When she did nothing else, he stood, brushing off evergreen needles and dirt. His arm was bleeding again. "Are the others still here?"

Niskenya turned her side to him and sank down on her belly. An invitation. The idea of trying to ride her without the saddle was daunting, but she could carry him faster than he could travel on foot, and she knew where they were going. He took a sword belt off one mercenary and strapped it on, then swung over her back, gripping tight with his legs as she stood. She loped off into the trees, putting forth a noticeable effort to keep her movement smooth for him. Her claws churned up dirt, the dust making him sneeze. Odd how it smelled warm, still holding the heat from the day beneath the surface.

They wove through the trees for a time in the darkness. Every step that took him farther from the castle – from Jethan – was another piece of glass grinding into his chest. Each of those steps also brought him closer to the moment he would have to tell Wedro that Chander was dead. A rumble rose from Niskenya. A deep, comforting sound.

He spotted figures moving in the trees ahead. The fact that Niskenya didn't slow told him they were friends and the weight on his shoulders lifted a little.

Merrin was the first to see the kanodrak. "Is that Niske?"

"It is." That was Avris, her tone listless and disinterested. A moment later, her voice rose. "And Kas!"

It looked as if they were preparing for something. They all wore their armor and had their weapons sheathed or nearby, with several horses ready to go. When he rode into their midst and hopped off Niskenya, they closed in around him, for once not shying away from the kanodrak. He spotted Wedro toward the back, lurking in the darkness, his shoulders hunched.

"What happened?" Darro reached him first. "I wasn't that far from the castle when the bears and my horse all spooked. I got lucky. The bears decided to make a run deeper into the woods rather than turn on me."

Kasiel grimaced, still watching Wedro. "I'm sorry about that. Edmund hit me with a blackout bomb. I was a fool for believing he wouldn't try anything while we still had his elixirs."

Wedro refused to look at him. The man knew. But how?

"It was pretty obvious something went wrong given how agitated Niskenya was before she disappeared, so we destroyed the elixirs," Kince continued. "They came after us just as we were finishing. We made a run for it, but one of them got a lucky shot on Chander's horse, dropping it out from under him. There were too many for us to fight unprepared, so we had to keep going. Then Niske showed up. We didn't expect to see her again with you gone, but she tore through them, giving us a chance to turn and fight." He glanced in Wedro's direction. "When we got back to where Chander had gone down, though, he was gone."

Kasiel touched Niskenya's shoulder. "Thank you for helping them," he murmured. Then he walked through them, coming to a stop in front of Wedro.

The other man finally met his eyes. He shifted his feet, hands clenching and unclenching. "He's dead," he said, nodding too fast, his voice sharp and tremulous. "I can feel it."

"He died quickly," Kasiel offered, for what little solace that might bring.

Wedro sank to the ground. His knees pulled in and his hands balled into fists behind his bowed head. His shoulders began to shake. Merrin, rarely the nurturing type, knelt next to him, putting her arms around him.

Kasiel turned to the others, the loathing in him spreading through his body like a sickness. Edmund would pay. "Edmund told me he'd captured all of you and that he would kill you if I didn't cooperate. He used Chander as an example." No point telling them he also did it as retaliation for the destroyed elixirs. Chander would have died either way.

"We were getting ready to attack the castle," Darro said, nodding toward the distant structure, "if you have a mind to join us."

"Why didn't you leave?"

"Because we're tehsheyn. You don't just walk away from your spirit family," Kince stated, his piercing gaze enhanced by the reflection of the moonlight. "You and Jethan are tehsheyn. Chander and Ahrin were tehsheyn. We're getting our family back and making these bastards pay for those we've lost. With the number of soldiers Niske helped us take down, we don't think they can have that many left at the castle. They don't have the facilities to maintain a large force."

The anger in Kince's voice resonated with the fury boiling inside Kasiel. He glanced around at them, getting supporting nods from everyone, even Wedro. "Good. I've got an idea."

Nerith shook her head at him. "You're bleeding and you're soaked. Get changed, then you can tell us your idea while I tend that arm."

He glanced at the wound. A slow trickle of blood still oozed from it. At his nod, Nerith showed him where they had stashed their packs. He pulled off the rest of Wedro's armor, then peeled out of his wet garments. When he had dry clothes on, he let her sit him down to care for the wound. Darro brought over his black armor and dark metal sword. Avris came to sit on the opposite side of him from Nerith and started drawing a comb through his hair.

He pulled away. "What are you doing?"

"I found these in your bags." She held up the little box that contained the ornamental ear cuffs from the khevarin.

"You dug through my bags?"

"I can't be trusted," she answered with a fleeting smile. "Can I braid your hair?"

Ignoring the coil of ingrained dread in his gut, Kasiel nodded. Nerith silently focused on bandaging his arm as Avris began weaving a set of two braids into his hair along the side of his head. Braids that exposed one of the cut ears he had spent his entire life hiding. While the two worked, they all discussed ideas for infiltrating the castle based on what Kasiel had learned. When Avris finished, she handed one of the ear cuffs to Nerith. They affixed the symbolic pieces in place as Darro, Kince, and Tath wandered off to gather what they would need to execute their plan.

It was strange letting anyone touch his cut ears. There was an intimacy and trust in it that shook him. These were the people he would fight for. The family he would die for if it came to that.

The two women helped speed up the process of donning his armor. They needed to make their move before morning. Midnight was fast approaching. If Edmund checked in on him prior to retiring for the night, he would soon discover that Kasiel had escaped, if he hadn't already. Not one of them commented on the danger inherent in their plan or suggested the possibility of walking away. This was personal for all of them.

"Now you're ready to fight." Avris traced a finger over the top of his ear and along the decorative wing, sending a shiver through him. She followed with a light kiss on the cheek before leaving to gather her weapons.

Nerith was less subtle. The kiss she gave him was deep and demanding. Then, without a word, she stepped away to strap on her short sword and crossbow. Kasiel walked over to place a hand on Niskenya's neck, needing to feel the comfort of their connection.

Kince watched him, brows pinching together. "Your plan doesn't involve any other beasts, danro. Is there a reason for that?"

Kasiel glanced over at him, unease dancing in his chest. "Edmund managed to block my ability with something he added to the blackout bomb."

"By the Break," Tath breathed.

"Well, we have no choice now, do we?" Merrin's

hand sank absently to her sword. "The Alliance could gain an even greater advantage if we lose our Ferals too. We have to stop the bastard."

Darro gave Kasiel a wary look. "If you can't control Niske, how can we trust her to follow the plan?"

The instant the question passed Darro's lips, the kanodrak lunged at him and snarled, forcing him to jump back.

Kasiel gave him a dry look. "I've never had any control over her. She's a partner, not a subordinate. You may want to apologize."

Darro swallowed and nodded. "Sorry, Niske."

The kanodrak backed away with a soft growl and sank down next to Kasiel to make it easier for him to mount.

They rode far enough to get within sight of the castle without being seen or heard by the guards. Brisk night air helped Kasiel focus on what they needed to accomplish rather than on his hatred for the man sheltered behind those stone walls. Once they had dismounted and tied the horses, Kasiel glanced around at the group. With Jethan and Chander absent, they were down to eight.

"We all know the plan." He met Kince's eyes. "Give my team a fifteen-minute lead."

"You've got it," Kince confirmed.

Kasiel looked at Darro, Merrin, and Wedro each in turn. "Are you ready?"

Nods all around. He held Wedro's gaze for a moment. Taking him inside was a risk. Having just lost his tehnaak, he might be reckless with his own life in pursuit of vengeance. And yet, the cold calculation in his eyes provided a strange reassurance. Wedro wanted revenge, but Kasiel got the sense he didn't intend to let his anger compromise this opportunity to take it.

After a moment, he started moving, staying inside

the cover of the trees as he led them toward the looming structure. The other three kept close behind him, sticking to the deeper shadows. When they reached the point where the main branch of the falls passed beneath the drawbridge and through the trees before crashing over the next drop, he stopped at the tree line. The current here, like in the secondary falls that had dragged him under the castle, was powerful. He snuck closer to the edge of the drop. It was narrow enough that they could jump across, though he wasn't sure how stable the rocks were.

Darro crept up next to him. Kasiel pointed to the potential crossing spot and the other man nodded. Two guards paced the top of the front castle wall. When they made their move, there would be a few seconds that the guards might be able to see them in the dark. Kasiel observed the two men, trying to reach out with his ability while he watched them. Still that devastating absence of any presence beyond his own thoughts.

As the two guards drew close to each other on their circuits, they paused to exchange a few words. Kasiel darted out onto the farthest rock and leapt. He landed on his target, struggling to keep his balance for a fraction of a second. Then he jumped again, reaching the opposite shore. Wedro landed almost on his heels. Merrin and Darro waited while the guards continued their circuits until one had his back to them and the other had passed out of sight. Merrin crossed next. She caught Darro's hand when he slipped on the second jump and pulled him the rest of the way.

Kasiel led them to the edge of the tree line. The narrow bank between the castle wall and the water would be enough for them to sneak along. They just had to make it across the brief exposed area from the tree line to the wall. He crouched down, waiting as agonizing seconds ticked by.

A familiar roar sounded from somewhere in the trees on the far side of the road. Niskenya. The two guards stopped their circuit, staring out into the dark forest, their hands drifting to their weapons. Kasiel made a break for it, the other three following close behind, moving as quickly and quietly as they could.

"I ain't getting paid enough for this," one guard grumbled above them.

"Horse shit! You're making more off the professor than you ever made on a job in your life."

"Yeah, but over half our guys didn't come back from that last chase, and what's he gonna pay us with if he hasn't got any product to send? Alliance ain't gonna pay if they don't get anything for it."

The other guard had no answer.

"And why'd those Vanrian guards get to go inside where it's safe?" the first guard complained.

"You are dumb as shit, aren't you? He locked them up because he's afraid they'll reconsider their allegiances now that some of their own kind are running around the area."

All of this sounded like excellent news to Kasiel as he crept along the castle wall. The riskiest stretch was going by the front gate, but with the drawbridge now raised, they could pass beneath the sightline of the gatehouse guards. That would make getting the other team in trickier, but it made things a little easier for them. For the moment, that had to be good enough.

Staying pressed against the wall, they worked their way to the far corner of the castle and ducked around through the narrow gap between the wall and the cliff. Darro waded into the edge of the pool where the current wasn't as overpowering, and leaned out, grabbing hold of the lower edge of the balcony. Without hesitation, he swung out, using impressive strength to haul himself up and catch hold of the balustrade. In one powerful move, he was up and over onto the balcony.

Merrin followed, swinging up with help from Darro. Then Wedro went and Kasiel came after, pleased to find that he had the strength to pull himself up despite the injured arm with a minor assist from Darro to speed him along.

Once they were all up, they huddled briefly.

"Given what I know of the layout, I suspect that door may give us access to the prison, though I'm hoping we'll also find a way to the courtyard through there." Kasiel pointed to the door he hadn't tried when he visited this balcony during his escape.

Darro nodded. "I'd guess so."

Shouts came from up on the wall. The other team was creating a distraction, shooting at, and hopefully hitting, the wall guards with their crossbows.

"Let's move." Kasiel hurried to the door and eased it open. This wasn't a proper entryway, but it was still a relief to find it unlocked. He got the impression from Danica that she and the servants were the only ones who used the space with any regularity.

They entered a dark hallway. Low light coming from a crossing hall a few yards down to their left revealed a set of stairs leading up to another door on the opposite side. Darro darted across and up those stairs. He stopped at the top, nudging the door open enough to peek through the crack. After a moment, he pushed it open a little more and nodded to Kasiel, confirming that it led to the courtyard. When Kasiel returned the gesture, Darro disappeared through the door.

It was hard not to follow and make sure nothing went wrong, but he had to trust his unit if this was going to work. With Wedro and Merrin still close behind, Kasiel crept down the hall toward the light. They had only made it a few feet when male voices reached them.

"Some of those Vanrian bastards are back. They're

shooting at the wall guards."

"How many?"

"Only two that we've seen."

"I'll take my bow and head up. Should be able to pick them off quickly enough. You two watch things down here."

Kasiel signaled for them to turn back. They retreated, ducking up into the shelter of the staircase and pressing against the wall. Brusque footsteps progressed along the hall toward them. Kasiel gave Merrin the front position. Wedro hesitated, meeting her eyes and gesturing for her to give him the spot. She shook her head. After a tense moment, during which the footsteps came ever closer, Wedro backed off. They eased out their weapons. Merrin waited near the wall at the bottom step. Kasiel watched her, the way her chest moved with slow, steady breaths, and how her shoulders remained relaxed, her sword hanging at her side.

The mercenary turned the corner, not expecting trouble or the blade that sank into his throat before he could so much as register that he wasn't alone. Wedro jumped forward as she pulled the sword free, catching the man to keep him from making noise when he hit the floor. Kasiel stepped in to help drag him up onto the stairs.

Moving faster now, they crept back down the hall, weapons at the ready. When they reached the end, Wedro tapped his shoulder. Kasiel met the other man's eyes. He pointed to himself, then toward the crossing hall. Kasiel hesitated. Trust. He had to trust them. He nodded.

Wedro peeked out enough to see around the corner. In less than a second, he ducked back, pointing to their right and holding up two fingers. A wildness came into his expression that any Feral would have envied. Having relayed the relevant information, he darted out of their hiding place. Kasiel and Merrin rushed after him.

One of the two mercenary guards in the room stood fiddling with a ring of keys as he stared down another hall. The other sat at a table, examining the fletching on a pile of arrows.

"Shit!" The man checking the arrows jumped to his feet, knocking the bench he had been sitting on against the wall with a loud bang.

The other guard startled, dropping the keys, and grabbed for his sword. He barely had it free of the sheath before Wedro was on him, a whirlwind of rage. Rather than try to follow that savage assault, Kasiel darted in after Merrin, who engaged the other soldier. The man lunged at her with a dagger. At the last second, she danced aside, letting him stumble directly into Kasiel, who brought his sword up just in time. The dark metal blade sank effortlessly through leather and mail armor, finding even less to challenge it in flesh and bone.

Kasiel twisted to the side, allowing the man to slide off his sword. He clutched at his chest as he hit the floor, eyes wide with that peculiar disbelief that came upon realizing death had never been more than a heartbeat away.

Wedro had the other mercenary pinned to the wall with his sword through the man's abdomen and was viciously driving his dagger into every vulnerable gap in his armor. Defensive wounds shredded the man's hands. Blood trickled from his mouth and his eyes were glossing over.

Merrin stepped in and caught Wedro's arm, interrupting another strike. "He's done," she said, the gentleness of her tone creating a dissonance with the brutality of the scene.

Wedro's arm sank to his side. He was breathing hard, his hands shaking with that surge of rage-fueled adrenaline. Merrin pulled his sword out and the guard collapsed.

Refusing to dwell on the dead men, Kasiel grabbed the blood-spattered ring of keys. "Let's find our people."

With Merrin and Wedro flanking him again, Kasiel followed a powerful draw that pulled him down the next hall. He passed the first set of doors without pausing and turned through the second door on the right. They entered a hallway lined with cells holding Vanrian prisoners, several of whom had fresh bandages on their arms. Upon seeing who burst in, most of them rushed to the bars, hope burning away some of the despair in their shadowed eyes. Kasiel ignored them, jogging to the end where Jethan was getting up from his cot to see what was going on.

By pure luck, the second key he stuck in the lock fit and turned easily. Kasiel threw the cell open, pulling Jethan out into a fierce embrace. His tehnaak grabbed on to him, all but falling into his arms. Joy and relief caused a tightening in his chest and throat, bringing tears to his eyes. The keys jingled as Merrin yanked them from the door to start freeing the others.

"Took you long enough." The break in Jethan's voice echoed the cascade of emotions surging through Kasiel. "I thought the plan was to rescue me before they got me here."

"That was the plan. It was poorly thought out and these Alliance callochs didn't go along with it for shit."

Jethan gave a weak chuckle and stepped back to look

him over. "Did you get dressed up just for me?" He dredged up a shaky grin. "You actually look as intimidating as your father at the moment."

Kasiel drew in a deep breath. They were far from done here, but victory felt much more attainable now. "That wasn't my goal, but I'll take it if it makes these bastards uncomfortable."

Jethan's eyes narrowed. "You've got something on your cheek." He reached out, then drew his hand back. "Oh. That's blood. Not yours, I'm guessing?"

Kasiel shook his head, becoming aware of the declarations of relief and gratitude as Merrin unlocked the other cells. He wiped his cheek, noting the resulting streak of red on his fingertips before he turned to look over the newly freed prisoners. Ten in all, including Jethan.

"Anyone fit enough to fight?"

Jethan stepped forward. "I can."

Kasiel arched a brow at him. "I disagree, tehnaak. You're weak as a kitten. I just hugged you. I know." He faced the others again. "No one who's been bled recently should be fighting. Anyone else, if you feel up for it, there are a few weapons available in the room down the hall." He caught Wedro's eyes. "Can you show them?"

Wedro glanced around at the mind-crafters, who had stepped forward and gestured toward the door with a jerk of his head. "Follow me."

As Wedro led them out, Kasiel moved to the next task. "Merrin, check the other halls. There should be a few more than this."

"Yes, Ahninveth," she replied, giving him his rank now that they had company. She turned and hurried out.

The remaining mind-crafters exited out into the central hall ahead of Kasiel, putting distance between themselves and the cells they had suffered in. Slinging an arm around Jethan's shoulders, he steered him along after the rest, watching to see which of them stumbled or dragged their feet. The ones who might need protecting if they encountered more of Edmund's men. Merrin had already found additional mind-crafters across the hall and was making quick work of setting them free.

Sudden disorientation compelled Kasiel to reach out and brace himself against the wall for balance as Niskenya unceremoniously pulled him into her head. He had a brief glimpse of one massive paw swatting down a mercenary like an insect out in the courtyard. That told him Darro had successfully dropped the drawbridge and raised the gate to let the others in. More importantly, it meant he had his ability back. The swell of relief made him giddy and lightheaded at once.

"Ahninveth," Merrin had returned and stood watching him. "I could use your input on something."

He glanced at Jethan.

"Go, tehnaak. I'm fine here with the others."

"I'll be right back," Kasiel said, reassuring himself as much as Jethan.

Merrin led him to the end of the hall, where a set of stairs ascended to the next floor. They turned through the last door on the left before those stairs. More Vanrians occupied the first three cells, but these weren't mind-crafters. They all still wore their armor and looked distinctly uncomfortable when he entered.

"Traitors." Kasiel's lip curled in a disgusted sneer. He approached the first cell and glared at the man inside, who took a hasty step back from the bars. "How are you feeling about your choices now?"

"Break-blasted mind-crafters," the man spat. "You're all too damned arrogant to see that you're the problem. You get priority treatment in everything. Vanris would be better off without you."

"And you were willing to sacrifice all of Vanris to

make that point?"

The man scoffed at him. "We wouldn't even be at war with the Alliance kingdoms if it weren't for the fucking mind-crafters."

The man in the next cell grabbed the bars, ignoring his fellow's ranting. "You're the dhomvalen's son. Is he here?"

Kasiel narrowed his eyes at the man. "No, he is not."

The man visibly sagged with relief. "Get us out. We'll help you fight them. We were wrong to do what we did. Give us a chance to make amends."

A woman in the third cell also grabbed the bars, nodding her agreement. "Yes. Let us help you."

They dared to assume he would be merciful because he wasn't his father. Each of them had been responsible for at least one of the mind-crafters they had just set free. Each of them was willing to see their own people made into livestock.

He turned to Merrin. "Leave them for now."

Insults and shouts of outrage pursued him out into the central hall. He watched Merrin lock the door behind them, then he cast out with his ability. He needed more information, and he had a way to obtain it now.

Reaching toward a familiar presence, he touched on Niskenya first, followed by numerous other creatures within the outer walls of the structure. While Merrin finished checking the last few sections, he bounced between rodents in different rooms inside the castle.

Through the eyes of an opportunistic mouse, he discovered most of the serving staff huddled in the kitchens. Nearly all the guards had rushed out to the courtyard to deal with his companions and Niskenya, who appeared to be holding their own when he found a rat to check on them through. He lingered there a moment, watching Nerith outmaneuver a guard. She deflected his attack with her sword, sweeping it up, and ducked under that arm to drive a dagger up into his armpit. Then she yanked the blade free and stepped clear. The maneuver was especially impressive from his diminutive perspective, hiding in a bush a few feet away. He would remember this moment the next time he considered doing something that might upset her.

He continued his search, jumping between creatures until he found himself with another mouse looking out from behind the edge of a stack of books at tables covered in flasks and a myriad of unfamiliar apparatus. Edmund was there, snatching up scrolls, journals, and other items and throwing them into a satchel. Three guards stood near the door, weapons out and ready.

Kasiel dropped back into his body, maintaining a distant connection to the mouse in the laboratory. The new members of their group watched him curiously.

"Wedro, can you lead them up to the courtyard? Keep the fighters in front in case you run into trouble."

Wedro looked confused. It took Kasiel a moment to realize why. As far as the other man knew, he still couldn't use his Feral ability.

"Darro and the others are in the courtyard," he elaborated. "They're still fighting, though I don't know how many they're up against at this point. I didn't have the best angle."

"So your ability is..." He trailed off, giving him a meaningful look.

Kasiel nodded.

"I'd rather go with you." An unspoken message hung heavy between them. Wedro didn't want to miss an opportunity for payback.

Kasiel glanced around, spotting Merrin.

"I'll take them up." She took a few steps toward the end of the hall in the direction of the courtyard entrance, a hand on the hilt of her sword.

He looked at the mind-crafters who had offered to

fight. "I need one additional fighter with me."

A tall blond woman stepped forward, hefting an axe she had found somewhere. "I'd be honored to fight with you."

Kasiel nodded. His gaze caught on Jethan. "Be careful."

Merrin grinned. "I won't let anything happen to your tehnaak, Ahninveth. Not after everything we went through to rescue his ass."

Taking her at her word, Kasiel headed toward the stairs at the end of the hall, ignoring the ongoing shouts from the three traitors. Wedro jogged up on one side of him. The woman with the axe came up on the other. Her pale gray eyes shone with a bloodlust as intense as that in Wedro's.

"What's your name?"

"Etris. I'm a Speaker."

"This is Wedro," Kasiel pointed to his other side. When he gestured to himself, she cut him off.

"Ahninveth Hahren Cavenos, or Kasiel to your friends. Your reputation precedes you, sir."

He had a reputation.

He itched to investigate that further, but more important matters required his attention, like making sure Edmund answered for what he had done. Reaching out to the mouse in the laboratory again, he peered out through its eyes as he jogged up the stairs. The disconnected visuals made his stomach turn, something he was becoming a little better at ignoring.

Edmund was still in there with his guards. Now he was tucking the satchel and other items in a hidden space behind a stone in the wall. It looked as if he was preparing to escape with the assumption he could come back when this was over.

At the top of the stairs, Kasiel threw open the door and turned left, breaking into a jog toward where he sensed the mouse. The other two stayed close on his heels, trusting his lead.

The mouse watched Edmund seal up the opening in the wall. One guard pushed aside a bookcase at the back of the room, revealing a hidden door. The man ducked into the dark passage beyond, holding a lantern ahead of him. Edmund followed with the unnoticed mouse on his heels and the other two guards closed the door behind them.

Kasiel ran faster.

They came around the next corner in time to see the same two guards out in the main hall now, locking the door to the laboratory. They brandished their weapons.

"Tight quarters here, Ahninveth," Wedro said. "We'll handle it."

When Etris nodded, Kasiel let them race ahead. He didn't love the stabbing and slicing part all that much anyhow. Holding his sword ready in case they needed him, he sank deeper into the mouse's mind.

The poor rodent bounded along at top speed, racing to keep up with the two men. Fortunately for the little creature, they didn't travel far before they turned a corner and stopped at another door. The guard threw the bolt and pushed it open, letting in bright moonlight as he leaned out. After a few seconds, he nodded and led the way out to a narrow path descending along the cliff behind the castle.

Releasing the mouse, Kasiel reached out again.

"Calloch!" Wedro snarled.

Focusing through his own eyes for a second, he saw Wedro hit the wall, wiping blood from his face before he charged at the guard again. Etris had her opponent on the defensive and had driven him down the hall.

They couldn't let Edmund escape.

Continuing his search, he found one of the large raptors that seemed common to the area and took control.

As he drew the bird toward the castle, he reached out to Niskenya, sending a respectful nudge. For a moment, he feared she might rebuff him as usual, then she let him in, not taking hold as she typically did, but allowing him to choose how much of himself he invested. Slipping in behind her eyes, he encouraged her to look around.

Merrin and several of the rescued mind-crafters were there now, their arrival securing the advantage for the Vanrians. Tath and Darro were fighting together against a desperate mercenary they had backed into a corner. Another mercenary tossed his sword at Kince's feet, his wide eyes locked on Niskenya as he pleaded for mercy. Kince, not the merciful type, kicked the blade away and swung his sword into the man's neck. The rest of the battle appeared to be winding down.

Ignoring his unsettled stomach, Kasiel switched to the raptor, spotting Edmund and the guard making their way along the gradual descent. He passed that information to Niskenya an instant before someone slammed into him. He started falling, bouncing fully back to himself. A hand caught his arm, keeping him from going down as the guard who had run into him hit the stone floor. The man didn't move again once he landed. Getting his feet stable under him, Kasiel looked at Wedro. Now that he was facing him, he could see the fresh cut down Wedro's cheek and through his upper lip that streamed red.

Spitting blood to the side, Wedro said, "Sorry, Ahninveth. Bastard tried to run."

Glancing past him, Kasiel saw the other guard, also on the floor, with the axe buried deep in his chest. Etris leaned against the wall with her hands on her knees, catching her breath.

He looked at Wedro again, wincing at the man's wound. "Put some pressure on that. Etris, see if you can find the keys to the laboratory."

As the two turned to their new tasks, Kasiel returned to the raptor and dove at the guard. The man fell back against the cliff face, trying to avoid the edge and the long drop to the bank of the plunge pool below. Kasiel could sense Niskenya sprinting around the perimeter of the large pool at the base of the falls. All he had to do was delay them a little.

The man swung his sword at the raptor when Kasiel made it dive in a second time. He had expected that, so he let the bird's instincts guide its dodge, narrowly avoiding the blade. When he swept around again, he caught the look of wide-eyed panic on Edmund's face. The professor recognized that this attack wasn't random. He knew Kasiel's ability had returned, and it frightened him. Watching his former father figure retreating from the guard and the bird brought an unexpected surge of malicious satisfaction.

He dove at the guard once more, forcing the man back a few steps in search of a wider place in the path to make a stand. Then a roar sounded behind the raptor. Kasiel swept around, spotting Niskenya as she sprinted from the trees. Despite her size, she didn't miss a step as she galloped up the narrow ledge toward the guard. Edmund turned and ran for the door back into the castle.

The limitations of the restricted space made it harder for Niskenya to reach past the guard's sword. With a snarl of frustration, she swiped out with one paw. His blade made contact with the inside of her leg. Kasiel gasped as he shared the flash of pain from her wound. She carried through despite the injury, striking him in the ribs. Her claws sunk into his armor and the flesh beneath, catching hold and throwing him away from the cliff wall out over the side. His shout ended abruptly when he struck the ground below.

Niskenya continued up after Edmund. The professor

reached the door and ducked back into the passageway, slamming it behind him.

Kasiel returned to himself. Etris had unlocked the door to the laboratory. Wedro stood by the opposite wall, a cloth he had found somewhere pressed to his face. Kasiel jogged over and entered the laboratory, hurrying to the bookshelf in the back. He shoved it aside and opened the door to the hidden passage.

"The kanodrak's not leaving," he called down the dark corridor. Niskenya snarled outside. "You have nowhere else to go, Edmund."

"Kasiel?"

The placating tone, full of false relief, that emerged from the darkness only fueled Kasiel's loathing. He made himself turn away and approach one of the tables. He moved around a few of the flasks and vials containing mysterious alchemical ingredients. Etris went to stand on one side of the passage opening. Wedro stayed in the main doorway, glowering hatred at the professor as he warily emerged with his hands up before him.

"I suggest you keep your thoughts to yourself. I find myself rather low on compassion right now," Kasiel said, not looking at Edmund. He raised his gaze to meet Etris's eyes and switched to Vanrian. "Take him out to the courtyard. The battle's over."

"Yes, Ahninveth." Etris grabbed Edmund's arms, twisting them around behind his back, and escorted him from the room.

Wedro hesitated in the doorway.

"Go with her. I'll be there in a few minutes."

When they left the room, Kasiel jumped to Niskenya for a few seconds. She was backing awkwardly down the path. Irritation surged along their link. He rebuffed it with gratitude. When she got a little closer to the bottom, she leapt off the side, landing with catlike precision. Then she pushed him away, denying him his view from behind her eyes. Kasiel answered her expulsion with a wave of stubborn affection.

He went to the hidden recess in the wall. It took a minute to work the thick stone facing free. Once he did, he raised it high over the floor and dropped it, breaking it in two. Edmund had stashed three flasks of blood in the secret space. He knocked those out, letting them shatter on the broken stone facing. That done, he pulled out the satchel and opened it, skimming briefly through the journals, diagrams, and notes tucked within. Placing the contents back in the satchel, he carried it from the room and out through the main entrance hall.

He drew the raptor in again, sending it to perch on the wall overlooking the courtyard to get a quick glimpse of the scene before he strode out the front door of the castle. In one corner of the courtyard, Tath and Nerith were tending to the wounded. Those who were healthy enough and free of serious injuries were moving bodies off to the opposite side. Except for the healers, everyone ceased what they were doing when he emerged. He stopped and grabbed a torch from alongside the entrance, then walked a few feet from the door and picked out Etris with his gaze where she stood holding Edmund.

"Bring him here."

Edmund lifted his chin in a show of defiance as she pushed him forward. With a forceful knee to the back of his leg, she drove him down to kneel before Kasiel.

Kasiel upended the satchel, dumping its contents onto the ground in front of Edmund.

The professor's eyes widened. "How did you find those?"

"Your bomb didn't work for as long as you might have hoped. I watched you hide them through the eyes of a humble little mouse." He lowered the torch, setting the papers on fire.

"No! My work!"

Edmund struggled against Etris's grip, but the woman was stronger than him, even after being imprisoned and bled who knew how many times. Or maybe it was the hatred the professor had cultivated in her that gave her the strength she needed to hold him.

"Behind you!" Etris shouted.

Kasiel spun, bringing the torch up in time to block Danica's blade with it as she burst through the doorway at him. He kicked out, catching her in the gut and sending her stumbling back. Tossing aside the torch, he drew his sword and leveled it at her.

"You promised you wouldn't come back here." She raised her blade, ready to fight him.

At one time, he would have assumed she could beat him. That was no longer true. Still, he had no desire to fight her. He lowered his sword. "I lied, Dani. I had to."

Tears broke free, streaming down her cheeks. Jethan walked past him and took her sword from her. She didn't resist. Darro, Kince, Merrin, and Avris joined them. Only Merrin appeared to have escaped the fighting unscathed, though a knot in Kasiel's gut unwound upon seeing that none of them looked seriously injured.

Danica hugged her arms across her chest and lowered her eyes.

Avris scowled at her and spoke to him in Vanrian, effectively blocking Danica out of their conversation. "What do you want us to do with her and the professor?"

"Bind and gag the professor. He's earned a trip to Vanris." Kasiel eyed Danica for a moment. "The servants are in the kitchen. Bring them out here and put her with them. We can let them go when we leave. Then burn everything. I want all traces of his research destroyed."

"What about the traitors in the cells below?" Etris asked.

"Leave them. They earned their fate."

No one disagreed.

Niskenya came up behind them then. Kasiel glanced down at her leg. The cut was still bleeding. He looked around at his companions. "I need to have her tended to."

Jethan put a hand on his shoulder. "Go, tehnaak. We can handle all of this."

He turned to leave, then glanced back, deliberately not looking at Danica. "Oh, and if we can send someone out to get Niske's saddle and untie the horses, I can bring them back here. We're going to need all of them."

Darro nodded. "Consider it done."

"Thank you." He guided Niskenya over to where they were still caring for injuries, not the least of which was the gash down Wedro's face that Tath was now working on.

Nerith saw them coming. Her trained healer's eyes promptly spotted the bleeding wound on the kanodrak's leg. She also gave Kasiel a visual once-over on her way to them.

"I'm fine. It's Niske that needs your care."

"Will she let me?"

The kanodrak lowered her head and shifted her stance, bringing the leg forward to provide easier access.

"I would say yes." Kasiel turned to Wedro as Nerith leaned down to inspect the wound. "Don't worry. I've been told facial scars make you more attractive."

Wedro breathed a tired laugh. "Calloch."

"Don't move, don't talk, and don't laugh," Tath hissed, giving Kasiel a chastising look.

"Sorry."

Kasiel wasn't sorry, though. He'd gotten a chuckle from Wedro. When the charge of battle had fully worn off, the grief of Chander's death would come crashing back in. For this moment, however, they could just be victorious.

CHAPTER TWENTY ONE

By the time they were ready to depart, flames licked out of nearly every window of the castle. An explosion of alchemical bombs had blown out a section of the wall, sending debris cascading over the cliff and causing a portion of the upper levels to collapse. The servants looked on, huddled together and cowering any time the Vanrians approached. They refused to accept that they would be spared, even when his unit set food and supplies aside for them while collecting goods from the castle to manage their increased numbers on the journey home. They mourned the loss of the place that had been their home and dreaded their perceived future.

Kasiel's group needed sixteen extra mounts with the addition of fifteen rescued mind-crafters and Edmund. Fortunately, they had acquired fourteen horses from the Alliance soldiers guarding the wagon and the wagon itself. They found more in the castle stable. Jethan took Chander's mount, an arrangement Wedro seemed able to tolerate, though his brief glimmer of better humor had long vanished. Niskenya objected loudly when Kasiel suggested riding a horse for a time to avoid worsening the cut on her leg. For now, he yielded to her terms on the condition that they brought an extra animal along in case her feelings on the situation changed later.

As they were getting those most in need of assistance

mounted, Danica ventured away from the group of servants and approached Kasiel. She stopped several feet back when Niskenya moved protectively close to him and growled.

He placed a hand on the kanodrak's neck. "It's all right, Niske. She's a friend." Was she anymore? She had tried to attack him, not that he could entirely blame her under the circumstances.

Niskenya huffed her skepticism, though she didn't follow when he moved closer to Danica.

"You can't leave us like this," she insisted.

He took a deep breath, searching for the objectivity that their long history sought to deny him. "You can follow the road or wait for the Alliance to send someone. They'll be looking for their elixirs soon, I imagine, and this smoke is bound to draw attention. Trust me, it's better this way."

"Is it?" she snapped.

"Yes. You're tired, Dani. When this is all over, you'll see that I was right." He tried to believe the words as he spoke them, but the haunted look in her eyes made him uneasy.

"Of course, I'm tired, Kas. I've been plagued with nightmares since Katovan. I don't even have to be asleep to have them anymore."

A burst of powerful dread twisted his gut. "Were you there when the other Alliance troops arrived?"

She nodded. "We had just gotten clear of them when the horrors came. I've never experienced anything so awful." A visible shudder moved through her. "I can't seem to get it out of my head. One of Edmund's mercenaries said your side brought a Frightener in."

The same Frightener, in fact, who had filled his head with terrors at one point. "And Edmund, does he have nightmares too?"

"I don't think so. He was unconscious when we

took him out of there." She glanced toward where Edmund sat on a horse, his hands bound tightly in front of him. Her brows pinched together. "What does that have to do with any of this?"

He remembered what Setera had said. If she hadn't extracted the memory of his encounter with his father's ability, it would drive him mad until he killed himself, or they had to terminate him for the safety of those around him. He glanced back, spotting Jethan, who had come up to stand near Niskenya, watching him as intently as the kanodrak was. With a quick jerk of his head, Kasiel beckoned him over.

"We need another horse."

Jethan frowned and answered in Vanrian. "She can't come with us."

Kasiel switched to Vanrian as well. Danica shouldn't be privy to everything they said. "Do we have any Evokers among the mind-crafters here?"

Jethan's eyes narrowed. "No. Mostly Speakers, Charmers, and Enkindlers, one Dampener, and a Frightener. Why?"

"She was in Katovan when my father went to confront the Alliance company there. She's got the same problem I had, and there's only one way to fix that."

Jethan glanced over at her, a flicker of pity in his eyes. Still, he shook his head. "You have to let her go, Kas. It's not your problem."

"He's right." Darro strode up, shamelessly acknowledging that he had been listening in. "We've got to go. Her situation's unfortunate, but we can't fix it."

Kasiel met Darro's eyes. "How do you think I escaped the castle without my ability?"

"What do you mean, escaped here?" Jethan asked, his brow bunching up like a drawn curtain.

"I'll tell you about it later," Kasiel answered, keeping his intent gaze on Darro.

"Shit." Darro blew out a heavy exhalation. "You know she'll be hated in Vanris. It will be miserable for her, assuming they don't kill her outright."

"She's already miserable, and it's going to keep getting worse," Kasiel countered.

Darro stepped away and waved to Merrin, who stood near the stable entrance. "Hey, Merrin, get another horse ready."

"Consider it done," she called back.

"Well, this should at least be interesting." Darro shook his head and strode away.

Danica took a tentative step closer to Jethan. "What's going on?"

Kasiel found her choice to approach his tehnaak instead of him a little unsettling. Jethan appeared to feel the same. He retreated a pace, deferring to Kasiel with a glance.

Flipping back to Pandrean Common, Kasiel said, "You're coming to Vanris."

"I don't want to go to Vanris." Her gaze flickered up to his exposed ear with the symbolic cuff attached and abruptly away again. She stared at her hands.

So that was it. Not his coloring or his tattoos or his mindcraft. It was his cut ears that finally drove her to accept that he had always been one of *them*. The enemy.

A flash of irritation swept through him. "We can get rid of the nightmares in Vanris, or you can stay here where they'll continue to get worse. It's up to you." He strode back and swung up on Niskenya, getting a spark of satisfaction from the way Danica's eyes widened when he did so.

When they struck out a short time later, Danica mounted up and followed.

·

By late the second afternoon, they were close enough to the border that the trees had thinned considerably. Kasiel led them as far as he dared, stopping them while they still had adequate cover to avoid notice until they made their run for the Break after dark. Even the weakest and most injured among them were sufficiently eager to get home that they had pushed for speed on the way here. With Niskenya selecting the best routes through the rocky landscape, and Kasiel using birds to scout ahead for danger and help guide their path, they had made excellent time. Now they simply had to wait for nightfall.

Edmund had earned himself a shallow cut across his throat to match the faint scar in the same place on Kasiel's neck. A sharp reminder to keep his mouth shut unless he fancied wearing a gag. Unlike the mercenaries who had treated Kasiel far less kindly, he allowed Edmund to travel without the gag if he followed the rules and didn't talk to anyone. That included Danica. With everyone else speaking primarily Vanrian, and Edmund off limits, she kept to herself. Not a prisoner, but still an outsider among them. With her as angry with him as she was now, Kasiel wasn't willing to risk Edmund convincing her to free him.

Kasiel was checking Niskenya's leg at their last rest stop before the Crimson Break when Nerith came up behind him.

"How is she?"

He glanced over his shoulder at her and stepped to one side, gesturing to the leg. "You're the healer."

Nerith leaned in to take a closer look. While she did so, Kasiel glanced around the group, a slight tightening of apprehension in his chest until he spotted Jethan off talking to a few of the rescued mind-crafters. The tightness eased a little.

"Are you all right, Kas?"

He managed to hide a mild startle. "Yes."

"You've kept yourself apart since we left the castle."

She wasn't wrong. He had watched Tath, Nerith, and now Wedro suffer through the losses of their teh-naaks. After losing Sylaryth and Kitrix himself, and nearly losing Jethan too, he had developed a constant need to track where his tehnaak was. He took a moment to locate the others as well, spotting Darro, Kince, Wedro, Tath, Merrin, and Avris before he could relax enough to answer her.

"I'm just focused on getting everyone across the border safe."

"Mm-hmm." She moved closer, drawing his gaze down to her.

"And having Edmund here is... unsettling."

"You can't escape the hatred and resentment with him here, can you?" She took another step closer. Her fingers brushed along his cheek in a light caress.

"No," he murmured, her lavender eyes drawing him in. He slid a hand back into her hair, letting his thumb trace the line of her jaw as he did so. "Not really."

The camp disappeared when she smiled and closed the remaining distance, capturing his lips in an ardent kiss. Her passion burned through him, making him yearn for more of her, and offering him an escape from his worries. Moving his other hand to the small of her back, he pulled her close, delighting in the shape of her pressed against him. His fingers traced a light line down her neck, eliciting a soft moan as he deepened the kiss.

"Want me to see if I can find an inn out here for you two?" Kince teased as he strolled past them, breaking the moment.

The comment earned light laughter from a few others around the camp. Kasiel drew back from her, appreciating the slight flush that warmed her cheeks.

"There are plenty of downed trees out here," Darro

added. "We could probably throw something together for you."

Kasiel shook his head at his companions, arching a brow at Darro for how far up on his thigh Tath's hand rested. Tath answered his look with a smirk and a good-natured wink. Then Kasiel's attention drifted to Danica, sitting off to one side by herself, knees pulled in to her chest. When their eyes met, she averted her gaze. He clenched his teeth and glanced away as well. Right now, he couldn't afford to become caught up in her plight.

"You were checking Niske's leg before you so effectively distracted me," he said, turning back to Nerith.

"It's as good as can be expected. It would be better if she could rest it, but that's not really an option now."

"If I wasn't riding her—"

Niske growled.

Kasiel gave the kanodrak a hard look, but the kanodrak was never wrong. Adnar told him that. If only that argument would hold up when they took him to task for bringing her along.

"Come with me."

He moved his hand into Nerith's and turned to lead her toward where Kince, Tath, and Darro had settled. Merrin, Avris, and Wedro were there too now. He caught Jethan's eye, beckoning for him to join them.

"So, will you be reporting all of this to the khevarin?" he asked.

She leaned into him, giving him a gentle nudge with her shoulder. "I have a funny feeling we'll all be telling Ahninveth Setera about this."

He squeezed her hand. "Seems likely."

As they gathered, several of the rescued mind-crafters also moved in closer. Jethan sat on Kasiel's other side. Simply having him there made Kasiel feel more complete. He was starting to understand what getting him back must have been like for his tehnaak. That concept of being whole again made more sense now.

"How do you want to approach the crossing?" Darro asked, skillfully predicting his purpose in bringing them together, although Kasiel had hoped to ask them that, rather than be the one put on the spot to answer the question.

He looked around at them all. Several nursed injuries or still suffered weakness from being bled near to death by Edmund. They also had the professor to keep in mind. Their prisoner.

"I had considered taking our strongest fighters to draw out the guards at the nearest watchtower while the rest of the group makes a run for the Break. Given how limited Edmund's production of his elixir was, there's a chance they won't have any here. Though, however we do this, we should proceed with the assumption that they do."

Darro's lips curved in an approving smile. "My thoughts exactly. We send a few fighters with the injured and our prisoners in case they run into trouble. The rest—"

"Danica isn't a prisoner," Kasiel interrupted.

"It's on you to convince them of that in Vanris, Ahninveth." Darro glanced at Danica, giving a small shake of his head. She scowled at him, and he winked at her before turning back to the conversation. "Regardless, we should take our best fighters out first and see if we can keep the watchtower guards busy. They'll get a signal off. We probably can't prevent that. But if we don't waste time, we should be able to get far enough into the Break that any reinforcements can't catch us."

"Exactly." Kasiel opted to let the subject of Danica go for now. Convincing Vanris not to imprison her when he was already in trouble for taking Niskenya was going to be difficult. The alternative was to leave her here and let his father's ability slowly drive her mad. Not much of a choice. "The wildcats I used before should still be in the area. I can bring them in to help us or send them with the other group."

Kince arched a brow at him. "So, you intend to help with the watchtower guards?"

"Shouldn't I?" Truthfully, he didn't want to fight more, but he would do what was necessary to see them safely home.

"It's your mission. For my part, I think you can handle it."

Kince's show of confidence surprised Kasiel a little. Next to him, Jethan shifted, a thoughtful frown tugging at the corners of his mouth. "What is it, tehnaak?"

"What if we send the other group out first to draw out the guards, then the second group can charge in to attack them after they emerge from the tower? That would give us a chance to surprise them and maybe even pick a few off with crossbows before engaging. Tath and Kince are both dead shots."

Darro was nodding. "I like that better. Gives us an advantageous position in addition to catching them by surprise."

"Then we'll do that, though you'll be with the group heading for the Break." He gave his tehnaak a stern look to discourage any argument.

Jethan scowled. "I don't like not being able to help more."

"You're not in top shape, and I'm unwilling to risk you right now. I hope you can forgive me for that later." Kasiel dredged up a grin for him, trying to hide his own unease. It had been easier to ignore his doubts when he had that all-consuming drive to rescue his tehnaak. Now that they were together again, his fear of failing them all gained potency. "Besides, I'm counting on you to save me from Adnar and the khevarin when we get back to Vanris."

Jethan gave him a wry smile. "I think I'd rather take my chances with the Alliance guards."

The uneasy laughter that met that comment heightened Kasiel's dread. The dhomvalen had sent them, but he had no part in the decision to take Niskenya. Still, they had to make it that far before it became an issue. Pushing those thoughts aside, he drew them into the process of deciding who would ride with what group. Once they figured out the teams, he brought up the last point that concerned him. Edmund.

He eyed them all, hoping his solemn expression adequately conveyed the gravity of his next words. "For those of you making the run for the Break, if it looks like there's the slightest chance the professor might fall into Alliance hands at any point, I need you to kill him. Don't let them take him back."

Edmund cleared his throat. "I would prefer—"

Kasiel cut him off with a glare that overflowed with loathing, though knowing he had been following their conversation in Vanrian formed a lump of ice in his gut. Edmund scowled back, but he didn't finish his sentence. Several uneasy looks told Kasiel he wasn't the only one disturbed by the professor's apparent knowledge of their language. Yet one more thing he had hidden from Kasiel as he was raising him.

Wedro was staring daggers at Edmund. "Don't worry, Ahninveth. I promise you they won't take him back alive."

The murder in the other man's eyes, made more convincing by the stitched wound on his face, might have bothered Kasiel another time. At that moment, he found it reassuring.

"Good. Let's all try to get some rest before dark."

After deciding who would take which watch shifts, the gathering dispersed. Nerith and Jethan met each other's eyes. Whatever passed between them in that glance, she excused herself. Jethan walked with him to where Niskenya had settled in to rest.

"I'm impressed by how much you've taken charge, Kas, especially for a Feral. When we first rescued you, I wasn't sure you had it in you."

Kasiel gave him a sideways glance. "What difference does being a Feral make?"

Jethan sat down and leaned against a tree while Kasiel settled next to Niskenya. The kanodrak moved her head closer to his leg, and he placed a hand on the bone plating that extended along the back of her neck. Jethan's gaze followed every part of their silent interaction.

"I don't know if you've noticed, but neither Adnar nor Kenna spend as much time with their tehnaaks as they do with their beasts, and not just because it's their job. They prefer it. That's how Ferals learn to work on the battlefield too, apart from human troops, always running their beasts. The connection Ferals have with the creatures they work with is, in some ways, more intimate than the bond they have with their tehnaak. It draws them apart from everyone else, makes them almost a little wild themselves." Jethan lowered his gaze, picking at the dead evergreen needles that carpeted the ground. "Part of me was a little worried about that when your ability awakened."

Kasiel considered his words, not wanting to cheapen Jethan's concerns with an impulsive response. His mental connection with Sylaryth had been something intimate and familiar in a way his bond with Jethan couldn't be. That was even more true with Niskenya. That didn't mean Jethan wasn't his foundation, or anything less than a vital part of who he was becoming. Did it? His tehnaak was the constant that gave him the courage and drive to keep pushing forward.

Before he could speak, he felt a polite tug on his awareness. Relenting, he let Niskenya pull him in behind her eyes. She lifted her head and looked across the camp at Kince and Darro. A strand of warm violet light extended between the two. It was the same with Avris and Merrin and the few pairings that had ended up in Edmund's prison together. The brightness of that violet light varied from pairing to pairing, but it was always present.

Niskenya got up then and started walking away. Several feet out, she stopped and looked back at him and Jethan, at the vivid violet light that connected them, shining like a beacon in the darkness. It was breathtaking.

Then the kanodrak passed a sense of hunger across the link and kicked Kasiel out of her head before loping off.

Kasiel grinned. "I don't think you have anything to worry about, tehnaak. Our bond is stronger than you realize. And this experience has given me a great deal of respect for what you must have gone through when you led the mission to retrieve me. Now," he said, reclining back in the dirt, "get some rest. We've got a potentially harrowing night ahead."

CHAPTER TWENTY TWO

They would come out closer to the watchtower this time. The dry forest stretched farther north there, allowing them to stay hidden within the limited tree cover longer. Since they wanted the tower's attention, it didn't matter that they would be making their move directly under the guards' noses this time. Wedro was ready to guide the team with the injured, including Jethan and their prisoner, into the slot canyons. Three of the ten mind-crafters with that group were in good enough condition to fight if needed. Danica was also, but no one wanted her armed, so Kasiel ignored her request for a weapon. He had an owl waiting to scout ahead of them and watch for danger in the narrow passages.

Kasiel had drawn on the family of wildcats, bringing the group into the shade of a rock overhang near the tower. The Alliance guards were unlikely to pay them any mind so long as they were merely lounging there. If the time came that he needed the cats to move in, the guards would already have other problems to occupy their attention. He primarily wanted the beasts in range to deal with local patrols or scouts that might be near enough to hear the tower's horn and reach them before the battle was over.

Once dark had fallen, Wedro's team prepared to split off and start their run first. Nerith would go with them.

Kasiel wanted a healer with each group, and he liked the idea of keeping Nerith and Jethan together, out of the fighting if possible. They would also be there to make sure Wedro didn't decide to pick off Edmund in the excitement. Edmund deserved it, but his fate was to be placed in the hands of the khevarin to answer for the wrongs he had committed against the people of Vanris.

Before they parted, Nerith braided back the side of Kasiel's hair again and helped him put the symbolic ear cuffs on.

"The perfect image of a Vanrian warrior." Jethan offered a nod of approval as he admired her finished work. "Be careful out there, Kas."

"What he said." Nerith leaned in and gave him a lingering kiss that sparked a flood of desire in him despite, or perhaps because of, the stressful circumstances. She placed a finger to his lips before she backed away, her mischievous smile telling him she knew what kind of reaction she had gotten. "There are many more of those waiting on the other side."

The other side, where they would throw him in the deeps for the rest of his life if they didn't execute him outright for taking Niskenya. How much would the rescued mind-crafters and the professor balance out that offense?

"Do me a favor, look out for each other." He glanced over to where Edmund waited on his mount, his hands bound. Somehow, the man still appeared smug as he regarded them all. Kasiel hoped he was at least quivering with fear on the inside. "As much as I'd like to see the professor take an arrow to the throat, try to get him across alive too."

"Don't worry about us." Jethan pulled him in for a brief hug. "We know what we need to do. You focus on your part."

Wedro joined them, the stitched cut on his face still

somewhat swollen, distorting his features. "Time to go."

"You're comfortable leading them through the canyons?" Kasiel asked.

"No. I've changed my mind." He smirked, then winced as the expression tugged on his cut lip. "Stop worrying, Ahninveth. I'll get them to our side. Just make sure you get your group there too."

He offered his arm. Kasiel took it in a warrior's handshake and immediately drew him into a quick hug. "No more injuries."

"You don't have to tell me twice." Wedro returned the embrace for a second, then pulled back and looked at Nerith and Jethan. With a jerk of his head, he gestured toward their waiting horses. "Come on."

Kasiel watched them mount up before heading over to where his group was getting ready. He swung up on one of the spare horses they had prepared for him, shifting around in the saddle to try getting comfortable there. The animal was shorter and narrower than Niskenya. It felt fragile by comparison. He was going to have to deal with it. Doing it this way would give the kanodrak increased freedom to fight, though he didn't like risking her again. No matter how often he tried to convince himself they could pull this off without her, they all recognized that she was their greatest asset in battle, injured or not.

He thought he understood now why she had objected to him switching to a horse before. Being separated from her made him uneasy. It was shocking how fast he had become accustomed to the comfort and security of her presence.

Niskenya, sitting a few yards away, glanced over at him. Her claws flexed, digging into the dirt. A hunger passed through their connection. Not for food this time, but for conflict. He didn't get the sense that she craved this battle as much as she was impatient to bring an end to the confrontation ahead of them. In that, he wholeheartedly agreed. The time had come to start the fight, so they could progress past this point of dreadful anticipation.

Kasiel closed his eyes and breathed in, inhaling the warm, dusty scent of the desert. The sound of hooves crunching on the gritty ground filled his ears as the first team moved out. He touched on the wildcats, the horses, Niskenya, and the owl waiting overhead. Slipping behind the eyes of the owl, he flew up, scanning the vicinity for patrols and other dangers. It was the sixth time he had done so in the last hour. Two pairs of soldiers patrolling east and west along the border had checked in about twenty minutes ago. They would be far out on their routes, heading away from the tower and not due to turn around anytime soon. At a full gallop, they could cover that distance in little time depending on the footing, so they remained a potential threat. The pair scouting the nearby slot canyons had started back from their circuit shortly before the others checked in at the tower. That meant they would arrive at the tower any second now.

Using the owl, he spotted the two guards riding from the canyons toward the watchtower. They were perhaps two minutes away. Reaching out with his ability, he stopped Wedro's horse. Opening his eyes, he saw the first team now halted, with Wedro at the front trying to kick his mount forward. When the animal didn't move, he looked back at Kasiel, figuring it out fast.

Kasiel held up two fingers.

Wedro nodded.

Signaling the others to follow, Kasiel urged his mount forward, moving into place to start their advance from almost directly behind the tower. They had the Dampener with them. If the guards weren't fortunate enough to have Edmund's elixir, she would be an extremely valuable asset. If they did have it, she would still be a useful fighter, but they would have to rely entirely on physical combat with the help of Niskenya and the wildcats. The other team had the Frightener, but he was one of those more recently bled. They wouldn't ask him to do much unless that group encountered significant trouble.

The patrol rode up to the tower and dismounted by the stable. Kasiel released Wedro's horse, signaling the other team to advance again. When they reached the point at which the trees thinned out to almost nothing, the group kicked their horses up to a gallop, sprinting for the border and the slot canyons beyond. Kasiel's party moved out, heading toward the tower at a slower pace for the moment to avoid catching anyone's notice too soon.

It was less than a minute before the noise of pounding hooves in the darkness had drawn attention. A horn blared from the tower and the two soldiers who had just returned from their patrol came around the side, already up on their horses again. They hesitated there, choosing not to pursue yet. Not a surprising decision, given that Wedro's group had a total of fifteen riders. Kasiel had ten with Avris, Merrin, Kince, Darro, Tath, and five of the rescued mind-crafters. The Alliance soldiers had no way of knowing that over half of those riding with Wedro weren't in any condition to put up a fight. With the uneven odds, they were wisely waiting for help, but shouts from the tower promised it was coming.

One of the two guards raised a shortbow. That was Kasiel's cue to intervene. As his group kicked their mounts up to a gallop, Niskenya surging ahead of them, he reached out to the two guards' horses. Both animals reared, and the archer dropped his arrow to grab his reins. Five more Alliance soldiers came charging out of the stable on horseback and Kasiel seized control of their mounts too, slowing his own horse to let the rest of his group pull ahead of him. Darro and Merrin took the lead while he turned part of his attention to looking through the eyes of the owl flying out with the first team.

Wedro's group was over the border and sprinting out into the Break toward the slot canyons. He swept wide once with the bird, scanning for threats, then jumped fully back to himself in time to see an archer near the stable firing an arrow at him. He twisted, and it struck his chest at an angle, deflected away by one of the dark metal plates on his armor. Heart pounding, he glanced back to see the archer calmly nocking a second arrow. Niskenya surged out of the night behind the man. A swipe of one massive paw sent him flying from the saddle.

In minutes, it became impossible for the Alliance soldiers to even consider pursuing the first group. All of them were on the ground now, having either jumped clear of or been thrown from their mounts. Kasiel sent their horses galloping away to prevent the soldiers from trying to use them again. His companions and the men from the watchtower, more of whom had come sprinting out of the structure, were engaged in full combat now. Kasiel kicked his mount forward, ready to join the fray, when fire erupted behind him.

The blast knocked the animal's rear legs out from under it and threw Kasiel from the saddle. He hit the ground hard, then rolled and jumped to his feet, tasting blood. Something warm and wet streamed down the side of his face. His horse struggled, trying to stand with both hind legs shattered by the blast. Its tail burned along with the brush within a radius of about two yards around where the firebomb had struck behind them.

Seven Alliance soldiers were charging his way. He

had missed them on his aerial searches with the birds. They could have been tracking his group for a while or simply been in the vicinity, hidden from view by the trees. Not that it mattered now.

The leader pointed at him. "That's the Warden's son! Take him down now!"

Kasiel drew his sword and channeled his own fear and surprise into their mounts. The horses reared and bucked, one twisting in the air so violently that horse and rider went over together. Kasiel strode toward them, rage moving in behind the fear he had used on their animals. On his way past, he thrust his blade into his horse's neck, putting the poor creature out of its misery. When he looked up, the Alliance group's leader was back on his feet after being thrown, his sword out, staring daggers at Kasiel. The man sneered and charged him.

They met in the midst of the fire that still hungrily consumed patches of sparse dry grass and brush. Flames danced along the ground toward the stable, searching for more robust fuel.

Kasiel lifted his lip in a silent snarl as he met the leader's charge. The first strike came fast. He deflected it but didn't have time to counter. The Alliance soldier was agile and strong, the intercepted swing vibrating up through Kasiel's shoulders. If that weren't concerning enough, the man's allies were free of their horses now and advancing, except for the one who had fallen with his horse and still lay in the dirt clutching a badly busted leg.

Blocking the Alliance soldier's attacks a few more times was already causing Kasiel's arms to fatigue. He needed an opening. Leaping back from a strike gave his muscles a momentary reprieve, but it also provided an opportunity for one of the other men to take a swing at him.

Knowing he couldn't bring his sword between them in time, he tried twisting to avoid the weapon. As he did so, a crossbow bolt whistled past and plunged into the soldier's cheek at a slight angle, bursting out the other side below his temple in a spray of blood and shattered bone. The man staggered back, his sword falling from his hands. Adding that to the list of sights he wished he had never seen, Kasiel spun to block another strike from his original opponent.

With a roar, Niskenya charged past them, a whirlwind of claws and teeth diving into the remaining four Alliance soldiers. The leader faltered, hesitating for a heartbeat at the panicked shouting and screams of his comrades rising in the night behind him. It was one heartbeat too many. Kasiel lunged, dodging the man's distracted block, and swung the dark metal blade into the side of his neck below the edge of his helm. The weapon sliced clear through, as if cutting a sheet of parchment. The leader's body wavered a moment after his head had fallen, then it toppled forward, forcing Kasiel to sidestep out of the way.

"Kas!" Avris jogged over to him, Merrin close behind her.

He focused on her, noticing that the surrounding landscape wasn't entirely steady in his vision. She cringed, reaching toward his head, then seemed to reconsider and pulled her hand back. Niskenya came up beside him, blood dripping from her jaws and spattered over her neck and chest. There appeared to be a few bits of flesh caught her in claws. His stomach turned unpleasantly.

"Is everyone all right?" he asked, his voice echoing in his head from a thousand miles away.

Avris narrowed her eyes at him. "At least as all right as you. We beat them, but we need to get out of here. Can you ride?"

Niskenya huffed softly.

Wavering a little, he wiped his sword clean on the dead man's surcoat and sheathed it. He missed the stirrup twice before managing to climb up on the kanodrak.

"That's a dubious yes, then." Avris turned to Merrin, gesturing to where their horses waited. "Let's go."

As they hurried away, Tath came riding over, eyeing Kasiel critically. "You've got a bit of a bleeder going there." She leaned back and pulled a piece of cloth out of her pack. "If you can manage it, try to put some pressure on that until we get someplace where I can do more for it." She handed him the cloth. "How do you feel?"

"I'm all right." Truthfully, he was dizzy, and his chest was tight, but he didn't see where it made a difference. They had to move. He pressed the fabric to the source of the blood still streaming down the side of his face.

"Sure, you are. Just stay close. Let me know if you start to feel like you might throw up or can't keep your balance."

The rest of them mounted quickly, eager to get away from the aftermath of the battle. His horse appeared to be the only one they lost. Etris had retrieved the packs off the animal and attached them behind her saddle. As one of their rescues, she had no gear of her own to carry.

The fire from the bomb had spread into the stables. Just as Kasiel reached out to see if any horses were still in there, six animals came bolting out, Kince chasing after them. He grinned at Darro as he sprinted to his own mount and swung up. The blaze would find plentiful fuel in the stable and make its way from there into the attached tower. Kasiel hoped it didn't spread too far beyond that, but they could do little about it now. The Alliance soldiers had set their own land and building on fire.

Reaching out to the owl, he spotted the first team still moving steadily through the slot canyon toward

Vanris. They weren't supposed to stop until they were within sight of a Vanrian watchtower. The wildcats he had lost connection with when the firebomb went off. Not being stupid animals, they had taken the opportunity to flee the chaos and return to their den. Fortunately, they hadn't needed the beasts for this fight.

He glanced around the group. One of the mindcrafters was favoring an arm, and another had a cut on her thigh, though it didn't appear to be deep. Darro had a split and swollen lower lip and a black eye. He looked more like he had gotten into a tavern brawl. When Kasiel received nods from all of them, he encouraged Niskenya to make for home. The kanodrak took off at a steady lope, working to minimize the bounce in her movement to help Kasiel keep pressure on his head wound.

As the brisk evening air parted around him, he could feel Niskenya's pain almost more acutely than he did his own. He experienced the warmth of blood trickling down the inside of her leg and from the opposite shoulder as vividly as if the wounds were in his own flesh. He drew a deep breath and sank his awareness into her, absorbing a portion of her discomfort. Her strength and determination flowed to him in response, helping him to stay upright in the saddle as much as his muscles did.

After a time, his arms grew too fatigued to keep pressure on the head injury, so he gave up trying. The cloth disappeared. He suspected he had dropped it somewhere along the way. With all the blood on it, a desert beast would undoubtedly make a snack of it. His wound had stopped bleeding at some point, as had both of Niskenya's, which told him they weren't too deep. It felt as though an eternity passed before they emerged from the slot canyon on the other side to find the first group waiting there for them.

Kasiel slid off Niskenya's back. He staggered when he landed, barely catching himself. In an instant, Jethan was there, supporting him with an enthusiastic embrace.

"We're not splitting up again, tehnaak," Jethan said, relief and a hint of anger giving a raw edge to his voice.

When he stepped back, Nerith moved in, scowling briefly at the trail of dried blood down his face. "At least you didn't lose these." She flicked one of the ear cuffs, trying to mask the worry that shone in her eyes.

Tension rippled through the group at the sound of approaching riders. A trio of Vanrian watchtower guards emerged from the darkness. Kasiel stepped forward, the action intended to bring their attention to him. With Niskenya behind him, the effort was unnecessary.

One of them gave him a gruff nod. "Ahninveth Hahren, it looks as if some of you are in need of healing. Our tower isn't far. You can take a couple of hours to deal with injuries and rest before we escort you to the city."

Escort?

It surprised him a little that they weren't trying to arrest him now, though it would be a poor choice with Niskenya there.

"How did you spot us in the dark?" His head throbbed when he spoke.

"All the towers have been on high alert, watching for you, but you were nice enough to announce your arrival for us." The guard glanced toward the south, and Kasiel turned to see the gleaming speck of the burning Alliance watchtower in the distance.

His thoughts fragmented, refusing to help him come up with anything useful to say, so he settled for, "You're welcome."

Avris covered a giggle with one hand, then stepped forward. "Just to keep the record straight, we did not set their tower on fire. They did that all by themselves with a firebomb."

The guard looked them over, his gaze lingering on

Edmund and Danica, one southerner bound, the other not. "Good to know. Whatever else you have to report, save it for the khevarin. This is well above my rank."

CHAPTER TWENTY THREE

The Vanrian watchtower guards gave them a generous few hours to care for injuries and rest, sending them on their way a little before dawn with a token escort of two soldiers. Given the events at the Pandrean Alliance tower across the Break, they didn't want to reduce their numbers beyond that and leave this tower more vulnerable than necessary.

Niskenya allowed Nerith to tend to her wounds, but when it came time to depart, she adamantly refused to let Kasiel ride one of the horses. Fighting her was pointless. He couldn't force her to come with them, and she wouldn't move unless he climbed on board. It appeared the kanodrak really was always right.

As they prepared to cover the last stretch home, the weight of their journey, the stress, and all the fighting they had done crashed down on Kasiel, compounding the ache in his head, in his entire body. Everything they had accomplished. The loss of Chander. The uncertainty that waited for them back in Etrion. All he could do was hope the backlash of his bringing Niskenya with them didn't fall too heavily on the shoulders of his companions. They may have opted to travel with him after he showed up with the kanodrak, but it was his choice alone to bring her. His and Niskenya's.

Danica glowered at him when they mounted up, so

he made a point of riding out ahead of her where he couldn't see her. At the recommendation of the watchtower guards, they tied her hands the way they had Edmund's. Arriving in Etrion with a free southerner in their midst, especially under the circumstances, had the potential to worsen their reception. They ignored Danica's fierce objections to being bound, and Darro silenced her by threatening to gag her if she didn't play along nicely. As guilty as Kasiel felt about putting her through it, he knew better than to believe they had much choice in the matter.

The sun was up when they reached Etrion, and Kasiel moved to the front of the group to lead his unit and their acquisitions home. He still wore the braids and ear cuffs. Regardless of what he had done wrong, he was Vanrian, and he had earned his place here. He would not ride meekly to the gate, not with a group of rescued mind-crafters and his tehnaak behind him.

The wall guards spotted them from far enough away that a sizeable company of soldiers rode out and surrounded them before they came under the shadow of the gates. With that escort in place, they continued to the entrance where Dhomen Branith and several of his city guards waited on their mounts, blocking the way in.

If the dhomen thought anything of the rescued mind-crafters and the southern prisoners in their party, his wary regard didn't show it. "Ahninveth Hahren Cavenos, you will come with us around to the kanodrak habitat. The rest of you will be escorted directly to the palace. Anyone who resists in any way will be subdued and thrown immediately into the deeps." He narrowed his eyes at Kasiel. "Is that understood?"

Kanodraks were too large for the lift and the tunnel passage between the canyons, so they had little choice other than to take him around to the habitat outside the walls. As much as he dreaded parting ways with Niskenya, the time had come for him to do so.

Kasiel inclined his head, unable to keep the weariness from his voice when he spoke. "Yes, Dhomen Branith."

At a curt gesture from the dhomen, Kasiel and Niskenya turned to ride to the outer habitat entrance. Branith and four guards fell in around him. He considered letting the guard horses panic at the nearness of the kanodrak, but it would serve no purpose beyond a moment of petty vindictiveness. The instant the animals started reacting to the massive predator, he calmed them, earning a gruff nod of gratitude from Branith.

Kasiel didn't look back at the others as he left, not even at Jethan. This wasn't the time to emphasize the closeness of the unit or give any of them a chance to offer him expressions of support. For now, some separation between him and the rest of them might work out in their favor.

"Will they be arrested, Dhomen?" Kasiel asked as they rode around the city, heading for the habitat entrance.

Branith gave him a sideways glance. "Everyone who left here with you will be arrested pending an investigation. The other Vanrians, some of our missing mind-crafters it appears, will be questioned and held under supervision until the investigation is complete. As for the two southern prisoners, knowing nothing about them or why you brought them here, I can only say they will be imprisoned at least until this is sorted."

"Thank you, Dhomen." He didn't feel like talking beyond that, preferring to finish the ride in silence.

Adnar waited inside the gate, mounted on his bonded kanodrak. Kasiel felt him attempt to touch Niskenya's mind as they approached, but she rebuffed him decisively. The ahndhomen's glower deepened in response. He let Kasiel and Niskenya in, his gaze homing in on the stitched wounds on her shoulder and her leg. Kasiel's injuries held no apparent interest for him. He turned away the guards with a curt dismissal. As they departed, he snapped one arm out, pointing toward the front of the canyon.

Niskenya broke into a casual lope. Kasiel could feel that she was as weary and sore as he was, but when he encouraged her to take it easy, pride and defiance answered him. She meant to prove to Adnar that she was in fine health, whether he wanted her to or not. Recognizing that he had little say in the matter, Kasiel merely tightened his grip on the saddle.

Four guards awaited them outside the bars at the front of the enclosure. Adnar dismounted and unsaddled his kanodrak, sending the beast back out into the canyon. Kasiel pulled Niskenya's saddle off and set it in the dirt. She turned to him, lowering her head to let him press his forehead against the hard bone armor that protected her face. He placed a hand on her neck and closed his eyes, feeling her worry, her desire to defend him, her confusion at the hostility even he could sense coming from Adnar and the guards. Her paw came up, deadly claws curling around his arm with a surprising carefulness.

"Aren't we supposed to be arresting him?" one guard asked in a low voice.

"Be my guest," another guard answered.

Kasiel ignored them. He stayed there, seeking the calm and courage he needed to walk away from her. With a deep breath, he passed patience, comfort, and affection across to Niskenya, then he stepped back. Adnar stood watching him, the anger in his eyes supplanted by a hint of sorrow and what might be a touch of empathy. He picked up Kasiel's saddle and gestured to the gate, the sharpness gone from his movements. Kasiel forced himself to turn and leave his companion.

Once he was outside the bars, the guards closed around him.

"You are under arrest, Lord Hahren Cavenos, by

order of Khevarin Seylin Markanis."

"I know."

He kept himself calm, trying not to distress Niskenya, and left with them quietly. They escorted him to the unpolished black halls of the prison below the main level of the palace. The rest of his unit was already there, each in their own cell. The guards took his weapons and sent him into a cell across from Danica. There was something unpleasantly familiar about looking at her through bars again.

She hurried up to the front of her cell, staring at him with wide, desperate eyes. The tenacious blacksmith's daughter, fractured by the brutal loss of her father, the destruction of her life, and the ongoing torment of worsening nightmares his father had given her that would drive her mad in time. He struggled to meet her eyes.

"What's going on, Kas?"

A guard smacked the bars with the haft of her axe, making Danica jump. "There will be no talking until you have all been questioned. The next one to say anything will be thrown in the deeps." She stared hard at Danica and repeated her words in Pandrean Common, a hateful sneer curling her lip as she did so.

Kasiel sat back on his cot. After removing the ear cuffs and pulling out the braids, he rested his head against the wall and closed his eyes. He wandered, using his ability to touch on creatures in the canyon habitats and outside the city. A sandhawk carried him over it all, showing him the fierce black city he now thought of as home from above. A mother tethdrak welcomed him, allowing him to observe her offspring as they frolicked around the juvenile enclosure. Kenna was there watching them. She leaned against the bars, a hint of worry tightening her eyes and subduing her smile. Niskenya greeted him warmly. She lay in the sun, belly already full of meat Adnar had brought her so she wouldn't have to hunt with her injuries. Kasiel passed reassurance to her, hoping she would relax and enjoy her rest.

While he wandered through the minds of other creatures, they led Darro out. He returned after an hour, and they escorted Kince away. Kasiel laid back on the cot and dozed. At one point, the sound of Danica whimpering in her sleep dragged him from his own. The guard hit the bars, jarring her from her nightmares. Later, a key clinking in his lock pulled him from a restless half-sleep. He wasn't sure how much time had passed or how many of his companions had gone in for questioning. When he sat up, surprise sparked through him at seeing Adnar standing outside the bars. The ahndhomen didn't look pleased.

"You're needed, Cavenos. Your kanodrak won't allow anyone to tend her wounds."

Kasiel couldn't stop a soft chuckle as he stood. Across the hall, Danica lay curled on her side on her cot, staring at the wall. He smothered his guilt as he emerged from the cell, focusing on those problems he could do something about, and fell in beside Adnar. Two of the guards moved to follow behind them and the Feral ahndhomen waved them off.

"I can handle this whelp," he growled at them.

Sharing an uneasy glance between them, the guards stopped, letting them leave. As they ascended into the main palace, the angle of light creeping in the windows told Kasiel it was mid-afternoon. Adnar stalked along in silence until they were out of the building. Then he gave a shake of his head.

"You're a Break-blasted idiot, Cavenos," he snapped, hesitating a moment before continuing with a hint of admiration in his tone, "but I've never worked with a better Feral."

"I hope that means I'm not bound for execution." Somehow, Kasiel sounded flippant when he said it. Not at all how he actually felt.

"There's nothing humorous about this situation." Adnar scowled at him, his gaze flickering briefly up to the stitched cut above Kasiel's left temple. "To address the concern hidden beneath your insolence, I doubt the khevarin would cast aside a Feral with your potential. Don't think that means you'll be let off easy, however."

The ahndhomen's words did nothing to unburden the weight pressing down on him. Adnar was the most apt to understand what had happened the night they left. He knew the kanodraks better than anyone. "No. I don't expect to be, but when I came—"

"Save it for your questioning." Adnar gave him a stern look.

As they rode down the lift a few minutes later, Kasiel reached out to let Niskenya know he was on his way. By the time they came through the passage to the kanodrak enclosure, she was waiting next to the gate. Adnar opened it for him. Niskenya bumped Kasiel's arm with her head the moment he was inside, nearly knocking him over. An affectionate rumble rose in her chest.

He breathed a soft laugh and placed a hand on her neck. "Niske," he murmured, "I appreciate the opportunity to get out of my cell, but you need to let them care for your wounds, even when I'm not here."

She lowered her head, pressing it to his chest. An ache spread through him that wasn't his. Regret.

Kasiel released a soft sigh. "You're not to blame, Niske. I didn't have to take you out of here. Besides, we'd have failed horribly out there if not for you. It should be pride you feel, not regret." He became aware of Adnar's intense scrutiny and took a step back from her. "She'll let them tend her now. She just wanted to..." He gazed into Niskenya's milky white eyes. She had brought him here to apologize. "To talk."

Adnar said nothing for several seconds. He looked

from Kasiel to Niskenya and back. Finally, he gestured toward the alcove in the wall outside the enclosure with a nod of his head. To Kasiel's surprise, Kenna came out, carrying supplies for attending to the kanodrak's injuries. She avoided Kasiel's gaze, and he didn't try speaking to her, despite how much he wanted to. Depending on how this all worked out, maybe he could ask her to teach him a little about caring for such wounds at a future time.

When they finished, Adnar took him back to his cell in silence. It was evening before they called Kasiel in for questioning. Everyone else who had ridden out with him on the mission to retrieve Jethan had already gone through the process. They escorted him to the warmly furnished room where Setera had interrogated him after he first arrived in Etrion. A fire crackled in the hearth. Full mugs of Vanrian Black Mead sat on the table. Simple touches designed to relax their subjects. Setera sat behind the table, another man and woman Kasiel hadn't seen before sitting on either side of her. Given his prior experience, he suspected at least one of the two was an Enkindler. All three had journals for taking notes in front of them. A guard stood at each of the doors with four more positioned at the corners of the room.

Setera gestured to the chair across from her. "Your name?"

As if she didn't know. A required formality, he supposed. He sat and claimed one mug of mead, taking a long drink. They weren't going to give him any in the prison. "Ahninveth Hahren Cavenos," he answered, swallowing his resentment for the name.

"Please, recount for us the events that occurred from the night of the battle, just before Lord Jethan Markanis was taken, to your arrival back here this morning."

Kasiel's chest constricted. He remembered coming to with the weight of Sylaryth's body pressing him into the dirt. Everything in the world that mattered – his companion, his tehnaak – all gone in an instant. He ground his teeth against the fresh pain, tears stinging his eyes.

Setera's regard softened, a hint of moisture rising in her eyes too. "I am sorry, Lord Hahren, but that is where we must start."

Kasiel nodded and drew a shaky breath. Then he told them all of it.

When they returned him to his cell a few hours later, warmed by the fire and two mugs of mead, he lay on the cot, ignoring the meal they had brought him. He had pushed all the anguish away to focus on getting Jethan back, and on leading them home safely, hiding that pain from himself. Not just the loss of Sylaryth, but of Chander, cut down in front of him for no good reason. Kitrix too, another sorrow to pile up on the rest. Tears crept quietly from his eyes, dripping along his ruined ears and into his hair.

At least Jethan was safe now. He and the other mind-crafters returned home. They had accomplished that. No matter how chaotic the process, they achieved something they could be proud of in the end.

When morning came, the heartache had settled in his chest. A hollow too immense to fill. He picked at the scant morning meal they brought. After that, he paced, aware of Danica watching him, a million questions hanging unspoken on her lips. He had questions too. Where was Edmund? Somewhere among the cells farther down along with his unit? What about Wedro and Nerith? Both locked in cells with no one there to help them through the loss of their tehnaaks?

A growl of frustration rose in his throat.

"Quiet, Feral," one of the morning guards snapped.

Kasiel tilted his head and glared at the guard, getting a thrill of bitter satisfaction when the man swallowed and took a step back.

It was nearing noon when four palace guards came to retrieve him. They led him to the chamber with the curved dais where he had faced the khevarin a few times before. Ahninveth Setera, Dhomen Branith, and Ahndhomen Adnar were there, with Adnar's tethdrak lying next to him. Adnar's tehnaak, Dhomen Nevias, was also there, sitting on his other side. Khevarin Seylin sat in an ornate, high-backed chair behind the center of the curved table. Otherwise, the room was empty, except for two guards posted inside the rear door leading from the dais. The other entrances had guards stationed outside them. Dhomvalen Arhk was conspicuously absent.

Kasiel acutely missed having either Jethan or Sylaryth at his side, but he would have to find courage on his own this time. Though not entirely on his own. He stretched his ability, seeking Niskenya and sinking part of his awareness into her welcoming presence.

It was Setera who got up and came around the table. "Ahninveth Hahren Cavenos."

"Yes, Ahninveth Setera." He kept his eyes on the edge of the dais, not wanting her in his head with Niskenya.

"Look at me when I am speaking to you," Setera ordered, her sharp tone offering no comfort.

He met her eyes, a flash of defiance, backed by the kanodrak, earning him an amused smirk from her that made him wonder if she might be something of an ally.

"You knew, when Dhomvalen Arhk Cavenos sent you on this mission to find your tehnaak, Lord Jethan Markanis, that he was acting without Khevarin Seylin's approval?"

"Yes."

At the table behind her, Seylin's lips pressed into a tight line.

"And yet you made no attempt to secure that approval yourself or bring his actions before the council?"

No point lying to an Evoker. "Yes. My tehnaak had been taken. The dhomvalen's support was more than I expected to leave with."

"And why..." she trailed off when one side door opened.

Arhk strode into the room. His white-blond hair, braided on the sides, its length cascading down his back in stark contrast to the long black and dark metal jacket that rippled around him as he walked. He came to stand next to Kasiel, facing the dais. Kasiel's pulse sped up. The khevarin pressed her lips into an even thinner line.

Arhk inclined his head to Setera. "You need not stop. I am merely here to ensure that you do not forget my son embarked on this mission with my support."

The Evoker glanced back at Seylin.

The look the khevarin gave Arhk was cutting. "We assure you, Dhomvalen Arhk, there is no danger of that. Proceed, Ahninveth Setera."

Setera inclined her head to the khevarin before facing Kasiel again. "Ahninveth Hahren—"

"Kasiel," Arhk interrupted, "Ahninveth Kasiel. That is the name he has chosen."

Setera's brows pinched together, her mouth hanging open for a second as if she had forgotten why they were even there. She shook herself. "Ahninveth Kasiel, why did you take the kanodrak?"

Kasiel was having trouble wrapping his head around his father standing beside him, not only supporting him, but his choice of names too. Facing the court at his side. He yearned to pinch himself to see if he might be dreaming in his cell. It was next to impossible to hold back a befuddled smile. Still, the dhomvalen couldn't defend his taking the kanodrak. In that, he was on his own.

"Niskenya wanted to come."

"Pardon. Did you say the kanodrak *wanted* to come?"

"Yes, Ahninveth."

Adnar rose from his seat. His tethdrak stood with him as if they shared a single mind, which, in a way, they did. "Khevarin Seylin, if I might be allowed to offer some insight."

Seylin exhaled heavily, her pale eyes flashing with irritation. "Speak, Ahndhomen Adnar."

"Ahninveth Hahren..." He looked at Arhk for a second. Kasiel caught the dhomvalen's slight nod out of the corner of his eye. "Apologies. Ahninveth Kasiel should not have taken the kanodrak. That is not in dispute. However, his ability to deny her may have been diminished by the fact that he and his kanodrak are spirit-bound."

The khevarin's gaze sharpened, piercing through Kasiel. Arhk looked at him with a hint of surprise that slowly morphed into a pleased, faintly covetous smile.

The khevarin turned to Adnar. "You are certain?"

"I am."

Seylin stood abruptly, shoving her chair back. The rest of those at the table hastened to their feet.

"Sit," she snapped at them, reinforcing the command with a curt gesture. As they did so, she strode around the table. Setera moved to one side, giving Seylin an open path to stalk to the edge of the dais. The khevarin stared down at Kasiel and Arhk. Her gaze eventually settled on Kasiel. "You make this extremely difficult." She scowled. "You make everything extremely difficult. We did not realize you would be so like your father."

Kasiel inclined his head. "Thank you, Majesty."

"That was not intended as a compliment."

"I know."

A smirk tugged at the corner of his father's lips.

Seylin glared a warning at Arhk. "We can strip you both of your ranks, Dhomvalen. Remember that."

Arhk schooled his expression to neutrality, though

his eyes gleamed with an inner fire that defied her threat. Kasiel longed for half of the man's self-assurance.

The khevarin moved slowly along the length of the table as she spoke. "Your unit returns here having rescued your tehnaak and fifteen other mind-crafters. You brought back knowledge of how the Alliance troops are resisting our abilities. You also delivered us this Professor Edmund Danovan, the man allegedly responsible both for giving them that power and for abducting our mind-crafters. According to every testimony from your unit and the individuals you rescued, your team destroyed the professor's castle with his research and his inventions inside. That includes a new blackout bomb he tested on you that could have completely crippled our mind-crafters in battle. Even our Ferals."

She stopped and looked at him. "In your absence, three watchtowers, two more of our military bases, and one of our towns along the border fell to Alliance attacks in which the elixir this professor created rendered our mind-crafters useless. Your mission, although not properly sanctioned, secured a critical victory for Vanris. One that may well turn the tides in our favor again. If you had accomplished this without stealing one of our most sacred creatures, we would be having a much simpler conversation right now."

Kasiel met her eyes, passing pride and affection to Niskenya as he did so. "We couldn't have accomplished any of it without Niske's assistance, Majesty. I'm confident my testimony and that of my companions supports that."

The khevarin offered no response to his defense. Instead, she met Arhk's eyes. "Guards, return Lord Hahren to his cell for now." Her emphasis on the name made it obvious the choice was deliberate. Arhk didn't correct her the way he had with Setera, but he met her gaze unwaveringly. "The other members of his unit may return to their homes under guard until further notice. It's time we interrogated this Professor Edmund Danovan. Dhomvalen, we expect you to assist Ahninveth Setera in that process." With that, she spun and strode toward the rear doors.

Arhk placed a hand on Kasiel's shoulder. "This will be over soon," he said in a low voice. Then he stepped up on the dais and followed the khevarin from the room, Setera falling in behind him.

Kasiel stared dumbfounded after his father until the guards escorted him out. If only he could get in that man's head.

CHAPTER TWENTY FOUR

When they brought Kasiel back to his cell in the lower halls of the palace, Danica rushed to the bars again. Her demanding, desperate gaze pulled at him.

He stopped outside the cell and turned to the guard. "Let me talk to her, please."

"You may speak now, Ahninveth, but not to it," the guard answered. "They haven't questioned it yet."

He glanced at Danica, frustration boiling over in him. "What happens if I do speak to her?"

"It goes in the deeps."

He had firsthand experience of how unpleasant the deeps were for someone with a Frightener's nightmares stuck in their head.

"You're welcome to do so," the guard added. "I would love to throw it in the deeps like the other one."

That gave him a brief surge of satisfaction. "They put the professor in the deeps?"

The man's tense posture relaxed in response to the pleased note in Kasiel's voice. "The calloch's not there anymore. They came to collect it just before your return."

Danica watched them, the frustration in her eyes growing. She had no clue what they were saying. He understood what that was like too, but at least he hadn't been a prisoner when he arrived in Etrion. The people he met in his first week here all put forth the effort to speak Pandrean Common to him, though many had obviously disliked doing so. He also had Jethan to support him during that flood of new experiences and information.

The thought of his tehnaak sent a wave of longing through him. Sorrow over Sylaryth and Chander pressed back in on the heels of that emotion, following him across the threshold into his cell.

A few minutes after his return, someone came to check on his injuries, putting fresh salve on his arm and the head wound. Guards arrived within the hour to escort the others to their homes. Each of them stopped at his cell, giving awkward hugs through the bars or brief words of encouragement. Avris pulled him gently against the cold metal and gave him a kiss on the forehead. The guards said nothing, though they didn't allow them to linger for more than a few seconds each.

"We'll get you out of here, Kas," Darro promised when he and Kince passed together.

When Nerith came by with Tath, she reached in and brushed her fingers through his hair, tidying it with a fond smile. Kasiel stepped up against the bars, the longing in his gaze enough to lure her lips to his for a soft, warm kiss. Tath conveniently shifted into the path of the guard who came forward to break them up, providing them with a few extra seconds.

Nerith bit her lip as she backed away, her mouth curving in a pleased smile. "I expect to finish that conversation soon," she said, giving him a wink as the irritated guard herded them on.

Wedro was the last to leave. He gave Kasiel a silent embrace, his eyes haunted and rimmed in red. He was the only one who didn't speak. Kasiel caught the arm of one of the guards escorting him out. The man stopped and met his eyes. He offered a sober nod before Kasiel could voice his concerns.

"We'll keep a close eye on him and Nerith, Ahninveth," he whispered. "They've arranged for both to stay with some of the others for now."

"Thank you." Kasiel released him.

When his unit had left, he noticed Danica staring at him, tears welling in her eyes, having watched from her lonely cell as his entire unit filed by, offering him their affection and support. He looked at the guard. "Let me talk to her, just for a minute. We might not have been able to rescue anyone if she hadn't helped us."

The guard considered Danica for several seconds before he nodded. "Two minutes, and I will throw you both in the deeps if you give her any information she shouldn't have."

"Thank you." Kasiel switched to Pandrean Common. "Dani, I'm so sorry about—"

She grabbed the bars. "Kas! Finally!"

"Just listen. I ah..." He glanced at the guard, trying to choose his words with care. "I took something I shouldn't have when I left here. Once that's sorted out, I can talk to them about your situation."

The guard smirked. When he spoke, it was in Vanrian. "Lucky for you, we value our mind-crafters almost as much as we value our kanodraks."

Kasiel gave him a sour look. "Not helpful."

The guard shrugged and switched to Pandrean Common. "Two minutes are up."

Kasiel threw up his hands in frustration. He shook his head at Danica, warning her away from the defiance he saw rising in her bloodshot eyes. He spent the rest of the day pacing, dozing, or wandering about in the minds of creatures in the canyons and beyond the city. As evening neared, four guards arrived and took Danica out. He tried to give her an encouraging look as she left, though he wasn't sure how successful it was.

An hour later, they came back for him and escorted him to that deceptively appointed interrogation room with its warm fire crackling in the hearth. Setera sat behind the table with the same two strangers that had helped her question him seated on either side of her. Danica sat across from her, eyes lighting with desperate hope when Kasiel entered. Two guards stood behind her chair in addition to those at the doors and in the corners. Kasiel made it to the edge of the table before one of the guards who had escorted him there placed a hand on his shoulder to stop him, leaving it there to keep him from advancing.

Setera addressed him in Pandrean Common. "Ahninveth Kasiel, is this woman, Danica Traven, the one who set you free after Professor Edmund Danovan took you prisoner?"

He attempted to rein in a burst of annoyance. "You know she is. You saw my memories." Her frigid look prompted him to add, "Ahninveth."

Danica's eyes widened at that, and she sank back into the chair as if trying to put distance between herself and Setera. Apparently, they hadn't informed her of the Evoker's abilities before this.

"Ah, yes." Setera spoke in Vanrian this time. She rested her elbows on the table and steepled her fingers in front of her. "Your memories did show her setting you free. That is not all I saw when you told me about your encounter with this girl. There is a much deeper history between the two of you that her memories confirm. You loved her once. She loves you still."

Her last words shredded him inside. Frustration swelled, making it hard to stand in place. Only the guard's hand holding his shoulder kept him from trying to approach Danica. The fact that Setera had switched to their language, blocking Danica out, meant she would expect him to do the same.

Did Danica really still love him? Even after all that had happened.

He hated everything about this, but fighting it wouldn't make the situation better for either of them, so he answered in Vanrian. "Whatever we had between us back when I was a naïve child in Fernwallow is irrelevant now. I brought her here because she's suffering from the effects of my father's ability. After she helped me, was I supposed to just leave her there to be driven mad and eventually die from it?"

Setera regarded him calmly through those icy blue eyes. "Yes. What did you think would happen to her here? Did you think we would allow her to walk our streets? Or did you think we would help her, then send her home?"

He lowered his gaze, ashamed to admit that he had assumed that. She was innocent. Edmund's ward, but not a part of his research. Dragged around the countryside and placed in danger simply because the professor hoped she might give him leverage over Kasiel. Edmund had led her father to his death, then he cast her aside to work with the servants in his castle. She deserved better, but maybe it had been foolish to expect the people of Vanris to see it that way.

Setera gave a shake of her head. "You are still a naïve child, Ahninveth. Someday, you will learn to think like a soldier. Until then, you would do well to defer to those who do."

Had Darro or one of the others mentioned advising him against this? Did it matter?

"Kas?"

Danica's tremulous plea for his attention cut into him, but he kept his eyes on Setera, and his mouth shut.

"That's a step in the right direction." Setera watched him closely. Given her ability, she had to know this was torture for him, and he resented her for that. "Khevarin

Seylin is still considering your case. It should come as no surprise that she sees this," she paused, gesturing to Danica, "as a count against you."

"What happens now?"

"You are about to be given a choice." Setera glanced at the guard by the rear entrance. "Let him in."

The guard opened the door and Jethan entered, escorted by yet another guard. A burst of joy chipped away at Kasiel's distress. His tehnaak looked better. Rest, food, and proper care had restored some of his color and strength. The intense sorrow in Jethan's regard, however, tempered Kasiel's brief elation at seeing him.

The guard behind Jethan placed a hand on his shoulder, stopping him at the opposite corner of the table.

When Setera spoke this time, it was in Pandrean Common. "Ahninveth Kasiel Cavenos, Khevarin Seylin Markanis would like me to extend you this offer. You may leave here with your tehnaak and return to your rooms in the palace. Your crime will be forgiven, provided you demonstrate an ability to follow orders in the coming days. All you must do is turn your back on this woman. Forget her, and trust in your country to handle the situation as appropriate."

"And if I—"

"No," Setera interrupted. "There will be no questions and no elaborations. Take the offer, or don't."

"Kasiel." His name crossed Danica's lips as an appeal. Out of the corner of his eye, he could see a few tears escaping down her cheeks. "Please."

One of the guards behind her chair squeezed her shoulder. Not in a gentle, reassuring way, but as a warning that made her wince.

Kasiel met Jethan's eyes. His tehnaak inclined his head in the barest hint of a nod.

It hurt to breathe. The walls closed in around him.

If he walked out of this room now, no matter what they did with Danica, he would have abandoned her. Years of friendship. Of love. Setera's stony regard told him she followed the trend of his thoughts. It was what they wanted. To destroy the connection that still lingered between them. His last meaningful link to his old life. But then, maybe this was what he and Danica needed. They belonged in different worlds, and he had to learn to trust the people in his.

Fighting tears, Kasiel returned Jethan's nod. Setera made a quick wave with one hand and the guards behind Jethan and Kasiel both released their grips. Jethan hurried around to him and took him by the elbow. Kasiel saw the guard forcefully holding Danica down in her chair as he let his tehnaak turn him and guide him from the room.

"No! Kas! I trusted you! Don't you dare—"

Danica's shouts ended abruptly when the door slammed in their wake. Kasiel jerked free of Jethan's grip and increased his stride, heading toward his rooms as fast as he could walk. A senseless ringing blared in his ears. He couldn't focus on the other familiar faces that waited in the hall. Someone might have called his name, but he didn't slow. Jethan caught up with him and put a hand on his shoulder.

Kasiel spun. "Don't touch me!"

Jethan backed off with his hands raised.

Turning away from the hurt spreading in his tehnaak's eyes, Kasiel continued down the hall as fast as his legs would take him without breaking into a jog.

"Let him go," Darro said.

"That's shit advice," Avris snapped.

Kasiel ignored them. Rage and pain waged war within him. Should he have left Danica at Edmund's destroyed castle to die? How could he do that to someone who had helped him? His best friend for much of his life. Someone who loved him. How could he abandon her now?

He threw open the door to his rooms and stormed through. His belongings, including his cleaned sword and armor, lay in a careful pile on the floor by the couch. The box with his symbolic ear cuffs sat on the table. When he stepped into the bedroom, he saw himself staring back at him from the full-length mirror. He looked disheveled from the journey and time spent in the prison cell without a chance to clean up. A hint of swelling and discoloration showed around the stitched cut on his head. The fury and cowardice in his eyes provoked loathing for the man in that reflection.

Kasiel strode to the mirror and yanked it over. It hit the floor with a loud crash, spraying glass across the room.

"Is this a bad time?"

Avris stood in the doorway to the sitting room.

"Go away." He put his back to her.

Glass crunched under her boots as she picked her way across to him. "Don't be a calloch."

He struggled with the urge to yell at her when she stepped over a corner of the mirror frame to come stand in front of him. Instead, he let her pull him into a firm embrace, his arms circling her as if his mind had lost all control of his body. He felt as if he were breaking apart inside, fragmenting like the mirror that lay in pieces around them.

He closed his eyes, clinging to her. Letting her hold him. More soft footsteps reached his ears from in the sitting room and the door between the two rooms clicked gently shut. Somehow, that became an endorsement, giving him permission to cry. A few tears came, though they were merely a fraction of the raging torrent that remained stuck behind a wall of confused emotions and exhaustion. A nudge in his mind brought him concern from Niskenya. When he let her in, her presence wrapped him in a blanket of calm affection.

"I can't get this right," he murmured into Avris's hair after a time.

She breathed a soft laugh. "Says the guy who went to get his tehnaak and returned with fifteen extra abductees and a war criminal just for fun." She pushed him back, holding him at arm's length. "Kas, the things you've had to learn in less than a year, most of us spent a lifetime learning. Give yourself a little credit."

"Danica..." He had to swallow, trying to ease the tightness in his throat so he could speak. "She was my best friend for twelve years. I couldn't have failed her more completely."

"There's nothing simple or fair about the choices you've had to make. You did the best you could, Kas."

Someone knocked on the door. Without waiting for a response, Wedro opened it and leaned in. "Jethan went to get some attendants to deal with the mirror. He said you can use his bathing chamber if you want. A bath is already being prepared."

"You could use a bath, country boy." Avris offered him a gentle smile. She put a hand on his back, applying light pressure to encourage him.

Kasiel went to his wardrobe, glass cracking under his feet, and pulled out a set of clean clothes. Wedro vanished from the doorway, and Avris followed him out. Nerith came in to take their place. She took the bundle of garments from him.

"Come on. I'll walk you there."

"Are you going back to being my palace attendant?" he asked, his attempt at a smile faltering before it fully reached his lips.

"No." She took his hand. "I'm your concerned lover."

He gave a weary nod and twined his fingers with hers. "I prefer that."

Anyone else who might have entered his rooms had already departed. When they reached Jethan's chambers, they were also empty, but the bath was full of steaming, scented water. Nerith insisted on undressing him, her light touch sending whispers of pleasure through his weary body. When she finished, she urged him into the tub, giving him a lingering kiss before leaving him alone.

It was the smell of food a short time later that dragged him out of the cooling water. He dried, dressed, and emerged to find Jethan reclined on the couch, reading a book, and eating a slice of apple. The rooms were nearly identical to Kasiel's, only with a lot more shelves around the walls, all crammed full of books.

"I hadn't realized you were such an avid reader."

Jethan sat up and set the book aside. "I had a lot more free time to fill before you showed up." He managed a wry smirk.

Kasiel glanced down at the arrangement of food but made no move to take any. "Did you know what they were going to do?"

"No. I was only told to keep my mouth shut and lead you out of the room if you accepted the khevarin's offer. They didn't tell me what that offer was, or that Danica was going to be there." Jethan gestured to a large, comfortable chair.

Kasiel met his eyes. "I'm sorry I got angry with you."

"Sit, Kas. You have nothing to apologize for." He reached for a wedge of juicy, black evalis fruit.

"I do."

Jethan brought his hand back to his side empty. "You came after me. You saved me from that bloodsucking professor. I think we're good. Now sit and have some proper food."

Kasiel sank down into the chair. "Why did they have

to do it that way?"

Jethan cut a piece off a slab of cooked meat and set it on a silver plate. He piled roasted potatoes, vegetables, and fruit on with it. When he finished, he set it on the table in front of Kasiel. "You were just tested, Kas. Like it or not, you passed."

"At what cost? What will happen to Danica?"

"I don't know." He nudged the plate a little closer. "It's not in your hands. Trust your country. Besides, you have other things to worry about. Before the execution—"

Kasiel sat straighter. "Execution?"

"I take it no one's told you yet."

Kasiel let himself fall back against the seat. "Edmund."

"Yes. They will try him, but there's little question about the outcome. The execution is already being planned. Anyhow, reinforcements have arrived from up north to help. Primarily Ferals and regular combat units. Day after tomorrow we'll be riding out with one of several companies as part of a campaign to drive the Pandrean Alliance back out of Vanris. Our destination is a town called Sharith that was just taken by Alliance forces. It was part of the deal to get you out. The dhomvalen and Ahndhomen Adnar even argued in favor of letting you take Niskenya along with your unit of tethdraks on this mission. The professor's execution will be set for after our return."

"That's what Setera meant by following orders in the coming days." More fighting. As much as he loved being a Feral, he did not love the carnage the beasts could create, but this was his place now. He was a Vanrian soldier. "So, we'll be deployed together?"

"Of course." Jethan smiled. "You'll have me, Niskenya, and a unit of tethdraks along with the unit that went south with you to rescue me. We're your unit now, Kas. We're being assigned to Dhomen Nevias's company. Kenna will be under her as well, along with another Feral by the name of Jhanik."

Everyone he cared about, in danger again.

Though his appetite had left him, Kasiel picked up the plate and made himself eat. It sounded as if he would once again need his strength in the coming days.

CHAPTER TWENTY FIVE

Soft knocking pulled Kasiel up from sleep. The light coming in the windows was bright, shortened shadows telling him it was almost noon. He vaguely recalled stumbling back to his rooms sometime around midnight. The attendants had cleaned up the glass from the mirror and a new, more ornate one, framed in dark metal with flowing silver accents, stood in its place.

He rolled over on his back and stared up at the high ceiling with its exposed, black-stained rafters. The knock came again, reminding him what had woken him. He sat up on the edge of the bed.

"Yes."

A male attendant stepped into the bedroom doorway. "Excuse me, Lord Hahren—"

Someone cleared their throat in the sitting room.

"Apologies. Lord Kasiel, Dhomvalen Arhk Cavenos is here to see you."

Kasiel fell back on the bed with a soft groan. "I'll be right there."

The man was kind enough to shut the door as he retreated into the sitting room. Kasiel got up and grabbed the clothes he had worn after his bath the prior evening. He pulled a brush through his hair, careful of the stitches on his head. When he stepped out, his father was standing near the windows, gazing out at the academy.

Arhk faced him. "Kasiel." He spoke the name with a hint of hesitation, as though still uncertain about using it.

"Father."

Kasiel couldn't have said what made him use the word in that moment, but Arhk gave him a long, unreadable look before he appeared to recall his purpose.

"Obviously, you will attend the execution after your return from Sharith. This man killed your mother, cut your ears, and remade your life to serve his ends. No one has more right to be there than you do. If you wish it, I can arrange for you to be involved in the execution itself."

The mere idea made Kasiel's gut twist into a thousand knots. "I destroyed his life's work and brought him to Vanris to face judgment. I'm confident he knows how I feel about those things now. That's sufficient."

Arhk inclined his head. "Very well." He took a few steps toward the door, the pressure of his gaze moving off Kasiel for a second. Then he stopped and faced him again. "What you accomplished in the south was more than I dared hope for. You have proven yourself to everyone."

"More than you dared hope for?" The bitterness in his own voice shocked him. He should have accepted the praise and left it at that. Instead, he forged recklessly ahead. "I don't think you believed I could do it, but you wanted me to try. I could see it in your face the night you gave me your leave to go after Jethan. You hoped I would either succeed or die trying."

The corner of Arhk's lip curved up a fraction. "I am pleased you succeeded, if that makes you feel any better about it." He continued to the door. "It is my hope that you will be at least as successful on this next mission."

Kasiel watched him leave. For some reason, civil encounters with his father were almost more confusing than the hostile ones. He looked around the room. A selection of food waited on the table. Jethan hadn't come by. Considering their late night, he might still be sleeping. Kasiel hadn't seen Nerith since she helped him into the bath, a stirring memory he did his best not to linger on. With nothing to keep him there, he grabbed two slices of bread off the platter, stuffing a pile of meat and cheese between them, and made his way to the canyon habitat as he ate.

Adnar was out working with a few tethdraks near the front of their enclosure. The Feral ahndhomen watched him as he made his way to the passage that would take him to the kanodrak canyon, making no effort to intercept him or call him over. Niskenya met him at the front of the enclosure. Not bothering with a saddle, Kasiel went inside and climbed aboard when she sank down beside him.

He spent the afternoon out there with her, letting her carry him around to her favorite spots. At a few of the prime vantage points, he reclined against her side to watch insects, reptiles, and other creatures that shared the canyon, simply appreciating her company and the lack of expectation.

The sun was dipping toward the horizon when they returned to the front of the enclosure. More clouds had moved in overhead than Kasiel had ever seen in the sky above Etrion. It struck him as appropriate to the day. Jethan waited outside the bars, casually flipping his dagger in the air and catching it by the hilt as if he had been there for a while. He sheathed it and straightened when he saw Kasiel, eyes lighting with relief.

"I was worried you two might have gone off on another adventure together."

Kasiel shook his head, avoiding Jethan's gaze as he slipped out through the gate. Niskenya gave him a mental nudge, and he faced her, putting a hand between the bars to rest it on her head for a moment.

"Thank you," he murmured, receiving a deep rumble from her in response. He turned and started toward the tunnel that led to the other canyon and the lift. "Let's go."

At the top of the lift, Nerith waited. She fell into step with them, claiming Kasiel's hand in hers. They returned to the palace together in relative silence. He appreciated the fact that they weren't pushing him to talk. He had gone to visit Niskenya partially to avoid uncomfortable conversations about yesterday with Danica or Edmund's coming execution. Perhaps he should have known they would understand.

As soon as they reached the private quarters in the palace, Jethan stopped and faced them. "I've got a few things to do for tomorrow still. I'll catch up with you two soon."

Kasiel released Nerith's hand and caught Jethan's arm, pulling him into a brief hug. Jethan returned the embrace before backing away.

"We're good, Kas," he said with a smile. "You two stay out of trouble." He winked at Nerith and left them.

When they entered Kasiel's rooms, most of the sconces along the walls had been snuffed. One still burned near the table where a platter of food and two glasses of Vanrian wine waited. In the bedroom, the dim light of a single sconce alongside the door flickered in the darkness. Kasiel continued through the doorway between the two rooms, noticing the open windows that let in the sound of rain pattering on the rooftops.

"Who..."

Nerith stepped around in front of him, interrupting him with her intense gaze as she slid a hand along his cheek. "I did. Are you..." she trailed off when he put a finger to her lips.

He met her eyes in the dim light, savoring the invitation

in them. She was willing to help him forget for a time. He moved his finger from her lips, replacing it with a kiss. She pushed his jacket off his shoulders, and they let it fall to the floor.

Maybe company wasn't such a bad thing after all.

•

The one benefit of leaving Etrion the next morning was that it didn't give Kasiel much time to dwell on Edmund's pending execution or on what they might have done with Danica. Nerith had left his rooms before dawn to change into travel clothes and collect her equipment. She would join Kasiel as part of his unit again under Dhomen Nevias.

Each of the three Feral ahninveths brought nine supports with them, including at least one healer and a Speaker. Etris, the rescued mind-crafter who had helped them in Edmund's castle, took Chander's empty spot, becoming Speaker for Kasiel's unit. Kenna had her tehnaak, Therin, and Jhanik, the Feral ahninveth who had joined Nevias's company, presumably had a Speaker in his unit, though Kasiel didn't know any of them well enough to say who it was.

Besides human troops, the Ferals had their beasts. Tethdraks for him and Jhanik, and cliff cats for Kenna. The units without Ferals had thirty-nine troops supporting each ahninveth or inveth leading them. Groups of three regular units combined under a third or fourth level ahninveth or inveth formed a union. Feral units remained apart, answering directly to the dhomen or ahndhomen leading the company. Two unions and three Feral units followed Dhomen Nevias. That put them right around two hundred and seventy fighters and mind-crafters, plus the beasts, each of which was worth at least two soldiers a piece.

Then they joined up with two additional companies at a military camp east of Etrion on the second day. The first was around one hundred and forty strong, with two more Feral units and one union. One Feral ran hounds, and the other had cliff cats like Kenna. The last was two hundred and forty strong, with two unions and no Ferals. That mass of soldiers was an awesome sight to Kasiel, who had never seen so many people and animals traveling together at once.

The dhomvalen rode out with Nevias's company as well, accompanied by three soldiers in black and dark metal armor who always stayed near him. Kasiel got the impression from eavesdropping on a brief exchange between Nevias and Arhk that the khevarin was unhappy with him going, but he appeared to do what he wanted much of the time, regardless of whom it vexed. Being Dhomvalen of Vanris, he was the ranking officer overseeing the entire army. That put him in charge of most military decisions.

With their numbers, the Alliance forces in the town of Sharith would undoubtedly spot them before they arrived. They might also have received word of Edmund's capture and the destruction of his research by then. If so, the desired outcome was that the news would shake them and undermine their resolve.

They were now within a few hours of Sharith, traveling in the shadow of a high plateau, and Kasiel had yet to say a word to Jhanik, the new Feral in Nevias's company. The man had both sides of his head shaved, the rest of his blond hair worn in a long, loose braid down the back. Part of his ke'hanoath showed along each side above his pointed ears where it would be hidden if he let his hair grow out. His strong, chiseled features and tall, muscular build irritated Kasiel somehow. He hated to admit that it might be petty jealousy over having another kanodrak rider in their midst, but what else could it be? Having not spoken to the man, he had no additional information to judge him on.

Jethan's attitude didn't help. He glowered at Jhanik's back as they watched the other Feral riding along with Kenna, joking and laughing. Did the man's predatory gaze linger on her a little too long? Was that merely because Ferals tended to develop such mannerisms? Or was there something else to it? Kasiel found himself yearning to intervene on Kenna's behalf. An impulse he suspected Jethan felt even more powerfully, although it really wasn't their place to assume she wanted an intervention.

Niskenya rumbled a low growl, reacting to Kasiel's irritation, though she seemed to have a dislike for Jhanik and his kanodrak that existed separately from his own. Kanodraks were solitary animals outside of mating season. He wasn't sure if she simply objected to the other beast's presence, or if something else about the man and his kanodrak bothered her.

At least they had removed the stitches from her wounds now. Apparently, kanodraks healed faster than most other creatures. Kenna told him this was because of a substance in their blood that the healers used in their stronger salves to speed up wound recovery, though they only ever collected it with the kanodrak's consent. He imagined that must be true. Taking blood from an unwilling kanodrak struck him as a life-limiting prospect.

Kenna glanced back over her shoulder at them. They both looked away, but not fast enough to pretend they didn't see her wave and gesture for them to come up. Kasiel met Jethan's eyes and his tehnaak shrugged.

"How bad can he be?"

Kasiel smirked. "I guess we're about to find out."

Jethan rode up alongside Kenna and Kasiel moved Niskenya up next to him. The two horses in the center immediately began fighting their riders.

Jhanik sneered at Kasiel. "Idiot. Any decent Feral knows you can't put horses between two kanodraks."

Kasiel strengthened his influence over the two animals between the massive predators, forcing them to calm down. "They seem fine to me."

Jhanik's glower darkened his angular features. "The dhomvalen's son and the khevarin's nephew. If you two had to work for your stations like the rest of us, you might respect them more." His gaze shifted to Kenna. "My apologies, Ahninveth Kenna. I need to return to my unit."

Kenna watched Jhanik urge his kanodrak over to where the rest of his unit was traveling. She turned to face them after a few seconds. "Huh. I envisioned that going differently."

"Maybe if he wasn't such a calloch," Kasiel muttered.

Jethan chuckled.

Kenna looked less amused. "Maybe if you weren't such a show-off, Cavenos. And he was right, you can't go hemming in horses with kanodraks without causing a problem."

"Clearly." Sensitive to his irritation, Niskenya stopped, allowing Kenna's cats and soldiers to pass around them until they were at the head of his unit again. Then she picked up her speed to match the others. Kasiel did his best not to notice Kenna glancing back at him periodically as she and Jethan engaged in conversation. Knowing that he hadn't handled the situation with the greatest level of maturity only compounded his irrational anger.

Nerith urged her mount up alongside him, her smile easing his temper. "I see you met Jhanik."

"Yes. A profoundly successful introduction." He didn't mean to show his sour mood to her, but she had a way of laying his truth bare with just her presence.

"Don't let it get to you. Jhanik was always a bit of a horse's ass."

That caught his attention. He drew her mount closer, keeping the animal calm as it approached Niskenya. "You know him?"

She glanced down at her horse, then up at him with mock indignation. "I don't think that's how you're supposed to be using your ability, Ahninveth Kasiel."

"I don't know what you're talking about," he answered with a wink.

"Indeed." She shook her head at him, a hint of color rising in her cheeks. "Jhanik and I grew up in the same town."

"Were you close?"

"He's not going to warm to you easily," she said, ignoring his question. "When the khevarin first offered your father the position of dhomvalen, Arhk turned it down because he wanted to focus on his family." She paused, casting him an uncertain look.

"It's fine. Go on." He wasn't entirely sure it was, but he didn't know that much about his father's past, and curiosity over how the other Feral played into it pushed him to try setting his emotions aside for the moment. Still, it was difficult imagining Arhk putting family before anything else, let alone his military advancement.

"Khevarin Seylin offered the position to Jhanik's mother. She's an accomplished Dampener. A few months after your mother was killed, and you were taken, Arhk sought an audience with the khevarin. He was convinced that what had happened was because of inadequate border management. Something Jhanik's mother was busy making changes to at the time. It didn't help that there had been several other incidents around the Vanrian border during that period that supported his case. I'm sure his being the khevarin's first choice for the position also came into play. Jhanik's mother was demoted and Arhk was promoted to Dhomvalen of Vanris. Being stripped of her rank amidst accusations of incompetence damaged her reputation and influenced how she and her entire family were treated after that."

"That explains why he might hate my father, but I'm not my father."

Her lips pressed into a tight line for a moment. "You're not, but I think Arhk losing his wife and son made it a little easier for them to stomach what he had taken from them. Your return probably hasn't been all that well received by his family."

Kasiel tried to imagine hating someone that much. "You know a lot about this."

"Yes." She averted her gaze. "Jhanik's father is my father's tehnaak. I got to hear him go on and on about it every time they drank together."

Kasiel's irritation intensified again. He did his best to hide it, though his next words had a curt edge to them. "That's a lot more than just growing up in the same town."

She drew a deep breath and slowly let it out. "I know. It's just that... Our parents were fond of the idea that we would become romantically involved at some point. It's part of why I decided to pursue my training as a healer in Etrion. I was willing to risk being sent to the front lines if it meant I could leave all that behind me."

"You weren't interested?"

"No. I'm not into spending time with callochs," she answered, a hint of exasperation sharpening her tone.

"You're with me."

She gave him a cross look. "You might have a point there."

He managed a hint of a smile until he faced forward and caught Jhanik glowering at them. The instant their eyes met, the other Feral straightened in his saddle and stared ahead, his behavior sparking a different concern.

"Was he interested?"

Nerith glanced up to where Jhanik rode, his rigid back to them now. "I don't know. Maybe a little."

"Well, at least he only has two reasons to hate me."

"Oh, I'm sure he'll find more. That's the kind of affable gentleman he is."

Kasiel gave her a flat look. "Thank you, Nerith. That makes me feel a lot better."

A silent halt passed along through the Speakers, bringing the entire force to a standstill with admirable efficiency. A group of riders, including Nevias, Arhk, the dhomens of the other companies, and Arhk's three dedicated guards, broke off from the front and circled around alongside the plateau. When they neared where Kasiel waited with his unit, Etris moved up next to him.

"Ahninveth Kasiel, Dhomen Nevias requires that you join them," she said, offering a slight nod to the dhomen as she spoke.

Niskenya moved toward the officers without awaiting input from him. By the time they reached the group, he had all their horses securely under his influence.

"Dhomen Nevias." He inclined his head to her, trying to ignore the shrewd gaze of his father.

"We're going up on top of the plateau. When we get there, I'd like you to use your vision to get us an aerial view of the town." She gestured toward a rough path that gradually ascended the side of the cliff. "Do you need another Feral to take over some of your beasts while you do this?"

Arhk's eyes were on him, curious and scrutinizing. The attention made him nervous, but he had managed far more difficult splits than what Nevias was asking for on his mission to retrieve Jethan. "No need. I can handle them."

"Good. Come with us."

Arhk urged his mount toward the path, his guards

and Nevias following him. The others didn't move. Before Kasiel could question whether that meant he should go next, Niskenya took the initiative and started up the cliffside behind Nevias. The remaining two dhomens came along after.

As narrow as the path was, he trusted the kanodrak, leaving her in charge while he reached out with his ability in search of a bird. By the time they approached the southeastern edge of the plateau up top, Kasiel had tracked down a sandhawk. He brought it in to land on his arm as they were stopping their mounts. Arhk glanced at the raptor, his expression curious. Nevias gave Kasiel an appreciative nod and gestured for him to join her when she dismounted. The other dhomens and Arhk accompanied them on foot to the edge of the cliff. Sharith was visible on the horizon, though too far away yet to make out many details with the naked eye.

"Ahninveth Kasiel," Nevias pointed toward the town as she spoke, "see what you can learn. Any information about the enemy or prisoners they are holding is of use."

Kasiel sank behind the eyes of the sandhawk as he sent it out over the cliff. That sudden drop stretching below him was exhilarating. The raptor let out a cry, responding to his elation. The disorientation caused by those changed visuals became less dramatic as he grew more accustomed to these transitions. He swept the bird in a wide circle to get his bearings, then sent it toward the town.

It didn't take long to reach his destination. A black stone wall surrounded Sharith, though it was less than half the height and width of the massive structure that protected Etrion. But then, the town itself was a mere whisper of that grand city. A high circuit around the perimeter showed him that the wall had taken damage in several places and an Alliance camp sprawled along the southern edge. Sweeping in closer to the camp, he noticed that less than a third of the soldiers milling about wore Alliance armor. The rest were wearing the mishmash of mail, leather, and bits of plate typical of mercenaries.

Arcing the raptor back around, he swept north into the town, dropping lower. The people out in the streets were also southerners, the majority in mercenary garb. Toward the center, roughly made cages constructed of wood and metal scavenged from nearby damaged buildings bordered a large square. In the middle of the space, they had erected two rows of ten wooden pillars, each with a Vanrian soldier hanging from it by their bound hands. The group of them appeared dead, riddled with arrows and crossbow bolts or wounds from blades, as if someone had used them as living practice dummies.

The hot burn of fury boiled up through Kasiel. He landed the raptor on top of a pillar and scanned the square. The cages held Vanrian men and women, most of whom were filthy, wounded, and listless, as if they hadn't had access to food or water in days. A town this size would have a lot more people, so there would have to be other prisoners somewhere, hopefully in better condition than these.

As he perched there, three mercenaries entered the square, leading a horse hitched to an open cart. Two of them cut down the first dead Vanrian soldier and tossed him in the cart.

At the next pillar, one mercenary slapped the face of the woman hanging there, chuckling when she groaned.

"This one's still breathing." He drew his dagger as he leaned in closer. "You're being greedy, sweetheart. It ain't your turn no more." He slit her throat and cut her down before she had stopped twitching.

Kasiel glanced at the cages. It sounded as if they meant to bring another round of prisoners out, and he could do nothing to stop it.

He kept the raptor there as a group of riders entered the square. In their lead was a woman as dark as Danica, with her long black hair woven into hundreds of thin braids and wrapped back out of her way. Her lack of Alliance colors suggested she wasn't a regular soldier, but her armor matched and appeared to be of a higher quality than that he saw on most of the mercenaries. The man next to her wore full Alliance gear.

She surveyed the scene Kasiel had taken in moments ago and grimaced. "What is going on here?" She shouted the question, the authority in her voice catching the attention of the man by the cart and his companions pulling down bodies.

"They're just Vanrians. Watching prisoners is dull work. You know how it is. We were just making a bit of entertainment, 'Tana," the man by the cart explained.

"Show some respect," the Alliance soldier on one side of her shouted. "This is General Itana Kedran." It surprised him to hear her introduced as a general. Why would the Alliance be promoting mercenaries as officers? "The Alliance has passed command of this town and all mercenary units here to her."

"And I will not tolerate this behavior," the general barked. "You are not animals. If I catch you acting like it again, you will be the next ones hanging from these pillars, understood?"

"Yes, General."

The three men bowed their heads, though Kasiel noticed reluctance in the gestures and a hint of defiance in their voices. They all deserved to hang from one of these pillars. If only this general would recognize that.

The woman narrowed her eyes at the three. "Stop playing with the bodies. Give the prisoners water, then split them into three groups of at least twenty each and take them to the three city gates. We have a better use for them."

One man pointed toward a large building at the front of the square. "The old ones and children too?"

"Grab adults from other buildings if necessary. I'll send more soldiers over to help." General Itana Kedran turned her horse and trotted off, all but one of the other riders leaving with her. The one who stayed sat his mount and watched the men as they went to work following the general's orders.

Kasiel launched the raptor into the air, completing a scan of the rest of the town. As it flew, he relayed everything he saw and overheard to the others on the cliff, embracing the indifference of the bird to help keep from coloring the facts with his emotions.

"Adnar didn't tell me you could also hear through your beasts, though I suppose it makes sense," Nevias commented, a faint edge of enthusiasm in her voice.

Kasiel winced inwardly. Adnar hadn't mentioned it because he hadn't told him. It was a discovery he hadn't been eager to share with everyone. Something that was his alone. In these circumstances, however, anything he held back could hurt their chances of victory. He wouldn't allow himself to regret revealing it when doing so might help save lives.

"They've put mercenaries in charge," the other dhomen growled under his breath.

"Yes. Both a good and bad sign. It suggests that the Alliance may expect to lose the town, which is encouraging. But letting mercenaries manage it may be a way to try giving themselves some deniability should we object to how our people were treated," Nevias said. "Ahninveth Kasiel, can you continue scouting with the raptor while controlling the rest of your beasts and your kanodrak?"

He drew the sandhawk away from the town, keeping the connection with it, and sank back behind his own senses. "Yes, Dhomen. I can manage the raptor and the tethdraks. Niske doesn't need my guidance." Nor would she accept it half the time he tried to give it.

"Good. I have a feeling I know what this mercenary general means to do with the prisoners, but it would be handy to have eyes on them. See what else you can learn while we finish our approach."

"Yes, Dhomen." Kasiel glanced over at Arhk where he stood gazing toward the distant town. Did it please him to see his son proving his worth? Did he even care?

Kasiel swung up on Niskenya as the others mounted their horses. An intoxicating sense of power came with riding the kanodrak, yet, even with that, his father's presence made him feel lesser. Why was Arhk here? If the Alliance mercenaries and soldiers had Edmund's elixir, his Frightener ability would be useless. Not that he couldn't fight. Kasiel had seen him do so quite effectively outside the Hall in Katovan. But they had hundreds of regular soldiers to handle combat who weren't as valuable to Vanris as Arhk was. Why risk it?

When they returned to the company, Jethan had left Kenna and was talking to Nerith, alleviating Kasiel's brief and apparently irrational concern that he would come back to find Jhanik with her. Nevias halted their group to the side of the main force and fell into a hushed conversation with the other dhomens and Arhk, the latter contributing little to the discussion. When they finished, she summoned the rest of the Ferals over. Kasiel glanced at Kenna as she rode up, and Niskenya instantly moved around on her left. Unfortunately, that put Jhanik on his left side since the other Feral made a point of not hemming in any horses between them.

The man running the hounds and the other woman controlling a group of cliff cats like Kenna's were both older. Kasiel didn't know if that meant they had more experience in battle or not, since they journeyed down from northern Vanris recently. There wasn't any fighting further north, but they could have served on the front in the past.

Nevias scanned over the five of them. "We want you and your beasts in the second line when we make our move on the city. Thanks to Ahninveth Kasiel's scouting, we have reason to believe the mercenaries in control of the town may try to use Vanrian prisoners as barriers or distractions. We cannot have your beasts killing off our people. You need to be extremely careful running them in. There is a camp on the south side of the city. If nothing changes by the time we get there, we will send both groups of cliff cats to make a run around and attack that camp. We will select additional units to join you in that undertaking."

Her gaze settled on Kasiel. "Ahninveth Kasiel, you can run your beasts from farther away. Since you have far less combat training, I want your tethdraks in the second line with the others, but I want you in the back.

Continue surveillance with the sandhawk and keep your Speaker close so you can pass along new information. Understood?" She moved her gaze over each of them to show that she expected an affirmation from them all. Once she had it, she dismissed them and turned to her Speaker.

Jhanik shifted his kanodrak closer to Kasiel. "Protecting daddy's little boy, I see. That's cute. You should still be an odrek, Cavenos."

Niskenya growled and snapped at him. Jhanik's kanodrak, a larger male, reflexively snapped back at her.

"I will have none of that," Nevias shouted, her attention instantly on them again. "If your kanodraks start fighting each other, I will demote you both."

"Yes, Dhomen," they answered together.

Jhanik sneered at Kasiel as his kanodrak began turning away. "As if your daddy would let her demote you," he said under his breath before riding off.

Kasiel scowled after him. "You clearly don't know my father," he muttered.

On his other side, Kenna chuckled. Kasiel gave her a sour look, and she shrugged. "That was kind of funny. What you said anyway," she clarified.

He managed a bitter smile. "More so if you ignore how true it is."

"Come on, Kas." She turned her horse around. "Let's get back to our units. You and Jhanik can irrationally hate each other when the fighting's finished."

"The hating wasn't my idea."

Kenna answered him with a dubious smirk.

They arrived within sight of the northwestern gate a short time later. The sun, sinking on the horizon, cast an orange light on a double line of prisoners bound before the entrance. They could see archers posted in the gate towers, on the narrow wall, and on surrounding rooftops. A speedy fly-over with the raptor let Kasiel confirm that the eastern and southern entrances also had human barriers in place. The camp to the south of town appeared abandoned now. Those troops must have moved inside the city, though, aside from those manning the gates, they weren't out in the open, which meant they could be lying in wait within the buildings.

Their force stopped out of range of the Alliance archers to revisit strategies. The officers gathered, including the five Feral ahninveths and several higher ranked inveths from each of the unions. A few of the other more experienced officers also joined them, Darro and Kince among them. Nevias didn't appear pleased about being right regarding how the enemy might use their Vanrian captives. The number of archers around the gates made a gradual approach impossible, but a rushed charge would result in losses among those bound before the gates or their own soldiers wary of hurting the prisoners.

"This is when things get ugly," Darro remarked, crossing his arms over his chest as he watched the discussion.

Kasiel glanced past him and Kince toward the setting sun. "Once it's dark, the sandhawk will be useless. They have terrible night vision."

"What of the other beasts?" Arhk asked from Kasiel's right.

Kasiel barely managed not to jump at the dhomvalen's unexpected arrival. Mere seconds ago, the man had been standing with Nevias. Shoving down the unease his father's presence always caused, he tried to focus on the question. "The tethdraks and cliff cats have excellent night vision."

"Better than ours?"

Of course, but Arhk had to know that, which meant he wasn't asking out of casual curiosity. It was a leading question, designed to show Kasiel something. But what?

He considered for a few minutes, peering at the distant gate and the double line of prisoners bound before it. The gates themselves were busted in from when the Alliance took Sharith. That was why they needed their human barricade in the first place, though they might have used the people regardless. Lacking a traditional barrier to hold the Vanrian troops back where arrows could pick them off, they were resorting to an alternate method. One that was arguably more effective than a gate.

"Archers and thrown bombs are the biggest threats," Kasiel said in a low voice, pondering aloud. "The beasts could jump the prisoner lines, but the archers would take a heavy toll before they got that close. Unless we wait until after dark, when the archers lose their visibility. The cats especially, given how quiet they are, might be able to move in relatively close before the archers could accurately target them. Then they would only have a quick sprint at full exposure. Our archers might get close enough to provide some cover fire. If we got enough beasts inside the barricade to wreak havoc on the defenders, we could give our troops an opportunity to move in and free the prisoners."

Arhk nodded thoughtfully. He gestured to the town with his chin. "That entrance is heavily guarded."

The mercenaries had far more soldiers around the northwestern gate. Kasiel had seen that when he last flew over with the sandhawk. "Naturally, that's the entrance being threatened. We breach the eastern gate after dark instead. Create a distraction there with cats and tethdraks while we move a smaller group of cats through the streets to attack from within at this gate."

Kasiel turned to see that Arhk had left. He spotted his father striding back toward where Nevias stood engaged in an intense conversation with the other two dhomens and one third-rank inveth. Kasiel looked at

Darro and Kince, who were close enough to have heard their exchange. They both nodded, falling in beside him when he strode forward.

"Dhomen Nevias." Kasiel caught her attention, glancing briefly at his father, who offered his usual unreadable gaze in return.

Nevias faced him. "Ahninveth Kasiel?"

"I might have an idea."

She beckoned him closer. "Tell me."

Kasiel's gut twisted into a million tiny knots before the dhomen's scrutinizing gaze. He forged ahead, detailing out the possibility of attacking the eastern entrance after dark and taking advantage of the natural stealth of the cats to move them through town to the northwestern gate. Nevias nodded as he spoke, her expression remaining neutral.

When he finished, Kenna took a step forward. "The cats could probably do it. The problem is that we don't all have your skills, Ahninveth Kasiel. You can control your beasts remotely. The rest of us need to be close to them to direct them. How are we going to move the cats through the streets if we can't go in with them?"

Kasiel met her eyes. "I can do it from outside the wall, if you'll let me run your cats."

Jhanik scoffed and the other two Ferals shook their heads emphatically.

Kenna held his gaze. Silence, weighted by the immense trust he was asking of her, lengthened between them.

Nevias started turning away. "Perhaps there is another way we can use the coming darkness to our advantage."

"No." Kenna nodded slowly. "Kas can run my cats."

For some reason, her words earned him a glare of pure loathing from Jhanik.

Nevias gave Kenna a long look, then turned a hard gaze on him. "Have you practiced controlling her cats prior to this?"

Kasiel still lacked confidence in many disciplines. This wasn't one of them. "No, but I have worked with cats in the wild a few times. I can do it."

"All right." Nevias held his gaze a moment before continuing. "You'll hit the east gate after dark with the cats. If you can get at least a couple of beasts through the town to the northwest gate, you should be able to create enough of a distraction to give us an opening there. Ahninveth Kenna, Ahninveth Jhanik, and two regular units will go with you to infiltrate the town from that side." Her gaze singled out the other two Ferals. "No one goes through that gate until Kasiel has confirmed that the northwest gate has also been breached."

She faced him again. "Ahninveth Kasiel, take your raptor in now, before it gets too dark, and pick out a few efficient routes for getting the cats between the two gates. Figure out where the dangers are. Make a plan. If you fail, we don't take the town tonight, and we risk losing some of our beasts and people for nothing. Do not fail."

Kenna came over to him as Nevias moved on to discussing the next steps with the other officers. She took him firmly by the shoulder, steering him away from the group. "Come on. We need to figure out how you're going to avoid getting my cats killed. I have a strong interest in making sure you plan this out flawlessly."

Afternoon wore into evening. They made a show of setting up a rough camp out of range of the archers to give their opponents the impression that they were still formulating a strategy. At one point, someone on the wall shouted for their ranking offers to come over and talk. Had they been Alliance troops, Nevias might have considered sending a representative, but she distrusted the mercenaries. She called back that the Vanrian officers preferred to remain where they were, but would be happy to host any Alliance leaders, should they wish to emerge. That offer met the same results. Arhk attempted to use his Frightener ability, trying to target mercenaries on the wall. Their lack of reaction confirmed that they were using Edmund's elixir.

As dusk crept over the landscape, a few arrows flew out from the town, landing far short of the closest target. The archers shot a few more down near the line of prisoners, eliciting startled cries from them. Defenders growing bored with waiting. If the Vanrian force didn't take the town tonight, they would need to try something else fast. The captives wouldn't last long exposed to the elements without food or water, let alone stuck there tempting the enemy archers.

CHAPTER TWENTY SEVEN

As midnight passed them by, Kasiel's unit, along with Jhanik's, Kenna's, and two regular units, made a wide arc around the city to the eastern gate, staying behind large rock formations and low hills that dotted the landscape. Wispy clouds overhead helped to further dim the starlight and the glow of the sliver moon. They made their approach on foot, except for Kasiel and Jhanik since their kanodraks created far less noise than horses.

Kasiel nudged Kenna's presence in the minds of her cats, feeling her reluctance as she relinquished control. He left her companion, Raxxa, with her. That would be asking too much. He split his ability across thirty-nine beasts now, not counting Niskenya who operated independently and as an extension of his own awareness. He cautiously moved them into position, bringing his tethdraks up after the cats once they were in place for their charge to the entrance. The archers among them snuck forward as well, ready to provide cover fire for the beasts. The mercenaries had erected a second barricade of wood and steel behind the double line of prisoners, but the cats and tethdraks could leap that with little trouble. They just had to make it that far.

Hand thrown bombs remained a significant threat, but the mercenaries wouldn't cast them at their own people. If the beasts could get in and over the obstacles fast enough, the close-quarter fighting around the entrance would hopefully mitigate that risk for them.

"Are you ready?" Jethan asked, glancing up at him.

Niskenya flexed her claws, digging deep into the dirt. Kasiel sank into her mind, appreciating her strength, abandoning himself to her absence of doubt and her fierce aggression.

"I am."

Kenna stood next to Jethan chewing at her lip, her brow furrowed as she peered at the torch-lit entrance to the town. One hand rested on Raxxa's head, seeking comfort from the beast, as Kasiel had often done with Sylaryth.

"Kenna." He waited for her to look up at him. "I'll try to keep them safe."

"Don't fuck this up, Cavenos," Jhanik said, riding up on alongside her.

Kasiel did his best to disregard the other Feral, sinking deeper still into his bond with Niskenya.

Kenna also ignored Jhanik's comment. She met Kasiel's eyes. "I know you will, Kas."

A few minutes passed in expectant silence until Etris joined them. Speakers needed to be within a certain range of their subjects to communicate with them, unless the subject was another Speaker, in which case they could connect across a much greater distance. Etris had been waiting for word from Nevias's Speaker on the other side of the town.

She met Kasiel's eyes now. "They're ready, Ahninveth."

He drew a deep, steadying breath. "Cue the archers and if you can, warn the prisoners. I'm moving the beasts in."

When she nodded, he sent the first set of cats sprinting for the town entrance. The captives threw themselves to the ground at Etris's warning, making their lines less of an obstacle. The second someone shouted an alarm from the top of the wall, the Vanrian archers started firing at those on the walls and rooftops around the gate. One cat let out a snarl of rage and pain when an arrow hit it in the shoulder, but the beast kept running. For now, Kasiel didn't hold it back. If he stopped it, he would turn the animal into an easier target.

The first two cats leapt over the human barricade and the constructed one behind it, barely missing a stride. More followed them. As much as he appreciated the power of the tethdraks, he could see advantages in the agility, speed, and silence of the cliff cats. In a way, the Alliance had done him a favor by using the prisoners at the gates. Because of that, he knew where those people were. He could give the beasts free rein to attack anyone they could dig their claws into once they were past that human shield, at least around the gates.

He slipped in behind the eyes of one cat, wincing as an arrow grazed its back in that instant of transition, and drove it up onto a rooftop with a series of powerful leaps. It took the legs out from under an archer up top with a single swipe of its paw, sending the man tumbling to the street below. He dared to stop the animal, taking a moment to look around and select targets to focus the other cats on.

Within seconds, he moved more of them up onto the rooftops and across to the top of the wall, efficiently eliminating that threat. He sent two tethdraks in, the muscular beasts lunging over the human barrier to begin tearing down the wood and steel barricade behind them. Still watching through the eyes of the cat, he dropped to the streets again and pulled four more of the swift felines along as he sprinted into the town, following a route he had planned out with the raptor earlier. It was different, seeing it from ground level rather than from above, but he had memorized the directions at each intersection for that reason. Straight, straight, left, right, straight, right, and so on.

Mercenaries raced out of several buildings in response to the commotion at the eastern gate, requiring him to veer off course for a few blocks, but he reached the northwest entrance within minutes. He sent three of the cats, including the one he was watching through, up onto the rooftops to take out those archers. Going up also meant the waiting Vanrian force would see them. The other two stayed low, charging into the midst of the troops at ground level.

He sent the lead cat across to the wall. The mercenary defender's shouts rang out as they faced that unexpected assault from behind. Kasiel winced with pain when any of the beasts sustained injuries in the fighting at both gates. The cat he continued to run with lunged on an archer atop the wall, tearing open the man's throat, then sprinted for the next one. An arrow sank deep into its side from a bowman on a nearby rooftop, sending a blast of pain through Kasiel. It made one last lunge, catching hold of the archer's armor with its claws, and dragged him over the wall with it. As it fell, Kasiel saw the cats and hounds of the other two Ferals charging toward the northwest gate. He pulled out the instant before the animal hit the ground to avoid the inevitable agony of the collision that awaited it.

An ache spread through his chest. *I'm sorry, Kenna.*

He dove in behind the eyes of another cat that had made its way to the wall on the other side of the northwest entrance.

"The gate! The Vanrian army is charging the gate! Turn around!"

The mercenary's shouts came too late. Vanrian soldiers surged in on the heels of the beasts. Numerous archers rushed up and set to work helping the cats. A smaller group slipped in under the cover fire to free the prisoners and move them out of the way. The second they were past the human barrier at the northwestern gate and were through part of the barricade, Kasiel raised an arm and signaled his side to advance.

"Kenna, take your cats. I'll bring back the ones at the far gate."

She said nothing, but he felt her slip into their minds, nudging him out. He let her have them, though he maintained a light connection to one, just in case. Kasiel sent the rest of his tethdraks in ahead of Jhanik's and the other soldiers.

Darro came up beside him. "We going in?"

That hadn't been the original plan. Nevias's initial orders had been for Kasiel to stay back and manage his tethdraks from afar while he scouted with the sandhawk. That wouldn't work in the dark. The raptor was useless here. His only purpose now was to keep his beasts on task.

The rest of his unit waited around him. Kasiel nodded. "We are."

Niskenya didn't hesitate. She let out a loud roar and surged ahead, angling for a section of wall to the left of the gate where several feet had been blown off the top by an Alliance bomb. Her muscles bunched, and he leaned low, holding on tight as she leapt over the break, coming down softer than he would have thought possible in the street on the other side. Ideally, they would stick with their unit, but the kanodrak could smell blood and feel the charge of conflict in the air. She disregarded most of his requests under normal circumstances. Battle, it seemed, exacerbated that issue.

Kasiel drew on his tethdraks. At least he would have support if he could bring them to him. Fighting broke out in the streets now, with groups of mercenary troops trying to stem the incoming tide. Archers leaned out of windows in various buildings, firing down on Vanrian beasts and soldiers. Kasiel sent his tethdraks after them. No ordinary door could withstand first contact with an enraged tethdrak.

Niskenya charged around a block, coming in behind a band of mercenaries. Kasiel held on tight, hands wrapped in the grips on the saddle, and let her handle the fighting. Her approach had closed the enemy in between them and Jhanik's unit of tethdraks. Kasiel called a few of his beasts in to join them as she reared up on her hind legs, laying into a mounted mercenary with claws and teeth. A warm spray of blood spattered his face.

Trying to convince himself it was a splash of sweat or some drops of rain, he placed his trust in the kanodrak, and jumped his ability between his tethdraks, searching for the rest of his unit. It only took a few seconds to find them a few streets over, fighting another group of mercenaries. They had part of one of the regular units with them, but a second band of mercenaries was moving in behind them.

He sent a few tethdraks that way and gave Niskenya some forceful mental nudges. When he broke past her battle rage, he passed along a sense of need and obligation. This fight was nearly done, and their unit required them elsewhere. She answered with a sting of regret and bolted in that direction. A burst of agony unbalanced him, though it wasn't physical. Several yards from them, one of the tethdraks he sent ahead had fallen through a pit trap dug into the street, landing on a bed of spikes. The intense pain and terror from the beast forced Kasiel to withdraw. He could do nothing for the poor creature, and he hated that. Rage boiled up in him.

The sound of a bomb exploding greeted him as he turned the corner, coming in at the back of one of the mercenary groups that had his unit surrounded. The band on the far side had thrown a firebomb into the Vanrian soldiers fighting behind his companions.

Several people thrashed about, screaming as the clinging flames burned through clothing and flesh. More lay in the streets, dead or dying.

Kasiel called in the tethdraks he had left to help Jhanik finish that battle and sent them around to the other end of this street. Then he leapt off Niskenya, letting her dive into the mercenaries along with the two tethdraks he had brought. He drew his sword, apprehension and reluctance overcome by the powerful need to protect his tehsheyn. Coming in behind them, he swung into the startled mercenaries with the dark metal blade after the beasts now in their midst caught their attention. A sting of pain surprised him when someone's sword point penetrated Niskenya's thick hide, but the wound wasn't deep. She spun about, ending the responsible enemy with a swipe of claws that raked through armor like it was skin.

With the aid of the beasts, he made his way to his companions. The tethdraks on the far end blazed a path through those mercenaries, meeting them in the middle.

Jethan grabbed his arm. "Kas, what happened to you?"

"Sorry. Niske got a bit overexcited."

Avris chuckled. "Yeah, we got that by how she jumped the wall like it was a sheep fence."

He spotted Etris and motioned her over. "Reach out to the other Speakers and let them know one of my tethdraks went down in a pit trap in the street. There may be more out there."

She gave a nod, her gaze turning inward.

Kasiel took a rapid visual inventory of the others. Everyone in his unit was present and still standing so far.

"Let's..." A brief lapse in Kenna's connection to the cliff cat he had maintained a link to caught his attention. Focusing in, he bumped her almost completely out of the beast's head, pushing her presence back so he could slip behind its eyes. Smoke from multiple bombs had her unit and possibly others socked in to the point that they were struggling to breathe or see. His sense of the cat put them a few blocks up on the west side of the town. "Kenna could use help."

Niskenya stopped next to him, and he swung back up in the saddle.

Jethan caught his leg. "We can't keep up. Where is she?"

"About three blocks up on the west side. I'll keep the tethdraks with you." Niskenya's intent to move swept across their link and Kasiel grabbed on as she bolted in Kenna's direction.

"Be careful," Jethan shouted after him.

Kasiel nearly laughed. As long as he was riding Niskenya, he was pretty sure he had little say in it.

As Niskenya loped up the street trending north, Jhanik came charging out of the next cross street up, his tethdraks strung out behind him. They both skidded to a stop, the kanodraks snarling at each other in surprise. Before Kasiel could think of what to say, movement on the next street over caught his attention. He turned in time to see a mercenary sprinting past, heading toward the south end of the town. Was the man fleeing? Or did he have another purpose? They still had prisoners at the southern gate.

He glanced at Jhanik, trying hard not to look at the other Feral as his enemy, at least not for tonight. "Kenna needs help. She's with at least one other unit two more streets up on the west side. They've been hit by several smoke bombs from what little I could see."

To his mild surprise, Jhanik inclined his head, his kanodrak already turning that direction. "I'll handle it."

"Watch out for pit traps in the streets," Kasiel shouted after him as Jhanik's kanodrak sprinted off, his tethdraks trailing behind him.

Niskenya followed the lure of Kasiel's curiosity to the next street over and turned south in pursuit of the mercenary. As they went, he drew one of his tethdraks with them, guiding it along close to the buildings in the direction the mercenary had gone.

Once he confirmed Jhanik's arrival through Kenna's cliff cat, he let her have the beast back. With the rest of his unit also on their way over there, he couldn't see how his presence would make a significant difference. He dropped deeper into his tethdrak's mind, keeping it to the shadows as he slipped behind its senses, listening as much as seeing. He slowed Niskenya, being more cautious now that he was leaving the active battle area.

As they approached an open square near the south gate, his tethdrak came close enough to spot the mercenary meeting up with a larger mounted group. The woman he had seen before, General Itana Kedran, was among them. Kasiel dared to encourage the beast a little closer, keeping it at the corner hidden from sight by a parked wagon. Niskenya stopped one street away at his urging, and he focused in on the tethdrak's sharp hearing while he counted the enemy numbers.

Itana gestured for the man Kasiel had been following to approach. "What is it?" she demanded.

"Vanrians have broken through the northwest gate, General."

"We have lost the northwest gate." She cast a look at another man on foot who stood leaned over with his hands on his knees, trying to catch his breath. Her eyes narrowed. "As well as the east gate." Her hands tightened on her reins. "Havaad-cursed Ferals," she growled, though a hint of something that might have been admiration crept through in her voice.

"What should we do?"

"Clear the barricades from the south gate. I'm calling for retreat before they take that end and trap us in here. We've got no chance with those beasts swarming the streets." She looked ready to punch someone.

"You're just going to give up?" the Alliance soldier sitting his mount behind her asked. "The Pandrean Alliance granted you rank and status to hold this town."

Itana turned on him and he flinched back, jerking his horse's reins so that the animal tossed its head in protest. "Only until more backup arrived! That was supposed to happen by yesterday afternoon. It appears they abandoned us the minute they knew their professor had fallen. You're a bold bunch when you think you have the advantage, but you turn tail awfully fast when things don't go your way. If your leaders have a problem with my retreat, they can choke to death on their blasted rank and status. You, however, are more than welcome to stay here and hold the town for them. I wish you the best of luck."

The Alliance soldier said nothing.

"What about the prisoners at the south gate?" the mercenary Kasiel had followed asked.

"We've no need of them now." Itana started turning toward someone else.

"So, we let them go?"

She glowered in the direction of the northwest gate. "No. There are more than enough pointed ears in this place. I'll deal with them when I get there. There might be time to leave a message for our Vanrian friends."

"Yes, General Kedran."

The man struck off for the south entrance, the other mercenary on foot going with him, along with eight of the seventeen riders Kasiel had counted. He watched the general sitting still on her mount, staring toward the sounds of fighting. He couldn't back away and leave her to kill the Vanrian prisoners, could he? Would Nevias expect him to? Would his father?

The general nodded to another man, who pulled out a horn and brought it to his lips. A blaring wail sounded out over the city, calling for retreat. The general turned her mount and kicked it up to a trot, heading toward the south gate. The remaining five riders began falling in behind her. Kasiel grabbed the saddle grips, drawing the tethdrak out of hiding as Niskenya sprinted after them.

The kanodrak covered the distance in seconds. The retreating riders heard them coming an instant before they plowed into the midst of the group, the tethdrak plunging in right alongside them. As Niskenya took down the horse and mercenary next to Itana, Kasiel lunged from his saddle, slamming into the general and pulling her from her mount. They hit the ground hard, Kasiel yanking her helmet off as they rolled away from each other.

Itana was on her feet faster. She had lost her shield in the fall, but the mace she carried was ready in hand. She wiped the blood from a scrape along her jaw, glaring as she circled out into a more open spot. Her movement put him between her and the chaos of the two raging beasts attacking her other soldiers. Kasiel drew his sword. He considered making the mercenary horses panic behind him, but his focus was already too divided with the tethdraks he was trying to control. This woman struck him as someone he would need to give a great deal of his attention to if he hoped to survive the encounter.

A flash of pain jarred him as the tethdrak took a stab wound deep in its shoulder. Itana chose that moment to attack, bringing the mace at him faster than anticipated. Kasiel barely had time to jump back out of the way, nearly falling over the leg of a dead horse as he did so.

His heart pounded as he got his feet stable under him again. Another mistake like that would be his last. A flash of anxiety threatened to freeze him in place, so he let some of Niskenya's blood rage flow through him, burning away fear and caution. It was like drinking too much mead, but instead of making him drowsy, it set a fire in him, filling him with reckless energy. Baring his teeth in a savage grin, he charged the general. They engaged in a deadly dance, striking and blocking in a rapid series of exchanges. Kasiel scored a few hits, but she moved too fast for him to catch the vulnerable points in her armor. Fortunately, she fared no better.

Unfortunately, he could hear the group of riders that had departed first coming back, having likely heard the fighting break out behind them. That would put a greater burden on Niskenya and the injured tethdrak. Taking a chance, he turned a portion of his attention to calling in more of his tethdraks, though it would take them a few minutes to reach him.

Another blast of pain hit him as someone drove a blade deep into the chest of the tethdrak with them. That jarring instant was all it took to give the general her opening. She lunged in, swinging her mace at his head. He tried to get his blade up to block her, but he wasn't fast enough this time. The mace slammed into his forearm with crushing force. An explosion of agony sent a flash of white across his vision. He heard his sword hit the ground a heartbeat before his knees did. Niskenya let out an earsplitting roar.

He expected the final blow to come crashing down on him, but someone rode around behind the mercenary general, leading another mount.

"They're almost here, General Kedran. We have to go."

She gave Kasiel a last look, then turned and swung up on her horse, kicking it to a gallop.

Kasiel curled forward into the pain, vaguely aware of Niskenya coming to stand protectively over him as the surviving mercenaries fled. She made a distressed chuffing noise, but he couldn't offer her any reassurance. He could only hope Kenna had gotten control of his tethdraks, because he had lost them.

More horses galloped up and the lead rider jumped down next to him.

Niskenya snarled.

"Let me help." It was his father's voice.

After a moment, the kanodrak stepped back and Arhk crouched in front of Kasiel. He glanced at the forearm, bent in ways it shouldn't bend, blood soaking the shirt sleeve beneath his leather armor.

"Ferals let their beasts do the fighting for a reason."

"She was going to...kill..." Kasiel swallowed. He couldn't get the words out. The pain was making him nauseous. A dizzying darkness threatened at the edges of his vision.

"The prisoners? Is that how this happened?" Arhk shook his head. "You can't save everyone, Kasiel."

"I... can try."

Arhk stood, beckoning to someone. "Send word we need healers to see to Ahninveth Kasiel. Now! Anyone mounted who can still fight, come with me."

His father disappeared from his line of sight. He heard horses and beasts charging off, then others came rushing over to him. Niskenya made more of her distressed chuffing noises, though she didn't interfere this time.

"Kas!" Jethan skidded to a stop beside him, sinking to one knee.

Nerith joined them. When she reached for his arm, he flinched back, sucking in a sharp breath at the pain the movement caused. She hesitated a few inches shy of touching it. "Oh, Kas." Her tone was less than reassuring.

Tath strode up, barking orders as she came. "Kince, Wedro, run ahead and get us two beds in the community hall where they're taking the other wounded. If it's too crowded, commandeer one of the houses."

Two beds?

"Merrin, help Jethan get him on his feet."

Kasiel tried to focus on anything beyond the agony. "My tethdraks?"

"Jhanik has them," Jethan answered, sliding a hand

under one arm as Merrin moved around to his other side.

"Jhanik!" He wanted to object more, but getting upset about it somehow made the pain worse.

"Don't worry about it right now." Nerith picked up his sword and stepped out of the way, moving closer to Niskenya.

He couldn't stop himself from crying out as they helped him up. Nothing he had ever done hurt like this. For the first time in his life, he longed to black out, but the dark threatening at the edges of his vision stubbornly refused to close in.

The walk to wherever they went from there felt as if it took an eternity. Kasiel let them guide him most of the way, his eyes squeezed shut against the flurry of activity around him that somehow seemed to aggravate the pain and nausea the same way getting upset had. He was vaguely aware of entering a building and being escorted up a flight of stairs.

"What did you do, find the nicest house in town?" Tath was asking.

"We needed three beds," Kince answered. "Therin took a substantial hit too."

At least that explained why Kenna didn't have his tethdraks. Still... Jhanik?

"Who else?" Kasiel forced the words out. Why had everything become so blasted difficult? Walking. Talking. Thinking.

"Avris got slammed into a wall by a bomb," Jethan answered. "She broke something in her shoulder and hit her head pretty hard."

He wanted to ask if she would be all right, but it was beyond him. Tath was speaking again anyhow.

"You know Kenna's unit has their own healers, right?"

"One of them got killed in the fighting." Wedro

sounded exhausted when he said it. Or perhaps disheartened was more accurate.

"Shit," Tath muttered under her breath.

They guided him into a room and sat him on a bed. Someone passed him a flask. He didn't even look to see who. He just accepted it and drank.

Nerith caught his hand and took the flask away. "Don't overdo it, Kas. You want to wake up eventually."

Did he?

Jethan helped him lie down.

"Where's Niske?"

"She settled out front. Doesn't look like she plans on leaving anytime soon. I'll go check on her if you like, tehnaak." Jethan had dirt across his cheek and in his hair, and a bloody scratch on the end of his nose, but he appeared otherwise unharmed.

Kasiel nodded. "Please."

Tath came and sat next to him, looking down at the arm. She shook her head. As his eyes slipped closed, he heard her say, "What a mess."

***

The throbbing in Kasiel's arm, awful though it was, wasn't what woke him. It was the hushed voices coming from over near the door. He couldn't convince his eyes to open or his mouth to move yet. It was far too much work. So, he lay there and listened.

"We have to take him back to Etrion with the other seriously injured soldiers," Tath said, her tone low and intense. "That arm needs attention that we can't safely give it here, and it needs it as soon as possible."

"We're keeping three Feral units here to help protect this place until defenses are rebuilt. I know the injury is severe, but if he leaves here, he'll have to be lucid enough to take his beasts with him." That was Nevias, frustration in her tone.

He could almost hear Tath shaking her head. "He'll

be in too much pain. Kenna's returning to Etrion with Therin. Kas ran her cliff cats and his tethdraks at the start of the battle. Couldn't she return the favor for the trip back?"

Nevias exhaled heavily. "I already asked her. Kenna and Jhanik are the only ones familiar with the tethdraks. They're taking turns keeping his beasts controlled for now, but I need Jhanik here. Running multiple species at once is apparently a lot more difficult than running one, and Kenna can't actively run the number of beasts at one time that Kasiel can. None of the other Ferals here can."

Couldn't they? That was news to him.

"Oh. Is that so?" The caustic edge in Tath's voice caught him by surprise. She was talking to their dho-men, after all. "It sounds to me like Kasiel's become rather valuable to Vanris. That seems like a compelling reason to want him to get the best possible care. If he's going to use that arm again, we need better tools and cleaner facilities. We have to get him back to Etrion without making it worse along the way."

That wasn't at all encouraging. "I..." His voice cracked. Why was his mouth so dry? He tried again. "I can take my tethdraks to Etrion."

When he peeled his eyes open, he found them both staring at him.

Tath recovered first. "I didn't expect you to wake up so soon." Her gentle smile wasn't enough to hide the underlying concern. "Trust me, Kas, you aren't going to want to make that journey without significant pain control, and you won't be able to handle your beasts when you're barely conscious."

"I'll manage. My being out of it makes Niske uneasy anyhow." He could feel her now. It was like having a kanodrak pacing through his head, the violent swishing of her tail knocking his thoughts into chaos. "You'll have less trouble with her if I stay conscious and I can solve your excess tethdrak issue." He took a breath, puzzled by how exhausting all those words were. "Now, can I get some water, please?"

Nevias continued to stare at him for several seconds after Tath left the room, hopefully to retrieve that water. "You know, your plan got this town back and saved most of the prisoners. It hinged on you being able to run the cliff cats through the city the way you did. Tath isn't wrong. You are important to Vanris."

Her last words caused an uncomfortable tightening in his chest, so he cast them aside. "Most of the prisoners?"

She approached the bed, glancing down at his arm, something he had yet to work up the nerve to do. "Archers took out a few before our people got to them, but most of them lived."

"And their general?"

"She escaped, along with many of those on horseback. The rest we brought down before they could get away. I can't help wondering why they didn't have more Alliance support with them."

For the first time, he noticed that the room they were in was very flowery and ornate, with an overabundance of lace everywhere. He closed his eyes to block that out of his head. He could visualize the general and her group again as he had seen them through the eyes of a tethdrak that was now dead. "She had only recently been put in charge of the town. I heard her saying that the Alliance was supposed to send reinforcements, but she suspected they defaulted on their promise because of the professor being taken." When he opened his eyes again, Nevias was gazing thoughtfully down at him.

She placed a light hand on his shoulder. "See, more of your work influencing our victory."

"With my father pulling my strings."

Her lips pressed together into a hard line for a second.

"No. Don't give him credit. Whatever the dhomvalen might have done to nudge you in the direction he wanted you to go, you were the one out there making things happen. If it hadn't been for your unit capturing the professor and destroying his research, it sounds like we would have faced a much different battle here. We lost enough as it was." She walked to the door before he could investigate that further. "Rest, Ahninveth Kasiel. You're going to need all your strength for the journey ahead."

CHAPTER TWENTY NINE

Nevias wasn't wrong. The trip back to Etrion was like a long, drawn-out nightmare. Kasiel rode Niskenya, something he fought Tath and Nerith over initially until the kanodrak herself intervened, snarling at the two healers as she sank onto her belly next to him to make mounting easier. The agony, even with the effort she made to keep her movement smooth, was nearly unbearable. Though some soldiers in the wagons suffered more severe injuries, they could deaden the pain with the healer's elixirs and rest. The primary difference between his journey and theirs was that he could use only light doses of those painkillers. Barely enough to do anything for the pain, but more would interfere with his ability to control his tethdraks.

Before departure, they braced, wrapped, and bound up the arm in a sling. Tath told him they needed to cut it open. It had broken in more than one place, and surgery was the only way they would be able to correctly realign the bones. Otherwise, he might never regain normal function in it, though she warned him that the outcome remained uncertain even with proper care. It sounded unpleasant and risky, but she assured him their master healers had the skills to do it. Until then, Kasiel bore his pain in silence. He didn't dare do any differently with his father there.

Why did you come?

That question rested on Kasiel's lips when he watched the dhomvalen riding along near the head of their company. One the insufferable man never gave him an opportunity to ask. He didn't have it in him to force an encounter. Given that Arhk couldn't use his Frightener ability in Sharith because of Edmund's elixir, Kasiel suspected he came with them at least partly to observe how his son performed. If that were true, was he disappointed that Kasiel had nearly gotten himself killed trying to stop the general from slaughtering the last group of prisoners? Would he write him off as useless now if the arm didn't heal right?

Kenna rode close to the wagon that carried Avris and Therin. Therin's injuries, like Avris's, came from a bomb blast that had thrown him into the side of a building. He had multiple broken ribs and severe burns. Guilt nagged at Kasiel. Had he missed an opportunity to help prevent those injuries by going after the mercenary instead of assisting them? Jethan and Kenna praised his decision to send his unit and Jhanik's to their aid, insisting that everyone in Kenna's unit might be dead now if he hadn't. They also assured him that following his instinct to pursue the mercenary was the only reason any of the captives at the south gate survived the night.

Maybe they were right. Maybe.

When they reached Etrion, he took Niskenya and the tethdraks to their habitats first. From there, he had an escort, not to the prison this time, but to the healer's building. A precaution meant to ensure he made it there without passing out. Once he arrived, they knocked him out and proceeded to repair the arm.

For the following week, they kept him confined to his room there to manage pain and monitor for infection. Each of his companions stopped in to check on him. They smuggled him pastries and brought updates on the campaign to drive the Alliance out of Vanris, which was proving successful between Feral involvement and enemy forces exhausting their supplies of Edmund's elixir. Jethan and Nerith all but moved into the healer's building with him, sometimes sleeping in his room. Avris, under similar mobility restrictions, came by for occasional games of dice, her arm braced in a complex frame to allow the shoulder to heal.

Today was the day the healers said they might permit him to return to the palace. Nerith had left before he woke to see to her duties. Jethan sat in a large chair next to the bed where he had fallen asleep again, stretching his stiff muscles. Kasiel, still struggling to escape the semiconscious haze that followed a night of sleeping on painkillers, lay propped up by a few pillows. An interim stage until he was awake enough to try sitting.

Without warning, the door opened, and a palace guard stepped in. She moved to stand on one side of the doorway after a brief scan of the room. A second guard entered, positioning himself on the other side of the entrance. Khevarin Seylin was in the hall speaking to one of Kasiel's healers. She wore a silver and black dress that draped elegantly over her curves, the simplicity of the garment doing nothing to lessen her regal presence.

Jethan scrambled to his feet and helped Kasiel into a sitting position as she dismissed the healer and glided in.

Her gaze settled on Jethan. "Lord Jethan, you may leave us."

Jethan stayed at Kasiel's side. "I'd rather not, Majesty."

"We weren't offering you a choice, nephew." Her glacial gaze remained on him until he lowered his eyes.

"I'll be right outside." He rested a hand on Kasiel's shoulder before leaving.

With a dismissive gesture, she sent the two guards out after him. The last one shut the door, closing Kasiel in alone with her. The room shrank around them. It wasn't a fair confrontation. He was barely awake and hadn't had anything for the pain since the prior evening.

"We have scheduled Professor Edmund Danovan's execution for tomorrow. The healer agrees you are well enough to attend."

Had she asked the healer, or merely given him her opinion on the matter? Kasiel's throat clenched. He made a noncommittal sound in response.

Seylin stepped up beside the bed, gazing down at his injured arm. "This is the price you were willing to pay to protect people you had never even met?" One delicate hand moved closer, her fingertips resting on the rigid bracing that kept his arm straight.

Kasiel pulled the arm tighter to his chest, his lip lifting in a hint of a snarl.

"Ah, my little Feral. So fierce." Seylin smiled, moving her hand away. "Son of the Dhomvalen of Vanris. We always knew you would have great potential."

Kasiel didn't have the composure at that moment to attempt diplomacy. "That wasn't the impression I got when we first met."

"You may feel that we treated you unkindly, but remember, Lord Kasiel, weapons are forged in fire."

Her comment made his stomach turn. "Is that what I am now?"

"Do not doubt it." If his bitter tone bothered her at all, her serene smile didn't show it. "If you develop some impulse control, you might prove to be as powerful a weapon as your father someday."

"And has he shown a great deal of impulse control? My father, that is?"

Her serenity cracked for a second, a slight tightening in her jaw telling him he'd struck a nerve. Then her smile returned, though it had a sharper edge to it now. "This once, we will assume the lack of respectful address is because you are under the influence of painkillers. Do not expect us to be so forgiving again."

Kasiel lowered his gaze, her words forcing him to acknowledge how brazen he was being. This woman could change his entire life with a command. End it, even. "I won't be so useful if this arm doesn't heal well, Majesty." He tried to sound more deferential this time, but the nagging fear that he might not regain function in the arm added bitterness to his tone.

"We have ordered that our best healers be placed in charge of your care, but you need not worry, Ahninveth. It is not your sword arm that makes you exceptional."

"My ability," he muttered, struggling to keep anger in check.

"Without your heart, even that would be worthless." She strode toward the door while his thoughts spun out of control at that unexpected response. "Focus on your recovery, Ahninveth Kasiel. We will need you again."

He wanted her out of the room, so he could gather his wits back about him, but curiosity, ever his downfall, forced a question past his lips. "Why did you come?" His own father hadn't bothered to pay him a visit.

She glanced over her shoulder at him. Infuriatingly elegant and unreadable. "To look into your eyes and see if your injury broke more than your arm. We are pleased to see that it did not." She left the room.

Jethan ducked back in immediately after she departed. "Sorry, Kas. I wanted to stay."

"She may be your aunt, but she's still the khevarin," he said, dismissing the apology. He reached out with his functional hand. "Help me up. This fucking arm is worse than useless."

"You two had a nice relaxing chat, did you?" Jethan smirked as he gripped Kasiel's hand and pulled him into a sitting position on the edge of the bed.

"It doesn't matter."

Once he was steady, Jethan moved back, regarding him with a furrowed brow. "You want to talk about it?"

Kasiel got to his feet too fast and wavered there. Jethan looked ready to intervene, but he waited, watching as Kasiel found his balance by pressing one leg against the bed. He stared at the wall and gingerly adjusted the sling. It wasn't necessary, but it gave him something to focus on other than the distress his lack of response was causing his tehnaak.

He gestured toward the door. "Come on, let's see if they'll let me out of this place."

The head healer in charge of his recovery consented to letting Kasiel return to the palace on the condition that he promise not to visit the canyon habitats until after a reevaluation of the injury at week's end. He agreed and negotiated them down from two daily visits with Healer Iatan to one, with the argument that Nerith would be around to check on his progress at least once a day. The head healer let it stand at that. It was no secret where Nerith spent most of her free time.

Not being able to visit the canyon habitats yet wasn't a significant burden. He could enter them anytime he wanted with his ability and had done so frequently to ease the boredom and frustration of recovery. He only had to reach out to Niskenya or one of the kanodraks. In fact, he had flown outside the walls more than once over the past week, soaring along with raptors he found around the vicinity to watch troop movements in and out of the city. Despite those adventures, he grew increasingly frustrated with the limitations of his injury. He couldn't imagine how others who didn't have that escape available to them managed.

Merrin and Avris joined them once they returned to Kasiel's sitting room. Avris was still spending her nights in the healer's building since she lacked the extra amenities that living in the palace provided, but they allowed her to leave for limited periods under Merrin's supervision. The two women challenged them to several games of dice, staying through the noon hour and picking at a platter of food until both Kasiel and Avris succumbed to increasing pain. After they departed, Kasiel took some of the painkiller and Jethan, more subdued than normal, helped him out of his shirt and left to let him rest.

When he woke again, it was to the unexpected sensation of someone laying on the bed next to him. Nerith's lavender eyes shone in the light of sconces she must have lit. One window was cracked, letting in the soft patter of a reluctant rain. He caught the aroma of what smelled like a roast wafting in from the other room.

He managed a half-smile. The full, welcoming smile he wanted to give her, the smile she deserved, eluded him. He hoped she would assume that was merely from the lingering grogginess of the painkiller.

Her answering expression overflowed with gentle affection. She took his hand. "Are you ready for something to eat? Followed by a much-needed bath?"

"I might be. Are you helping with that second part?"

Her cheeks colored, a mischievous sparkle in her eyes. "Maybe."

She got up and came around to lead him out into the other room. He dreaded that she might have to cut his food for him, but the palace kitchens had prepared everything in bite-sized morsels before delivering it. Yet another perk to being the dhomvalen's son, even if his father's love would never be one of them.

While they ate, attendants brought in hot water for the bath. When it had cooled enough to be usable, Nerith led him to the bathing chamber. After helping him shave, she slowly undressed him and arranged a stool alongside the tub with a pillow on it to rest his arm on. At first, she used a sponge, but soon abandoned it in favor of sliding her hands over his skin, down his chest, his stomach, and lower. In the clear water, he could do nothing to hide what her attentions were doing to him, and her self-satisfied smile told him it was all quite intentional.

When she leaned in to kiss him, he pulled her over with his good arm, dragging her into the bath with him. With a startled cry, she scrambled back out and stood glaring at him, her clothes weighed down and dripping with water.

"Kasiel Cavenos! You need to be more cautious with your arm."

He stared back at her and laughed. The maneuver had caused him a little pain, but he had been careful to keep the arm out of harm's way. "If that's all you're upset about, I'll consider it a success. You should probably get out of those wet clothes."

"You're the worst."

He splashed water at her. It was far too late to worry about spilling on the floor. She met his eyes and slowly began peeling off the wet garments, somehow taking control of the moment back from him in a way that he couldn't object to. When she finished, he was once more entirely in her thrall.

She leaned in, pressing her soft lips to his as he slid his usable hand over the curve of her waist.

When she moved back, he murmured, "I might need help getting ready for bed."

Nerith smiled. "Only if you let me do all the work. I wouldn't want you hurting that arm," she whispered, kissing him again.

He wholeheartedly agreed.

•

For a time, the physical pleasure she shared with him had pushed the worst pain to the sidelines. Never fully eliminating it but decreasing its hold on him. Later, she hung up her clothes by the fire and brought him more of the painkiller. Then she crawled back into the bed with him, laying on her side, and pressed her naked body against his, all while being careful of his arm. She touched her lips, soft and warm, to his shoulder. Then her forehead took the place of her lips. She lingered there a long moment, a heaviness entering the room.

"What is it?"

She drew a trembling breath. "It was awful seeing you there in the street, so obviously in agony. For a minute, it reminded me of the moment I saw Leysa struck down. But at least you were alive. When we cleared up the mess Kenna's unit was in, and you weren't there..."

He squeezed her hand. "I'm all right." That wasn't entirely true, but it was all he could think of to say. What if he had been in her position with her or Jethan being the one who had vanished amidst the fighting?

"I heard they set the execution for tomorrow," she murmured. "If you need anything..."

He kissed her head, at a loss for words.

"I love you, Kas." She pressed closer to him, resting her cheek on his shoulder.

He squeezed her hand again, unable to admit the same in return. Instead, he slipped into Niskenya's mind – she rarely blocked him out anymore – and let the kanodrak carry him through the canyon until he drifted to sleep.

The next morning, Nerith left early after caring for his arm and giving him more painkiller. Their mission had been a small part of the campaign to push Alliance forces out of the Break, so the healers had a large number of injured to attend to and needed all available staff working.

Kasiel slept through much of the day, willingly succumbing to the drowsiness caused by the healing elixirs. Jethan stopped in for a time and coerced him out to stroll around the gardens for a little light exercise. Kasiel slipped into all but forgotten habits, telling his tehnaak about many of the familiar plants there and their uses. Knowledge he had gained from Edmund during his years in Fernwallow. The process turned out to be unexpectedly cathartic.

Afterward, they ate together. Then he retired to his bed, alternately dozing and skipping around between beasts with his ability until Nerith returned to help him prepare for the evening's big event. An occasion he would have happily missed.

"Don't you need to change?" he asked, watching as she dug through his wardrobe and pulled out black trousers and a white shirt with delicate silver and purple embroidery, designed with wide sleeves to accommodate his injury. She finished it off with a ceremonial, sleeveless black tunic with a purple lining and silver embellishments.

"I won't be there. They restricted attendees to the city's elite and the mind-crafters who were taken by him, along with their tehnaaks. I'm afraid I don't fall into either of those categories. You will have Jethan with you, though."

At least he would have his tehnaak.

"It feels wrong dressing up for the execution of the man who raised me."

"I know." She squeezed his hand. "Maybe it would make it easier if you try to focus on some of the less pleasant things he's done."

Kasiel said nothing. He let her help him tidy and dress, attempting to seduce her from her task a few times for the distraction it provided. Though she brushed him off, he was rewarded with the sparkle of a smile in her lavender eyes that lifted his mood a little. Once she had him dressed and the sling situated for his arm, she turned her attention to braiding back the sides of his hair along his scalp and placing the dark metal wing ear cuffs. When she finished that last touch, he took one of her hands and put it around his waist, moving in to catch her lips in a soft kiss.

She relented for a moment, melting against him, until he brushed his tongue across her lower lip, and she pulled back, giving him a chastising look.

"There's no time for that."

"I'd rather stay here with you," he said, leaning down to steal another soft kiss.

"Kas." She freed her hand and placed a finger to his lips, stopping him from doing it again. "You have to go."

Someone knocked on the door.

He heaved a sigh and stepped back from her. "Come in."

Jethan opened the door, entering with Ahndhomen Kastus behind him. Not exactly the escort Kasiel expected. But then, he had no prior reference for attending executions. Knowledge he could have gone his entire life without acquiring.

Kastus looked him over once. "You're ready?"

Nerith placed a hand on his left arm, her touch gentle and reassuring.

"I am," he said. It was a lie. He turned to Nerith. "Thank you."

She slid her hand into his and gave it a squeeze. Then she picked up his sword belt from the couch and helped him strap it on before he strode to the door, not overly thrilled to have the weapon's weight resting there again.

They walked to a central section of the palace he had yet to visit. Every time they took him to some place new within the complex, he was awed anew by how massive it actually was. On this occasion, the hallway they came down opened on a wide, curved entrance hall lined with white marble statues of men and women in armor. The centerpiece was a Vanrian soldier with a tethdrak at his side, standing facing out from three sets of ornate double doors along the inside of the curve. The statues stood on a floor of polished black stone with swirls of silver and white throughout.

People were heading through those three doorways slowly, guards blocking the passage of each individual until an attendant checked their names against a list, ensuring that they were permitted to be there. Some Kasiel recognized as mind-crafters from the group they had rescued. Most were unfamiliar, though he had seen a few around the palace.

Before they ventured out into the entry area, Kastus took them down another long hall. They moved at a brisk pace, turning right into a crossing hallway halfway down.

"Kasiel!"

Edmund's voice behind them jarred Kasiel from his tenuous state of forced calm. The burst of conflicting emotions sent a pulse of pain through his arm. Turning to look back to the left down the hall they were entering, he saw Edmund in chains, being escorted by six guards. The guards stopped, deferring to Kastus's group. Edmund stared at him, fingers absently tugging at the cuff of the simple white robes trimmed in red and gold that they had given him. Pandrean Alliance colors, meant to mark him as the enemy perhaps, or possibly pay some peculiar homage to his origins. They had trimmed his hair and given him a clean shave, but his features were listless and drawn. He looked old and diminished. Vulnerable.

A flicker of hope lit his dull eyes. "Kasiel! You can't let them do this."

Something snapped inside Kasiel. Jethan grabbed for him as he stalked toward the man, but he twisted away, evading his tehnaak's grasp. The guards in front crossed their spears, blocking him before he could come close enough to touch Edmund. He didn't push it. Instead, he stopped and glared at the professor over the spear hafts.

"You're wrong. I can, and I will. I will watch until the last flicker of life fades from your eyes. And who knows, I might even enjoy it."

Edmund shrank back from his fury, the blood draining from his face as his last effort to save himself crumbled before Kasiel's harsh words.

As he turned away, Kasiel noticed more than one of the guards offering him respectful nods. Ironically, he hated them for it. He was raw inside, as though a tethdrak had raked its claws through his chest. When he rejoined the other two, Kastus resumed leading them down the hall without a word, as if nothing had happened.

Jethan leaned close. "Are you all right?" he asked in a whisper.

"Do I seem all right?" He adjusted his arm, wincing with a flare of pain.

Jethan didn't answer. They both recognized that he could do nothing to make this evening easier.

With barely more than a glance at the guards, Kastus escorted them through a set of simple double doors at the end of the hall. They opened to a large auditorium with spacious seating arranged as if for a show, set along a slow decline that ended before the stone stage at the front. A staircase curving up against the near wall led to a balcony level with five sitting areas divided by privacy walls. A matching set of stairs led up on the far side of the room. Khevarin Seylin, Ahninveth Setera, and Dhomen Nevias already occupied the central section above with four palace guards standing at the back of the partitioned area.

Kastus turned them up the staircase. At the top, they proceeded to the section to the right of the center. Kasiel strode to the balcony railing, ignoring the chairs, and stared down, watching the guards escort Edmund in. The sound of people talking as they filed in became a buzz in the background. Jethan came to stand close beside him, a silent pillar of support.

They placed Edmund against a stone wall erected near the middle of the stage, clamping a metal collar that was affixed to the wall around his neck. His wrists and ankles they locked into similarly mounted metal cuffs. When he opened his mouth to speak, one guard shoved a gag in place, silencing him.

Kasiel looked away, scanning the crowd below. Rescued mind-crafters and their tehnaaks stood among finely dressed officers and other elites of the city. He spotted two figures being escorted to the front near the stage by another group of six guards. Kasiel recognized

Danica immediately with her ebony skin and braided mane of long black hair. The man beside her, wearing Alliance colors, had dark, cropped hair that exposed his rounded ears.

"Who's that?"

Kastus followed his gaze. "A messenger from the Pandrean Alliance. He arrived two days ago to make us an offer for the professor's life."

That came as something of a shock. "And this is our answer?"

Kastus nodded.

"What did they offer?" Jethan asked.

"They proposed removing all of their troops from Vanris in exchange for the return of the professor."

That was a significant concession, though Vanris appeared to be accomplishing the same results without the Alliance's assistance, albeit not without cost. The khevarin and her advisors evidently hadn't been foolish enough to consider it. Edmund back in Alliance hands meant more advancements in the enemy's ability to fight their mind-crafters. It was an offer they couldn't afford to accept. That aside, the messenger's presence provided him with a glimmer of hope.

"Are they sending Danica back with him?"

"Not your concern, Cavenos." Kastus's tone said that was the end of that part of the conversation.

They waited, watching as the room filled in. Adnar and Kenna entered, the ahndhomen with his tethdrak and her with her cliff cat, Raxxa. They took up positions on either side in front of the stage Edmund stood bound upon. Unnecessary from a security standpoint, given the number of guards around the room, which meant they were there for ceremonial reasons, or just to intimidate the southern messenger. Would they have asked him to stand there if he still had Sylaryth?

The speculation brought a fresh surge of loathing

for the man chained up below. What caught him unprepared was the wave of sorrow that crashed in on the heels of that hatred. Improbably, two of the most prominent individuals from the majority of his favorite childhood memories were in this auditorium with him now. One about to die. The other...

He shifted his attention to Danica, watching her as she scanned the room. Her gaze eventually made its way up to him. Kasiel schooled his expression to neutrality, knowing someone would notice if he reacted to her. She narrowed her eyes in a hate-filled glare that pierced through him, then hastily averted her gaze.

Arhk and one of his guards, both in black and dark metal armor, strode out onto the stage. The guard approached Edmund, taking a second to tuck the professor's dark hair behind his ears before moving off to stand in one corner. With the curve of the balcony, Kasiel could see the khevarin when she walked to the front of her sitting area, Setera and Nevias coming up to flank on either side of her. A Speaker's voice asked for silence in his mind and a gesture passed among the guards around the room, the combination ending all conversation in the auditorium. All eyes turned up to where Seylin stood looking down on them.

"People of Etrion. Blood of Vanris. We have gathered you here on this auspicious occasion to witness the enforcement of our justice. This evening, we have also been granted an unusual opportunity to demonstrate our answer to crimes against our people to a messenger from the Pandrean Alliance. Executions such as this are rare in Vanris. It does not please us to stand in a position where we believe this is the just and proper ruling. However, once you have had the opportunity to hear the crimes of which this man is guilty, I know you will all stand behind our judgment. As such, once sentencing and punishment have been carried out, though the fire in your blood may burn hot, we ask that you allow the Alliance messenger in our midst to depart unharried so that he may deliver our answer to the message he so graciously brought to us."

Seylin gestured to the crowd with one hand, glancing at Setera as she did so. "Ahninveth Setera, if you would."

Setera inclined her head to the khevarin and stepped forward. "Professor Edmund Danovan," she said, projecting her voice over the room, "You have been found guilty of the following crimes: Accessory to the murder of Dhomvalen Arhk Cavenos's wife, Ellaris Cavenos. The abduction of the dhomvalen's son, Hahren "Kasiel" Cavenos, and subsequent cutting of his ears, in addition to research conducted upon him over the course of the ensuing twelve years. Abduction and imprisonment of at least sixteen Vanrian mind-crafters and ongoing torture in the form of forced collection of their blood. The development of weapons of war that brought about the death of hundreds of Vanrians in recent attacks."

She then proceeded to slowly read off a long string of names of mind-crafters taken by Edmund and some of the many Vanrians who died because of his creations. While she spoke, Edmund's eyes widened with panic, and he strained against his bonds, dignity abandoned before the overwhelming desire to live.

"The punishment for your crimes," Setera continued, "determined by your actions and treatment of our people, to be carried out immediately, is death by bleeding."

Edmund struggled, his protests muffled by the gag in his mouth. Danica stepped toward the stage, only to have a guard sweep his spear out in front of her. The Alliance messenger, aware of the precariousness of their position, caught her by the arms and drew her back beside him.

Arhk looked up at the khevarin.

She answered him with a solemn nod.

In a flash of motion, Arhk drew his dark metal sword and swung it at Edmund's head. A precise, effortless cut. Blood welled bright red from the top of his ear where the dhomvalen had neatly sliced the edge off. Kasiel cringed inwardly, reliving for an instant the agony of having his ears cut as a child. He fought the urge to put his hands over them. Edmund cried out through the gag, eyes going wild with pain and terror as Arhk stepped around him and did the same on the other side. His skill was apparent in the matching precision of that cut. As Edmund threw himself against his bonds, the dhomvalen moved close enough to whisper something into one of the professor's wounded ears that made his eyes flood over with desperate tears.

After a second, Arhk leaned back and brought the tip of his blade up again. He grabbed Edmund's arm, and, with an abrupt motion, sliced it open from the inside of his elbow halfway to his wrist. Another flash of remembered pain swept through Kasiel, followed by a burst of fresh, real agony in his broken arm. He clenched his teeth, fighting the urge to turn away as Arhk repeated the process on Edmund's other arm. Then the dhomvalen stepped back and tilted his head as if admiring his work, a drop of red falling from the tip of his blade.

Blood ran from both of Edmund's cut ears, a mere trickle compared to the heavy torrent pouring down over his hands and streaming to the floor. He thrashed ineffectively against his bonds, the realization of his inevitable death stealing all color from his face.

Edmund. The man who taught Kasiel to read and write. Who smiled patiently as he quizzed him on how to identify different plants in the woods. The man who cared for his hurts and comforted him when he cried for twelve years. The same man who had deliberately kept him ignorant about anything relating to who he was.

Who tried for all that time to awaken his ability, just so he could help the Alliance kill Kasiel's people.

Kasiel reached out to Niskenya. He had lied to Edmund. He wasn't going to watch the life fade from his eyes.

Carry me.

The kanodrak didn't hesitate. She welcomed him in and surged to her feet, bolting out along the canyon floor. The auditorium faded away as Kasiel immersed himself in her, watching the high canyon walls speeding past, listening to the chittering of night insects and creatures, and smelling the sunbaked dirt as fat raindrops started falling upon it. The wind moved over their scaled skin. He felt the flex and extension of each muscle as if they were his own, the slight sting of healing wounds being strained.

She shared her strength and her fierce confidence. The warmth of her protective affection cradled him. He reveled in the sensation of cool spots of dampness on her skin as more rain pattered down, contrasting the lingering heat radiated by the ground under her paws. She let him share in all of it selflessly, taking him far from the grim reality around him.

They raced together through the canyon until a touch on his arm and Jethan's urgent whisper pulled him back. "Kas."

The first thing he saw upon returning to himself was Edmund hanging limp in the shackles, his features slack. Blood created a great pool beneath him. He could hear Danica sobbing where she stood turned away from the front, her face buried in her hands. A solemn silence engulfed the room, the Vanrians holding respectful vigil even for such a hated person.

Arhk hopped down from the stage and approached the Alliance messenger. The man took an involuntary step back.

His voice carried in the silent space. "There is your answer." The dhomvalen stalked down the aisle then and out through the central set of doors, looking far less pleased than Kasiel would have expected under the circumstances.

Jethan touched his arm again, jerking his head toward the rear of the sitting area. Kasiel glanced at Kastus. When the man nodded, they left the section and made their way down the stairs, slipping out the side door where they had come in. Neither spoke until they were back in the hallways near their private quarters.

"You left, didn't you?" Jethan asked.

"I'm sorry." He lowered his gaze. "I couldn't—"

"It's fine. I'm glad you had that option." He stopped and faced Kasiel. "If you want company..."

Kasiel shook his head. "Get some rest."

Jethan considered him for a moment, his brow furrowing. Finally, he nodded. "You too, tehnaak." He sounded defeated.

Kasiel hesitated. His tehnaak wanted to help him, but Kasiel couldn't accept it yet. He didn't have it in him to do what he should do and let Jethan in. He reached out and gave his tehnaak's arm a half-hearted squeeze. The smile he offered felt as false as he imagined it looked. Without another word, he headed for his quarters, the ache in his arm almost as intense as that in his chest.

CHAPTER THIRTY ONE

When morning came, he awoke to Nerith frantically pulling on her clothes. She had come in the night, silently crawling in next to him and pressing close, asking for nothing. He lay there, watching her move. A healer trained to fight, like all the others who shared her vocation. Skilled, dangerous, giving. She noticed him as she slipped on her shoes.

"Don't look at me like that. I have to get to work."

He managed to sit up on the side of the bed with minimal pain. She walked to him, stepping in between his thighs and kissing him. He pulled his arm close to his chest, but she was careful not to put any pressure on it, as he should have known she would be. His other hand, he slid around to the small of her back, trying not to become aroused by their deepening kiss and failing completely.

When she ended the kiss, he kept his hand there, not letting her leave yet. "All I have to do is look at you to get this?"

"Pretty much." She kissed the tip of his nose, sliding a hand behind her back to grab his wrist as if considering moving his hand away. "But your body seems to want to make me late for work."

He let go of her and cleared his throat self-consciously.

"Don't be embarrassed. It's a sign that you have good blood flow."

He shook his head. "And now it's leaving, and so are you."

Her light laughter brought a flush to his cheeks for a moment, then memories of the previous evening chased that warmth away.

Her smile softened. "Do you need help getting dressed before I run off?"

As much as he wanted to say that he could manage, he knew exactly how frustrating it was to get his clothes on with one usable arm. He nodded. "If you don't mind."

She had just finished fastening his trousers for him when someone knocked firmly on the main door. Leaving him with his shirt hanging in his good hand, she scurried out to answer it.

"Oh, Kenna, that's..." Her pause piqued his curiosity. "That's unexpected. Since you're here, could you help Kas with his shirt? I really must go. I'm running late."

"Can I what?" Kenna sounded indignant, as if Nerith's request had insulted her somehow.

Kasiel stepped into the doorway to the sitting room to see Nerith vanish through the main door past Kenna, flashing him a quick smile before she passed out of sight. The other Feral looked at him, her expression darkening.

"Morning. What did you..." He trailed off when she stalked inside, and a cliff cat followed her. The massive feline padded over to him, head-butted his thigh hard enough to knock him back a step, then lay at his feet.

"I knew it! Adnar was right. You Break-blasted calloch!"

Kasiel held up the hand still holding his shirt in a defensive gesture. "Hold on. What's going on? This isn't Raxxa."

"No. It's one of the cats you ran to the northwest gate in Sharith. He's been acting depressed since we returned. Adnar suggested I take him to see you. I thought he was crazy, but no, one of *my* cats bonded with you. Who takes a person's cliff cat, Kas?" She shouted the question, and the cat stood, positioning itself protectively between her and Kasiel.

He shook his head, trying to deny the rather compelling evidence. "That can't be right. I run tethdraks."

She snapped a hand out to point at the cat, who growled back at her. "It's your problem now. I'm done here."

"Wait! Kenna, you can't just leave him here."

"Can't I? Maybe he'll help you with your stupid shirt." She spun and stormed out the door, nearly slamming into Jethan. She glared at him too and stalked away.

"Um. Why is she so upset?" Jethan stared after her. When he turned, his gaze lit upon the beast in front of Kasiel. "That's a cliff cat."

"Thank you for the biology lesson." Kasiel cautiously reached out to the cat's mind. His effort earned him a welcoming wave of pleasure. The cat started purring, though it kept its eyes on Jethan, daring him to make a threatening move.

"You bonded with one of her cats?"

"Other way around, and it wasn't on purpose."

"Well," Jethan grinned at the cat as he spoke, "I guess you better name him."

"No."

The cat, deciding that Jethan wasn't a threat, settled back down, laying across Kasiel's feet.

"All Ferals have a companion, Kas. You were going to end up with one again at some point."

His chest tightened, a desperate panic taking hold. "I run tethdraks."

"From what I've seen, you can run anything. I don't imagine one cliff cat in the group is going to break you. What's the problem?"

"I've already got Niske," he said, trying to ignore the cat's purring.

"Kanodraks aren't the same. Even I know that."

The amusement in Jethan's eyes transformed Kasiel's anxiety into anger. "I don't want a companion," he shouted.

The cat sprang to its feet again, hackles going up. It turned to stare at Jethan, perhaps reassessing him as a threat.

Jethan took a careful step back, all traces of humor vanishing. "What's going on here, Kas?"

Kasiel reluctantly set a hand on the cat's head, encouraging it to calm with a thought. It responded instantly, moving to sit beside him, though it kept its gaze trained on Jethan. "It's nothing."

Jethan's eyes narrowed. "You know, for a little while, you were willing to confide in me, but I feel like the closer you get to Niske, the farther you get from me."

Defensive anger tightened Kasiel's back and shoulders, a flare of pain in his arm giving his temper an extra boost. "Leave her out of this. This isn't that Feral problem you're so worried about," he snapped.

"Then what is it? How did I lose your trust?" A sharpness entered Jethan's tone, the hurt beneath his frustration threatening to break free.

He couldn't meet Jethan's eyes. An ache spread through his chest that he understood the cause of all too well. An ache that he had buried for a short time, but that hadn't truly left him since the night Sylaryth died. Arhk's words played back in his head, telling him he couldn't save everyone. His father was right, and he hated that truth. He feared it.

The cat's tail started lashing to-and-fro, a low growl

rising in its throat.

Jethan took a step closer, one hand tightening into a fist. "Blast it, Kas! You can't cut me out like this. I'm your tehnaak."

Kasiel met his eyes. "That's just it. This tehnaak thing seems like a brilliant concept at face value, but we're soldiers, Jeth. Like it or not, we lose the ones we care about. Sylaryth, Ahrin, Chander, Leysa, even Kitrix. I thought I lost you once too." His voice cracked as he said the next words. "I don't think I can stand that again."

Jethan's expression softened, the aggression in his posture disappearing. "I get that. I do. Now that you're here, I can't imagine living through the pain of losing you again, tehnaak." Jethan's voice cracked now, and he swallowed, pausing to collect himself. "It's a fear we all live with. But there is something different about your relationship with Niske. What is it that lets you stay so connected to her? Aren't you afraid of losing her like you lost Sylaryth? Like you almost lost me?"

Kasiel answered with a bitter chuckle, touching lightly on the kanodrak's presence that remained constant in the back of his mind now. "I'm terrified of losing her. But she's in my head all the time, Jeth. She doesn't give me a choice."

Jethan stared at him for a few seconds as if processing that. "So, you're saying I just need to be more of a stubborn calloch about it?"

Kasiel opened his mouth to object to that conclusion, then he shrugged instead, the sling holding his arm weighing heavy on his shoulders. "I don't know."

Jethan shook his head, a hint of fondness warming his expression. "We could have years together, Kas. Or we could have mere days. Do you honestly think that keeping me at arm's length will make you feel better about it if I die? Or do you think it'll just make you feel worse because you refused to let us make the most of the time we had?"

Kasiel sighed. A dark sense of defeat clawed at him, and yet, part of him was glad to have the folly of his behavior thrown in his face. "Sometimes I just wish we could go live farther north, away from the fighting."

"Wouldn't that be fantastic? But—"

"I know." Kasiel cut him off, a twinge of guilt in his chest as he did it. "The khevarin made it exceedingly clear I'm not done fighting for Vanris."

Jethan looked down. "Ah."

If only he could see an end to the war on the horizon. Kasiel couldn't imagine it, though. How was Vanris ever going to convince the Pandrean Alliance kingdoms that they could trust mind-crafters? After his experience being delivered into the hands of mercenaries by a Charmer, he couldn't even pretend that he didn't see the Alliance's point. It made finding a resolution to the conflict nearly impossible as far as he could see.

He dropped deeper into the cliff cat's mind, surprised by the animal's willingness to let him do so, and gazed out of its eyes, noting the sorrow in Jethan's expression and the hang of his shoulders. He had a tehnaak. Someone in his life who would support him through anything for as long as such was possible. Niskenya would stand with him just as fiercely, a partner of a different kind. Ready or not, he appeared to have a Feral companion again too. He even had a woman who loved him. His future here would never be dull.

It was hard to believe now that, less than a year ago, he had been content with the simple life Edmund gave him. If the professor had succeeded in awakening his ability, he didn't think he would have stayed in Fern-wallow for long. Or maybe he would have. Absent the expectations and responsibilities placed on his shoulders in Vanris, he might have found a peaceful expression for his Feral ability. He could almost imagine doing nothing more aggressive with it than sitting in the shade of a tree, letting his mind run with the forest creatures.

And while he sat beneath those trees, Edmund would have learned from his awakened blood how to create the elixir. The companions he loved now might have died because of the professor, and he would never have known they existed. His peace would have come from a place of ignorance. Of missing out on relationships he now couldn't imagine living without.

"I don't suppose you'd consider walking to the cliff cat enclosures with me?" Kasiel asked.

Jethan looked up at him, a hint of his defiant nature sparking to life in his eyes. "The healers didn't say you couldn't visit those."

"To be fair, I'm pretty confident that was just because they didn't think I had a reason to."

Jethan reached for his shirt. "If your new friend won't eat me, I can help with that."

Kasiel sent a touch of reassurance to the cat and nodded to Jethan. "He'll be fine." When they finished, Kasiel rested his hand on Jethan's shoulder. "I'm sorry, tehnaak. I won't try to push you away anymore."

Jethan grinned at him. "I know you won't. Because I'm not going to let you."

Kasiel found a faint smile in return and followed him from the room. As they turned down the next hall, he spotted Arhk and his guards heading out.

"Fa... Dhomvalen Arhk," he called.

The group stopped and waited for them, Arhk arching a brow at the cliff cat, though he didn't ask. "What do you need, Ahninveth?"

Kasiel honestly wasn't sure why he had called after him. He considered his father as he closed the distance. He and his guards were in their full armor, as if preparing to head out on another mission. "Where are you going?"

"I am afraid that information is above your rank, Ahninveth."

"When will you be back?"

Arhk's head tilted to the side slightly, as if Kasiel's sudden interrogation puzzled him as much as it did Kasiel. "When I accomplish my task. Is that all?"

Was it? "Yes."

Arhk started turning away.

"No."

He stopped again, his brows pinching as he regarded Kasiel.

"What did you say to Edmund after you cut his ears?"

Arhk's shoulders rose and fell as he took a deep breath. "I told him the ears were for you."

That moment was when Edmund fully realized he was about to die. Kasiel had seen it in his face. Something in the answer shook Kasiel, though he couldn't determine exactly what it was. Had the professor's last thoughts been of him? Had he regretted what he did to Kasiel and his family at all in the end? "I..." His thoughts wandered back to what he had been thinking about before they left his room. "Will this war ever end?"

An enigmatic smirk curved Arhk's lips. "We shall see. Rest and heal while you can, Kasiel." He turned and strode away then, his guards falling in behind him.

"What do you think that meant?" Kasiel asked.

Jethan stood next to him, watching his father walk away. "No clue. Do you want to bring your new cliff cat to the Twisted Vine later?"

Only his tehnaak would have already moved on to planning an evening at the tavern in the aftermath of that odd exchange. "Not yet. Besides, Nerith said I can't drink while I'm still taking the painkillers."

Jethan grinned at him. "That's fine. You can watch."

He clapped him on the good shoulder and resumed walking.

Kasiel chuckled and started after him with his unexpected cliff cat at his side. "You're a calloch."

"I am," Jethan answered much too cheerfully.

THE END

Kasiel's Glossary

Vanrian terms I've learned

Calloch	Rank ball of monkey shit. A favored insult in Vanris.
Company (military)	The units and unions under the command of a single dhomen or ahndhomen.
Crack a stone	Popular Vanrian phrase meaning to open and drink a stoneglass bottle of Vanrian Black Mead. Vanrians love that stuff.
Danro	Someone who is lost / out of place / doesn't fit in (me).
Evalis	Black fruit used to make Vanrian Black Mead. Imported from the original Vanrian homeland.
Ke'hanoath	Each Vanrian's individual story represented in symbols tattooed somewhere on their person.
Kenis Seed	Medicinal plant component used for sedation.
Mindcraft	Unusual abilities possessed by some Vanrians to manipulate the minds of humans or animals.

Mind-crafter　　Someone with a mindcraft ability.

...na sek　　Appended to an officer rank when a promotion is temporarily granted for a specific mission.

Stoneglass　　A light metal alloy that looks like stone and is extremely durable. Primarily used to make bottles for Vanrian Black Mead... naturally.

Tehnaak　　Spirit siblings, bound to each other through a ritual of some kind and raised together.

Tehsheyn　　Spirit family.

The Deeps　　Vanrian solitary confinement.

Union (military)　　A grouping of three regular units combined under a third or fourth level ahninveth or inveth.

Unit, Regular (military)　　A group of thirty-nine soldiers under a single inveth or ahninveth.

Unit, Feral (military)　　A group of nine soldiers and up to twenty beasts under a single Feral ahninveth.

RANKS & TITLES:

Khevarin	Ruler of Vanris – the rough equivalent of a king or queen.
Dhomvalen	Protector or warden. A Vanrian military leader who answers only to the khevarin. (My father.)
Dhomen	A Vanrian officer – the rough equivalent of a general in the southern kingdoms. There are four levels.
Ahndhomen	A Dhomen who is also a mind-crafter (slightly outranks a dhomen). There are four levels.
Inveth	A Vanrian officer – the rough equivalent of a captain in the southern kingdoms. There are four levels.
Ahninveth	An Inveth who is also a mind-crafter (slightly outranks an inveth). There are four levels.
Inren	A Vanrian common soldier. There are four levels.
Omren	A Vanrian mind-crafter common soldier. There are four levels.
Idrek	A Vanrian recruit – soldier in training.

Odrek	A Vanrian mind-crafter recruit – soldier in training.

Other things of interest

Anso nut butter	Made from tree nuts grown in Fallend. So creamy. I wish they had this in Vanris.
Havaad	A god worshipped in parts of the southern kingdoms, particularly in Sarket.
Pandrean Alliance	An alliance formed between the three southern kingdoms of Delaphine, Sarket, and Fallend to fight Vanris.

Mindcrafting disciplines

Charmer	A mind-crafter who can manipulate an individual or small number of individuals to go along with their suggestions.
Dampener	A mind-crafter who can interfere with the way people's minds perceive their senses, effectively taking away the sight, sound, smell, and/ or touch of individuals or groups.

Enkindler

A mind-crafter who can inspire positive or negative emotions in individuals or groups.

Evoker

A mind-crafter who can see and sometimes alter a single individuals surface thoughts and memories.

Feral

A mind-crafter who can connect with, influence, and control the minds of animals or groups of animals.

Frightener

A mind-crafter who can access the fears of individuals or groups and cause them to see terrifying visions, sometimes permanently scarring their minds.

Heartsmith

A blind mind-crafter who can tap into people's deepest thoughts and emotions in an abstract way to read the story of who they are in order to tattoo it upon their skin.

Speaker

A mind-crafter who can speak into the minds of individuals or groups, limited somewhat by range and visibility (less so if their subject is also another Speaker).

New creatures I've encountered

Cliff Cat

Large wildcats native to the mountains in Vanris. Some Ferals use them in combat. They have a deep blue-gray coat with darker blue stripes down the spine along either side of a ridge of longer hair. Their eyes are sapphire blue, and their tails end in a puff of hair the same blue as its stripes. They tend to be around waist high to a man at the shoulder.

Kanodrak

Impressive Vanrian predators brought to Pandrea from the original Vanrian homeland. Taller than a horse and used as mounts by a few Ferals. Vaguely feline with a silver-grey, scaled hide and milky white eyes. They have bone armor plating that starts at the nose and runs along the spine to the base of their long tail. Their massive canine teeth extend well below the lower jaw.

Sandhawk

Desert hawks commonly seen in southern Vanris and around the Crimson Break.

Tethdrak

Vanrian predators brought to Pandrea from the original Vanrian homeland. Some Ferals use them in combat.

Built a little like a hound, but reptilian. Adults are mid-rib high to a man at the shoulder. The thickly muscled limbs and torso are covered in light shades of red and brown scaling with spiked plates along the length of the spine and thick tail. Two backswept horns extend from the head and their massive jaws bristle with sharp teeth.

Werdyn Cat

Large wildcats common in northern Sarket. Broad swaths of charcoal fur tipped in white puff out around its face with tufts of white at the top of its ears, giving it an owl-like appearance. They have scales beneath their fur and a coat that repels water. Tend to be more active in inclement weather.

Places

Andaro

Capital city of the kingdom of Sarket.

Crimson Break

War-devastated, desert region between Vanris and the southern kingdoms.

Crimsondale

Town where the incident that started the war happened. Now part of the Crimson Break.

Daco

Town south of the Crimson Break in Sarket. Some animal in this region probably found and ate the missing tops of my ears.

Delaphine

Western kingdom on Pandrea. Home to the Delaphinian people.

Doran

The northern capital of Vanris.

Etrion

My home. The southern capital of Vanris. (Do you really need two capitals?)

Fallend

Southern kingdom on Pandrea. Home to the Fallenese people.

Fernwallow

Small village in Fallend where I grew up.

Katis

Vanrian military base slightly southeast of Etrion.

Katovan

Destroyed town in the Crimson Break. The Hall that survived there is in an agreed upon neutral zone sometimes used for negotiations.

Pandrea

The continent.

Sarket

Western kingdom on Pandrea. Home to the Sarketi people.

Sharith

Vanrian town east of Etrion.

Vanris	Northernmost kingdom on Pandrea. New home to the Vanrian people after volcanic activity drove them from their original island home.
Vareyl's Warning	Black crags that create a natural border between northern and southern Vanris. Called Vareyl's Gift before the war.

People

Kasiel Cavanos	Me (also known as Kasiel Danovan and Hahren Cavenos)
Edmund Danovan	Man who raised me
Danica Traven	Blacksmith's daughter, best friend, and first crush
Garrick Traven	Blacksmith in Fernwallow
Barden	Leatherworker in Fernwallow
Nix	Mercenary (bad person)
Loak	Mercenary (also bad)
Lorin	Mercenary (him too)
Jethan Markanis	Vanrian omren (My tehnaak – a Charmer)
Kince	Vanrian inveth (Darro's tehnaak)

Darro	Vanrian inveth (Kince's tehnaak)
Avris	Vanrian inren (Merrin's tehnaak)
Merrin	Vanrian inren (Avris's tehnaak)
Tath	Vanrian inren (a healer)
Ahrin	Vanrian inren (Tath's former tehnaak – a healer)
Wedro	Vanrian inren (Chander's tehnaak)
Chander	Vanrian inren (Wedro's tehnaak)
Arhk Cavenos	Dhomvalen of Vanris – My father (a Frightener)
Seylin Markanis	Khevarin of Vanris (an Enkindler)
Kastus	Vanrian ahndhomen (an Enkindler)
Kenna	Vanrian ahninveth (a Feral / Therin's tehnaak)
Adnar	Vanrian ahndhomen (a Feral / Nevias's tehnaak)
Farren	Vanrian dhomen
Setera	Vanrian ahninveth (an Evoker)

Therin	Vanrian soldier (a Speaker / Kenna's tehnaak)
Nerith	Vanrian inren (a healer)
Ganok	Vanrian Heartsmith
Ellaris	My deceased mother – killed when I was taken
Leysa	Vanrian inren (Nerith's tehnaak)
Tarik	Vanrian city guard inveth
Nevias	Vanrian dhomen (Adnar's tehnaak)
Iatan	Vanrian inren (a healer)

ACKNOWLEDGEMENTS

If you've been in my life while I was working on this series, you know how completely it pulled me in. Kasiel's story has been an extraordinary adventure for me as well as an escape from difficult things. I am grateful to him and his companions for the joy they brought me while I shared their story on these pages. There are also many people who deserve my appreciation, so I will try to capture them all here.

To Linda, who was my first reader as always and provided so much support and valuable feedback throughout the process. I can't imagine doing this without you.

To Kai, who took the brunt of dealing with my constant distraction and obsessive need to write at all hours of all days, and still allowed me to read the book to him out loud. Thank you for your patience.

As always, my best friends and beta readers, Rick and Ann, who somehow continue to stand by me regardless of where my crazy goes. You are now, and always will be, my tehsheyn.

To my additional beta readers, Todd and Jordan, your feedback was invaluable. You are greatly appreciated. And to all the ARC readers who have joined this journey, thank you!

As always, I want to acknowledge the fantastic team who helped me put together the finished book. Robert Crescenzio, my incredibly talented cover artist whose vision helps bring these books to life on the covers. Melissa Nash, the fantastic map designer who helped Kasiel's vision of the land come to life. Alexander Lockwood, my fantastic editor, fellow author, and now friend. Brian Short, my amazing formatter, whom I would also like to thank for your excellent company on many coffeeshop writing days. I love working with you all.

To my other friends and family, know that I love you and value your place in my life even if I don't call you out specifically here.

Last, but certainly not least, to my readers. To me, books are a collaborative effort between the author and their readers. Without you, this world would only ever come to life in my head. I hope you enjoy experiencing it as much as I did and will continue along the journey as the rest of this series releases into the world.

AUTHOR BIO

Nikki started writing her first novel at the age of 11, which she still has tucked in a briefcase in her home office. She lives in the magnificent Pacific Northwest with her wondrous cat-god. She feeds her imagination by sitting on the ocean in her kayak gazing out across the never-ending water or hanging from a rope in a cave, embraced by darkness and the sound of dripping water. She finds peace through practicing iaido or shooting her longbow.

•

Thank you for taking time to read this novel. Please leave a review if you enjoyed it.

•

For more about me and my work visit me at http://elysiumpalace.com.

OTHER NOVELS by NIKKI McCORMACK

CLOCKWORK ENTERPRISES
The Girl and the Clockwork Cat
The Girl and the Clockwork Conspiracy
The Girl and the Clockwork Crossfire

FORBIDDEN THINGS
Dissident
Exile
Apostate

ELYSIUM'S FALL
Dark Hope of the Dragons
Dark Savior of the Dragons

STANDALONE WORK
Golden Eyes
The Keeper

SILVERBLOOD RAVEN
A Path of Blood and Amber
A Path of Secrets and Dreams
A Path of Storms and Reckonings

HEART OF VANRIS

Kasiel ducked back, narrowly avoiding the arc of Dhomen Farren's swing. He darted in behind it, attempting to take advantage of a brief opening. Before he finished the attack, he knew it was going to be too slow. Too slow and too clumsy. Farren's parry and retaliation were lightning quick and anything but awkward. Kasiel's practice sword hit the ground, the strike that had disarmed him leaving his wrist stinging despite the protection of the bracer.

"This is impossible!" He followed the declaration with a string of curses in both Vanrian and Pandrean Common as he tried to shake feeling back into his fingers.

Farren stood watching him. A couple of braids hung behind his pointed ears, keeping his long white-blond hair back out of his eyes. The sharp red lines of his ke'hanoath tattoos climbing up his throat added an edge of threat to his countenance even when he was still.

The dhomen remained silent until Kasiel ran out of vulgarities. "Are you finished?"

"No," Kasiel snapped.

He kicked the training sword, sending it skidding across the sandy practice ring until it hit the low border at the side. Irith, his cliff cat companion, leapt the outer fence and sprinted after it, pouncing on the weapon as it rebounded toward the center. With the sword securely pinned under his paws, the big predator sat and began grooming one shoulder. He paused with the tip of his tongue still hanging out to look at Kasiel, the expectation in his bright blue eyes making it apparent that some recognition of his valiant efforts should be forthcoming.

Kasiel stared at the cat for a second, trying to rein in his temper, then he faced Farren. "Why are you wasting your time on this, sir? Any inren in the city could hold their own against me right now." He was being generous. Even a new recruit could probably beat him in single combat now.

Farren drew a deep breath and released it before answering. "What you are trying to do is extremely difficult, Ahninveth. Learning to fight left-handed is not something you're going to master overnight."

Kasiel clenched his right hand at his side. Three months and it remained weak, the nerves still not responding normally in places. "That doesn't answer my question. Why are *you* doing this?" He strode over to collect the practice sword, paying the toll of a good scratch behind Irith's ears to get the cat off it.

"Maybe I want you to have the skills to defend yourself when you're out running your beasts in battle. I believe you can succeed in this. Besides, the dhomvalen didn't give me a choice." He passed his practice blade to his left hand and flowed through a few elegant combat forms with it. "My being left-handed might have played a part in that."

Kasiel stared at him. The man wielded a sword in his right hand like he had been born with it there. This was the first time he'd seen him use the other. "Why don't you fight that way?"

"I do... against my enemies. Most people aren't accustomed to fighting a left-handed opponent, so it can give you an advantage if you're good at it. I don't fight that way with my students until they're more advanced because they'll typically be facing right-handed foes."

A flush of shame warmed Kasiel's cheeks. This man trained with both hands to better prepare his students. Here he was, complaining about having to train with his left hand when what he was actually angry about was being injured in a fight he shouldn't have charged into to begin with. Although, several residents of Sharith might feel differently, given that he had stalled the Delaphinian general long enough to save their lives. That aside, he was being bitter and childish.

He couldn't seem to control his quick temper. Maybe losing Sylaryth and almost losing Jethan still played a part in that. Those experiences weighed on him, sometimes haunting his dreams. Watching them execute the man who had raised him might also contribute to the problem. Not that Edmund hadn't deserved it with everything he had done to Kasiel and to the Vanrian people, but his emotions around all that remained a tangled, confusing mess. It could also have something to do with the way they forced him to abandon Danica after being foolish enough to bring her to Etrion for help. He still didn't know if they had cured her nightmares before sending her back with the Alliance messenger. No one would talk to him about it.

With a thought, he sent Irith out of the ring and faced Farren again, raising his blade.

"Ready?" Farren asked.

Kasiel nodded.

The combat instructor came at him like a lethal whirlwind. When Jethan showed up an hour later, Kasiel was bruised, sweaty, and struggling to keep his temper leashed, but he had made progress. In the final twenty minutes, Farren had failed to disarm him again, despite Kasiel's fingers being somewhat numb from all the hits he had taken on that arm.

A woman wearing the simple black and purple attire of a palace attendant accompanied Jethan. Her gaze homed in on Kasiel as they approached.

He urged Irith to his side, putting a hand on the cat's head when he sat there. The bond they shared wasn't as strong as that he and Sylaryth had developed, but maybe it would get there in time.

"Ahninveth Kasiel." She inclined her head. "You are required in the palace. Lord Jethan as well."

Farren held a hand out to take his practice sword. "You did well today, Ahninveth. I expect more improvement next time."

Next time. Not tomorrow. Farren must think the summons heralded a journey of some kind. A ball of dread formed in Kasiel's gut. "Of course, Dhomen." He handed Farren the sword, then faced the attendant. "Lead the way."

She nodded before heading back toward the palace, trusting them to follow.

Jethan fell into step alongside him. "You look tired, tehnaak. You want to skip the Twisted Vine tonight?"

Kasiel gestured to the woman in front of them with his chin. "We may not get much choice depending on what this is about."

"True."

He watched the woman for a moment, his thoughts turning to Nerith. She had been an attendant in the palace when he first met her. The khevarin had orchestrated that encounter in order to spy on him, but something genuine had grown from it.

"Are there rules about who can marry who in Vanris?" As the question tumbled out, he realized how it would sound, but it was too late to stop it.

"You mean, do nobles have to marry nobles or something like that?" Jethan grinned and bumped him with an elbow. "Why, are you already thinking about making a certain someone your future bride?"

His cheeks were instantly ablaze. "No. I..." His gaze rose to the towering black pinnacles that speared up from the rooftops of the palace complex as he collected his thoughts. "I guess I don't even know what I am here."

"You are considered military nobility, given your father's status."

Kasiel looked at him, unnerved by the comment. Why did the concept of being nobility of any kind make him so incredibly uncomfortable? "Really?"

"Would I joke about such a thing?"

"Is there anything you wouldn't joke about?"

Jethan chuckled. "Well, I'm serious this time."

They followed the attendant to a side entrance into the palace. It was warmer inside. It didn't rain often in this region of Vanris, but it had been chilly enough in recent months that when it did, they actually got some snow, though the coldest part of winter was past. While fighting Farren, Kasiel hadn't noticed the chill, but now that the sweat on his skin had cooled, it felt good to get inside. The cliff cat, with his heavy blue-gray coat, seemed to enjoy the brisk weather, requiring a little mental encouragement from Kasiel before he would come through the door with them.

"You qualify as royalty though, don't you?" he asked as the cat stepped inside and shook the dust from the practice ring onto the polished marble floor.

Jethan shrugged, his interest in the conversation waning the moment Kasiel brought up his status. "I am. Part of the extended royal family."

"So, are there restrictions on who we can be with?"

"Not really. Not unless you have far more influence on the future of Vanris than either of us do, though arranged marriages aren't unheard of regardless of rank or status. It depends on the circumstances. But Nerith is a healer now. That puts her in a well-respected position."

Kasiel's face warmed again. He stared hard at the back of the woman guiding them. Did she find their conversation amusing? "I didn't say anything about Nerith."

"Not by name."

Jethan's teasing tone didn't help Kasiel's composure. "We'll talk about it later."

"All right, tehnaak. Whatever makes you happy." A faint, self-satisfied grin lingered on Jethan's lips.

Kasiel rolled his eyes. Jethan wasn't wrong. Nerith was the reason for his questions. She was a healer now. Vanris highly valued its healers. Was that enough to make her an acceptable match for the son of the dhom-valen of Vanris? Did he care if it didn't?

The woman stopped outside the war room adjacent to the large chamber where he had gone before the khevarin and her council several times since he came to Vanris. The first time for the results of his assessment testing, then to face judgement for the night they helped catch the men who assaulted Nerith and again for rescu-ing Tath without seeking permission in Katovan.

The attendant stepped to one side, and one of the guards by the doors nodded to Kasiel and Jethan, his eyes lingering a moment on Irith before he opened it to allow them entry.

Dhomvalen Arhk was notably absent, but Adnar, his blond hair hanging loose over his shoulders, stood at the far end of a long table across from a stern-looking dhomen Kasiel hadn't met yet. The new man's dark blond hair, pulled into braids along both sides of his head, was streaked with gray, his blue-gray eyes as hard as steel. The only other person there, aside from guards positioned around the room, was Khevarin Seylin, ruler of Vanris, her white-blond hair pulled into a single loose braid that showed off both finely pointed ears. Her cool blue eyes focused on him as he entered. Not once in the unexpectedly long walk from the door to the end of the table did her gaze shift to Jethan or the cliff cat.

Kasiel absently touched the back of his right hand, where two more symbols had joined the original tattoo that showed her appreciation for catching Nerith's attackers. Of the newer ones, his entire unit shared the first. A recognition of their service to Vanris in destroying Edmund's research and bringing the man to Etrion to face judgment. He thought of it rather cynically as the symbol of his obliterated childhood. The other, he alone had received to honor his efforts in Sharith, getting them into the city without losing more than a few of the citizens the Alliance force had been using as human barricades.

The way the corners of the khevarin's mouth curved up in a brief flicker of a covetous smile reminded him of their conversation after Sharith.

"Remember, Lord Kasiel, weapons are forged in fire."
"Is that what I am now?"
"Do not doubt it."

Her response had left him ill at ease. Being a soldier was never his ambition. Edmund would have done his best to discourage such notions if he had ever had them. Now that he had a growing number of people he cared about in his life, he had that many more reasons to hate this war. Perhaps fear of losing them was another thing that contributed to his sharp temper of late.

When they stopped at the table near Adnar and knelt, Seylin finally released him from her gaze. She gestured for them to rise, then glanced at the Feral ahndhomen.

Adnar inclined his head to each of them. "Ahninveth Kasiel. Lord Jethan. This is Dhomen Sorval."

"Dhomen." Kasiel and Jethan acknowledged the other man together, both bowing their heads.

"You run tethdraks?" the dhomen asked, eyeing

Irith curiously.

"Yes, sir."

"This is the first time I've seen a Feral whose companion wasn't one of their preferred beasts."

"This was Irith's idea." The cliff cat's purr filled the room when Kasiel set a hand on his head.

"I see. You were responsible for getting our force into the city in Sharith?"

Where was he going with this? "Yes, sir."

"Our scouts recently reported a small company of Alliance troops gathering southeast of Etrion at the Sarketi border. We drove them out of Katis and our base just before you took Sharith back. From there, we kept after them, pushing them out of the ruins of Riftwater in the Break. They had been using that location as a base for some of their operations in Vanris. It now looks as if they are preparing to go back in there. What I need to do is figure out what they're after and, if necessary, keep them out of Riftwater until I can accomplish that."

His hard gaze shifted to Adnar for a moment before he continued. Did that mean this was the ahndhomen's idea? Had he recommended Kasiel's unit?

"Etrion is light on troops with so many out providing defense and helping rebuild after the Alliance's invasion. There should be units returning within the next few days, but I need to move on this now. I could use the combat power of your beasts and your unique scouting abilities. I understand you're still recovering from your injuries, but Ahndhomen Adnar assures me you have some excellent fighters in your unit who can provide you protection while you run your tethdraks."

A dark unease stirred in Kasiel's chest. "Does that mean you want my full unit, sir?"

"Not your healers," Seylin answered for him. "Dhomen Sorval has enough of our healers already. There is no reason to put yours at risk for this mission."

Relief washed away his anxiety. Nerith and Tath would get to stay out of the fighting this time. He was more than happy to stand behind that choice. "When do we head out?"

Respect found its way into Sorval's slow smile. "The company rides out in the morning."

"We'll be ready, sir." Kasiel might have appreciated Adnar's firm nod of approval more if he hadn't noticed the satisfied smirk that tugged at the khevarin's lips.

After receiving all the details for their coming mission, Kasiel and Jethan were dismissed. Irith's tail switched back and forth as they strode down the halls, the big cat picking up on the fresh tension in Kasiel. As happy as he was that Tath and Nerith wouldn't be involved, the rest of his companions would be back in harm's way, Jethan included.

What had his father said?

"You can't save everyone, Kasiel."

The truth in those words haunted him as unceasingly as the moment Itana's mace struck his arm. Whenever he did the exercises to strengthen his arm, he could see that powerful blow sweeping down again and hear his father's words.

"I guess we should go tell the others."

An uncomfortable edge in Jethan's tone pulled Kasiel's from his morose thoughts. Maybe it was the prospect of possibly heading into combat again that made Jethan sound uneasy, but he got the feeling there was more to it. "What's wrong, tehnaak?"

Jethan shook his head, his nose wrinkling as if he smelled something foul. "It's just the way my aunt was watching you, like she'd found a new favorite pet."

"Ah, that. I'm kind of getting used to it. From where she's standing, I'm just another tool in her arsenal." Another weapon to be deployed.

"Yes, but you're so much more than that. I hate that

she can't... that she *won't* see you for who you are outside of your potential as a weapon."

Kasiel smiled at his tehnaak. "Usually, I'm the naïve one."

Jethan shook his head at him, a reluctant grin cracking his features. "True. I prefer it that way."

When they arrived at the tavern, the rest of the unit was already there. Tath sat at one end of the bench against the wall, Darro's arm wrapped around her shoulders. Then Kince and Wedro with Etris at the far end, the Speaker looking ill-at-ease among them. She was welcome as part of their unit now, but Chander's loss still hung heavy over the group, and her discomfort made it clear how obvious that was.

Merrin, Avris, and Nerith sat across from them. The three women had become closer since their mission to rescue Jethan, though a slight tension rose between Avris and Nerith whenever Kasiel was around. He suspected Nerith knew he and Avris had slept together. It hadn't been a manifestation of romantic love, just a dash of attraction and the intense need for comfort. Still, it had changed his relationship with Avris, creating a closeness and physical ease between them he didn't share with the other women in the group.

Jethan claimed a spot next to Avris, bumping Nerith down to sit between him and Kasiel, who took a seat at the end of the bench to accommodate Irith. Once they had settled, each with a mug of Vanrian Black Mead before them, Jethan turned to Kasiel, waiting on him to break the news. It was an odd thing, considering this unit had been under Jethan's command when he first met them all on their mission to bring him to Vanris from the southern kingdom of Fallend. Now they were his unit.

"We're being sent on a mission," he began, capturing their full attention in a few words. "We'll be going out into the Break to the ruins of Riftwater under Dhomen Sorval's command. There's an Alliance company gathering south of there. The goal is to keep them out of the town and see if we can figure out what they're after. We leave in the morning." Nerith's fingers wound through his, tightening on his hand. Dread twisted in his gut. She wouldn't like what he was going to say next. His gaze moved to Tath. "The dhomen has enough healers in his company, so they want our healers to stay behind."

"What?"

It wasn't clear whether Nerith or Tath exclaimed the word first, but Nerith aggressively extracted her hand from his and both women stared at him as if this were his fault.

Kasiel cringed inwardly. "The khevarin doesn't want to risk more healers if it's not necessary." At least he had someone else to place the blame on. An individual they couldn't argue with.

"That's horseshit," Tath snapped. "We're a unit. We should go out together."

"Do we get to take your kanodrak?" Kince asked, ignoring the tension at the table.

Kasiel seized on the question, eager to escape the anger of the two healers. "I assume so. I won't go without Niske."

Nerith hit his arm. Slight as she was, she packed considerable power into that swing. "You won't go without her, but you'll leave me here?"

Kasiel rubbed his arm and looked at her, catching Avris's smirk from further down the bench before she hid it behind her mug of mead. Jethan leaned back a fraction and gestured to Nerith's head, raising his brows as if to ask whether Kasiel would like him to use his Charmer ability on her. Kasiel negated the idea with a subtle shake of his head, trying not to laugh at his teh-naak's audacity. That would only raise Nerith's ire.

He met her eyes. "You know I would rather have you with me."

"Do you think I can't tell when you're lying?" Nerith countered, her sharp tone making it clear how she felt about that.

He drew a deep breath, his gaze flickering to Darro and Tath, who were engaged in a quiet conversation punctuated by several light kisses. Tath was smiling. He sighed and met Nerith's eyes again.

"You're right. I'd rather keep you safe, but it's not because I doubt you. I've seen you fight." He leaned in and gave her a light kiss, encouraged when she didn't avoid it or pull away. Drawing back a fraction, his lips still almost touching hers, he said, "Can we talk about it later?"

"It had better be a very compelling conversation." She kissed him then, a soft lingering kiss that reassured him they would move past this.

After two hours spent enjoying the unit's company over tavern food and a few rounds of mead, they split up earlier than usual. They had responsibilities the next morning that required them to be awake and alert. Kasiel, Jethan, and Nerith went to drop Irith at the habitat for the cliff cats together. Jethan split off when they reached the private quarters in the palace.

By the time Kasiel had pulled out the clothing and equipment he would need for the next day, Nerith was curled in his bed, her eyes closed. She looked peaceful. Knowing how fierce she could be, he found the image endearingly deceptive. He stripped down, snuffed out the last wall sconce, leaving one candle burning next to the bed, and climbed in beside her.

"Kas?" she murmured.

Good, she was still awake. He didn't want to leave with this conflict hanging between them. "Yes."

"If you find yourself compelled to try saving anyone

out there, could you do me a favor?"

He rolled onto his side and brushed a lock of hair away from her eyes. Those unusual lavender eyes that he could happily gaze into for hours on end. "What favor?"

"Before you go charging in, make sure you'll be able to save yourself too. You're still recovering from the injury to your arm. You're not in any condition for heroics."

She was right, but he couldn't promise her that. If someone in his unit was in trouble, he knew himself too well to believe he would stay out of it. "Would you even like me if I didn't try to protect the people who are important to me?"

"I don't like you, Kas. I love you." She traced a line of the tattoo on his cheek with one finger. "And I love how you care so deeply, but I don't want to lose you. Promise me you'll remember that."

That was something he could give her. He doubted he would ever forget the way she was looking at him, or the words she had just said. "I promise," he whispered, taking her hand and pressing his lips to her palm.

"And Kas?"

"Hmm?" He leaned in to kiss her neck, sliding one hand down her side to the curve of her waist.

She turned her head a little to the side, giving him better access to the soft skin there. "Do you love me?"

"Of course." He kissed down her neck to her collarbone, moving in toward the hollow of her throat.

"Of course, what?" she asked, the question punctuated by a soft gasp as his hand slid over to her belly and down.

He drew back to look at her. "Yes, Nerith." He placed a light kiss on her lips. "I love you." It felt unexpectedly good to admit that. To see the resulting sparkle of pleasure in her eyes. He gave her a mischievous smile and slid his hand lower, eliciting another gasp from her.

She matched his smile and pulled him in for a deeper kiss.